Beggarman's Country

JAN WEBSTER was born in 1924 in Blantyre, in the heart of the Lanarkshire coalfields. Her father died when she was fifteen.

She was educated at St John's Grammar School, Hamilton, and Hamilton Academy. On leaving school she worked as a journalist on the *Border Mail*, Kelso; the old *Glasgow Evening News*; the *Scottish Sunday Mail*, and for Kemsley (now Thomson) Newspapers in London. While still a teenage reporter in the Glasgow Northern Police Court she met her future husband, Drew Webster, now London Editor of United Newspapers and former lobby correspondent. The Websters live in Croydon, Surrey, and have two children.

Jan Webster sold her first short story at the age of seventeen, and has had many published and broadcast since then. Her hobbies include gardening, American history, and looking at paintings. *Colliers Row*, her first published novel, was the first of a trilogy; the second book in the series was *Saturday City* and *Beggarman's Country* is the third.

Available in Fontana by the same author

Colliers Row
Saturday City

JAN WEBSTER

Beggarman's Country

Collins
FONTANA BOOKS

First published in 1979 by William Collins Sons & Co Ltd
First issued in Fontana Books 1980

© Jan Webster 1979

Made and printed in Great Britain by
William Collins Sons & Co Ltd, Glasgow

DEDICATED TO THE MEMORY OF
MY MOTHER AND FATHER

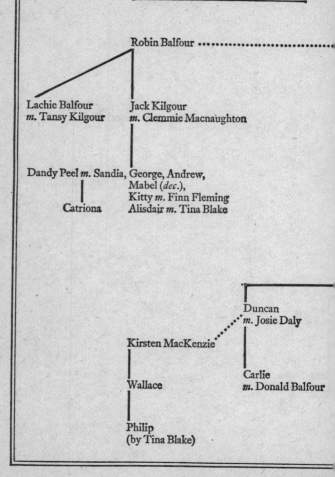

FAMILY TREE AT 1920

Robin Balfour

Lachie Balfour
m. Tansy Kilgour

Jack Kilgour
m. Clemmie Macnaughton

Dandy Peel *m.* Sandia, George, Andrew,
Mabel (*dec.*),
Kitty *m.* Finn Fleming
Catriona   Alisdair *m.* Tina Blake

Duncan
m. Josie Daly

Kirsten MacKenzie

Wallace

Carlie
m. Donald Balfour

Philip
(by Tina Blake)

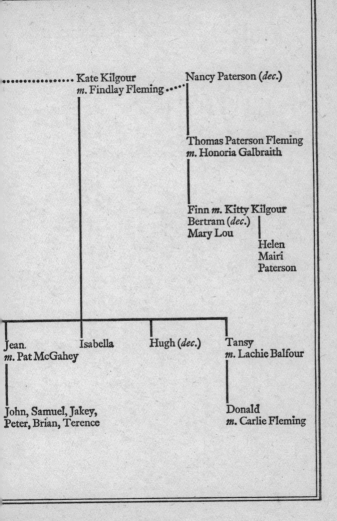

Kate Kilgour ·················· Nancy Paterson (*dec.*)
m. Findlay Fleming ·····

Thomas Paterson Fleming
m. Honoria Galbraith

Finn *m.* Kitty Kilgour
Bertram (*dec.*)
Mary Lou

Helen
Mairi
Paterson

Jean.   Isabella   Hugh (*dec.*)   Tansy
m. Pat McGahey   *m.* Lachie Balfour

John, Samuel, Jakey,   Donald
Peter, Brian, Terence   *m.* Carlie Fleming

Part One

CHAPTER ONE

Pass through the Lanarkshire village of Dounhead with its small greystone cottages, pit rows, scattering of shops and two kirks and you came on the outskirts to Dounhead House, cosseted by trees and high stone walls, spangled by a free-flowing burn and guarded at the imposing gates by two stone lions.

Round the wide circular drive on this cold day in 1920 a handsome dark blue car moved at a fast, erratic pace, a red-faced excited boy at the wheel. Honk-honk went the horn, rooks scattered in noisy outraged confusion and a leggy, pretty girl in high button boots, tartan ribbons in her hair, first ran after the car, then waited in a trance of anxiety till the vehicle finally returned to the front door.

When it stopped, she was suddenly galvanized into action. She raced forward, dragged the tall, raw-boned boy from the wheel and as they struggled and the boy fell over, rained blows down on his shoulders and back. Yelling, he dodged out of her grip, backing away from her and not allowing her near him until he saw her rage was ebbing.

'Patie,' she cried at last, 'what did you do that for?' Her face was pink with fright and anger. 'You bad, wicked boy. It could have crashed and then what would Daddy have done? It belongs to his guest.'

The boy's breath grated in his throat. Patie, born Paterson, rubbed ruefully at a scraped knee. 'I was only trying it out. Peter Frensham wouldn't mind. He knows I'm a car man. He's seen me drive ours.' He glared at her with an irrepressible sense of shaky triumph.

'Yes, but that was on his estate and Daddy sat beside you. You really shouldn't make things difficult for us just now. Daddy has enough on his plate.' Her tone, grown-up, was still breathlessly shrill. Pushing him towards the stone steps, she made him sit down while she took out her own clean handkerchief and dabbed at the graze. 'I didn't mean you to fall over.'

'It's nothing,' he said magniloquently. 'Don't fuss.' He gazed at the car with a critical, expert eye, letting out a long, juddering breath. 'I wouldn't have cared that much if I had crashed it. He didn't help Father before the war when times were bad. It was Grandpa who did that. Now the factory's going well and our cars are in demand, he wants to give England the benefit of our experience.'

'You're just parroting Grandpa.'

'Well, he *knows*.'

Mairi Fleming subsided next to her brother and gazed thoughtfully in front of her. Her eyes were large, a pale, washed blue and her hair a soft maize with underlying dark strands. Her mouth, thin-lipped but mobile, with a distinct Cupid's bow, was perhaps her most distinctive feature, barely closing over strong, white teeth.

'It isn't just a question of business,' she said, with troubled seriousness. 'Grandma says it's what's going to happen to Daddy, if he doesn't take an interest again. Maybe amalgamating with this Birmingham firm would be good for him.'

'Would you like to go to England?' demanded Patie fiercely.

'No. But I'd go to please Daddy.'

'I wouldn't. I'm to inherit the works some day. Grandpa says so. It won't be long till I can go in and help Father –'

'Don't be silly. You're only twelve.'

'I'm an *old* twelve. I'm not a child any more. Anyhow, whatever anyone says, I'm leaving school at fourteen.'

'Patie,' she protested, sighing. 'I wish you weren't such a worry to me.' The adult note underlay everything she said and just for a moment a flicker of something that might have been a response sobered his expression. 'With Mother gone, and Helen, there *is* only me. Don't you see that?'

He nodded. He had heard the words so many times since the influenza epidemic, in its third and last thrust in February, 1919, had taken first his sister and then his mother as almost the last of its 200,000 victims. Sometimes even now he didn't believe it. They had all had it. Why had his mother and Helen been the ones to die?

He missed the big old house in Glasgow with its parties and fun and visitors, for although living with the grandparents at Dounhead House was satisfying in many ways, especially now that they'd also bought over the neighbouring farm, they didn't like to have as many people around as his parents once had. His father might prefer it here, but Patie longed obdurately for the small things like the games he'd played with his Glasgow pals, the banter they'd exchanged, the cigarette cards they'd swopped. The confusion in his mind made him restless, wild, so that he did things at times that were silly and dangerous. Like taking Peter Frensham's car.

It had been heavier to handle than he'd thought and just for a heart-stopping second or two he had feared he wouldn't be able to turn it in time at the gates. Maybe the fact that its engine had been developed from an airship starting motor had something to do with it. The Fleming engine was altogether better. He knew every inch of the Fleming car's construction and although there were refinements he might make here and there, he was sure that none of the other dozen or so contemporary Scottish makes could touch it.

'Do you miss them still, Patie? Mother and Helen?'

Startled out of his reverie, he nodded slowly. 'Do you?'

'Yes, but I don't cry now. Do you?'

'No. I never cried.'

'Father still does. Grandma says it was the shock. Coming so sudden. She says Mother and Father were made for each other and it might have been more merciful if he had gone too. She doesn't mean it, of course.'

'That would have made us total orphans.'

'Yes.' She put a skinny, protective arm round his shoulders. 'I'm sorry I hit you. Come on in and I'll wash your knee and get you a bandage. Don't tell them we fought,' she added judiciously. 'Just say you fell over.'

In view of his escapade with the car, he saw the wisdom of this. He supposed he was lucky that he hadn't been spotted from inside the house. Not that he would have cared. Something in him went looking for trouble these days. But the need for his dinner was uppermost now. His big, rangy frame needed constant stoking. He could smell hot, tasty chicken broth, roast mutton and something deliciously lemony. Since there were guests, Cook would be sure to provide something special in the way of dessert.

When Mairi had bandaged his knee, they both washed their hands and faces and tidied their hair, then fidgeted in the large hall waiting for the dinner gong. Foggy Highland scenes and seascapes gazed mildly down at them; draughts nibbled their ankles. Just as it seemed they couldn't wait a moment longer, Nellie the maid sped out from the kitchen, her face red, her cap almost over her eyes and banged the big brass gong. Another day she might have permitted Patie to do it. Today she was wrapped in sweaty preoccupation. She raced back to the kitchen to reappear with a huge tureen of steaming soup which she carried into the dining-room. Patie's mouth watered.

Grandma Honoria appeared from the morning-room, her hair freshly coiled, shooing them in ahead of her. Then came the men, the light, heady fumes of whisky emanating from their breath, their watchchains gleaming and boots creaking. Their grandfather, Paterson Fleming Sr, with his two sticks. Their father, the gaunt widower, Finn. Sir Peter Frensham. And lastly the dark-suited, saturnine business acquaintance they knew simply as Grant, busily dousing his pipe.

Finn Fleming had never had much flesh on his bones. 'One of Pharaoh's lean cattle,' was his mother's description of him. But now his grey tweed suit seemed to hang as though from the broomstick shoulders of a scarecrow. His fair hair was liberally sprinkled with grey, his moustache gingery white. His movements were slow, even the picking up of the soup spoon seemed an effort. His mother, hooding her look of concern, ladled a full plateful of the soup and handed it to him. 'Eat up.' Even with guests she could not stifle the injunction.

'You see how she bullies me.' Finn addressed Peter Frensham with a lantern-jawed smile.

'She's right,' said Frensham. 'We're all going to bully you unmercifully. It's what you need. That's why I want you to consider this proposal of ours.' His look embraced Frederick Grant, mopping up his soup with relish, the ends of his straggling moustache decorated with leek, at which Mairi stared with covert fascination. 'You need to be bullied into a new challenge. And, by George, this is it. Come in with us and you'll have no time to mope.'

Finn gazed at his friend enigmatically, feeling something stir through his bones again; the old passion to produce cars that were good cars, better than anybody else's. Grant claimed he could raise all the necessary capital, find the site and enrol the work force. Frensham? Finn had no illusions, Peter was offering his name. Decorated war hero, baronet, he was the darling of the society columns. The war had changed the former pleasure-seeker into an allegedly serious, if hard-up, 'businessman'. *Flâneur* was the better word, Finn thought. Yet he couldn't be too hard on him. In the early days, when it had been a question of getting a spindly car chassis together in a back garden shed, it had been Frensham's money and interest that had encouraged him. You didn't forget things like that, even when he brought someone like Grant to see you, with his talk about amalgamation and mass production and setting up in England.

Frederick Grant finished his soup, wiped his moustache and turned in a considerate manner towards Honoria.

'You see, Mrs Fleming,' he explained, bringing her into the conversation, 'what is happening is that Ford are planning to bring the latest assembly line techniques over from America, Morris means to swamp the market with what are called "family cars" and the first mass car, the Austin, will be on our roads next year at the latest.'

'What do you mean by assembly line?' demanded Honoria.

'Well, instead of cars being individually tailored, as you might say, by craftsmen, all the parts will be mass produced and assembled on a much greater, more ordered scale. It'll do for cars what Singer's sewing-machine and the divisional labour system did for clothes. Every process will be hastened.'

'But will that be a good thing?' asked Honoria innocently.

Paterson, her husband, shook his head. 'How can it be a good thing,' he demanded, with truculence, 'if it takes engineering know-how and the car trade away from Scotland?'

'You can't deny physical facts,' argued Frensham. 'Glasgow's too far away from the auxiliary industries in the Midlands.'

'Give us time,' growled Paterson. 'We haven't got over the war yet –'

'But they're not prepared to wait elsewhere! You can't hang around waiting in the mysterious belief that things will just improve of their own free will –'

'Hold on,' commanded Paterson, raising a magisterial hand. 'This country still has the best engineers. Bar none. This country has been building cars since somebody first thought of putting a chassis on four wheels. I mind when John Stirling drove his motor carriage from Hamilton to Carlisle and back in twelve hours. That was in 1896, the year of the pneumatic tyre, and it was considered a great, a shattering feat. Which it was for the times.'

'With respect, sir,' said Frederick Grant softly, 'we are now past the era of experimentation. The motor-car has arrived. Not just for the privileged few, but for anyone who can scrape up a couple of hundred pounds.'

'Standards will go down,' maintained the old man stubbornly. 'Good engineering is about keeping up standards. I'm not ready yet to admit we have to take the trail south to survive.'

'Grandfather is right.' Every eye turned towards Patie, whose spoon had just rattled down on his plate with a decisive sound. His face had gone bright red. He could feel the iodine make his leg throb and something was tickling his throat. He cleared it away roughly. 'We should keep the work here in Scotland. We've been bled enough.'

Peter Frensham gave an amused laugh. 'Where does he learn this sort of talk?'

Patie rounded on him furiously. 'We *can't* afford any more emigration.'

'Going to England isn't emigration.'

'It's worse. It's treachery.'

'Finn,' appealed Honoria, 'can you not silence that child? He doesn't know his place.'

Finn glared at his son. 'You are here to eat your dinner,' he said heavily. 'Not to give your opinion. Now get on with it.'

'I thought it was a free country,' said Patie defiantly.

Finn looked round the table with apologetic embarrassment. 'I ask you to excuse my son. If he goes on, he will be asked to leave the table.' To Patie he grated, 'This conversation is for adults. I'll speak to you later. Now be silent, sir.'

Patie hung his head over his soup plate, but it was Mairi's turn to take up the cudgels. Straight-backed but near to tears, she demanded, 'If the talk is not for children, why are we here? Anyhow, Patie's twelve and I am fourteen. Surely I am not a child?' Apart from a slight quiver of the lips, she certainly didn't look it then.

'I don't know what's got into the pair of you!' Honoria's glare was baleful, the more so because of the mild smirking satisfaction she had just spied on her husband's face.

'I think maybe you should both get down from the table,' said Finn evenly. 'You may ask Nellie to give you the rest of your meal in the kitchen.'

'Grandpa!' Mairi appealed to Paterson. But her grandfather made a deprecating gesture towards her, hiding his true feelings behind his table napkin.

Mairi looked at her brother. Without another word, they folded their napkins, scraped back their chairs and with heads held high left the room, almost as though they'd rehearsed it. There was a moment of embarrassed silence, then Finn waved dismissively to indicate to his guests that the contretemps was over. 'I'm afraid they've become horribly spoiled since – well, since you know what.'

14

Frensham and Grant made deprecatory noises. 'He's a spunky one, that,' Grant laughed, referring to Patie. 'He'll make or mar the firm one day, that's for sure.'

'Yes. Well, he doesn't understand the issues involved,' said Finn.

'On the contrary,' interposed Paterson sardonically. 'He understands only too well.'

Grant turned towards Paterson. 'You must realize, sir,' he said persuasively, 'that I've done my homework before coming here. The signs are there that industry generally is on the decline all over the West of Scotland. The pits aren't what they were. The cotton trade is all Lancashire's. Even the big ships will be built elsewhere than the Clyde. The warehouses are stuffed with goods but no one has the money to buy.' He let out a gusty sigh. 'We've relied too much on the heavy industries. We haven't learned to modernize or diversify. If we'd had the right kind of foresight, the supplies for car manufacture would be here. Not in the Midlands.'

'We're too far from our main markets,' Finn admitted gloomily.

Paterson glared at them in perturbation. 'I'll not let you put the old country down. Patie may be a child, but I think he's got the right attitude. A fighting one.'

'That's funny, coming from you,' Finn answered, softly but swiftly. 'A man who had to go to America to get his ideas realized.'

'Aye,' admitted Paterson. 'But I'm back here now and I'm not shifting.'

'I understand your feelings, Mr Fleming.' Grant poured oil on the troubled waters. 'But you have to accept that the investment can't be raised here. It's a hard fact; Scots'll invest anywhere but in their own country.'

Half an hour later Nellie brought the cleared pudding plates and a progress report out to the kitchen. 'Let them get on with their blethers and their bannocks and cheese,' she addressed the subdued two at the big scrubbed table. Then forcefully: 'Do you two have to sit there as though someone had stolen your scone?'

They regarded her moodily. She was a sturdily-built woman in her late twenties, reconciled to a career in service now the one lad she had fancied had been killed in the war. Her maternal concern was all for the people she worked for and her warmth such that no one minded when that concern slipped over into familiarity. Today she felt the preoccupations of the house lie heavily on her mind. More change afoot and these motherless youngsters still not settled after the last, terrible upset.

She buttered two hunks of gingerbread liberally and placed them in front of them. Mairi pushed hers towards Patie, her face set and pale. 'You should hear the way they're going on in there!' Nellie addressed her. 'To listen to them you'd think Scotland was down the drain already. Your father's looking out of the window at Dounhead pit and saying it's running down like the rest of the country.' She took an angry breath. 'And I thought the war was supposed to have solved everything.' Her irony was deep.

'What we had after the war was a false dawn. That's what Peter Frensham said.' Mairi spoke at last.

'What does he know?' Patie's scornful words were muffled by the gingerbread.

'He said we mustn't allow sentiment to cloud our judgment.'

'Well, Grandpa's on our side.' Patie kicked at the cross struts of a chair till told by Nellie to desist.

'What will it be like in England, if we go there?' Mairi's chief worry was out at last. 'We won't know anybody.'

'You're nearly crying again,' said Patie, with a brotherly lack of feeling.

'I wasn't,' she spat at him.

Judiciously, Nellie placed herself between them. Looking down on Patie's ruffled fair hair and intransigent face, she said with some seriousness, 'Behave yourself, you great loon, or get out of my kitchen.'

'It isn't your kitchen,' he pointed out. 'And *I'm* not going anywhere.'

Nellie gazed down at him more in sorrow than in anger. 'You,' she said, 'would argue with your shadow.'

'Who will tell the children?' asked Honoria. The guests had long since departed and she had sat listening to the two men, Paterson and Finn, hammer out their plans before reaching a final decision.

'I think you should tackle Mairi,' said Finn. 'Would you do that for me, Mother?' He looked over at the broad-bosomed, comfortable figure. There was still colour in the thick grey hair. But she was seventy-five, like his father. He knew that these days since Kitty's death he had asked too much of her. Still she seemed sharp, vigorous, quick to

16

realize the subtleties of almost any situation and certainly of this one.

'Yes, I'll do it.'

'And I'll tell the laddie. Send the laddie down to me.' Paterson's commanding look brooked no rebuttal.

'Don't you think I should do it?' asked Finn.

'I think he'll take it better, coming from me,' said Paterson. Finn looked as though he were about to argue, but gave in. He realized that since Kitty had gone he had abnegated most of his responsibilities towards his children. Two wild, argumentative creatures they had become, too. The one as self-willed and opinionated as the old man himself; the other secretive, her eyes following him at every turn, pleading and supplicating for something it was not in his power to give to her. Her mother and her sister. He felt that strange, sickening response to his children's needs, a turning away from the hurt in which he was included. If he couldn't cope with his own grief, how could he help them? Catching sight of himself in the bevelled mirror above the sideboard, he saw the night stubble shadow his skin with a grey look. *Grey ghost.* He said weakly, 'I'll talk to him tomorrow. Make him understand.' He poured himself a whisky and said, 'I'll take this up with me. Help me to sleep,' and avoided his mother's cautioning helpless face.

Honoria followed him slowly up the broad, turkey-red stairs with their shining brass rods, clinging on fast to the polished oak banisters. What a day it had been for decisions and she had not even had her customary after-dinner nap. But there was a feeling akin to relief inside her. It was just possible that Frensham and Grant between them were going to pull Finn out of this mourning. She had thought for a time that no one could. The blow had been so savage, swift and unexpected. Helen had sickened first, then after her death poor Kitty had not been able to put up a fight against the virulent disease that had, after all, killed off strong young men in as little as two hours.

But now the Fleming mettle was showing through again. Honoria remembered the times when, first married, she and Paterson had touted for work all over America, until her husband had finally sold his expertise as a railway engineer. Talk about mettle! It was a wonder they had ever survived the hardship of those early days. No, they weren't the sort of family who went under. Thank God for that. She was glad that Paterson had realized in the end that going south might prove his son's salvation.

She knocked on Patie's bedroom door and went in. As long as they went upstairs at eight, they were allowed to stay up longer reading or playing games. It was a routine that had started in the early days after the double bereavement and it was established now. Patie looked up from a model steam engine he was making from treacle tins and thread bobbins.

'Grandpa wants to see you.' She saw the start of apprehension in his eyes. 'It's all right. He's got something to tell you. Something important.' She brushed the hair back from his eyes. 'Go down now.'

She went next door to Mairi's room. The door, as always, was ajar and Mairi appeared to be simultaneously knitting and reading a book propped up in front of her.

'Time you were in bed,' said the old woman gently.

Obediently Mairi put down her knitting and began to unknot the ribbons in her hair.

'No, leave that a minute,' said her grandmother. 'I want to talk to you.' She patted the window-seat. 'Put the light out and come and sit here, by me. This is what we did in the old days, before we lit the paraffin lamps.'

The girl did as she was told and together they stared out at the moonlit landscape. The trees with their knots of rooks' nests were clearly discernible and further off, the dark hump of the pit bing and the lights of the village. It had the tranquil reassurance of all familiar scenes.

'Mairi,' Honoria began, 'your father has decided to go in with Mr Grant and is going to Birmingham almost immediately.'

'But he hasn't asked us if we want to go.'

There was a small pause, then Honoria said gently, 'Well, that is what I'm here to talk about. He doesn't think it would be a good idea to uproot you and Patie again. Not when you're both settled in at school and all that sort of thing.'

She felt rather than saw Mairi propel herself from her seat and blunder about the darkened room, bumping into the furniture.

'He's going without us? To *England*? He doesn't care about us! No one loves us any more. Not the way Mama did.' Honoria could hear that Mairi was crying; and as the child blundered past her in her rage and distress, one warm tear fell on to the back of Honoria's hand. She raised it to her mouth, feeling its saltiness.

'Now you know that's not the way of it,' she protested. 'We all love you. Your father most of all.'

'He doesn't! He doesn't! It's no good your saying he does, when I feel it inside here –' Mairi thumped her chest – 'that he doesn't. He wouldn't be going away without us, if he did.' She gave a great cry of protestation and fell down on her bed, sobbing loudly and, it seemed to Honoria, more than a little dramatically. But then she was at an age when what you felt and what you thought you ought to feel were inextricably mixed up in your mind. Even allowing for the girl's natural distress, Honoria felt an irresistible tide of bitter-sweet amusement rise up in her. There were times when she could remember very well what it was like to be fourteen and convinced your feelings were the very axis on which the world spun. Strange. That she could remember, that is.

'Come on now,' she coaxed. 'Calm yourself. It won't be so bad. Your father will come home quite often. I'm counting on you to help with Patie, you know. Nellie will help and there's Cousin Carlie in the village.'

'I didn't think you approved all that much of her.' Suddenly the histrionics were over and Mairi was sharp and sour.

Smiling faintly in the dark, Honoria rejoined, 'It's her politics I don't approve of. But now she's at least put all that Suffragette nonsense behind her, I don't mind so much. She's family. That's what I'm getting at. And she thinks a lot of you, not having children of her own.'

But Mairi was weeping once more. 'Daddy doesn't want to be bothered with us, does he? Nellie says now Mother's gone, he doesn't want to bother about anything.'

'Nellie should have more sense.' Even in the dark, Mairi knew her grandmother's face was angry. 'Now listen. Your grandfather and father have worked things out carefully between them. Grandpa is explaining things to Patie at this very minute. The Glasgow works are to be closed down but some of the plant is coming to a new, small factory here in Dounhead, which your Grandpa will supervise with the help of a good manager. Until Patie is old enough. It will make custom-built cars and your father will still keep an eye on things.

'The rest of the plant, the Fleming name, those men who want to go south and your father's money as opposed to your grandfather's – all that goes to Birmingham as part of the new deal.' Honoria's voice changed slightly. 'Your grandfather would not have agreed except that he sees your father needs the challenge. And you have to look at it that way, too, Mairi, for your father has had so much to bear.'

'But going to England.' Mairi's voice had ceased to be self-pitying and was now flat and angry. 'You know Grandpa says Scotland's just becoming an annexe to England. Why does Father make things worse?'

'You're just saying that because you're not going with him, aren't you?'

'No. Patie feels the same way as Grandpa. Daddy'll come back with an Oxford accent, talking down to everyone the way Peter Frensham does.'

Honoria laughed. 'I don't think that's going to happen.'

'We shall see,' said Mairi, in a hard tone. 'Please may I put the light on again?'

In the glare after the dark, she kept her face averted from her grandmother, moving things about pointlessly on her dressing-table. The old woman rose to go. She could see Mairi's expression had closed down and was giving nothing away. Misgivings about whether she was wise to take on the responsibility for looking after these two assailed her. It was difficult to know what went through Mairi's head at the best of times. There was a big five-year diary with a clasp and key lying at her bedside and it was obvious she poured many of her thoughts into that. She liked poetry, reciting and acting and it was part of the enigma of the adolescent girl that while she was often awkward and jagged in her everyday relations, on the stage she had a certain grace and no shyness.

Honoria kissed her granddaughter and moved slowly towards her own room, her bones suddenly stiff and weary. She was glad of the stone 'piggy' Nellie had wrapped her nightgown round, but even in bed she couldn't relax till she heard the sound of Patie's tread on the stairs and the click shut of his door. The chances were he'd been even more furious than Mairi at what he would see as his father's defection. They were young; they would learn life never offered any simple options and would come to understand eventually it was their father's health and survival that were at stake.

Funny how in her sleepy ruminations the well-shaped, narrow head that was Patie's slipped and dissolved into her recollection of Paterson when she had first met him. Headstrong and passionate the pair of them, sharing the same

Christian name, with Finn the disparate link. What a mystery the generations were, dying and resurrecting like spring flowers. She tried to see into the future – how it would be for all of them. How long would she be spared? She began her habitual prayers, but before she could finish them the blessed warmth of her bed eased through her bones and in an instant her thoughts scattered like quick rain on the far hills of sleep.

'If you go to see your Cousin Carlie, keep away from the Rows,' said Nellie. She wrapped the large woollen scarf twice round Mairi's neck and tied the ends at the back. The effect was muffled and comical. Crossly, Mairi unwound the scarf and, winding it once only, tucked the ends into the belt of her navy Melton coat. 'Don't fuss me, Nellie,' she said sharply. 'I'm not an infant.'

'It's bitter out there,' said Nellie, 'and you've just had a cold. Have a bit of sense, do. What would your father say if he thought I neglected you?'

'He probably wouldn't care.'

'Would you listen to her?' Nellie appealed to the ceiling. 'Now, did you hear what I said? You don't want to be catching the scarlet fever.'

'You think I'll go into Tina Mackenzie's for sweeties. That's it, isn't it? But she's clean enough, Nellie. Most folk in the Rows are.'

'She shouldn't be running a shop in the Rows, anyway,' grumbled Nellie. 'Who gave her the permission? A right hand-to-mouth existence it is for her and that bairn. We could do without her sort coming out from Glasgow.'

'What sort do you mean?'

'Her sort with their illegitimate bairns.'

Mairi pulled on long fur-backed gauntlet gloves. Fleece-lined, leather-palmed, they were beautifully warm and luxurious. She stroked the pale grey rabbit fur reflectively.

'You come from the Rows, Nellie,' she pointed out.

'Aye, so I know what they're like. Smelly middens and outside cludgies. Men washing their bare backs at the windows.'

'Your family's still there. Your mother and father and Nicol.'

'Aye, well, never you mind our Nicol. If he tries to talk to you, don't you listen.'

'I think he's all right. He always speaks to me. He's very

nice.' Mairi stood very still, petrified in case Nellie should guess the real strength of her feelings for Nicol. For never a day passed but he was in her mind. She didn't know how to define this predicament. Love? There was too much of terror and prohibition for that. What it was struggled towards definition through a welter of doubts and hesitations. Knowledge that Grandma would be outraged.

'He'll speak to you, but he'll sneer behind your back. He's got no time for the likes of you or your family. Come the revolution, he'll chop off your head.'

Mairi stared at Nellie. Sometimes it was difficult to tell whether she was serious. 'You're joking,' she said uneasily.

'Well, maybe I am,' agreed Nellie, only half-relenting. 'Away you go. Home before dark now, and don't talk to any strange men.'

Mairi was glad to be out of the house with its afternoon somnolence. Her grandfather rose early and worked all morning, supervising the new factory near the farm sheds, but after dinner, both he and her grandmother retired to their bedroom where, with the big, banked fire giving off an intolerable heat, they slept till it was time for tea.

She would have gone down to the farm with Patie, but they were expecting the delivery of young bullocks this afternoon and she had developed a morbid fear of all cattle. She hated the way they snorted and bellowed and slobbered, pawing the ground and showing the whites of their eyes, and had never got over being chased by a particularly alarming specimen, half-demented with rage at having been shut up in the delivery truck. Funny she should remember about that now, when she'd just been talking to Nellie about Nicol. He'd been up helping at the farm that afternoon and he'd cornered the animal, allowing her to run for the safety of the house as fast as her inadequate jelly legs would allow.

That was when she had started to think about him. Up till then she had never really spoken to him. But he had reassured her in a very gentle, understanding way, neither shouting nor laughing as Patie would certainly have done. It was as though his face in its caring and intensity was photographed on her mind, so that she could conjure it up whenever she was bewildered or lonely or just sad. Sometimes it was as though Patie and she had no father, so little was Finn in touch these days, and when she felt particularly bereft or let-down it was Nicol she conjured up for comfort, Nicol she made speak words of love and reassurance. But

22

the strange watery feeling she had inside was like nothing she had ever felt towards anybody, certainly not her father.

She could only confide in her diary, 'Saw N.C. today. Looked at me that way again. Think I love him. Could it be?' Her grandmother would kill her if she knew. She did not even mention the conversations she and Patie often had now with Nicol when he came to do casual work at the farm. It was all politics between him and Patie and sometimes one or two of the farm hands and even the foreman joined in. Since going to Bellnoch Academy, where the Greek master was Robin Chisholm, a recognized Lowland poet and Home Ruler not averse to spreading his views in class, Patie had become obsessed by what he saw as the injustice to Scotland of two Home Rule bills summarily put aside during the war. Patie loved arguing, often just for the sake of it, as Nellie said, and Nicol, amused and half-annoyed by his vehemence, shamelessly led him on. Sometimes Big Eck the ploughboy, lost in the maze of more sophisticated arguments than his own, yet stubbornly pro-Lloyd George, lent a physical element to the debates by offering to take on anyone who disagreed with him and he and Patie would have wrestling-matches that started off half-serious and ended up in mud and acrimony.

Once Nicol had broken off and glancing at her had said, 'This doesn't interest Mairi.' She adopted the role of political cynic, saying none of it mattered and he demanded once to know what *did* interest her. When she answered 'Poetry', he quoted Yeats's *Innisfree*, swinging on the big farm gate, a length of straw hanging from his mouth, his face lively and triumphant. He made her tell them what her favourite was and she had come back with Keats's *Endymion* because they had just read it at school. And he had smiled at her and said, 'They don't understand, do they?' meaning how both of them felt and it had been like having her heart sewn up in a great silken web, his words the stitches and his smile the seal.

Another time they had all sat in the evening sunshine on a grassy bank behind a hedge and discussed the war. Nicol had been called up for the last eighteen months of the conflict and had been shell-shocked and wounded in the leg. He had said with a bitter fury that made his limbs restless and his black eyes spark like coal that too many had died for too little.

Then he had gone on to describe what it had been like

23

during the last great German push when it had looked for a short time as though the unbelievable might happen and the Germans win. With a curious, hallucinatory hysteria, some of his comrades had begun to tell tales of dead friends coming back to join in the fighting. Haig had put up his 'Special Order of the Day' – 'Every position must be held to the last man. There must be no retirement.'

He had killed his first German in hand-to-hand fighting – a young soldier 'who might have been Eck or Patie. He didn't look evil or different to me – just a man' – and then shortly afterwards the coalbox had landed on their trench, killing everyone but him. In the hospital at Etaples, a young VAD with a toffee accent had read poems to him. On his way back to Britain, he had seen the first of the Americans arrive, fresh lambs to the slaughter.

'Show us your wound,' Patie had pleaded, and after some hesitation he had pulled up his trouser leg to reveal a great deep channel of a scar that had made Mairi draw her breath in a sob of horror. Swiftly he had covered the scar again, saying the physical pain hadn't been the worst of it. She had seen something in his eyes then that had brought pity up in a flood that threatened to all but drown her. She had wanted to touch and hold him, find words that would wipe out some of the horror of his memories. She knew then that her age was immaterial. She was committed to these feelings whether permissible or otherwise.

Nellie was funny about her brother. 'He's off the Connors,' she would say, meaning her mother's side of the family, the argumentative rebellious side that had been Irish two generations back, while Nellie was all inhibited Presbyterian Chambers. But even though she criticized him unmercifully, the note of pride and puzzlement was there. Pride because he hadn't followed his brothers heedlessly into Dounhead pit; puzzlement because what his role was to be was not yet clear. In a hospital in Edinburgh for soldiers suffering war trauma he had met the poet Sassoon and others whose rage and disillusion had turned them inside out and re-made them, sometimes into identities they could barely live with. This was what Nicol's Communism was, Nellie averred: a way of getting back at the blundering generals and double-dealing politicians like Lloyd George, whose 'homes fit for heroes' seemed the biggest blasphemy of them all.

What perturbed Nellie most of all was that Nicol didn't know his place. He had appointed himself unofficial spokesman for the Rows, for servicemen without pensions and war widows without food and was putting himself forward as a councillor: all this before he had found any sort of regular employment. In his shabby clothes he bearded the county officials in their dens. At the age of twenty-one he threw his weight about both at home and in public, addressed street corner meetings like a veteran. He had received no more education than the rest of the family, yet he was already a somebody. Different. It was partly to do with his looks, his dark, dramatice eyes, partly his voice and partly to what had happened out there in France. When nearly everyone in your battalion had been killed, and you had witnessed the process, maybe you did feel there was some magical property in your survival.

But it was his lack of balance that gave birth to Nellie's deepest reservations. She had seen him in his black depressions when he first returned from the front and watched the struggle to formulate answers from the chaos of feeling. Her mother had said it for her: 'He's like a man possessed.' She repeated the phrase with a morbid satisfaction to Mairi. It added a romantic thrill to what Mairi felt.

As she walked towards Cousin Carlie's, Mairi's mind was busy trying to sort out the complexities of the other relationships around her. Although she was related to them, for instance, she wasn't allowed to visit Tina Mackenzie and her little boy Philip. That wasn't because Tina was poor but because, as her grandmother put it, she had Transgressed.

It was a wonder, indeed, they allowed her to visit Cousin Carlie, in view of Grandfather's attitude towards Carlie and her husband Donald Balfour, who was Labour Member of Parliament for Dounhead and next door to a Bolshevik in Paterson's eyes. No good pointing out to Grandfather that Carlie and Donald were anti-Communist and jealous of the old traditions of Co-operative Labour. The roots of his antagonism more probably lay in his attitude to the man he referred to as That Damned Old Radical – his half-brother and Carlie's father, Duncan, who had held Dounhead for Labour before Donald and who now lived with Carlie, his wife Josie having died a year before.

Grandma said there had always been trouble between the two, who had shared the same father but had different mothers, right back from the time they had fought over her own favours when little more than children. There was the nub of it – Honoria still spoke of Duncan with a fondness that infuriated her husband. But she was strongest in this matter and family ties were maintained. Mairi thought it amusing how after all these years her grandmother could look so pleased and animated when she recalled how the half-brothers had fought over her. Shrewdly, she guessed also that Duncan's standing in the community as the grand old man of coalfield politics niggled Paterson's touchy ego, for in terms of money, influence and the provision of jobs his own achievements were measurable but only grudgingly acknowledged.

Mairi let all these deliberations go as she lifted the latch on the gate to one half of 'Tarbert Villas', the greystone, semi-detached house with pebbled path and cream, lace-edged blinds that was now Carlie's home. She felt a little lift of spirits, for Carlie and her late mother, Kitty, had shared some happy times in the house at Kelvinside. She even remembered the day Carlie and Donald had come in to announce they were getting married and she, Mairi, had insisted there and then she wanted to be a bridesmaid in a tussore dress with frills. It made her smile to think of it.

As usual, she went round to the back door to gain informal entry. The old man was napping here, too – she could see him in the front parlour as she passed, the *Glasgow Herald* spread magisterially over his face.

Carlie was writing at the kitchen table as Mairi tiptoed in, but she looked up with a smile. A sheaf of correspondence lay before her.

'Hello, stranger. Haven't seen you for a while.'

'I've had a cold.'

Carlie pushed her work away from her. Her untidy red hair always made Mairi want to take a brush and comb to it, but she knew that even if she did it would look as bad as ever half an hour later. That was Cousin Carlie. Maybe later she would suggest giving her a water-wave – she was very good at crimping waves with her fingers. She had done it for her mother sometimes.

'I'll make some tea.' Carlie smiled, happy to see her, but sounding a little weary. 'I've just been waiting for the excuse. You've no idea the problems people write to Donald about. He could never answer all of them himself.'

'What kind of problems?' Mairi was watching greedily as Carlie delved into a paper bag and produced some delicious-looking teabread – snowballs, Paris buns, crumpets. The Co-op van drawn by the big, feathery-footed Clydesdale must recently have called. Grandma never bought from the Co-op on principle but Mairi felt a distinct partiality for its buns.

'Just what you'd expect. Men not able to find work. Women getting behind with the rent and having to sell their furniture. Sickness. Legal problems.' Carlie stirred the coal fire on which the big black kettle rested and chanted, 'Boil, boil, darn you, boil.'

'Carlie,' said Mairi thoughtfully, sinking her teeth into a snowball, 'I'm all mixed up about whether I should go into Tina Mackenzie's shop or not.'

Carlie glanced at her sharply. 'Where's the problem?'

'They don't really like me going near the Rows at all. Grandma says it isn't fitting for someone from the big house.'

'And how do you feel about it?'

'Well . . . she *is* a relative, after all.'

'Your aunt by marriage, to be exact.'

'Yes. But the marriage was a farce, wasn't it? What do you know about it, Carlie?'

'Well, I don't know what happened exactly. Nobody does. Although he's a clever doctor, your Uncle Alisdair's a strange man. Turned in on himself. I don't think Tina was ever really in love with him. She married him because she'd nothing better to do at the time.'

'And then your brother came along and they fell properly in love with each other.'

Carlie gazed into the fire, her thoughts miles away. Her expression when she finally spoke was subtly altered and sad. 'Yes, my poor brother. Or half-brother, rather. You might as well know the lot of it. He was my father's illegitimate child by a woman called Kirsten Mackenzie, and the boy took his mother's name. He and Tina fell in love, started seeing each other, broke up and came together again. Tina says if it hadn't been for the war, she would have resisted him. As it was, she felt she might never see him again. And she was right, wasn't she? He was killed and all she has to remember him by is her little boy. But at least she has that.'

'I see.' Mairi tipped the fire-irons with the toe of her boot. 'It doesn't seem very bad to me. She calls herself Mackenzie, doesn't she, not Kilgour? So she must have loved your brother very much.'

'Yes, I think she did.' Carlie smiled briefly. 'You're how old now, Mairi?'

'Nearly fifteen.'

27

'Yes. Getting old enough to decide for yourself. I'm not suggesting you should ignore what your grandmother says. Just keep an open mind about things. Don't judge people too harshly till you know all the facts.' She laughed. 'In fact, it's better not to judge people at all. Leave that to the Almighty.'

'I think I *will* go into her shop. And speak to her if I meet her in the street.' Mairi looked pink-faced but decisive. 'After all, Grandma isn't God.'

'Tina's had a bad time of it,' said Carlie quietly. 'I had to bring her out from Glasgow when she lost her job as a housekeeper. She was so run down and ill she couldn't get another. Good thing there's houses to spare in the Rows, even for folk who don't work at the pit, but even so, she lives from hand to mouth.'

Carlie gazed thoughtfully at the girl, her grey eyes understanding and sympathetic. 'What about you? How are things working out for you without your father?'

'It's just – ' Mairi's pent-up frustrations burst out. 'I love Grandma but she's so old-fashioned. She makes me wear a chemise *and* a liberty bodice, and such big hems on my clothes. And she thinks I should be happy to leave school and just be at home. It's what girls did in her day. I won't do it – I'll teach elocution or be an actress or a shorthand-typist. Or *something*. I don't want to waste my life. You understand, don't you, Carlie?'

Carlie nodded slowly. 'It amuses me,' she said, 'how people think women have nothing left to fight for, now some of us have the vote. But we're still second-class citizens. Glasgow Corporation sacks its married women. Cambridge won't give its female students the satisfaction of a degree and Donald tells me the London Hospital won't have women medical students because "unpleasant subjects" can't be taught to mixed audiences. They'll take women nurses, of course, for all sorts of unpleasant tasks no man would do – but that's apparently a different matter.'

'It isn't fair,' Mairi agreed. 'I'm going to be like you, Carlie. A free woman.' She blushed and laughed a little. 'But I want to enjoy myself, too. Do you know my cousin Catriona Peel goes to dances already in Glasgow? She's spoiled, of course. I want to learn to dance to jass – '

'Jazz,' corrected Carlie gently. She leaned over impulsively and patted Mairi's hand. 'Don't be in too big a hurry, that's all. Work hard at your lessons, learn all you can, because it's education in the end that's the passport to a free life. And when Grandma gets you down, come to me and talk things over. I like young life in the house. You see, I'm restricted, too. I have to look after my father, when I'd rather be in London with Donald. But it won't be for long.' She looked quickly out of the window. 'The old man's fading.'

When Mairi finally took her leave of Carlie, she walked towards the Rows still not certain of her course of action. It was difficult going against Grandma but she really was very rigid in her ideas. Even Daddy had admitted that. And how could Grandma insist on you going to church on Sunday and then forgetting the lesson of charity on weekdays?

Maybe her motives weren't as pure as all that, of course. There was always the chance of seeing Nicol Chambers if she walked down the Rows. And then, the whole ambience of poverty fascinated her, drew her like a magnet. Somehow, since her mother had died, she had lined up mentally with the have-nots. What was it like not to have enough to eat or be able to buy decent clothes or take a bath? Did it alter people in some subtle way she hadn't understood before so that they were different, really different, from the likes of her?

If they were, they seemed to be able to bear it. The grubby, sometimes barefoot, children, playing about near the germ-laden drains, were full of noisy, cheeky life. They hurled rude unabashed comments after her which she elected not to hear. An old woman hirpling over the frozen ground, a shawl over head and shoulders, gave her a friendly, toothless smile and said, 'Hello, hen,' obviously recognizing her.

Some of the cottages had front doors left ajar while the women gossiped and she looked in on cosy interiors with cheap, crudely-coloured linoleum and hooked rag rugs. They looked both simple and cramped. How could whole families live and sleep and wash and eat in one room, with no privacy? Even the thought made her uneasy and wish she had never started out down the Rows. But it would look odd if she walked back now. If she continued towards Tina's shop there was another way home. Feeling feet and hands cold, she stumbled on.

She passed the Chamberses' house and could see Mrs Chambers, massive in a print overall, sitting by the window peeling potatoes into an iron pot. No Nicol. Her heart lurched in an excess of disappointment. She had hoped for one of their conversations, ostensibly formal and friendly but full of hidden tugs and tides and glances.

She was at the corner now and Tina's shop was the first at the beginning of the next Row. In the space between the Rows, boys were having a noisy game of 'football' with a tin can and the ex-soldier they called the God Man was standing preaching to the wind, his black hair blowing hither and thither, the ramshackle two-wheeler he referred to as God's Bike laid at his feet. He'd fought at the Dardanelles, they said. Outwardly he looked no different from the day he'd 'listed but his eyes registered nothing as Mairi hurried past.

Mairi felt for the twopence she carried inside the palm of her right glove. Shyness overcome by curiosity, she stepped into the ramshackle space that was Tina's shop. Faded curtains on bamboo poles screened off half the room, obviously the living quarters. The other half contained a shabby counter with trays of home-made toffee balls and sugar tablet and an earthenware plate holding a large, spicy fruit dumpling, sold at a ha'penny a slice. There were a few packets of cigarettes, some headache powders and a large sack containing the main purchase of the Rows' housewives, potatoes.

A small boy appeared as if by magic from below the counter, saying in brisk grown-up fashion, 'Yes?' And then looking abashed. He wore a grey jersey with the elbows well-darned and his boots had been lovingly polished. Philip. Her cousin. Though he would not know it.

'A pennyworth of cheughers,' said Mairi, meaning the toffee balls, 'and a pennyworth of peppermint tablet.' She looked down at the child. 'Wait a minute,' she temporized. 'Are your hands clean?'

The child spread two exceedingly grubby small paws for inspection.

'They're not *very* clean,' he admitted. He spat on them and rubbed them on his trousers, then held them up again. 'Is that better?'

The curtain parted again and a small, dark woman presented herself, looking instantly proudly defensive. At closer quarters, Mairi was impressed by her neat and pretty look. She gave a quick taut smile and dismissed the child, completing the transaction briskly. 'You're Mairi Fleming, aren't you?'

Mairi nodded.

'How are your grandparents keeping?'

'Very well, thank you,' said Mairi automatically. She had just looked through a gap in the curtains to the set-in beds and fireside beyond. On a ramshackle chair she saw the figure of Nicol Chambers, making toast by holding a thick doorstep of bread up to the glowing bars of the steel grate. Embarrassment rooted her to the spot.

He looked up and his smile and speech were imperceptibly delayed. 'It's Mairi Fleming!' he said, turning the toast. The note of surprise was unmistakable. 'Bring her in, Tina. Maybe I'll get *her* to sign the petition.'

Tina held the curtains aside so that Mairi could pass through. 'He's brought in this petition for the Hands Off Russia campaign,' she explained, with an awkward smile. 'But if he thinks I'm going to sign it, he can think again.'

'Why should I sign it, then?' demanded Mairi. 'I'm not a Communist, either.'

He shook the papers tantalizingly at her. 'Do you think it's right that sixteen of her former allies should be trying to impose their various wills on Russia?'

'I don't know.'

'Or that the King of Britain should send a message of congratulation to the Poles when they invade the Ukraine?'

'I've told you: I don't know.'

'But does it sound fair to you?'

'Not very.'

He gave Tina a triumphant look. 'See, Mairi sees the light, even if you don't.' He handed the girl a stub of pencil, urging, 'Put your name down there.' From an obscure sudden impulse, perhaps wishing to be different from Tina, who obviously had no interest in politics, she signed her name with a flourish of initials. 'There, if it will shut you up.' She felt grown-up, forward and a little scared. It was the King's congratulations that had done it. He should mind his own business, she felt, and keep Britain out of any more fighting.

Tina spread the toasted bread with margarine and handed it to the little boy, who nibbled at it shyly, as though unused to having strangers watch him eat. Nicol rose, awkward on his lame leg, and said, 'Well, I must be going, Tina.'

So he called her Tina. Even allowing for the familiarity of the Rows, it seemed to Mairi to exceed the bounds of what was proper. But then, she thought with a spurt of righteous, disowning anger, the Chamberses were rough and common and even though Nicol was sure he knew how to put the world to rights he didn't really – couldn't really – know what was what. And why should it trouble her? Why was it her face that was reddening?

'Thanks for the coal,' Tina said. 'It was good of you, Nicol.'

Outside Mairi didn't know what to say. But Nicol seemed to feel the need to explain. 'I scrounged a bag of coal from the pithead for her. You can't do without heat this weather. Not with a bairn in the house.'

'I see,' said Mairi gravely. She thought his face looked white and unhealthy and there were red rims all the way round his eyes. 'Have you not found a job yet, then?'

He gave the funny little hop he used sometimes to steady himself on his good leg. 'You can tell Nellie I'm doing some work for the *Dounhead Courier*. Penny a line. Better than nothing.'

'You? Writing?'

'Aye. Me. Writing. Did you think I still used hieroglyphics like the cave men?'

Her face burned at his sarcasm and ready tears sprang to her eyes. That he, who was always her ally and protagonist, should speak to her like that! She looked away and far off down the road saw the figure of the leerie, touching the gas lamps with his long pole, setting little oranges of life glowing in the dusk.

'I didn't mean that,' she said, barely audible.

'No,' he said instantly. 'I know you didn't.'

She brought her eyes up to meet his and saw that his good humour was restored. He grinned. 'You're the product of your privileged background, girl. You can't help that.'

'Don't patronize me.'

Still he grinned. She felt angry, miserable and even a little frightened, all at once. She said, out of her discomfiture, 'I must run. Nellie said to be home before dark.'

'Don't keep our Nellie waiting, then.'

'No.' And she ran, not as a child might, but as she had seen women do, self-consciously, from the knees, splaying her feet delicately behind in a little seductive, kicking movement that suddenly didn't feel foreign to her any more.

Smiling grimly, Nicol Chambers leaned on his stick and watched her go.

Tina watched the little tableau from the window. The implications of her own friendship with Nicol Chambers had been written all over Mairi's face. So perhaps she should stop encouraging him to hang about the shop.

But it wasn't easy. He had time on his hands and the shop was convenient. And there was something between them, Nicol and herself, a rapport and a liking. She knew she tidied her hair for him, put on a little rouge for him, wore a smile for him. Where was the harm in it? Or if he touched her waist or arm occasionally and looked into her face with a challenging male stare? It wasn't important in the way Wallace had been important. It was a way of getting through the day, of facing up to tomorrow.

Poor Mairi! Finn Fleming had gone off to England six months ago and left his son and daughter with the old couple. From what Carlie said they already had their hands full with the boy Patie, who was into every mischief conceivable. The girl, though tall and well-formed, looked somehow forlorn. She had lost her mother at a bad age. She had responded to Nicol's magnetism too. He liked the girl, he had once told Tina. She had quality. When Tina had pointed out the inegalitarian nature of that remark, he had laughed and assured her class barriers no longer existed for him. He saw Mairi simply as another human being, not a pampered young woman from the big house.

Remembering how the girl's pale skin had warmed and ebbed with colour when she'd seen Nicol sitting by the fire, Tina felt a swift pang of sympathy for her. And something else she couldn't quite define. She was too amused to call it envy.

CHAPTER TWO

'How do I look?'

Patie Fleming stood in the kitchen doorway, his eyes fixed imploringly on Nellie, his gangling youth's body encased in bright, almost orange Harris tweed, a new gold tiepin under his knitted tie, new brown brogues on his feet and his fair hair slicked back carefully with water. There was already the intimation of a moustache on the upper lip, while a first chin shave had taken off more pimple heads than stubble, leaving the delicate skin looking angry and cratered.

'First class,' Nellie adjudicated, suppressing a smile. 'Away you go and don't keep your grandfather waiting. He's fidgeting about on the drive there. It'll be a black mark if you're late on your first day at work.' She picked up a pair of discarded short trousers from a pile of used clothing in front of her. 'Wait a minute,' she cried. 'Is it all right if I get rid of these old things of yours? You've a cousin in the Rows who could make use of them.'

He broke away momentarily from his own preoccupation. 'You mean Philip Mackenzie? He's far too small.'

'His mother can make them down for him.'

'Oh, all right. I don't mind.' Giving her a last anguished look, Patie went out to join his grandfather. He had never thought this morning would actually come, but now that it had, school in retrospect seemed a haven of ease and certainty. There had been ructions, of course, when he'd insisted on leaving. His father had made one of his rare sorties north to try and talk some sense into him, his grandmother had been coaxing and Robin Chisholm, the Greek master at the Academy, had called him a short-sighted idiot and worse, for he regarded him as one of his best pupils. Only his grandfather, old Paterson, had said nothing, allowing him his own way, saying truculently he was the sort who would only ever learn from his own mistakes. It was a rare experience for Patie to be reflective, but the mood was forced on him this morning.

His grandfather said nothing as he joined him. As he grew older Paterson Senior grew increasingly irascible and his temper had not been improved this morning on learning from his foreman that forty or so beasts on the farm would have to be slaughtered, victims of the foot-and-mouth that was breaking out everywhere. Add to this the fact that Finn had been proved all too infuriatingly right about the running down of the Scots economy and the richer financial pickings in the south, though that was not to say all was entirely well there either. All he had invested in the future, thought the old man now, was this skinny lump of a lad, too like himself when young, sharp and clever but bumptious too, full of the certainty he knew what was best for him. Blissful in his ignorance.

'You're going to learn it all from the bottom up,' he said now uncompromisingly. 'If you'll not stay on at school, you'll have to study at home at night. With a tutor for maths and drawing. I'll not put up with less than your best and you might as well know it.'

'Yes, Grandpa,' said Patie meekly. 'What are they to call me in the works?'

'They'll call you Mr Patie,' the old man decreed. 'And don't forget to let them know from the start who you are. Don't be over-familiar. It's a great mistake.'

'All right.' Patie's words were coming out increasingly lacking in enthusiasm. His grandfather stopped in his tracks and at last sensing his alarm said more kindly, 'The first day will be the worst, you know.'

Getting no response from this, but sensing an ever-deepening uncertainty, verging on gloom, he reminded Patie firmly, 'What about the day your father decided to go south? You said then we should keep the flag flying here. Do you not still think that?'

'Yes. I do.'

'Well then. We'll show them, eh?'

'But orders have been poor.' He was only reiterating the old man's words.

'That's when you have to fight back. When your back is to the wall.'

'You know what Nicol Chambers says? He says we should have Home Rule. Things would get better if we had our own economy.'

'First time I've ever known that Communist talk sense. Throwing his weight about, now he's a councillor, is he? Where was he giving you the benefit of his normally doubtful wisdom?'

'He comes up the farm sometimes. *Do* you agree, then?'

'What about?'

'About Home Rule for Scotland?'

'I stay above politics. But if the Irish have got their Free State and the League of Nations says that the Jews must have Palestine as their National Home, maybe it's time Scotland ran her own affairs too.'

'That's what I think,' said Patie. 'But Robin Chisholm thinks it might already be too late. That we've just sort of merged into the English culture.'

They had reached the factory beyond the byres. A long, low building with a corrugated iron roof, it had a temporary look about it. Inside, it was cold and noisy.

The old man indicated some new overalls lying on a chair in his tiny office. 'Put these on,' he ordered, thundery-browed. 'Mind what I said. You've to learn the lot. So's Robin Chisholm, by the sound of it. And this is the day you get your hands dirty.'

Nellie Chambers lifted the latch on the Rows door and entered the habitual scene of easy squalor her parents had engendered for most of their lives. Her father, wheezing in a chair by the fire, opened a lizard eye as she went in. Her mother, cutting turnip into an enamel colander, rose and stirred a pot of soup over the grate before giving her her attention. Vast, sagging, slippered, enveloped in a grimy print overall, her mother seemed to devote her life entirely to the preparation and doling out of food. Usually one or two grand-children were present, taking turns at being cuddled against the huge, grubby bosom and fed with sticky titbits. But Nellie was glad to see there were no visitors today. She had come to do her fortnightly chore of family washing and would presently take the wash-house key round to the chill edifice behind the house, light the boiler, tuck her skirts up into the legs of her knickers, don a sacking apron and have a satisfying session with tub and scrubbing-board. It might be a funny way to spend your half-day off, but she rather enjoyed the steam and suds, the approbation of passing neighbours for the way she looked after her parents and the final reward of clean linen blowing on a line between Rows and wash-house gable. Now that Nicol was on the Council, it was important to keep up some kind of appearances. Not that he was any sort of conventional councillor, for there were scenes at every meeting he attended and a peppery Unionist, Major Halliday, had attempted to have him thrown out more than once. Terms like capitalist oppressor and Communist oaf were bandied about the once-august council chamber and glee-fully reported in the papers.

Nellie dumped the bundle of second-hand clothing she had carried from Dounhead House down on the cluttered table, momentarily repelled by the worn-out grimy poverty of the room and at the same time feeling guilty because she had come to love the order and comfort, the cleanliness and plenty, of the place where she worked.

'Where's Nicol?' she demanded.

As she spoke, the latch clattered again on the door and her brother came in. 'I've brought you some of our Patie's old things you can take down to Tina Mackenzie, if you like.'

'Take them down yourself,' he said calmly.

'From all accounts, you know her better than I do.'

'What's that supposed to mean?'

'Take it any way you like.'

'I talk to the woman. Why shouldn't I? She's a cut above

36

some round here. You can have a decent conversation with her.'

Nellie's expression softened slightly. 'It wouldn't have anything to do with her looks, would it? Ah well, there's some good things there. She can make them down for the wee fellow.'

'She'll be duly grateful.' Nellie didn't miss the irony, but he looked at the clothes and eventually promised he would take them to Tina.

As their mother ladled out plates of the steaming barley-rich soup, Nellie studied her brother covertly. She remembered the weeks just after the war when he had been little more than a shaking, nervous bundle of bones, his eyes burning with pain and fright. A mild case of shell-shock, they'd said. Someone had given him a suit and he wore a collar and tie in an attempt at 'nattiness'. The collar points were frayed, like the shirt cuffs, and his boots were cracked across the toecap and down at heel, so that his sketchy attempt at respectability did not quite come off.

Quite how the Chambers family had managed to produce someone like him she didn't know. Her other brothers and sisters, all married and left home, aspired to a station in life no higher than that of her parents. She herself remembered being what was called smart at school, but if she'd once hungered after something better than service she chose to forget it now.

Nicol had always been secretive, clever, different, a throw-back, her mother chose to believe, to one of her own brothers who had become a schoolmaster. He'd always managed to find books to read. Although he'd gone down the pit before joining the Army, it had been against the advice of his teachers who had tried to raise the possibility of university, knowing full well there was no way in which it could be accomplished.

She felt the usual ache behind her breastbone when she thought of Nicol, an ache halfway between frustration and sorrow. At least now the limp was less pronounced and he mostly did without a stick. But it was no life at all for him, stuck between his ambitions and the dull, grinding sameness of the Rows, his penny-a-line work for the paper giving him a little status but nothing in the way of prospects. The best that could be said was that he had plenty of time for council work.

When Nellie had departed for the wash-house, Nicol

wrapped up the cast-off clothing and took it down to Tina. In a small lidded canister he also took some of his mother's soup. 'The lassie aye looks to me as though she could do with some nourishment,' said Mrs Chambers, though this was her pronouncement on nearly everybody.

Philip, who had recently started school, was not home yet and Nicol surprised Tina nodding by the fire, the parlour-shop without customers during the quiet part of the afternoon. She looked pale and he suspected she had been crying, though she greeted him formally and pleasantly as always and invited him to take a seat on the other side of the grate.

'Don't be offended now,' he said hastily. 'As well as some soup from Ma I've brought you clothes that our Nellie said might come in handy for the lad. From the big house.'

He saw her chin go up, but she looked at the clothing, feeling the good quality, and although her expression was set and resentful, she admitted she could do something with it. Without comment she poured the soup into a bowl, rinsed and dried the canister and handed it back.

'Is there something the matter?' he demanded.

'No. Nothing.'

'You don't seem yourself.'

'Can I make you a cup of tea?'

'No, no. Just sit and rest when you get the chance. I've got to go and see Carlie Balfour in a little while. Ask her when the next election campaign is due to start.'

'Do you think her husband'll get in again?'

'I should think so. It's going to be easier for Labour all round this time.'

'Why do you say that?'

'Because Catholic voters don't need to support the Liberals any more, not now they've got the Irish Free State. The Independent Labour Party'll get their vote this time and that'll make all the difference.'

She was scarcely listening to him. He said, with a hint of impatience. 'There's something you're not telling me. But just as you like. I'll away about my business.'

'Nicol.' The conciliatory note in her voice stopped him. 'You can see I'm not making a go of it here, can't you?'

'It's been hard for you,' he agreed.

'It isn't a living. It's a mere existence – and scarcely that. And I've got the chance of going back to my husband. He's approached me through Carlie Balfour. I'm thinking of taking it.'

He sat down again. 'I thought all that was behind you.'

'He's offered before – to have me back. You know he was the doctor who helped my poor Wallace out of his pain? Wallace was carried into his casualty station, dying of his wounds. Alisdair came to me afterwards and told me how it had been. He was decent. Very decent.' Her mouth worked and trembled. 'Considering I'd gone off with Wallace and ruined his good name.'

'How could you ruin his name? Only he could do that.'

'He felt it bitterly.'

'But you told me once he mistreated you. When you were together.'

A shadow crossed her face. 'There were faults on both sides. I can see his side now – '

'I wouldn't be in too much of a hurry to go back to a man like that.'

'I could handle him now. He wouldn't be able to bully me. And if I went back, you see, Philip could have a proper schooling. I want the best for him. Alisdair isn't set against him, you know. They've met and he's quite fatherly with the little chap.'

He gave her a long, considering look. 'You must do as you think best.'

She got up and put her hand familiarly on his shoulder. 'You've been a good friend to me, Nicol. I've few enough. That's why I'm telling you this.'

There was a small, quivering movement down his jaw-line, then his hand came up and caught hers. 'More than a friend, Tina. What about the times you let me into your bed?' He felt her hand withdraw. 'No, don't shy away from it. We never talk about it afterwards, do we?'

'I'm not proud of it.'

'I didn't think you were,' he said ruefully. 'But it was loving-kindness, wasn't it, there in the dark? At least it was for me and I didn't think I made you do anything you didn't want to do.'

'A slice off a cut loaf's never missed. Isn't that what they say?' Her voice carried a bitter crudity he had never heard before. 'It wasn't me you were thinking of when you did it. And I wish to God we never had.'

'What do you mean?'

She gave him a half-smile. 'You had been talking about Mairi Fleming all evening, the first time. How sensitive she was; how you could talk to her about things nobody else understood, but you hung back from kissing her. Or were you thinking of that VAD woman at Etaples? She was the first, wasn't she?'

'I told you what I felt for *you* too, Tina. It isn't just nothing. You *give* to a man – '

She rounded on him swiftly. 'Oh, aye, I give. I was easy. I was here. Handy. They're probably saying I led you on.'

'Don't talk like that.'

'Like what?' she taunted. He was silent and she said at last, with weary exasperation, 'I'm far too old for you. I know that. We're better just to be friends. Let what's past be over.'

'How can you go and live with a man you don't love?'

She moved away from him, taking down aired washing from the brass chain strung across the fireplace, folding it with exaggerated care. Her voice hardened. 'What kind of love are we talking about? You think it's what you read about in your books, don't you? Maybe it is, once in a while. But even that doesn't last. Death takes away, or people get ground down with poverty. And then it's comfort that matters. Food and clothes and a fire.' She laughed suddenly. 'I've never told you – I'm one of those women that want a fur coat. Silk stockings. I think I could grow to have a great affection for a man who gave me these things.'

'It's a kind of prostitution,' he said, and she laughed for he looked like his sister Nellie then, a sharp disapprobation sitting uneasily on his features.

She nodded. 'I might as well sleep with him as with you. That's what I've decided.'

He got up and held her arm, hurting her. 'Don't,' he said, white-faced.

'I'll leave you to your Mairi. She's seventeen now. Old enough for courting. See if you're brave enough to try the lassie from the big house. You and your talk about being equal.'

'What if he knocks you about again?'

She ran her tongue around her lips, as though they'd suddenly gone dry.

'This time I'll not leave him without taking a penny. This time he'll pay for it.'

'Poor bugger!'

'Aye, but he wants me. More than you do.'

He put up his arms to hold her, but they fell back down by his sides in a helpless gesture. She handed him back the empty soup canister. 'Put the sneck down on the door as you go.'

Alisdair Kilgour stopped the car on the outskirts of Dounhead and drew a flask from his jacket pocket, unscrewing the silver top with his scrubbed surgeon's fingers. He wasn't just shivering with cold. It was the familiar feeling of solitariness, of being totally alone. Just recently it had been getting harder to bear and he'd been resorting often, too often, to the glass, the bottle, the hip flask. Stupid, but you had to blur it somehow. He doubted if he'd have done anything about Tina, if it hadn't been for this feeling of cosmic misery. Even if he felt hurt and resentment again when he saw her, anything would be better than this. And if, miraculously, things worked out, and the hurt went, then he'd have a wife again like other men and a ready-made son. Children were a distraction. He'd teach the lad golf and tennis and take him sailing.

He took another furtive sip, his thoughts bottomless. Why was he so bad at the social side of things? He had a colleague, a jocular, secure, family man, who assured him he always said the wrong thing to nurses, spoke to children as though they were little old men. Inept. Had it something to do with his physical make-up? He was craggy, solid, like an uncompromising rock and his face registered nothing of what went on inside him. When young he had wanted it to look good, good in the righteous sense the Bible talked about. His mother had shovelled righteousness at him like porridge. Porridgy was what he was now. Wholesome and dull like porridge.

And bad at living. He had thought the war would finish him off; was convinced he'd actually had a death wish. But it had been Wallace Mackenzie, the man Tina had gone off with, who had been the one to die. And he the one to witness it. Agonizing and without mercy it had been, too. There had been no morphine to ease his passing.

A lot of people had given up churchgoing since the war. But he still went. Hung on to the feeling there had to be Something, a Someone, a Right and a Wrong. That being so, it was right he should try again with Tina, forgive her. A ripple of sensation ran through him, something almost like ironic laughter, but jarring like despair.

He would have to try and explain how he felt to Tina. After all, he'd knocked her about. When he looked back

41

now he saw he must have had some kind of nervous breakdown. His mother's death, the pressure of his final exams
and then Tina not letting him near her. What else could
explain the times he'd tried to establish mastery by striking
her? Even now he could feel the terror of his control slipping. It was like watching a moving picture in his mind of
someone else, a stranger. Yet all he'd wanted were her arms
about him, the closeness of mind and body which she'd held
at bay with that trapped, ferocious look in her eyes. Christ,
he was a glutton for punishment. Here he was, on the point
of asking her yet again to come back to him. He turned the
car down Balniel Street and stopped outside Carlie's cottage.

Good old Cousin Carlie! He'd always been able to count
on her. She'd offered the cottage as neutral ground, with
herself as mediator, and had even promised to make sure
the old man was away for the day, with friends. Leaning
over to the back of the car, he lifted up two stiff bunches
of chrysanthemums, one for Carlie, one for Tina. It seemed
to him as he scrunched up the pebble path that his feet
slipped on shifting ground.

'Hello, Tina.'

'Hello, Alisdair.'

Carlie had shown him, with a smile of encouragement,
into the front room. It smelled of damp and soot and lack
of use, but a fresh fire smoked up the chimney. Carlie took
a handful of sugar from the bowl on a tray and threw it on
to the tiny flames to encourage them. 'It'll soon warm up,'
she assured them. She was wringing her hands, nervous as
they were.

Tina had taken care, as always, of her appearance. Her
blue suit had been sponged with vinegar and so carefully
pressed there was not a wrinkle to be seen. Her simple tussore
blouse was freshly laundered and the collar smoothed over
her jacket lapels. She had no jewellery. Her dark hair was
parted in the centre, taken back in a chignon and softened by
a wispy fringe.

His heart began a whole concatenation of leaps and bumps
at the sight of her, leaving him weak and trembling. Strange,
he thought, how this is the one, and I don't know the reason
for it. But poverty faded. Her looks had lost their lustre. She
looked ill. The blackbird sheen had gone from her dark hair
and her skin had the pallor brought about by bad nutrition.
Yet the big, reflective eyes, the smile that was so special and
unexpected, still wreaked their old merciless havoc. He'd

played mild, flirtatious games with some of the nurses he'd worked with, clever, capable, responsive women worth twice this timid, uncertain creature, yet she was the life enhancer, she was the one he wanted. He knew it all over again and it shook and disarmed him.

'Shall I leave you together?' Carlie enquired. 'I'll go and put the kettle on. Let me know when you're ready for a cup of tea.'

'Do you want Carlie to stay?' He played his first card, that of caution, circumspection, keeping his voice formal but gentle.

Tina looked uncertain, then shook her head. 'There's no need.' She smiled at Carlie. 'I don't suppose we'll bite each other.'

She picked a straight-backed chair and he sat on the edge of the horsehair sofa, pulling up the knees of his immaculate pinstripe trousers, nervously stroking his moustache.

'Well, have you thought about it, Tina?'

'Yes, I have.' She looked quickly away and back at him, then burst out with a deliberate cruel directness, 'I don't love you, Alisdair. It's only fair I should tell you that. And I couldn't put up with the sort of thing we had before. You taking your hand to me, I mean.'

His big, boyish face had begun to shine with perspiration and embarrassment. He could feel all his good resolutions depart as shaky humiliation took their place and on top of that, blind masculine pride and anger. The recipe as before. So it was hopeless, after all. He half-rose from his seat, but she put out a placatory hand and waved him down again.

'No, I *had* to say that. I made up my mind I would be honest with you. But that's not to say I don't have any feeling left for you. And I never forget for a moment what you did for poor Wallace.'

Suddenly he came over and knelt in front of her, taking her hand and gazing at her as though he were trying to analyse all that was in her mind. Her mouth quivered at the unexpected tenderness of the gesture and his emotional balance was as quickly destroyed. He made a smothered sound and buried his head in her lap, his arms going round her and drawing her to him with urgent, desperate, claiming movements.

'Don't,' Tina pleaded. Her hand touched his hair, but her back was stiff. 'Please don't. Let's talk about this thing sensibly. We can't afford to make any more mistakes.'

43

'Yes.' He backed away from her, shame-faced, taking out a spotless handkerchief and putting it to his eyes. 'I get easily moved. Since the war. Terrible, isn't it?'

'I don't think so,' she said calmly. 'Don't worry. I understand. I don't think the less of you for it.'

'Would you come, then?' he asked, humbly, after a pause. 'Do you think I should?'

He nodded. 'Yes, I do. About the business – of what I was like before, you know, losing my temper and so on – it was unforgivable. I went through some sort of nervous crisis I didn't know how to handle. Mother dying, the exams, wanting to do well and on top of it all, thinking you didn't love me. I couldn't take it. But it doesn't excuse it.'

'I felt – frozen.' In her turn she tried to explain. 'I couldn't make you understand though, could I?'

'You could have your own room, this time. Until you wanted – '

As though she hadn't heard him, she broke in very rapidly, 'I've been crushed since coming here. Such poverty. I'm not used to it. The other day they said at school that Philip was to get free Virol. That finished me. He's too thin. Undernourished. And I have to take cast-offs from the cousins at the big house. And cadge coal.' Her hands began to work together but her control burst and she wept. 'I can't go on like this. I've no pride left.'

'Then it's a deal?' His chest rose on a great, heavy sigh that was half relief, half pity. 'You can come back with me today, if you like. You'll be warm, looked after. And so will Philip. He'll be treated like my own.'

She sat very still then, and he was like someone carved out of stone, waiting. At last she looked up and gave an almost imperceptible nod. 'Yes. All right.'

Carlie came in then, bearing the teapot, looking from one to the other warily. 'It's been settled?' When she saw the answers from their faces she kissed them both. 'It'll work out,' she told them. 'You'll see. What have we got in the world but our love for one another? Imperfect though it may sometimes be.'

When Tina left to go back to the Rows and put a few belongings together, and wait for Philip coming in from school, Carlie said to Alisdair, 'She's been through a bad time. You'll have to be patient with her. She doesn't belong in the Rows and they resent her for that.' She looked down. 'I'll miss Philip. In some ways I feel he's almost half mine!

But she wouldn't let me buy him things – jealous, you know. Possessive. I suppose it's natural.'

He looked at her speculatively. 'You should have had one of your own.'

'It's as well I didn't. Donald needs all the help I can give him. And he's coming home again soon, for the general election. I can't say I'm looking forward to another campaign so soon.'

'Go on with you! It's in your blood. You know you'll enjoy it.'

Tina stepped back into the cottage-shop in the Rows, noting the fire was going out in the grate and thinking that it did not matter. All she had to do was get some clothes together, Philip's few playthings and any little personal knick-knacks. That's what Alisdair had said. Presently he would drive down in the car to pick up her and Philip, and that would be that. An event the Rows would talk about for days to come. Tonight there would be no worry about how many lumps of coal she put on the fire. Tonight there would be enough food on the table for her to pick and choose. The sheets would be smooth and the carpets soft. And Alisdair's big, wary boy's face would be watching her. Waiting for a sign.

She was breathing rapidly, almost as though she'd run a race, as she pushed things into a heavy leather case she dragged from under her bed. How pathetic and touching were the few pieces of clothes she packed for Philip – nothing new, all of it patched, made-down, second-hand. She reached under the bed for the other thing she was determined to take with her. Wallace's kitbag. She would have to try and squeeze it into the case. It wouldn't do to let Alisdair see it.

It had been sent to her as his registered next-of-kin. In it were his diary, a photograph they had had taken together in Argyle Street, Glasgow, and one of Philip as a baby. His tin mug, his puttees and a balaclava. Three of her letters. That was all. When she'd first got it, she had kept going through it, reading the brief entries in the diary, gazing at the photographs, holding the knitted helmet, hoping for something, some feeling, some message, some contact.

Even today she couldn't stop herself doing it all over again. The fast breathing turned to weak stupid tears and she left the kitbag, rose, and tidied the room as best she could. *Leave it*, Alisdair had said. *Carlie'll get rid of it all for you.* But she packed the tea caddy and, absurdly, took down the brass chain from the fireplace and wound it round her fingers, as though she were saving string. Last Christmas Philip had hung his sock on it and she'd put some trifles in to please him. Sometimes when the room had been warm and the counter had been busy, it had been good in here. Philip and herself. Not often. But sometimes. Like the times with Nicol Chambers . . .

She had not heard the child come in and now he had gone straight to the kitbag and was riffling through it, crying, 'Mammy, what's this? Whose mug is it? Look, it's me in this photo.'

She snatched the bag from him and put the contents back inside.

'Don't touch it,' she said shortly.

He began to whine. 'I want to see it. I *want* it.'

'Look at you!' she cried. 'You come in from that school filthy. Can't you keep yourself tidy?' She was aware of the rising shriek in her voice and at his look of alarm relented and said, 'The kitbag belonged to your daddy. You shall have it when you grow up.'

Philip defiantly snatched the kitbag again and sat down with it across his knees, his look at once absorbed and seeking. He took out each item, turning it over carefully in his hands, like a dealer sizing up goods. 'You mean, these were my own daddy's? When he was in the war?'

She nodded. 'That kitbag went all over France. Sometimes I expect he used it as a pillow, to lay his head on. They had to sleep in the trenches. In the mud.'

'And this is you and him?' The grubby fingers pointed at the photograph. 'Where am I? Was I not borned yet?'

'No.' She shook her head, smiling in spite of her annoyance with him. 'That was taken before the war, one day when we'd been to hear the band in the park, and the sun had made my skin burn, here, under my eyes.'

'I wish I still had a daddy. Like the other boys.'

'You did have a daddy. Who loved you very much. He went to the war to save this country from the Germans. Some of the boys had daddies who didn't need to fight – they were maybe too old, or not fit enough. But if it hadn't been for your daddy, this country would not be free. Now, come on. We are going somewhere today. Let me wash your face.'

He didn't hear her. In the way of children, he had completely cut off from everything but his own present absorption, and he was going through the kitbag again, just the way she had, she thought, as though looking for something.

'What was his name?'

'Whose name?'

'My daddy.'

'His name was Wallace.'

'I don't want him to have died. I want him. Here.' He was standing up, the socks falling down his skinny, dusty legs, hugging the kitbag to him as though he would never let it go.

'Give it to me.'

'It's mine. It's my daddy's, so it's mine.'

'No!' she screamed at him. She took the bag from him and stuffed it into the suitcase, slamming down the locks. She scarcely knew what happened over the next few seconds, just that something snapped, some resolution, some intent. She found herself standing outside the house, tears streaming down her face, her head turning from side to side, grinding sobs and sounds issuing from her throat.

She began to stumble down the Rows, making no effort to stem the tears that rushed down her face. 'Ah, Wallace!' she heard herself saying. 'Ah, Wallace. Wallace.'

'Tina. Tina! What is it?'

Someone had her by the arm. Concerned brown eyes stared into her face. She was outside the Chamberses' house and Mrs Chambers, huge and alarmed, stood in the doorway. It was Nicol who held her, shook her, eventually put an arm round her and led her into the house.

'What is it?'

'What ails you?'

She couldn't tell them. She could only sit in the big, rackety chair, head bent into her arms, almost to her lap, while the grief for Wallace she had thought left behind engulfed her once more, drowning her like seas, stifling her like the dark. She could hear screams and shouts that were her own and yet had no consciousness of making them. Someone pulled back her head and held a burning liquid to her lips. She spat it out, flailing her arms. And then Mrs Chambers called her name, very sharply, and when she looked up threw a cup of cold water over her face. She drew a long sobbing breath and sat up, pushing the wet strands of hair out of her eyes, no longer shrieking or sobbing, but drawing her breath in long, painful rhythms,

47

saying his name quietly like a tide going out. 'Wallace.'

'Here, lass.' It was Mrs Chambers again, this time with a cup of tea in her outstretched hand. 'Take a sip of this. You're going to be all right. The da's keeping an eye on the bairn.'

From a chair on the other side of the room, Nicol looked at her with his dark, brooding eyes. Tina addressed him: 'I'm not going, Nicol.'

'Not going where?'

'He's coming for us. In the car. My husband. Alisdair. I'm not going. Tell him for me, Nicol. I don't want to see him.'

Old Mr Chambers came in, holding Philip by the hand. 'There's a gent down at your house. A gent with a car. Says he's come for you, lassie.'

'Tell him, Nicol,' Tina beseeched. Her hand was grasping convulsively at the fringe of his mother's plaid. He came and stood in front of her. 'Are you sure it's what you want?'

She straightened and took a deep, shivering breath. 'Yes, I'm sure. Tell him I'm sorry. Very, very sorry. Tell him I can't, will you? Tell him I'm sorry, but I can't.'

The war, the war, the bloody war, thought Carlie Balfour, shutting the door on a sleeping Tina the next morning and setting off home to catch up with her own domestic duties. Strange how it's still with us, laying its sourness over everything. How could it ever be over, when there were men who would never be able to work again and no work for the 'lucky' ones who were fit enough to look for it? And how could it be over when there were women like Tina, inconsolable for the lovers who would never hold them in their arms, ever again?

The night shift was coming up from Dounhead Colliery, black resurrected men walking over the tussocky grass between pit and Rows, cheerful in the daylight, handing over the dry remains of their bread and cheese to the children who ran after them asking 'Any chuck, mister?' At least, thanks to a levy on coal production, they were having their own Welfare Hall constructed. For a while in the war the mines had been nationalized, now they were being handed back. Either way, the wages they gave seemed to be minimal, stingy, for the risks involved. Her father and grandfather had done their best to improve the miners' lot. Once Donald's family owned the pit. She was glad they had sold out so that his mother could live abroad, which was the life she had chosen. Donald was better at fighting than administering. He wouldn't have made any better a collier boss than his father before him.

'How was she?'

She was startled out of her reverie by Nicol Chambers, whose dark eyes fastened on her face with a troubled, demanding sympathy. She felt a swift, defensive anger against him, because she had heard the rumours about him and Tina and knew he had that same attraction for women that her own Donald possessed, that something that was part looks, part personality that took sense and breath from women. Even the sensible ones. Perhaps especially the sensible ones.

Noticing he carried gloves and wore a tiepin under his frayed collar, presenting the Rows version of the Edwardian knuts she had seen in London before the war, she felt her anger melt at his shabby armour and said at last quite kindly, 'She's in a poor way, Nicol.'

'Did the doctor come? What did he say?'

'Neurasthenia. Anæmia. He's put her on chemical food. But I think she's just giving up.'

'We'll not let her do that.' He fell into step beside her.

Carlie said shortly, 'The best thing you can do is keep away from her. I wish she had been able to go with Alisdair. He wants to look after her, you know. Properly. Not many men could be as big at heart as that. But if she won't try, he won't pay.'

'It wouldn't have worked. You can't make yourself love somebody. Love's a question of chemistry.'

She gave him a quick, sideways smile. 'Perhaps you're right. She said a funny thing to me last night, after the doctor had been. She said, "Wallace was my husband." And he was, if not in letter, certainly in spirit, and she's not over him yet.'

'Who's keeping an eye on Philip?'

'I am. He's coming to me for his dinner break.' Her eyes betrayed the pleasure she felt over this.

'And Donald's coming home this week-end? For the election campaign? Is he going to let me help him, do you think?'

She stopped, gazing at him with a wary mixture of affection and exasperation. 'We've been over all this before, Nicol. We've voted to keep Communists out of the Labour Party.'

'We agree more than we disagree.'

49

Her expression closed and hardened. 'It's a question of approach. Ours is the inevitability of gradualness. Yours would mean revolution and misery. We don't want that.'

'You'll never dislodge capitalism, except by force.'

'Well, I've seen enough of the Russian model for revolution,' she said grimly. She had gone to Petrograd with a Suffragette party in 1917 and had brought Donald back from his wartime engineering mission there, dying on his feet from starvation. Even under the moderate Kerensky government there had been fear and looting, massacre and suppression. A feeling of hidden terror that still had the power to water her limbs. And since then, stories of the murder of the Kulaks, in their thousands if not their millions. 'We don't want any of that here.'

'You can't keep Marxists out of the Labour Party.'

'We can try.'

'It's always the same,' he said angrily. 'When we send someone down to Westminster, they get in with the money boys there. It's all culture and theatres and Tory soirées. They forget what it's like up here. We should be solving our own problems. It can't be done at a range of four hundred miles.'

'You're not suggesting my Donald's like that?'

With a quick respectful glance at her red hair, he said, 'I don't know. They're all too far away for us to see.'

She began to laugh then, seeing a certain justice in his impatience.

'You can tell your Donald this.' His tone sharpened. 'They've just made me agent at the pit. And that's going to mean trouble for him and for the government. We've taken enough and wages have to start going up.'

'*You* tell him. I have enough to worry about.'

CHAPTER THREE

Mairi Fleming was walking along the road towards Dounhead House thinking of her recent meeting in the village with Nicol Chambers, and how satisfactory it had been in every respect, when she heard a car klaxon behind her and turned to see Robin Chisholm in his Dalgleish-Gullane.

Reluctantly pushing Nicol away from her thoughts (he

had been friendlier than he had been for ages), she looked up at Robin in the big rangy car and found herself saying automatically, 'Hello, sir.' Since she had not taken Latin or Greek at the Academy, he had not taught her, but school was still close enough for the old respectful epithet to come out.

'No need to "sir" me now, Mairi.' He had a thin, wiry frame and a big, bony, serious forehead, from which heavy dark hair waved back like the ploughed furrows in a field. Only the eyes were exceptional: full of a deep, broody intelligence. Mairi, like everybody else, had come to accept the fact that he wore the kilt at all times, rare enough in Lowland Scotland. 'Want a lift? I'm going up to see that grandfather of yours. Or Patie. This machine needs something done about its steering.'

She settled herself in the seat beside him. 'They don't do repairs,' she pointed out. Chisholm gave an ingratiating half-smile. 'This is just a small favour, for me. Tell me, you're related to Balfour the Labour man, aren't you? When is his election meeting? There's a few things I have in mind to take up with him.'

'Thursday night. In the Co-operative Hall.'

'Will you be there?'

'I might,' she said cautiously. She was beginning to enjoy the ride, feeling more at ease. She had left school some time ago, after all, and Robin Chisholm surely wasn't yet thirty and not all that old. Satisfaction at being seventeen and in grown-up territory went through her with a pleasing thrill that was still novel.

'I hear you may soon be starting to teach elocution,' Chisholm pursued. 'Is that right?'

Mairi nodded. The fact that he was interested was very gratifying for someone who only a year before had been treated to his hectoring disciplinary tones in the school corridors. He was, besides, despite his reputation for eccentricity – the kilt and his Home Rule campaigning – something of a minor celebrity as a poet and writer. She had recently tried to follow his views in a Glasgow evening paper on a strange new poetic work called 'The Waste Land' and he had been very funny writing about an Irishman called Joyce whose *Ulysses*, it seemed, came out like something in a child's scrambled word game.

She said, 'My grandparents say I can have a room downstairs for a studio – that's when I get my teaching diploma.'

She did not say how surprised she had been at their helpfulness, but felt it probably had something to do with keeping her away from Glasgow and shorthand-typing.

'I've heard you.' He gave her an appraising glance. 'I've heard your reading at the Caledonia Society. Something from "Childe Harold's Pilgrimage", wasn't it?'

She felt her face redden. 'Yes. "Waterloo".'

' "There was a sound of revelry by night," ' he quoted, with relish. 'The audience seemed to enjoy all that Byronic stuff about Cameron's gathering and the war-note of Lochiel.'

' "How in the noon of night that pibroch thrills, savage and shrill." ' She quoted it now, surprising herself, and was rewarded by his open, appreciative grin.

'My, how you've grown up, Mairi Fleming! But I'll tell you something. When I spoke to Sixth Year Assembly it used to be as though I was talking to you and no one else.' He grinned. 'It was a nice feeling. Will you come out with me some time? I'll take you to Glasgow, to the theatre. What do you say?'

'I don't know,' she said confusedly. 'Oh, look, we're here.' She got down with undue haste, not looking up at him, and saying hurriedly, 'I'll find Patie for you.' Afterwards she knew very well she had been lacking in poise, though not in rudeness. But there had been something in Chisholm's attitude that had annoyed her. A suspicion of conferring favours from the Olympian heights. Besides, he was *quite* old. His kilt dipped at the back over his skinny knees. She didn't like his sort of hair. And there was Nicol. After all the months of waiting, hearing the rumours about him and Tina, telling herself she was stupid and impractical, after all that, they'd spoken today like old friends. Something had gone click! again, and even just talking to him had filled her with a silly, mindless happiness which she wouldn't, couldn't exchange for the sake of further friendship with Robin Chisholm.

Watching his sister's retreating back, Patie came out of the workshop, wiping oily hands on a rag, and faced his former teacher quizzically.

'Nice old car,' he opined. 'Improved de Dion, basically, isn't it? Made by the Haddington Motor Engineering Company.'

'Steering's gone,' said Chisholm.

The old man had materialized from the office. 'We don't do repairs,' he said gruffly.

Chisholm ignored him. 'I see Balfour's back for the election.' He spoke obliquely into the space between the boy and the old man. 'His socialist peers will soon be running the country. If they don't get in this time, they'll do it the time after. And then there'll be no more grand old cars like this. Individual enterprise'll become a dirty word. We'll be England's scudgies when we're not licking Russia's arse.'

'You have a strong command of the language,' said Paterson drily. He gave a full-throated bark of enjoyment and capitulated. 'Leave your bloody old car and we'll fix it for you.'

Chisholm smiled. He turned to Patie. 'You were a Home Ruler at school, weren't you? Be sure you come to the meeting on Thursday night. Bring Mairi. If Balfour's going back to Westminster, I'll water his socialist cant with some strong Scotch medicine. We'll see how he likes it.'

'I wonder you don't stand for Parliament yourself,' said Paterson.

Chisholm stroked the car bonnet affectionately. 'We have to bide our time. You know the bit about the tide in the affairs of men. Willie Shakespeare had it right, once or twice. Our tide's not yet. But it'll come.'

'How is he?'

Donald Balfour looked at his wife as she came into the room after checking that her father was sleeping.

'Peaceful.' At the rue and sadness in her face, he held out his arms. 'Come here, Carlie.' He kissed her brow and mouth. 'He can come to no harm. Tina will watch him. I need you with me on the platform.'

She put her arms round his neck and relaxed in his embrace. 'Oh, I'm so glad to have you home. I can face anything with you here, even – '

'He's just old and very tired.'

She wiped tears away carelessly. 'Once all this excitement was his. It was him on the platform, my mother polishing his shoes and making his tea.'

'And he'd want you to do the same for me.'

She brightened, making the effort. 'Here, turn round.' She took a clothes brush and scoured the shoulders of his ageing serge suit and followed that by straightening his tie and pin while he submitted with the air and demeanour of a martyr.

'Donald – ' she said hesitantly. He lifted one eyebrow. She

53

looked at the face she knew and loved above all else. Its strengths and its weaknesses were knitted into her own being so that when he was threatened it was like her own life laid on the line. 'Donald, I think it's going to be rough down there tonight. Nicol Chambers has told me as much and Mairi says Robin Chisholm is out for trouble.'

'Let them come. It's a free country.'

'Yes. But – ' How could she say to him: 'I think you look frail. I think the shoulders I've just brushed in that shabby serge are too narrow, too insubstantial, for the burdens you carry. I hear you cough in the night and your lungs refuse to expunge their harshness. I remember you when you were a little boy and they said you were delicate, and I remember when I stirred those rags in a room in Petrograd and they were you.' In the end she said nothing. Words were inadequate and unnecessary between them. He put his hand under her chin in a wordless gesture, then handed her her hat and permitted himself the time and luxury of watching her put it on in front of the overmantel mirror, enjoying the small feminine gestures of impatience and vanity as she coaxed her hair up under the brim.

The hall had filled up substantially when they mounted the platform. Carlie could smell the now-familiar mixed odour of public meetings – carbolic soap and boot polish mingled with sweat and stale clothes, cheap essence of violets with whisky and beer. There were a number of women in plaids, one or two with babies, a couple of miners still in their pit dirt but many more scrubbed up and watching Donald with attentive expressions. Carlie noted Patie and Mairi sitting beside Robin Chisholm and two rows in front, Nicol Chambers doodling into a notebook. She wished then that Donald had been able to bring up one of the big guns like Ramsay MacDonald, but they had either been already booked or Donald's independent, quixotic line was not to their liking.

When 'Ginger' Murray, his agent, had introduced him, Donald gave what Carlie thought was a well-judged, constructive speech, pledging help in the pits, as always, but extending his brief to lighter industries so that Dounhead would not fall into the old, distressing reliance on coal and steel only.

Chisholm rose to heckle him persistently, but it appeared to be mainly counter-productive for those around him silenced him with angry shouts. But he stood up before the applause for Donald's speech had died away and this time he refused to sit down. The crowd rose, braying, to its feet, some wanting to eject him bodily and others crying for fair play and free speech. Dodging a furious old miner who was wagging his fist in his face, Chisholm took a running leap on the edge of the platform. Donald held up his hand for quiet, what he hoped was a patient smile on his face.

Chisholm said angrily, 'I've listened to Balfour here tonight and what he says may be all right as far it goes. But you know and I know that Scotland is going to end up bottom of the heap again. Whatever he says.

'Do you know how many people are leaving Scotland, this very day? We're a nation of less than five million people but there are already about twenty million calling themselves Scots living all over the world and they went *because there was nothing here*. Does it not give you pause for thought? We've done more, possibly, man for man, woman for woman, to build the modern world than any other nation and what have we created for ourselves *here*?'

'Not much,' shouted a wag, and as the laughter died away Chisholm took up the slack on his oratorical reins. 'Does it ever occur to you that what we are nowadays is a sort of annexe of England? What about our language? Sanny Batters down there –' pointing to the wag –'learned Lallans at his mother's knee and now he's made to feel ashamed of it. Ashamed of a vocabulary rich and varied and his birthright, but it's not English, so it's judged inferior.'

'Away hame, Robin,' someone shouted, and another invited, 'Gi'e us a lend of your kilt.' Nicol Chambers was on his feet now, eyes blazing although all that could be gathered above the din was his reiteration that 'the worker had no fatherland'.

Blandly, determinedly, Chisholm went on, 'Even Marx has praised what he calls "healthy nationalism" –' with a glare at Nicol –'but we don't need a German-Jewish intellectual to tell us that if we don't do something, we'll remain a province of London. Our cities are deteriorating before our eyes, our villages are emptying as fast as folk can get to the Broomielaw, and we have neither a proper urban nor a country life, but something hybrid and attenuated, something in between.'

A scattering of applause, and Donald finally seized his chance to reassert himself, agreeing that much of what Chisholm had said was true, but arguing that a Labour government would by its very nature take up neglected areas first.

When the meeting was over, Carlie went down into the hall and invited Mairi and Patie back to supper at Tarbert Villas. She turned to Robin Chisholm with a bright, sociable smile and said, 'You'd be welcome to come too, if you feel like it.' As he nodded his acceptance, Nicol Chambers to Carlie's surprise joined the group. 'Am I included, too? I'll not eat much.' 'You'd better not,' said Carlie, mock grimly.

As they walked towards the promise of food and warmth, Patie argued with Robin Chisholm that Scottish education was still best.

'Do you remember what Dickens said about the headmaster in *Hard Times*?' Chisholm's tone was ironic. ' "If he had only learnt a little less, how infinitely better he might have taught much more." We're too broadly based, especially in the universities. We've lost our intellectual vigour. Not our fault. War and emigration have done it to us.'

Mairi was conscious of Nicol Chambers tugging at her to hang back. 'That ape Chisholm!' His face was dark with annoyance. 'Cassandra in a kilt.' Mairi began to giggle irrepressibly. 'He's a Lowlander, like me,' Nicol went on. 'Chances are he's descended from some Norman baron who slipped over the Border on a dark night with his Yorkshire henchmen. Only the wildest Highlanders are entitled to the kilt, and he's neither wild nor Highland.'

'I wouldn't say he wasn't wild!' protested Mairi. 'He seems fanatical enough to me. He'll not be happy till we've severed all relations with the south and stopped up the ports of emigration.'

'He's got his eye on you.'

'Don't be silly.'

'I don't blame him. So have I.'

So it had worked, she thought. The new beige dress with its shorter hemline, the square neckline, the tambour embroidery. The pale stockings. The wide velvet bow at the nape of her neck. They had all worked together with some wild stray magic this unlikely evening. 'All went merry as a marriage bell.' She recollected her Byron once again, feeling vaguely sorry because if Robin liked her, then it was a pity for him.

In the dark she saw Nicol's face, the eyes almost hypnotic with their dark gleam. His hand, bony and firm, caught hers and held it as they walked. And although she hoped that nobody saw, she could feel this contact change the very structure and functioning of her being.

Carlie Balfour raised the heavy Ayrshire blankets and the cosy patchwork quilt and snuggled up against her husband in the commodious brass and iron bed. She knew Donald was lying in the dark as wide-eyed as herself, waiting to talk about the evening's happenings.

'There *is* something in what Robin Chisholm says,' she averred. 'I feel it. Every time I walk down the main street, or along the Rows. It's an emptiness, a feeling of things and people gone away.'

'You have to make allowances for a war. Of course, there are people gone away. Half a generation of men.'

'Yes.' She acknowledged the words soberly. 'But it's more than that. Not just apathy. Cynicism.' She hugged his ribs. 'People I talk to have given up on Parliament. They really don't think the politicians can help. In some ways Labour are to blame, Donald.' At his protest, she nudged him reassuringly but went on, 'Yes, they are. They take the solutions out of the people's hands, as it were. It's not so much *we'll* put things right any more, as *they* ought to do it for us.'

'You sound for all the world like the wife of some Tory ironmaster,' he said, stiffly.

'You know I don't mean to. It's just that I am beginning to think we do need Home Rule. We'll be overlooked otherwise, treated like machine-minders and beaters for the Glorious Twelfth. A subject race.'

'I never thought to hear you talk such twaddle.' He was leaning up on an elbow now, angry.

'We *don't* talk like the English. We stifle our own words because we think they sound ignorant and wrong. How can that be? I can think of dozens of words that have no equivalent in the English language – '

'Well, maybe it is time for a cultural stand. I don't deny you that. It could happen without severing the economic ties. We would have gone down sooner, you know, if we hadn't joined Parliaments. We got a share in the Empire, a chance to administer India, colonize Canada . . .'

'And all London asked in return was that all the men who made their mark took the trail south and stayed there.'

'You can't blame the English for the Scots desire to get on.'

'Why can't we get on in our own country?'

He sighed at this, drawing her into his arms and kissing her hair and cheek. 'I wish I knew the answer. Something to do with the tightness and narrowness of our society. The libertarian impulse must be realized elsewhere. Something to do with Calvinism and the perpetual social criticism it implies. I sometimes think the role of the kirk and the role of Karl Marx are similar. He studied eighteenth-century Scots social thought, you know. He might have been influenced by the insistence of communal responsibility for morality.'

She lay digesting this, quiescent in his arms.

'Do you realize, woman, that I'm home again? The times I've lain in my bachelor bed in London and longed for you! What are we doing discussing politics when we could be making love?'

'But it's important!'

'Aye, so is this.'

'I wish we'd had a bairn, Donald.'

'You are my bairn and I am your bairn.'

She smiled. 'That's true.' She kissed him.

When they had been close and she had fallen asleep, breathing lightly and rhythmically, he lay feeling a post-coital tenderness that verged on sadness. What he had to do took him away from her far too much. Not just in the physical sense; but essentially. For what were politics if not a loving and caring for the unspecific mass, for the general instead of the particular. The way he felt now, he could have taken her off to an island, Mull, or Eigg or somewhere else bleak and splendid, kept her to himself while they walked in the brash winds and felt the soft rain, and afterwards made love again and again till he knew nothing but her red hair and soft pale skin. He grinned luxuriously to himself in the dark, his mind but not his lips saying her name, his body aware of her warm certainty next to him.

As sexual euphoria relaxed and remade him (strange how by giving you recreated yourself always) Robin Chisholm's gaunt, serious form rose unbidden in his mind. It was diffi-cult, for all the man's sincerity, to take his talk of a new Home Rule party, a national party, seriously. He was what his mother would have called a big sapsie, almost a figure of fun in his long, unbecoming kilt, his hand-knitted socks and his buckle shoes.

Yet it wasn't as simple as that. Take the question of vocabulary. His father, Lachie Balfour, had been university-educated and never used the Lallans, except in teasing mood, whereas his mother, Rows-born Tansy Fleming, had a fund of pithy, colourful expressions she brought out in moments of stress. Carlie used colloquialisms all the time. Stealing a person's vocabulary was like stealing his birthright. Yet the writers of the Kailyard School had surely used the Lallans to create a pawky, cosy, semi-literate prototype who was somehow negligible, or would have been if he had had any semblance to reality. The papers were full of examples. And language should surely be a tool of precision?

He didn't want a Kailyard Scotland, full of singing kilties and drouthy Harry Lauder-like worthies. People weighed down with their Scottishness. What did he want, then? He didn't want world revolution with Scotland hanging on to the Comintern's whirling coat-tails, like some of his Marxist friends. There was going to be a collapse of the Liberal vote in the coming election, of this he was sure, and Labour with over 400 candidates might do spectacularly well, though it would probably be a Tory victory. He stubbed his specula-tive toe on the hard fact reiterated by Chisholm: the last vestiges of any kind of independent Scottish decision-making were gradually being whittled away by the Whitehall machine, whichever Party was in power. If the hopeful projections of a Labour government in the year to come had any basis, it still remained true that the machinery of government as well as the actuality of government would remain in London. It jarred. It jarred. As much as Robin in his sapsie kilt.

'Father? Are you awake?'

Carlie went into her father's bedroom at Tarbert Villas. Although he could no longer read, his books and papers took up the shelves of two walls and memorabilia nearly all the rest of the space. By his bedside lay the calfskin volume of Burns he had first given and then got back from Kirsten Mackenzie. Sometimes he called Carlie 'Kirsten' or 'Bonnie bird' and even now it gave her pain, on her mother's behalf. Poor Josie! She had not been the sort to lay a spell on a man, not being beautiful, or educated, or clever. Yet her stoic dignity had meant something.

The old warrior opened his eyes. 'Is it morning, then?'

'A good morning.' Carlie beamed down at him, her pleasure unrestrained. 'Donald's in again, Father. But it's better than that. We've got 142 in all told. The Liberals are down to third place.'

He pushed himself up, accepting the breakfast tray with shaking old hands, striving to clear his brain. 'Tell me again.'

'Donald's got in again, with a better majority. The ILP have got ten seats in Glasgow alone, five elsewhere, and the trade-union men have won nine more for Labour.'

He took a sip of tea. 'Tom Johnston got in?'

'Yes. Jimmy Maxton, Manny Shinwell, Davie Kirkwood. The Clydesiders. It's bound to make a difference—'

'Parliament'll never be the same again!' Duncan chuckled. 'Changed days, lass, eh? Since I was the only rebel on the scene!'

As the day wore on, Carlie thought again of her father's words, the sensation it had been when even one Labour man had got in. And now there were so many. The Rows were alive with the news and there was a kind of fighting euphoria abroad, those with doubts to express caught up in ceaseless argument with others who saw Jerusalem round the corner.

The door-knocker went ceaselessly with congratulations and exhortations of what had to be done now at Westminster —a job secured for this one's husband, a house and a cure for TB for the next, pit nationalization for the next. One fat old widow with nothing left to hope for waddled up the garden path to weep inarticulately on the doorstep, till Carlie brought her into the warmth of the kitchen and made her a cup of tea.

'Are you going to the station to see them off?' Nicol Chambers met Mairi coming from the grocer's, where she had been handing in her grandmother's weekly order. His smile went over her face like the touch of fingers and she blushed and looked down at her new strapped shoes.

'My grandparents wouldn't like it.'

'What have they got to worry about? Their Government's still in power.'

'They weren't too happy about me going to the election meeting and Patie and I both got a row for being late in.'

'You'll have to learn to be responsible for your own decisions.'

She looked at him defensively. 'It's different for a girl.'

'There's women pressing for all kinds of things now. Widows' pensions, equal rights in the Civil Service.'

'You'll be telling me next about Marie Stopes.'

She had wanted to shock him, and succeeded.

'You know about her?'

'About birth control?' Mairi no longer felt one down, so

she smiled at him a little more confidently. 'Yes. Doesn't mean to say I approve, of course.'

'Of course not.'

'You're funny,' she said, faintly irked. 'I expect you're just like every other man. You think a woman's place is in the home. Having babies.' She sounded like Carlie Balfour, and he knew it. He grinned.

'Come to Glasgow. There's going to be a great send-off for the Clydesiders. Your grandparents can think you're looking at the shops.'

'I could say I needed books for my elocution. In fact, I do.'

'Well then.' He beamed at her. 'It's going to be an occasion you'll never forget.'

As she continued with her shopping – tobacco for her grandfather, pan drops and the *People's Friend* for Honoria – Mairi knew that despite the risks she would do anything Nicol asked her. When she was with him, she was so happy all her senses vibrated like a harp in a breeze. That feeling was worth trading in almost anything for – even the occasional moment of self-doubt. It was like being in another country, full of soft airs and half-heard beautiful songs. Like the island in *The Tempest*.

Later, before the day of the Clydesiders' departure, she allowed certain fears to surface. If Nellie knew she was seeing Nicol, she would almost certainly tell her grandparents. And if Patie decided to be mischievously indiscreet, she could be in trouble there also. He had already made his disapproval plain. Well, if he let the cat out of the bag she wouldn't be able to restrain herself from wrecking his precious crystal set. That would teach him. But it wouldn't come to that. He could be jealous and intransigent but he did believe still in their united front.

The trouble was, going against what was expected of you was like asserting yourself in a new guise, a grown-up version of the Mairi in whose skin she had been so comfortable for so long. This new Mairi felt as stalky and vulnerable as an Easter daffodil. But it seemed she had no more say as to her blooming than flowers did in their season in the sun.

Carlie could not believe it when she walked through the station concourse on Donald's arm. Hundreds of people had turned up to see their heroes off to Westminster, in some cases making their own vociferous contingent from Dounhead appear very small beer indeed.

She spotted young Emmanuel Shinwell and long-haired, delicate-looking Jimmy Maxton, each with their crowd of well-wishers making progress towards the train difficult if not impossible. More and more people poured into the station by the minute, someone in front was playing a mouth-organ and a man in a muffler near her had tears pouring down his face yet still was smiling.

Carlie felt herself caught up in the emotionalism of the moment. It wasn't just this present triumph she was thinking about: somehow she was also remembering the day Ivy Thompson's man had died down the pit and the Hussars had come out to quieten the rage of the men. Her mother's face bobbed up in her mind – no, not just her face, but her whole stance, somehow indomitable, waiting, refusing to be cast down. And the night her father had first been returned to Dounhead, and old Grannie Kate had come into the hall with snow beading her bonnet. And the hunger in the Rows and the fight for the women's vote in the early days in London . . .

She felt Donald's hand tighten on her arm. They had reached the compartment where he had to enter the train and she felt the usual wild selfish desire to keep him with her.

'Take care,' she said. 'See you soon.'

'Let me know when anything happens.' They both knew he referred to her father. She nodded soberly, afraid to say what was in her heart in case she broke down.

'There's Mairi over there, with Nicol Chambers.' Donald raised a hand in salute and Carlie motioned the young couple to come over. But they did not seem to be able to make any headway through the pushing, jostling crowds. Donald climbed up the compartment steps, reappearing at the window and giving a boxer's salute as a cheer went up for him.

Someone had started to sing the 23rd Psalm, raggedly at first, but the sound thickened and grew as more and more voices took it up.

'Good old Davie!' somebody shouted. David Kirkwood, veteran of many a George Square rally, was making his victorious way to his carriage.

'When we come back,' he told the crowd, his hand up-raised like the prophet, 'this station, this railway, will belong to the people!'

Carlie's eyes met Donald's. Already bloodied in the West-minster arena, he would need all his steadiness to counter-balance the wild heady arrogance of such as these.

The guard's whistle blew and slowly, separating itself from the importunate tide of well-wishers, the London train snaked out of the station. Carlie waved to the mass of arms and scarves that trailed from it, no longer knowing which belonged to Donald, unable to see for the tears that would not now be stemmed. She tried to find Mairi and Nicol in the crowd, but they were no longer to be seen.

'It won't work,' said Mairi, wiping the luscious juice from a Ca'doro apple tart from her mouth, 'because, you see, Communism thinks people can be unselfish and sharing but we're not born like that. We're not perfectible.'

'We have to try.' Nicol had cut a potato scone into two and was nibbling at it absently. ' "To each, according to his need. From each according to his ability." '

'And who decides what I need? I might need more to eat than you and I might wear out more clothes, and would that be fair?'

She stopped, aghast, as he poured the tea from his cup into his saucer.

'Nicol! You can't do that!'

'Why not?'

He blew on the tea, drinking it imperturbably. A large woman in a fox fur at the next table clicked her tongue and turned her head away with a jerking movement.

'You see . . . it worries me,' she said slowly. 'I think you have to improve from inside, as an individual. I don't think you can have improvement thrust upon you.'

'Oh, go back to your kirk,' he said, suddenly surly. 'You know it's only for the well-off and well-dressed. It's irrelevant in this day and age.'

'No. You have to be answerable to somebody, and Grandpa says it's better God than Lenin.'

He changed the subject abruptly. 'Do you want to go to the pictures? Will they expect you home early?'

'I told them I might go with my cousin Catriona Peel to see Garbo.'

'Clever,' he acknowledged. Restored to favour, she beamed at him happily and unobtrusively pushed her share of the bill across the table.

When they came out of the picture-house in Renfield Street, they were still arguing about the existence of God.

'God is simply the moral sense you were brought up with,' he insisted and she replied, 'No, God is stronger than me, outside me, above me.'

'Kirk-goers only care about the impression they make. About keeping up appearances. They're the biggest bunch of humbugs in the town.'

'Because Christians fall short doesn't mean the church does.'

'But charity. "The greatest of these is charity." Where does that come in?'

She was thoughtful, beaten, and burst out: 'People don't seem to be able to break through barriers . . . Oh, you might be right. I don't know.'

As they walked towards the station, they looked down dark cobbled alleyways and saw couples caught up in urgent embraces. Their steps slowed down, they moved closer and closer till his arm was about her waist and her light weight pressed against him. Then he turned her gently down a narrow passageway and his arms were about her totally and his voice sounded close in her ear: 'You are good, at least, Mairi. Good and innocent. And I want you.'

'Nicol.' She stood quiescent in the circle of his arms, heart bumping so loudly he could feel it. He gave her a little reassuring hug, but his own expression had changed, become urgent.

'Can I kiss you?'

'Do you want to?' Her voice shook.

'More than anything.' She felt his lips lightly, then strongly on hers. 'Oh, more than anything.' Now the pressure would not give up, she could smell the damp Glasgow drizzle on his coat collar, the faint odour of somebody else's tobacco and then her senses took off and it was as though she floated weightless through the dark and mysterious Glasgow night.

He stumbled slightly away from her, groaning. 'I'm frightened I'll crush you.'

She could feel herself smiling in the dark. 'I won't crush.' She put out a hand and drew him back to her, her fingers touching his face. 'Nicol, I want to say it. I think I love you.'

She could judge that his expression had altered, from exultation to something more sober and cautious. In alarm, she said, 'What's the matter? Don't you – '

'Aye, I do. But have I a right to? You're that innocent and I'm a renegade and a rebel. Sometimes a black-hearted bastard. I know it. Come on. While there's time let me undo what I've just done.'

'No. Kiss me again. I've said I love you. I don't care –'

'But I have to care. I'm older.'

Her arms dropped to her sides as though full of lead. 'I was afraid it would come to that. It's because I live at the big house, isn't it? And all your talk about being equal doesn't really work, when you get down to it.'

'I've got nothing to lose,' he said helplessly. 'It's you that stands to lose everything.'

She did not know where the next question came from and would have called it back as soon as she uttered it. 'Was it different with Tina Mackenzie, then?'

She thought he would never answer. Then in a flat voice he reiterated the name, almost as though it didn't make sense. 'Tina Mackenzie?'

'She was before me, wasn't she? And maybe others.'

'Mairi.' He sounded commanding, almost like Nellie telling her to behave herself. 'You have to accept me as I am. Nothing before was ever like you. And that's the truth.'

She began to move away then, walking up the vennel and into the street, and he came a few paces behind, his look desperate. Then he caught up with her again, pulling her arm and saying, 'You have to show you trust me, you know. It's hopeless without that.'

'You're right. I *am* too young. We're too different. I don't know anything and you know it all. You're *experienced*.' They stopped and their eyes met, pain and defensiveness in his, pride and belligerence in hers.

'What I did, I did. It's past.'

'Oh, but if we're really close, we could share anything. But you tell me nothing.'

'Some things a man doesn't tell.'

'If that's the way of it –' her head went up – 'then I'm going home by myself. Leave me. Don't walk with me.' She took off at an almost running pace.

When he got to the station, he could see her standing at the far end of the platform, but made no move to join her. He was torn between a towering anger and a desperate wish to laugh at her wilfulness but in the end what held him back was the fear of more rejection. She had unmanned him, left him not knowing who he was or where he was.

Mairi watched the hands of the station clock creep round,

mind and eyes both a blur.

'Good evening, Miss Fleming.' She scarcely heard the greeting above the hiss and rattle of the train approaching the bumpers. 'You're a late traveller, are you not?'

She turned a hastily alarmed face and saw a watchful, curious Robin Chisholm. He helped her enter the train and sat purposefully down beside her.

'Did you see the big send-off earlier for our heroes of the left?'

She nodded. 'Then I went to the pictures with – with a friend.'

'That lot were better than the pictures. Most of them'll be earning decent money for the first time in their lives.'

'Four hundred a year's not exactly a fortune.'

'It will be for most of them. I wonder if it'll change their ideas of equality for them.'

There was a grudging, railing note in his voice that annoyed her. 'You sound so cynical,' she charged him. 'Surely you wish them well?'

'Two million unemployed,' said Robin Chisholm, with unrepentant blithe irony, 'and they think they'll solve *that* with a hymn or two. Sure I wish them well. They'll need it!'

Mairi gazed at a picture of Rothesay Bay under the luggage rack opposite and said nothing. As though it were happening all over again, she could remember the feeling of Nicol's mouth on hers. She took in very little of Robin's subsequent conversation. She was mad to see Nicol again. To be with him. Not to be with him had become a kind of death.

CHAPTER FOUR

'Come in here.'

Honoria Fleming's tone was uncompromising. She stood at the door of her own private sitting-room on the ground floor, waiting to be obeyed. Mairi walked past her, refusing to cast down her head, her eyes bright with defiance.

The old woman had not long wakened from her afternoon nap. Her face was still puffy, the eyes like little bright currants in the folds of pink fire-warmed flesh. She sagged down again in the cushioned wicker chair, groping for the bag of striped humbugs down the side. From the heavily banked fire a large cinder clattered on to dark green tiles. Mairi lifted the firetongs to replace it but her grandmother said sharply, 'Never mind that. You've been seeing Nellie's brother, it seems. What sort of way is this for Finn Fleming's daughter to behave?'

'Finn Fleming doesn't care what happens to his daughter.' Still kneeling straight-backed by the hearth, Mairi turned an unwavering, challenging gaze in Honoria's direction. She could feel her heart race with panic and fright. Who had told the grandparents? She rejected Nellie and Patie in turn, knowing neither of them could have guessed at yesterday's escapade. Unless Patie had been speaking to Robin Chisholm. Something in the latter's face last night had told her he must have seen her and Nicol together earlier. She could not identify that look completely: but something had made Robin behave the way he did, as though he wanted to vent his anger on any target that came to hand.

Mairi noticed with a start of shock that the hand carrying a sweet to Honoria's mouth was trembling. 'I'm going to put a stop to it. There'll be no scandal here while I'm answerable for you. You're going to stay with your Aunt Sandia for a while. I've arranged it over the telephone. Catriona Peel has more sense than to get herself involved with – with men, and maybe she'll be able to teach you something I can't.'

'You haven't asked me –'

'Asked you what?'

'Whether I want to go to Aunt Sandia's.'

'I'm not giving you the option.' But her grandmother's tone softened slightly. 'You think I'm an ogre, don't you? But I'm doing it for your sake. You haven't done anything silly with Nicol Chambers? Nothing you'll regret?'

Mairi's face flamed. 'It wasn't like that at all –'

'It's always like that. You're seventeen and at seventeen the tide runs strong. It's all too easy for a girl to get into trouble.'

'I don't know what you mean.'

'I think you do.' Honoria gave her a long, searching look, then said, 'Your grandfather and I both feel a spell in Glasgow would be good for you. Catriona knows a lot of young folk, goes to parties and so on. It's time you met a wider variety of people. Dounhead's a small, inward-looking place, with nobody of your own sort. It turns people like

Nicol Chambers into somebody important.'

'Nicol *is* my sort. He's far better read than Catriona's stupid friends. All they can talk about is golf and sailing.'

'He's from the Rows. A useless agitator . . .'

'But so was Grandpa from the Rows. What's wrong with that?'

'Your grandpa is off better stock. His family all did well for themselves. And Nellie works for us. It puts her in an awkward position.'

'Did Nellie tell you?'

'No, she did not.'

'Who did?'

'I'm not at liberty to say.'

Mairi shook the fire-irons. 'I'm not going. You can't make me.'

'You'll force me to get the minister to talk to you then – '

'You wouldn't, Grandma.' One glance at Honoria's set face told Mairi that she would. She began to sob then, knowing she was beaten. With the tears running down her face, she ran upstairs, locking herself into her bedroom and beginning a long, passionate, blotchy letter to Nicol, apologizing for running away from him the night before, telling him they were sending her away and imploring him to write to her.

'They can't keep me away for ever,' she wrote. 'And I won't change, if you won't.' She signed herself after much deliberation but no doubt 'Yours eternally', gazing at the words and feeling such sorrow and desperation it was as though her heart were breaking.

'Mairi.' There was loud, peremptory knocking on the door and Nellie's voice cut through her reverie. 'Open this door, Mairi. I want to talk to you.'

She sealed the letter and tucked it carefully away in her handbag before turning the lock.

'Did you tell Grandma about Nicol and me?' she demanded.

'I did not.'

'Who did?'

'How should I know?' Nellie stared at the tear-stained face.

'I *would* have clyped, if I'd known. Mairi – ' she gave a great, exasperated sigh – 'you want your head looked at, taking up with somebody like my brother. He'll never have a tosser to bless himself with. You – well, you're class. Used

68

to the best. It would finish off your grannie if you went to live in the Rows.'

'Nellie, people are all the same. Can you not see that?'

'No, I can't,' said Nellie, with sudden vehemence. 'That brother of mine's dangerous because he thinks he knows it all. He's Mister Trouble. You're better away from him. Take it from one that knows.'

'Go on up,' said Aunt Sandia, with an encouraging smile. 'Catriona's in her bedroom. She'll be so pleased to see you. Poor wee soul – I think she gets a bit lonely sometimes. Being an only child.'

Relinquished from her aunt's warm, bead-encrusted bosom (Sandia still seemed to smell of flour and baking soda from the tea-rooms she had once run) Mairi took the last few thick-carpeted stairs at an eager run. From the far end of the corridor came the strains of music – Aunt Sandia had explained they had bought Catriona a portable gramophone so that if it was too cold to go to church – Catriona had a delicate chest – she could play hymns while her parents were at the service.

The furthest door opened now to Mairi's knock and her cousin dragged her quickly in and shut the door carefully behind her. Catriona Peel was a couple of inches smaller, broad and chubby where Mairi was willowy, sandy of hair and eyebrow where Mairi was maize-fair. The two girls gazed at each other with open, smiling pleasure. Catriona was smoking a black cigarette on the end of a long jade holder. She made elaborate passes at the air to dispel the smoke, coughed once and said on an irrepressible giggle, 'If the mater finds out about this, she'll have a wally. Like one?'

'No thanks. What are you playing?' Mairi turned towards the dainty gramophone, perched dangerously on the edge of a handsome walnut dressing-table laden with cut crystal dishes. Catriona turned the handle and the music picked up pace once again. 'A tango. My favourite.' She grabbed her cousin and led her in long, stretchy steps across the well-carpeted bedroom floor.

When the music stopped, they flopped gasping and laughing on the bed. 'Mairi, we'll have fun, won't we? I wish I'd had a sister, I truly do – ' She stopped, aghast. 'It's worse for you, having had one and then losing her. Oh, Mosses, I'm a tactless besom.' She swooped on Mairi and gave her an impulsive hug. 'You must tell me *all*. No romance has as yet entered my barren life. You are beautiful, of course, and all I have's character. As yet. But I'm working on it.' She picked up a swansdown puff from the dressing-table, dipped it into a crystal bowl holding face powder, and made light patting movements all över her flushed, freckled face.

'"*Tous les jours, à tous points de vue, je vais de mieux en mieux.*" Or to peasants like yourself, "Every day, in every way, I'm getting better and better." Better-looking, that is.' She stared at Mairi's bosom. 'Heavens, you've got big bumps too.' Heaving up her dress with its handkerchief-pointed hem, she demonstrated a width of stiff white material wound tightly round her upper regions. 'You have to *flatten* yourself, darling. It's terribly unfashionable to have a plateau in front. The flatter the better.'

Mairi gazed down bewilderedly. 'I'll never be flat,' she equivocated.

'Think flat,' Catriona advised her succinctly. 'You will be.'

'Catriona.' Mairi lifted the needle from the gramophone to indicate it was time the conversation took a serious turn. 'I'm terribly in love, you know. I don't know what to do about it.'

'What's it like?' Catriona had pulled her small, round face into a semblance of earnestness as she sat down close to her cousin, her eyes trying desperately to read Mairi's face for the answer.

'I don't know. It's – it's a bit like being born again. It's – it's like living on a different plateau.' She grabbed Catriona's hand and began absently separating the fingers, a game they had played as children. 'When you're with the person, you don't want it ever to end. And the times in between aren't like living at all.'

'Crumbs,' said Catriona, 'you have got it badly. But Maisie – ' she lapsed into the old childish diminutive she had forgotten her cousin hated – 'he's not well set-up, is he?' She searched for as delicate a way of putting it as possible. 'He's, well, he's *poor*, isn't he?'

Mairi gazed at her dispassionately. She was very fond of her cousin. Plump and roly-poly as a child, over-indulged by her doting parents, Catriona had never been too much of a spoiled brat, but had been sunny and malleable by nature, the instigator of many hilarious games and adventures and a playmate of wit and imagination.

She was still roly-poly, with a face that came close to being homely except for its mobility. But although her figure was chubby and unprepossessing, Catriona had acquired a certain sophistication beyond her years, possibly from mixing largely with her parents' friends. She had an open, cheerful confidence that contrasted with Mairi's more reflective nature and a puppy-type, uncritical outlook that was always endearing. Just as well, for Mairi could feel herself going over to the defensive about Nicol.

'I don't believe money's important,' she said now. 'I mean, what a person is should come first, and Nicol is the sort of person you want to talk to all the time. I mean, he's thought about things.'

'He's a Communist, you mean,' said Catriona, reproachfully. 'Really, Mais, I wonder at you. They're not our sort of people at all. Politics are very boring.'

'You can't go through life with your head stuck in the sand, like an ostrich,' Mairi protested hotly.

Catriona stuck her sandy head into the pale blue eiderdown and gave a muffled laugh. 'Why not? I believe "there's a divinity that shapes our ends" and all that. I mean, Mais, the war showed how little time most of us will have here on earth. Why shouldn't we enjoy it? Poor people have fun, too.'

'If you became poor, would you like it?'

'I might not mind. If I still had my health and strength. I shouldn't sit about and moan. I'd go out and buy bones and make good nourishing soup for my children and learn to make down my old clothes for them.'

She sat up, red-faced, and gazed at Mairi with a half-assumed seriousness. 'But why go in for being poor if you don't need to? I don't see the sense of it.'

'You used to be like this when we were children,' complained Mairi. 'You think everything's a bit of a game, don't you? Well, falling in love isn't games, Cat. Nicol isn't a game.'

'Do you think I haven't been in love, then?'

'I know you haven't.'

'I might have been. When we were at the theatre last week, someone Daddy knew introduced his son who's training to be a lawyer. Hamish, his name was.'

'Was he nice?'

'He had a little twitchy nose like a rabbit and he dropped his ice-cream all down his waistcoat.' Catriona fell back in a paroxysm of remembered mirth. Then she sat up, making an effort at seriousness and said, 'I shall know him when I see

71

him. My fate! My love! Meantime, darling, can we have fun? You won't go on about Nicol all the time, will you? I've promised the parents I'll take you out of yourself a bit. You can help me plan my birthday party. We're having music, eightsome reels, Dashing White Sergeant, the tango by special request of me. And it's to be held at the Wellington Rooms – rather grand, don't you think? All part of the master-plan to help little Catriona make a brilliant match.'

Sitting in the back of the chauffeur-driven car on its way to the Wellington Rooms in Sauchiehall Street two weeks later Mairi watched as her bright-faced cousin gazed out at the beginning of a snowstorm and tried to stir up some small flame of enthusiasm in her own bosom for the night before them.

Catriona had done her best. They had tried to persuade Aunt Sandia that Nicol could be invited, without Honoria knowing, but she had turned the idea down flat. She was a good sport, but not that good. Instead, as Patie would be coming from Dounhead, Aunt Sandia had issued an invitation to Robin Chisholm to come along with him.

This convinced Mairi that Robin Chisholm had been involved somewhere in the revelations about her Glasgow outing with Nicol and that it had been for nefarious reasons of his own. She was determined now that she would worm a confession out of him. Anger against him was mounting in her mind, quite spoiling any previous light-hearted anticipation. Who did he think he was? Some sort of guardian angel? Even the new pale blue satin dress with its dropped waist and shot-silk roses, specially made for her by Catriona's dressmaker, failed to melt the ice in her mind. While Catriona looked out at the snow and compared it to blossom or confetti, Mairi deliberately made herself think of things bleak and cold – the frozen sheep at the farm, the children who had no warm boots or clothing and Nicol who had difficulty keeping his balance on the ice because of that great ugly seamed scar up his leg. Nicol who had cheap gloves and hand-me-down shirts. If they married, she would sew them where they were frayed. She was quite a neat needlewoman.

'Mairi, we're here, I said!' Her rosy face framed by an ermine collar, Catriona hopped out on to the slushy street. Both girls wore capes, galoshes and gaiters and were well protected from the chills. As they scuttered towards the doors of the Wellington Rooms, Mairi turned at the sound of music somewhere in the dark. Further up, outside the lighted windows of a department store, an ex-Servicemen's 'band' played 'Mademoiselle from Armentières'. The sound chilled and repelled in the bitter night. There were three men, one blind, one without a leg and the other one-armed. She stood as though riveted to the spot, not hearing Catriona's repeated cries to 'Hurry up'. She opened the clasp of her bag and felt for her purse. Two half-crowns and some coppers lay in it and she took all the money out, running up the street to the source of the music and clattering the coins into the tin mug held out before him by the blind man. She stared into his face and his sightless eyes, blue and flickering, stared through her and beyond. 'Thank you,' said the one-armed man, who played a mouth-organ. She saw that he was dirty and unshaven but he had bright dark eyes that looked contemptuously, she thought, at her finery and embarrassed face.

'God bless you.' His voice was as rough as sandpaper, barely audible.

'What were you doing?' Catriona demanded as she got back to the rooms. Mairi scarcely heard and did not answer. Instead, she followed Catriona to the powder-room, where they divested themselves of their outdoor things, combed their hair and surreptitiously powdered their noses. Her mind was in a whirl.

Inside the large hall where the party was being held everything was colourful and jolly. As Christmas was approaching, the ceilings and walls had been decorated with streamers, evergreens and balloons. Round the edge of the dance floor tables were set with mounds of food, galantines and trifles, sandwiches and exquisite small cakes. Rumpitty-tump sounds came from the drummer in the band and a fiddle sent a thin, keening note into the laughter and conversation. Aunt Sandia and Uncle Dandy, like many of the older folks, were already seated at the tables, waiting for the young ones to appear and get the dancing started.

Mairi spotted Robin Chisholm almost at once. Although he had arrived with Patie, the latter had deserted him almost immediately so that he could claim as partner a fair, flushed girl in a pink net dress. Robin Chisholm stood by himself calmly taking in the scene.

'He's rather *interesting*-looking,' said Catriona in a small breathy voice.

'Come on. I'll introduce you,' offered Mairi grimly.

After that, the dancing began and Chisholm claimed both girls in turn. When it was the Dashing White Sergeant, he had one on each arm. Mairi could see Catriona was quite smitten by him. She flirted and coquetted outrageously, hanging on his arm when the point came for him to whirl her round, her face upturned to his quite shamelessly. By contrast, Mairi kept her own expression restrained and unsmiling. She did not intend to spare Chisholm her catechism, party or no party, dance or no dance.

They were all seated round the same large table for supper but he contrived to be next to her.

'You seem a shade subdued,' he challenged her.

She made sure none of the others was listening and said, 'Is it any wonder? You told my grandmother about Nicol Chambers and me, didn't you?'

'I told your brother. I make no apology. I felt your guardians should know. Nicol Chambers has a certain reputation.'

'How dare you!' She could feel the angry flush mount her face. She fastened her eyes on his in a furious upbraiding glare, but he did not quail before it. He was prevented from answering her by the others' chatter and there was no further opportunity for an exchange till the supper was over. Then he held out his hand for the next dance and she had to accept or look ungracious.

Although excellent at the reels and other Scottish dances, he was inept at the newer quickstep. They settled for an unambitious shuffle to the music and he said in her ear, 'What do you mean by it, getting involved with a rag like that? A girl of your breeding and background, taking up with a semi-literate anarchist who's had what little brains he's heir to scrambled in the war.'

She was so angry her breath was taken away. She tried to move away, but his grip tightened on her, his face as set as her own.

'Your guardians should lock you up, that's what they should do, till you've learned a bit of sense. And I'll not apologize. I know your worth. You're a splendid girl with a fine mind and what do you think will happen to you if you end up in the Rows?'

'Have you no pity to spare for Nicol?' She was totally involved in the argument now and oblivious of the people around them. 'Whatever you may think, he has a good mind too, and he's had to feed it on what he can get.'

'He'll pull you down into the Kailyard politics and dull your edge with his ranting polemics.'

'He *feels*,' she said, disdainfully. 'He *feels*. That's what's important.'

'You really are a stupid, gullible girl. It seems I've over-estimated you. I had thought you and I could be friends, the sort who strike sparks off each other. I could help you develop your powers of analysis, teach you some metaphysics. You could have made a name for yourself as an elocutionist, an actress. I might have written a play for you.'

Something in his voice stopped the harsh retort on her lips. She could feel his grip lessen on her and when she stared into his face she could see he was labouring under the stress of strong emotion.

'How old do you think I am?' he demanded. 'I'm twenty-seven. There isn't such a gap between us in age, and mentally there need be no gap at all.'

'Your age doesn't matter,' she said helplessly. 'But I'm not interested in you, Robin.' Somehow it was totally easy to use his Christian name. 'I'm not interested in you at all.'

They concentrated on the dancing for a brief space of time, while all sorts of sensations chased themselves through Mairi's mind. Amazement, fury, pity. Above all, blind denial of all Robin Chisholm had said about Nicol. *Nicol*. She began to think she would drown in the fear of losing him, while this implacable creature who held her would not lift a finger to help.

'Let me go, Robin,' she demanded, with a strength and finality he could not misunderstand.

He danced her till they came to the exit to the foyer and led her out there where one or two other couples were cooling off and non-dancers were indulging in banter with friends.

They were both panting slightly as though they had just run a race. He put his head down, then raised it with a look that momentarily pierced her armour.

'I am trying to tell you –'

She refused to make it easy for him.

'You know what I'm trying to tell you. Do I need to spell it out?'

'I can't forgive you for what you said about Nicol. He's worth ten of most of the men I know.'

'And you know so many!' He permitted himself the ghost of a smile. 'All right. Leave him out of it. It's you I don't want to see making a mistake. I don't want you pulled down. Chambers wouldn't be loyal to you, apart from anything else.'

'That's where you're wrong.' She didn't know how she managed to make her stiff lips say the words. 'You are so wrong. I really do not want to speak to you any longer, Robin. Excuse me.'

She made for the powder-room, her legs as wobbly as if she had just recovered from 'flu. How dared he? How dared he use the remains of the authority he had once held over her at school to speak to her in that way about a life that was her own? She could never feel anything for him, he was hard, selfish, self-important, sure, where Nicol was bruised feeling and need like herself. Nicol was an extension of herself; when he was hurt, she cried, as she began to do now. They could not take him away from her. All the authority in the world could not do that.

Her feelings were in a greater turmoil than at any time since she had been sent away from Dounhead. Her aunt had told her that two letters from Nicol had been returned to him unopened. That had outraged her but hadn't threatened her in the way the general growing conspiracy against them had begun to do. The next thing would be her father coming back from England and maybe – Catriona had hinted as much – dragging her off there to keep house for him.

She could feel the cold of the wash-basin press through the satin of her dress. The old woman keeping an eye on the cloaks at the far end of the room eyed her suspiciously. From what seemed light years away came the sound of the music and dancing, now a wild eightsome reel with the men stomping and screeching:

'Who's the best set in the ha'?
Eee-aye-ee-aye-ee-aye-aw!'

Suddenly her mind was made up. She had given all her silver away to the street musicians but she still had a pound note tucked inside her purse. It would take her to Dounhead. She didn't know why she had vacillated so long. She wanted to be with Nicol. They weren't going to stop her. She got her coat, pulled on her galoshes, buttoned her legs into their warm gaiters and slipped and slithered across slushy streets to the station. No one had seen her go and before the outside doors flung themselves shut behind her, she glimpsed through glass Robin Chisholm dancing with Catriona. He looked like a man under sentence, but Catriona was pink and laughing.

They were like two people a thousand miles away.

When she alighted at Dounhead, the snow had turned to a hard, driving sleet that made deep pin-cushion marks on the white railway bankings. It was colder than she had ever known in her life and she regretted the thin satin dress under the thick cape and cardigan. She pulled her deep fur collar up so that it almost made a hood for her hair and set her face against the sleet and wind. She had no option now but to make for the Rows and hope that Nicol would be at home. All the way there she rehearsed what she would say, but there was no way of making it sound matter-of-fact or undramatic. 'I've come back.' 'I'm not going home — ever.' She began to be past caring about that.

It was Mrs Chambers who answered the door, shiveringly, her hair, loosened from its fat bun, indicating that she was already preparing for bed.

'Aye, lassie, what would you be wanting?'

'To speak to Nicol, if you please, Mrs Chambers.'

'He's no' here. And should you no' be in Glasgow, with your auntie?'

'Can I come in a minute?'

Reluctantly, Mrs Chambers pulled the door open a little wider to permit entry. The old man watched from the fireside.

'If I let you in here, they'll say I'm encouraging you,' said Nicol's mother fiercely. 'And I would rather you left our Nicol alone. Go to your grannie's, lassie.'

'Where is Nicol?' Mairi persisted. It was odd how in the warm her teeth began to chatter and her feet turn to ice.

'He's gone down to the pit. I'll tell him you came. Away you home now, before you catch your death o' cold.' The old woman's voice held a vestige of pity. Then suddenly it changed to wide-awake alarm. 'You're not having a bairn, are you? He's no' put you in the family way?'

'I'm not that sort of girl.' What sort of girl was she, though? She had come here as though she had taken leave of her senses. And now there was no going back.

The voice came from the chair by the fire, where a black whippet shared the tatty cushions. 'Come over and get a heat.' Nicol's father rose, gesturing to Mairi to take off her cape. 'The mother'll get you some cocoa.' His tone brooked no denial.

She felt as though everything in her began to melt at his concern, melt and dissolve into a blur of sensation. The flames from the cheerful fire in the grate danced up and down in a myriad of colours so that she was reminded of the kilts and dresses whirling round in the reels and waltzes at Catriona's party. Had she really left it like that, without telling anyone? It seemed a thousand years ago. And what would they be thinking now? She could visualize the concern and panic on their faces and the enormity of her actions suddenly struck home. She said to the old man with a new desperation, 'I must see him. I must go to the pit.'

Mrs Chambers had rammed the big black kettle down over the flames, her face set but no longer angry. 'You'll have something hot first, then you can go.' The old man said resolutely, 'I'll take you there myself.'

Ignoring his wife's warning of the consequences, he wrapped a huge checked scarf across his chest, shrugged into a filthy old coat, pulled on a cap and great heavy tackety boots, while Mrs Chambers made a mug of cocoa and handed it to Mairi without a word. She warmed the lining of the girl's cape before Mairi shrugged it on again. After this largely silent pantomime, old man and girl looked at each other. 'I'm ready,' he said. 'So am I,' Mairi replied.

It was not far to the pit but even so the struggle against the wind taxed the old man's lungs, so that he had to stop frequently, turn his back to the buffeting and wait till the bellows, as he put it, were once again in working order.

She wanted to say she was sorry, but the words seemed pointless. When they reached the pithead she had half-expected to see Nicol straight away, but the under-manager, agog with curiosity, told them he was down at the coal-face, investigating a complaint about loading.

'Ye canna see him unless you go down there yourself,' he pointed out, with a grim satisfaction. Old Chambers had vouchsafed no explanation for the visit, beyond saying it was urgent. A gaggle of men were making towards the cage, ready to go down on a safety check.

'Have you ever been down a pit?' Joe Chambers looked at the distraught girl with a strange, unfathomable expression. 'You should know what you're getting into.'

The under-manager circled the duo, alarmed. 'She's not

going down there. It would be as much as my job's worth.'

Mairi ignored him. All she could think of was that she was getting nearer to Nicol: that, and answering the challenge in Joe Chambers's eyes. 'I'll go down if you go down.'

They started towards the cage. 'At least, put these on.' The under-manager ran after them with helmets. He had no love for Nicol Chambers. If there was trouble, he would have to carry the can. In any case, he was an indiscreet – his wife said foolish – man who enjoyed letting matters run their course. It would be interesting to see what transpired when they all came up again.

'Are you not feared, hen?' The man standing next to Mairi in the cage grinned up into her face. He was toothless but not more than forty, his shoulders broad and his gaze a steady one. 'Your stomach'll stay behind when you drop, you know.'

'I'm not feared,' she answered, in the same idiom. But her fists were balled so tightly the fingernails cut into her palms.

The rest of the men did not speak. She remembered some of them were superstitious about women. They kept their faces turned away. When the cage dropped it was like nothing she had ever experienced in her life before. Limbo. 'We're going down three thousand feet, near enough,' said the friendly miner. 'You can tell your weans when you have them that you've been down to the bowels of the earth. So to speak.'

When the lift stopped and the men got off, Mairi saw what looked like roads radiating off in various directions. They looked about twelve feet wide and were tall enough to stand up in with comfort. The organs of her body seemed to assemble themselves back in their normal places. Everything down here looked ordered. It was a strange, eerie, other-worldly atmosphere. Yet not totally alarming. She heard creaks from the conifer wood props, shouted greetings from one man to another and a persistent cheerful whistling above the grind of the coal trucks.

Joe Chambers pulled her in the direction of one of the roads where a small knot of men was emerging. With a start of joy and fear she saw one of them was Nicol. He came hurrying forward with an expression of total incredulity.

'Aye.' His father nodded as though in answer to an unspoken question. 'She wants you. Nothing would do but I had to bring her. Are you finished down here? We've plenty to settle up there.'

'Mairi.' He looked down at her, still with disbelief and with a sort of measured, dream-like tread they made back towards the cage. This time, going up, it was like waiting to be re-born, a feeling of soaring through time and space to the unknown that was almost an exaltation. In the cage, his hand grasped her arm so hard she almost cried with the pain. The under-manager watched them emerging, his small ferret eyes gleaming with the prospect of spreading the tale. Nicol dismissed him with a nod.

He waited till they had walked out of the shelter of the pithead, and then till his father had walked on ahead and turned a bend in the rutted path, before he pulled her into his arms and, holding her so close that there was almost no point where they did not touch, kissed her lips and her eyes while his breath grated and gasped in his throat.

'Mairi, no going back. No going back, mind. Promise. Promise.'

'I promise.' She was suddenly so tired and cold yet deathly happy it was all she could do to keep her legs moving. Back in the house, Mrs Chambers sat with her outdoor coat on over her nightdress. She had built up a roaring fire and set the table with four of her best cups and saucers.

It was she who said shortly to Nicol, 'You'll have to go up to the big house. Go round the back and tell Nellie. They'll have to use the telephone to Glasgow and let the lassie's auntie know where she is. She sleeps here tonight.'

He nodded. She was conscious of the others taking over all decisions, of taking off her cape and drinking tea, of hearing him go out and come back again, of the old man undressing modestly behind his chair and climbing on to a creaking, hard chair to enter one of the set-in beds. The dog, named Diana, followed him, settling over his feet.

Mrs Chambers handed her a starched, cambric nightgown with tamboured neck and sleeves. 'It'll fit you,' she urged. 'It was for our Nellie's bottom drawer.'

She saw Nicol's look as she took the gown. She had to undress too, behind the chair, while he looked delicately away. He was to sleep with his father and she had to climb in behind the vast bulk of Mrs Chambers in the other set-in bed. The blankets rubbed harshly against her skin but their warmth was undeniable.

'Good night.' She could see, above the mound that was

Mrs Chambers, Nicol's hand go up to douse the gas. His voice came to her as though from a great distance, and it was as though her being floated down, down again, and then up, as it had done in the pit cage.

'Tomorrow we see about the wedding.'

Overnight the story of her defection from the big house became news throughout the Rows and curious, inquisitive faces floated past the window, while little knots of women congregated on nearby doorsteps to exchange the latest tit-bits.

Her grandmother sent Nellie to tell her she must go home at once to discuss the situation, but nothing Nellie could say would change her mind. She sat on the hard chair between the two set-in beds, her face pale and set with the determination not to give in. Eventually Carlie arrived, looking red-faced and harassed, and persuaded her that it would be best all round if she went to stay at Tarbert Villas. This she agreed to, because she trusted Carlie.

It was Patie's turn next. Their verbal battle was like an exchange of rifle fire, designed to wound and hurt. He could not get over the fact that she was prepared to leave him on his own with the grandparents. When he saw that she could feel nothing for anyone, outside her obsession with Nicol, he became fierce and cold and bitter, reminding her of Grandpa Paterson.

'You don't think Father will allow it, do you?' This was his trump card. But she used Carlie's telephone to ring her father in Birmingham.

'It doesn't matter what anyone says,' she told Finn. 'I intend to marry Nicol even if we run away to Gretna Green.'

He was preparing to go on a business trip to the States. His voice sounded strained and distant. 'If you've found the man you want, then I won't stand in your way. I can't come to the wedding, unless you're prepared to wait till I come back.'

She stood stock-still, shocked at the suddenness of her victory.

'Mairi?' Finn's voice came, thin and attenuated over the wires. 'I wish your mother and I had not wasted time before we married. We had too few years together. But wait till I get back and we can talk about it.'

She wasn't prepared to concede even this. She had gone with Mrs Chambers that morning to pick her wedding dress at the Dounhead Co-op Drapery Department. It was of cheap 'art. silk' but pretty, with ripples of small frills from a dropped waistline and they did not have to pay for it till the end of the quarter.

'I'm not waiting, Daddy.'

There was a long silence, during which she began to think he had simply put the phone down and walked away.

Then he said in an almost businesslike way, 'Very well, I'll not stop you. Your allowance will continue, in the normal way. I'll see you when I get back.'

'No allowance, Daddy. Nicol won't have it.'

'As you say, then. Goodbye, Mairi. Do as you think fit.'

She stood on the verge of hysterical laughter, yet with a persistent savage sadness somewhere inside. He had once been a funny, loving father, full of jokes and good humour, on whose sharp knees she had perched to feel the bristle of his morning chin. And after her mother and Helen died, there had been nothing. He had been unreachable, his eyes sliding away like cold river water. Still was. She gave a little muted moan of pain as the tears came. For a moment when he had said that about the years with her mother, she had thought with a lift of spirit that he understood. But it was more likely he didn't really care what happened to them now. She was just another problem to dispose of, and the American trip was more pressing.

Her grandparents were not at the register office wedding, but Carlie and Patie came. Patie's face was puffy with emotion. He had defied his grandparents to attend and afterwards he pushed a badly wrapped present into Mairi's hands. It was a magnificent punch bowl of Edinburgh crystal, an unlikely ornament for the sparsely furnished Rows cottage into which they intended to move immediately.

'Patie,' she said pleadingly. She was nearly as tall as he was. Blue eyes looked into blue eyes. 'I have to live my life.' He looked away.

It took six months for the grandparents to come round, but in the end Honoria paid a visit to Mairi. She came at dusk in order not to be conspicuous.

'It isn't much, but it's home.' Mairi's face gleamed with pleasure as she drew her grandmother over to the seat of honour by the fire. 'It once belonged to the under-manager, so it has two rooms. And its own water-closet.'

Honoria gazed round at the familiar Rows kitchen, pleasant in the firelight. Two beds set into the wall, a big deep stone sink with a brass faucet, a steel range with a coal fire, a hand-hooked rug with a chair either side, a big scrubbed table and a dresser with cups on hooks. When she'd been the minister's daughter, she'd been inside many a home like this. But she'd never thought Finn's daughter would end up in one.

'Wait a minute. The gas needs a new mantle.' Mairi took a delicate, cobwebby semi-sphere from a small cardboard box and affixed it with great care to the gas bracket. 'Nicol says I'm better at this than he is – they cost a penny each, so you have to be very gentle.' She held a taper to the mantle and the little room sprang into warm comfortable life. Honoria settled back in her chair, feeling its cheap springs creak and sag. 'It's not what you're used to,' she said at last.

'No, but it could be worse.' Mairi placed a kettle over the coals and set out cups and saucers. 'I'm glad you came. You can see I'm surviving.'

Honoria looked at the girl's gently rounding figure. 'I came because I heard about the baby,' she said. 'I was angry at the marriage and there's a lot I would like to take up with your husband, but the baby alters things.' She drew a handsome hand-crocheted shawl from a bag on her knee and spread it out for Mairi to admire. 'Will it keep the little mite warm, do you think?'

Mairi sank to her knees, gathering up the shawl and holding it to her face, smiling.

'I'm happy, you know, Grandma. Every day of the week I'm happy. I've got Nicol and that's what I wanted.'

Honoria heaved a sigh. 'No money to speak of. Another mouth to feed.'

'We manage. Our lives are very full. Nicol makes a bit extra from his journalism and once the baby's here I can give elocution lessons in the front room. We're young, after all.'

It was a mild yet invincible expression that gazed up at Honoria and the words took her back to the early days of her own marriage. *We're young.* Maybe the struggle to make it together was the best of it. She sighed again, more conciliatingly, and vouchsafed the fact that it was a splendid cup of tea.

Carlie had crept down to the cottage in the Rows at daybreak to look again at Mairi's daughter, Eleanor. Fair down of hair. A look of placid, pink accomplishment that had made Nicol laugh with pride and pleasure. And then coming back, hearing rasping stentorian sounds from her father's bedroom, had had time to think: a birth, a death, before she knew the certainty of her father's going.

And then there had been a cold grey day, soft rain from dawn till dusk, and people weeping. Standing all the way along the Rows and the main street of Dounhead to watch the cortege, weeping. Politicians from afar, dark-clothed and well-fed compared to the mass of folk in the street. Donald's arm through hers, his hand clasping her hand, one and indivisible. She the one who leaned this day, the day of her father's going.

Part Two

CHAPTER FIVE

Six years ago Mairi had married. Six months ago, the old
man, his grandfather, on whom he had patterned himself,
had died. Then, shrivelling overnight like a leaf in frost, his
grandmother too. Now what was to happen to him? He had
to find an answer.

Patie Fleming stopped at Harvey the baker's in Dounhead
main street and bought pies and tea-bread to take to his
sister. The grey-haired woman assistant, civil verging on the
obsequious, said how sorry she was to hear about the old lady
dying so soon after his grandfather. Tying up his purchases
carefully, doing her best to hide her curiosity, she said without looking at him directly, 'There'll be some changes made
at the big house now.' He did not enlighten her, merely
thanked her, smiled and tipped his cap. To her assistant
hot-footing out of the back shop for news after his departure,
she said vexedly, 'You'll get nothing out of him. He's too
big a toff. But everybody knows the old woman took it
hard when their Mairi married Nicol Chambers. And then
there's that young one with his racing cars and his gambling.
That's what went for her.'

'She was well over eighty, the old body,' said the assistant
more charitably.

'She never got over it,' the grey-haired one insisted. 'I
mean, would you? Red Nicol never out the papers, with his
rows in the council and his fights at the pit. Have you heard
the latest? He's away to Canada to see what's happening
about the unemployed miners they sent out for the harvesting. There was talk they were keeping them in cages.'

'Wild talk.'

'Well, it's what I heard.'

'Just Red Nicol whipping it up again. I don't believe the
half of it.'

Patie had been aware of the women's curiosity. It followed
him everywhere. It was what he hated about living in a
small town. Its twitching curtains and gossiping women
with the deprived, hungry, angry look of those to whom
nothing of moment ever happened. Just the same, despite
the criticism he felt he was probably subjected to, he didn't

want to leave the area. Dounhead was where the factory was and where he still dreamed of making the best cars in Britain.

Uncomfortably, he knew this had become more of a dream and less of a reality. He and his grandfather had turned their backs for too long on economic realities, had concentrated on quality rather than cost. And now his father refused to pump any more money into the company and in fact wanted it closed down. He had tried arguing that there were still those who wanted custom-built cars with their own style and elegance but he was forced to acknowledge they were becoming thinner on the ground all the time.

It had been tempting, when things got too much, to turn to the challenge of building his own racing car. At the back of his mind was the thought that if he could do a successful job, it would bring publicity and custom to the factory. It had started almost as a sort of joke, when he had souped up one of the Fleming Flyers, entered for a trans-continental rally and come in second. After that it had been Brooklands, and then the public as well as his own imagination being fired by Malcolm Campbell and Henry Segrave attacking the speed records in their Sunbeams. Someone had offered him two aero engines and a super-charger at a challengingly low price, on the premise that he would carry out his boast to build a racing car with which one day he might be able to challenge the aces.

No one in the family had been keen on the idea. His grandfather had insisted that no car could overcome wind resistance past 180 miles per hour, but since the old man's death both Campbell and Segrave had proved this was not so. Another big reservation had been finding tyres that would stand up to great speeds but Dunlop had now come up with some of a guaranteed life of three and a half minutes at speeds about 200 mph.

It was a lonely obsession, however, and he had been sobered when Parry Thomas in his beautiful white stream-lined 'Babs', the car he admired most of all, had been instantly decapitated when the machine overturned on the Pendine Sands. It was at times like that when he took off for the races, gambled too much but found at least a different focus for his restlessness. For a time. Always the car came back to haunt him, like a tormenting mistress.

As he turned now towards his sister's house at the end of the Rows, he saw a small boy emerge from the door and scuttle off in the opposite direction. Philip Mackenzie.

'What did he want – ?' he asked Mairi, frowning.

She looked at the child's slight, running figure and shook her head. 'Half-a-crown till Friday. Tina's eternal song. I wish she wouldn't send Philip, though. He blushes and stammers and hates it.'

'Poor little bugger,' Patie agreed. 'Carlie says she sends him to the pawnshop as well. Some upbringing.'

'It's worse for Tina. She's used to better things.'

He handed over the pies and tea-bread, gazing at her critically. In the six years since her marriage she had changed in some subtle way, had lost the hauteur of the girl from the big house, become softer, broader in speech, at once more ordinary yet still extraordinarily attractive in her looks. 'I wish you wouldn't wear a pinny,' he reprimanded her.

'What's wrong with it?' But she began to remove the offending print overall.

'It makes you look like one of them.'

'Never.' There was no heat in the argument. It was just part of his constant campaign to remind her of her origins. She smiled at him, patted his face, unwrapped the pies with grateful murmurings and set them to heat in the oven.

'I've had my dinner. With Eleanor, before she went back to school.'

'You can always eat a Harvey's pie.'

'And you can always eat *two* Harvey's pies.' She smiled at him, trying to mask her concern. 'I'm glad we've got a chance to talk without Nicol putting his oar in.'

'Do you miss him?' he asked abruptly.

'Of course! But when he's here, he does the talking!'

'What's happening in Canada, then?'

'I'll have to wait till he comes back to get the truth of it. It was just that some of our politicians out there for the Empire Parliamentary Association saw some of the men penned behind locked railings at Winnipeg, with an armed guard.'

'What had they done?'

'They hadn't committed any crime. Just hadn't been up to the job they were sent out for, helping with the harvest. Some of them went because they'd heard the food was good on the ships out. But there's no law which turns an un-employed miner into a farmer, is there? What worried Nicol was the Dounhead men who'd signed away the right to parish relief for the families they'd left behind. Some of the

87

wives and children are near enough starving.'

'I thought the idea was that most of the men would settle down out there?'

'Yes, but their return passages were guaranteed if it didn't work out. Trouble is, the tough ones make it; the weak ones and the misfits are the ones we'll get back on the Labour Exchange.' She sighed. 'Nicol won't come back till he's sorted things out for every man jack of them. Eleanor and I take a back seat, as usual.'

He waited to see if she would confide anything more about her marriage. Because of the kind of man his brother-in-law was, there were obvious strains. Yet even when she was being critical her face lit up when she mentioned him, always affecting him with a sense of something lacking in his own affairs. It wasn't that he didn't like girls, but he was naturally wary. Happier in male company where confusions and uncertainties could always be papered over with jokes and repartee. *Time enough,* Grandma had always said. Other things would have to fall into place first. He had always thought it would be a car of his own making. Now all that was in the balance. He had read the message in Mairi's face. She knew what he was here to talk about.

Prevaricating, he said, 'Does Eleanor like school?'

'She loves it.'

'She should be at the Academy. I would pay the fees.'

'Nicol wouldn't stand for that! She's fine where she is. Happy as a lintie.'

'God, I wish I was,' he broke out at last. He spread his hands apart and curled his fingers into menacing claws. 'If I had him here, do you know what I'd do to him? I think I'd murder him.'

'You don't mean Nicol, I take it!'

'No, you know who I mean. The man that calls himself our father. The shit and reprobate who's taking away my livelihood.'

She sat down at the table opposite, gazing at him broodingly. Now in his twenties, he was forbiddingly good-looking in the way of some Scotsmen, the extraordinary bone structure and breadth of shoulder giving him a presence in excess as yet of his mental capabilities. She looked and saw a great, unhappy lump of young manhood. She didn't pretend to understand him nowadays. He had moved into a totally masculine world of cars, golf, horse-racing and drinking, and since three years ago had been involved with people like

Robin Chisholm in a rabid kind of nationalism. At that time Glasgow Corporation's Extension of Boundaries Bill had been thrashed out in London, to the scandalous financial aggrandizement of the lawyers involved, and tales of the 'dripping roasts' filling legal ashets had given a new boost to the Home Rulers, already angered at the way Scottish affairs were always decided in the south. When Patie got into his political stride, he liked to point out that unemployment was seven per cent worse in Scotland than England, maternal deaths fifty per cent higher, infant deaths twenty-five per cent and army rejects six per cent higher.

Political argument was not something that disturbed her; in fact, it was salt to her daily diet. But the unrest and perturbation in Patie, of which the politics were only a partial expression, did worry her greatly, feeling as she did that her marriage, her desertion as he had seen it at the time, might have been responsible for his failure to get his life together. They would have to have grown apart some time. The short, intense period when they had been flung together like castaways after their mother's death had burned their concern for each other deep. That would always exist, but every time she saw him now, it was as though she had to dig that bit harder for understanding.

Cutting into a hot, savoury pie, she said, 'Why don't you just go with the tide for once? If he wants to close down the Dounhead factory, it's for good economic reasons. And don't talk about our father that way. Whatever he's done, he's still our father.'

He looked at her with what was almost desperate assumed good humour. 'Has Nicol taught you nothing? Mairi, Mairi, Mairi, it's not just *me* losing sight of what I set out to do. It's what's happening in the country. Emigration's not just increasing, it's a bloody galloping consumption. Eight per cent. Not counting the deserters to London.'

'You can't call folk deserters who're just looking for work. For bread.'

'And how can they get bread if we can't keep factories going here? He knows – ' he thumped the table with the side of his hand, like a guillotine – 'he *knows* that making cars wasn't the whole idea. It was making cars *in Scotland*. That was the old man's dream. Now it's sell up, shut up, get out.'

'What about the showroom idea? A showroom and garage in Glasgow. He thinks it would be less precarious.'

'Sell other folks' cars? I don't think that's very funny.

And I was counting on you to see it my way.'

She rose to put more water in the big brown teapot.

'Nicol always says you can't argue with facts. It's a fact you've been losing money. It's a fact that Grandpa's will left everything to Father. It's a fact that he can do what he likes.'

'He hadn't the guts to close the place when the old man was alive.'

She said abruptly, 'The fault's not all his.'

'What do you mean?'

'I can say this to you, because I'm your sister –'

'No! If you're going to preach, I'm going.'

'You've got to listen, Patie. Work and horses don't go together. He knows about your gambling. Frensham must have told him how much you lost at Ayr races.'

'Frensham can talk! He lost twice what I did. Come to that, it was Frensham who started me off.'

'So Father has to keep an eye on him, his business partner, as well as you. Somebody has to be practical.'

'I can give up gambling whenever I like.' He was red-faced, cornered, and got up to move about the room like some clumsy young stallion. She watched him with a gentle remorselessness.

'Take the offer of the showroom,' said Mairi quietly. 'It doesn't mean you'll never do the other thing. It just means you have to wait till the time is ripe.'

He had begun to sweat with anger.

'I'm not giving up.' Abruptly, he sat down again. 'What about the racer? What about the record?'

'Patie, what am I going to do with you?' It came back to her that she had used the self-same words the day he had recklessly taken Peter Frensham's car and driven it when he was only twelve years old. 'These are *dreams* you have. You can't make them come true without money. Can't you see that?'

His face had closed down, mutinous and stubborn.

'Everything starts as a dream in somebody's head. If I wait for a favourable time, I'll wait for ever. If we had Home Rule, things would be different. I'd get help from the government.'

Helplessly she argued, 'But the second Home Rule Bill in two years has just gone the way of all the rest. That's just a dream too.'

'Maybe an army's what's needed, then.'

'A civil war? Don't talk so daft. Just ask the Irish where that gets you.'

'I'm joining the Scottish Nationalists. We'll maybe be governing our own country sooner than you think. Has Nicol not impressed on you how serious things are? I suppose he's too busy speaking for his masters in the Comintern.'

'I'm not answering for Nicol's politics,' she said slowly.

'The banks are hiving off to Lombard Street one by one. Didn't you know that? And the government of Scotland is now under the London Civil Service. The country's dying. They're doing now what they couldn't do when they cut off Wallace's head. Conquering Scotland.' He pushed his face under hers. 'The day I heard about the Nationalists starting up was the best day of my life. I'm going up to see Robin Chisholm and find out what you do to join.'

Mairi saw that Patie's frustration was gathering a momentum she could not stop. In one way, she was almost relieved to see he had at last focused his discontent. In another, she was afraid of his recklessness. Robin Chisholm was on the conservative wing of the new party. He had even persuaded her cousin Catriona to join, although she had done so for personal rather than political reasons. But there were hotheads and rebels with whom Patie was far more likely to identify.

She sighed. Sometimes she wondered what it must be like to live with people who weren't out to change the world. Dull, maybe? She stood on tiptoe to kiss her brother's temple.

'I don't see Scotland going under while you're around,' she said pacifically. 'But make your peace with Father.'

He shook his head, then reached for his cap. 'That — traitor. He'll see the stuff I'm made of, never fear.'

She watched him stride off, her face clouded. Somehow every issue Patie touched was coloured and distorted by his angry restlessness. She saw what he was getting at, knew as well as he did that something had gone from their lives. How was it that nobody could come up with an answer for revitalizing the country? Then she realized that answers abounded. It was who would put them into practice that was the worry.

Patie Fleming left his car on the brow of the road and slithered down a bank of slippery heather and gorse towards Robin Chisholm's cottage. There were two more vehicles on the grassy verge by the side of the road; one of them he recognized as his cousin Catriona's little Voisin. So it looked as though some kind of meeting was taking place. He felt his former impetus give way to shyness: some of Robin's friends were intimidating in their learning. Cosmopolitan, Robin called them. They'd gone away from the Kailyard, been places and seen things. And then his stubborn pride and anger reasserted themselves. He wasn't going to be put down by anyone, least of all half-Englified intellectuals who yah-yah-ed at him about what was best for Scotland. Just the same, he remembered the queue he'd passed for *The Jazz Singer* which had reached the Dounhead flea-pit, the Rialto. Maybe he should have joined it. It might have been worth seeing.

He stopped in mid-slither, something about the sunlit evening view passing into his consciousness and soothing away his reservations. It extended over a tawny burn to pastureland and low hills, with some three miles away the kirk spire of Dounhead Parish Church rising above the untidy huddle of dwellings with an elegance it did not affect close by.

Chisholm and his mother had moved into the cottage – in reality three knocked into one – after his father's death. One end of the former labourers' dwellings was used now by Mrs Chisholm for modelling in clay. A gaunt, striking woman who wore cloaks and wide-brimmed hats, she had retreated into what the world saw as mild eccentricity since her husband's passing. Patie could see her working intently as he passed a window, but she did not raise her head. It was rumoured she had little patience with Robin's politics and would rather he stuck to writing poetry.

Patie was about to lift the brass knocker on the main door when a movement in the copse beyond the burn caught his eye. A flutter of fur-trimmed stole collar being tossed over a shoulder materialized further into his cousin Catriona. She gave him a hard, unsmiling stare and turned away her head, making off along the half-trodden track that led further up the little leaps of hillside.

Intrigued, he bounded after her. 'Cat, it *is* you!' He caught her arm. As always, she was dressed with scrupulous attention to fashion. The first to wear – and discard – Russian boots, the first to pluck her eyebrows, she now wore a beige wrapover coat, fastening elegantly with a single carved button over her left hip, and trimmed with soft, flattering fur on the hemline and attached stole collar. Her pretty light-coloured shoes were already stained from the dew on the grass. She turned her plump little face towards him, topped by its new Eton crop and ridiculous pencilled eyebrows, and glowered.

'What's up? Aren't you talking to me?'

'I'm finished with men. I'm finished with Robin Chisholm,' she spat out vehemently. 'I came out all the way from Glasgow and it's the same as ever; they sit in there putting the world to rights and I might as well not exist.' Tears of rage dampened her rounded, childlike cheeks. 'You can go in and tell him that. Tell him I never want to see him again. We're finished. Napoo, too-ra-loo, goodbye-ee.'

He began to laugh. He had never been able to take anything about Catriona seriously, even her furious spitting rages when he had not played games properly when they were children. But like Mairi, he was very fond of her. He matched his long, laconic stride to her short one as they climbed towards the crest of the hill and the rustic seat that had been placed there. He took his jacket off and placed it so that her clothes would not be marked and found most of his own ill humour dissolved as he looked at her.

'Are you serious about that big kilted sausage?' he demanded irreverently. 'Personally, I can't see what the attraction is. Not for someone like you, who enjoys dancing and having a good time. Cattie, there must be plenty of bachelors around who wouldn't ignore you.'

'But they're not Robin Chisholm, are they?' she demanded illogically. '*I* don't know what I see in him. I don't even like men in kilts, for a start.' She took a scrap of hankie and dabbed her eyes, then with a gold compact from her handbag repaired the redness at the tip of her nose. 'He's – what's the word? – pedantic –'

'Stuffy?'

'If you like. It must be the attraction of opposites. I want to know what makes him tick.'

'You puzzle me. I don't think you love him. I think he's a challenge to you.'

'What are you doing here, anyway?' she demanded obliquely.

'I want to join the Party. You know my father wants me to close the works at Dounhead? Finish making custom-made

93

cars? I don't know — I just thought that Robin might have some idea as to how I could keep going. I want to build the racer.'

'But you've been a naughty boy,' she said severely. 'Mairi told me you'd been at the races and lost far too much. You're just like all men. You can't see what side your bread's been buttered on.'

He began a helpless, sputtering fit of laughter and slowly Catriona's face lost the despairing lines that so ill became it and sparkled with responsive fun.

'At least you keep a sense of proportion,' she said. 'You don't think you're Lord God Almighty. That's what gets me about him — Robert the Bruce or Rob Roy Macgregor down there. He never lets up for a moment. I suppose I'm too frivolous for him. He thought I was quite amusing to start with. Now I simply bore him.'

'Maybe it's time you made the break with him, then.'

She looked down at the pale beige shoes, saying nothing. When she looked up again, directly at him, there was an expression he had never seen before. Half-humorous, half-resigned. 'You know the way these burry things — soldier's buttons — in the wood there stick to your hair and clothes? That's what it's like. I can't get rid of what I feel for him. I've tried. Honestly.'

'Would you like to marry him?'

'Yes.'

'Why?'

'It's difficult to explain. It's because of what he is and what I am. You see, I've been brought up spoiled. I only have to ask Pop for something, and it's mine. That's the way it's always been. Clothes. Car. Dancing lessons. Trips abroad. And up to a point it's fine. But I'm not totally vacuous, Patie.' She looked at him appealingly. 'Under the fluff, I do have a brain. Perhaps I should have gone to college. Become a teacher or something. But I don't need to earn my living.'

'I don't see where this is getting us — '

'No, wait a minute. If I married Robin, people would have to take me seriously because they take him seriously. D'you see? I would grow into a different person.' At his expression of disbelief, she laughed, but insisted, 'No, I would. I would like to be mistress of my own home, not just a little ray of sunshine for the parents. Not that I mind being that. But I could run a household. Furnish it with taste. Entertain the right people. Oh, I'd be good for him, Patie. He might not see it, but I would.'

'The trouble with Robin,' he said slowly, 'is that he's self-contained. All his life is lived up here – ' he tapped his head. 'He's got his poetry and his politics and maybe he doesn't need a woman.'

'You mean he sublimates his sexual instincts?'

He looked a little shocked at her frankness.

'Where did you hear that?' he said prudishly.

'It's a respectable theory. Nuns do it, priests do it, maybe poets do it. He's kissed me, though. I think he's just a bit inhibited. Maybe I could uninhibit him if we were married!'

'He's had women. I do know that.'

The colour flooded into her face. 'How could you know?'

'Men talk. Some women are pretty free with their favours, since the war. They go with a man for the night and that's it.'

'Have you done it, Patie?'

'This isn't proper talk between us. Let's drop it. You just should know that he wanted Mairi – '

'I do know that – '

'And that when she went with Nicol he tried the field.'

She had been rosy and now was quite pale. 'You're right. We should drop it.' She stood up, her envelope handbag falling to the ground from her lap as though her fingers were too weak to grasp it. She tottered on the uneven ground and he put a hand out to steady her.

'Forgive me,' he said. 'I don't want to shock you, but these are things you should know. I've never thought it fair to keep women in ignorance.'

She managed a somewhat tremulous smile. 'Look, we'll go down again,' she said. 'You want to talk to him, don't you, about the racing car? Maybe he does know people who would be interested in backing you. I would put some money in myself, if it would help. We could have a consortium.'

'No, please,' he protested. 'I don't want you getting into something just because Robin might be involved.'

'You're quick.'

'Yes. Well, I think you should cut your stick with him. Find somebody else.'

She looked at him as though his words refused to make sense.

'You don't understand. But then, why should you?'

'Meaning?'

'Meaning you haven't ever felt what I feel. Have you?'

'I don't trust women.'

'Ah, now we are getting the truth! Why don't you?'

He shaded his eyes, trying to spot a lark they could hear trilling invisibly somewhere in the sky. He was reluctant to discuss his feelings further, but she tugged at his arm so that he had to turn round and face her. She was moved by the disconsolate expression in his eyes.

She said softly, 'Come on, Patie. It isn't as bad as all that.'

'I'm stifled,' he burst out at her.

'I think you're avoiding my question,' she said gently. 'Why don't you trust women, Patie? You went into your shell a bit when Mairi married, didn't you? But you can't go on being Nellie's little boy at the big house for ever.'

'You're a stupid bitch,' he said, not unkindly. 'You don't understand how men function. They need to succeed on their own terms, first and foremost.' He tapped her head. 'What have you got up here? Cotton wool? Do you never think of anything else but LURV?'

'And do you ever think of anyone but yourself?'

The bird that had been singing dropped now like a stone into the field next to the cottage, its song over.

He put his hand under her arm to help her over the rough, tussocky grass as they approached the house. They had gone back to the honest intimacy of childhood.

'Never mind,' he said at last, his annoyance evaporating. 'I suppose I'm quite fond of you. Chisholm needs his head looked at. You're not all that bad.'

She gave him a subdued grin. 'Cousins don't count,' she said.

Mairi washed Eleanor's face and neck at the kitchen sink and dried the tender skin gently. The child was so like Nicol, even to the once-blonde hair that had now darkened, that it made her mouth quirk as she dropped a quick kiss on a damp cheek. Eleanor turned like a small slippery minnow in her arms, smiling and holding up her arms so that the blue pleated skirt with its flannel bodice could be slipped over her head, and on top of that the jersey Mairi had knitted in the long evenings while Nicol had been away.

'When is my daddy coming?' She knew the answer to the oft-repeated question,

'Tonight.'

96

'But first we're going to see Uncle Patie?'

Mairi nodded absently. Ever since Patie's visit she had worried about his course of action. Secretly she had hoped he would take his father's offer and start the showroom in Glasgow. With a good manager there would not be too much responsibility and perhaps Patie would forget altogether his notion of a speed-car. But she knew her brother. If he had made a decision that would please her, he would have been to see her before now.

At Dounhead House, Nellie greeted the child with kisses and promises of treats. In a strange way she seemed to regard herself now as châtelaine of the place, dressing up after lunch, speaking in a rather refined manner and reverting to the vernacular only when Patie was late for a meal or aggravated her in some other way. But she also did the work of two women, kept the place immaculate and ruled the gardener and cleaning woman with a rod of iron.

Officially, of course, the house belonged to Finn, who had pointed out that Mairi was free to live there with her family, as well as Patie, till he decided whether to sell. It was doubtful if he ever would. The price would not be great, the farm was well managed and showing a small profit and it seemed like an act of treachery to let the old place pass out of the family grasp ever again. Mairi would not live there, even if Nicol entertained the idea, which he did not. It was too full of Grandma with her gentle iron will and Grandpa vague and irascible in his last years. She had aspirations towards a small stone villa, but nothing grander.

Patie was being waited on by Nellie as Mairi and the child entered by the kitchen door – they had come to the back of the house in search of Tibby, the cat, on whom Eleanor lavished an unrequited affection. Mairi sipped a cup of tea while Patie finished his meal and Nellie went off with Eleanor to explore the garden.

'What happened?' Mairi demanded. 'Did you see Robin Chisholm?'

He balanced on two legs of the solid kitchen chair and gazed at her, deliberately enigmatic, teasing. 'I'm going on with the racing car,' he said, at last. 'The old man can close down the works as soon as he likes. All I need is a shed and a good mechanic. I've got the backing I need.'

'What do you mean, backing?' she demanded with deepening suspicion.

'I spoke to Robin. He introduced me to Sir Marcus Repton,

the tea merchant, and Willie Peat, the multiple grocer. They're prepared to put up a bit. So is Robin himself, and Catriona. Sponsoring, they call it. If I hit the headlines, some of the limelight falls on them.'

'I don't like it,' she said precipitately. 'You could get yourself killed. You know that.'

He gave her a blithe, laughing look of complete confidence. 'No car would ever get the better of me. You don't have to worry.'

'But you know I will! I wish you would settle for something – something less up in the air. More ordinary.'

'That comes rare, from someone who burned her own boats so thoroughly.' He was inviting her to join in his joke.

She smiled reluctantly, as though it hurt.

'How long will it take?'

'Not long. I've got the engines I want already.'

'You didn't come up with enough to keep the factory going then?'

He faced her inscrutably. 'I might have had more difficulty convincing them about that. The racing car took their imagination.'

'You mean you talked them into it?'

'I'd like to bring the record to Scotland.'

'And you've joined the Party?'

'Of course. It all hangs together. We'll show the world we're not finished yet. Only just beginning.'

Going home, her unease about Patie was vanquished by the stronger, more positive emotion of anticipation. When Nicol had first gone to Canada she had felt a small treacherous sense of release, because his life and personality dominated the cottage in the Rows to such an excess that there were times when she felt swamped.

There was always someone at the hearth night or day, talking and arguing or seeking help. She had grown used to strangers' faces, strangers' smells, strangers' demands, tolerating them because always above their heads was the smile that struck straight to her innermost being, like love-making in a glance. It was a strong emotional pitch at which to live – always the dramas of others to be shared, solved, lived through. She was getting better at it and the more she became involved, the more rewarding it seemed.

But tonight it would be just the three of them. And he would have such tales to tell. About the ship and the sights of Canada. There would be little gifts for Eleanor and herself, chosen carefully because every penny counted.

Going down the drive from her old home, she swung Eleanor's arm and danced a step or two, knowing there was no one to see them. They sang 'In and Out the Dusty Bluebells' and 'Bee Baw Babbity' and other chants the little girl was learning in the school playground. Before they reached the road, she showed Eleanor how to do the Charleston. When they came to the new council houses, the slum clearance, they met the chip-van and horse beginning their rounds and she bought Eleanor a pennyworth of hot, vinegary chips, a rare treat, restraining herself from taking more than one because Eleanor gloated over her paper bag of delicacies like a miser with his gold.

Neither of them liked walking through the depressing slum clearance area. The new houses that should have looked spruce and fresh and cared for were already almost rundown because of the deep, ineradicable poverty they sheltered. In some, the fences had been uprooted for burning in the grates. And although some of the gardens were carefully, defiantly tended, others were a sea of mud and rubble. There were curtains at some windows and none at others and a few windows were even broken or boarded up. *Cancer of Empire*, William Bolitho had called the Glasgow slums a few years before, describing the 'drabbled women', the fireplace like an enclosed iron altar, the teapot everlastingly on the boil: 'bed, hearth and chair: humanity's minimum.' Mairi knew very well that behind most of those doors in Dounhead nothing had changed.

Back in her own house, she looked round with a quick surge of gratitude. This last week she had scrubbed and polished with an almost manic energy so that everything should be looking its best for Nicol's return. Nellie had given her some pretty shadow tissue which her grandmother had purchased not long before her death, but never used, and she had made curtains and chair covers which transformed the kitchen. She had black-leaded the grate and rubbed up the shining steel parts with a cloth rung out in cold tea and dipped in fine ash, finishing off the job with fine emery paper. *The iron altar.* But with good coal burning brightly there could never be a more welcoming, warming sight. It was what she wanted for Nicol coming back from his long, daunting task.

At seven o'clock the latch clattered on the door and he came in, three wary, deferential men in near-rags behind him. When they had embraced, and with Eleanor fast in his arms, he gestured the men in towards the fire and said, 'Make us some tea, will you, Mairi? These lads are chilled to the marrow.'

She tried not to let her disappointment show. He was home, after all, filling up her life again, and quick to explain.

'Chip, Jazz and Harry here came back on the ship with me. But we had to bring Ned McCafferty back in a wooden overcoat. He died on the way across. We have to go down and tell his wife tonight. I don't relish the prospect.'

'What happened to him?'

'He should never have been passed fit in the first place. Some blackguard down at the Labour Exchange is going to have to answer for it to me. The man took fits.'

'They wanted him off their books. He had too many bairns,' volunteered the man called Harry.

'He worked at the same farm as me,' said Jazz, a thin, alert young man who moved around as though listening to some syncopated beat inside his head, hence the name. 'We were treated like pigs. He hadn't the strength to lift a hoe. I'm not saying it was like that everywhere. We just happened to be unlucky.'

'You can say that again,' said Chip, blowing gratefully on a saucer of tea, to Eleanor's bright-eyed interest. 'My farmer was a good man. Jean Benois, a French Canadian. I could have stayed. I don't know why I didn't except that this—' he indicated the bright fire—'this is home and when all's said and done, there's no place like it.'

Mairi's defensiveness melted. There were muddy boot traces on her polished linoleum, the sharp, sour smell of old clothes in her well-scoured room, but the thin scarecrows of men in their poor clothes were looking more human already.

'Which of us goes to see Mary McCafferty?' asked Harry.

Mairi saw Nicol put down his cup and almost imperceptibly square his shoulders. She knew what was coming. 'I'll go. You men get back to your families.'

'I'll come with you,' she said quickly. She brought two paper bags full of biscuits from the kitchen press. 'I'll take these for the children.'

'Why did you want to come?' Nicol demanded as they made later for the slum clearance. They had left Eleanor with her grandparents, showing off a paper parasol he had bought for her on the boat home.

'To be with you.' Hanging on to his arm, she smiled at him.

'Did you miss me?'

'What do you think?'

In the darkling street their lips met. 'Hold your nose,' he said grimly. 'We're nearly there.'

The woman who opened the battered door in the big, barrack-like new house was a gigantic size. Dirty stockings cascaded down her ankles to huge, holey slippers. A vast print overall covered her body and a toothless mouth folded itself grimly under a thatch of straight, greasy hair. Infants crowded round her feet, holding on to her pinny, while behind her in the passage a sea of dirty little faces seemed to stretch to infinity.

Her eyes were hard as she surveyed her visitors. 'Aye?' she demanded.

'Can I come in, Mrs McCafferty?' asked Nicol. 'I'm the pit agent that went to Canada –'

'I ken who you are.' She stared at Mairi, then moved her large bulk slightly. 'Youse might as well come in. If youse can get in.'

Mairi had never seen such squalor. The children were ingrained with dirt, their clothes filthy and ragged and evil-smelling. One or two of the older ones had made some attempts at keeping clean, but the little ones were obviously used to urinating where they stood, for rivulets of white ran down their unwashed legs and feet and the stench was overpowering. A baby slept deep in a scarred, dilapidated pram without covers. Yet the faces that crowded round the visitors were innocent, uncowed, friendly. Mairi handed the biscuits to an older girl and the rest immediately swarmed round her like gannets in a fish market.

'Have you come about my Ned?' enquired Mrs McCafferty. 'He's not back yet –'

He told her then, as gently as he could while Mairi covertly studied the heavy features for some traces of the young girl that must once have been. Mary McCafferty's face did not change at the telling, except for a further hardening of the eyes and folding of the mouth, which she habitually covered from time to time with her hand, conscious of her lack of teeth.

'Ah, well,' she said, her breathing coming so rapidly Mairi

thought she would have a stroke. 'The bastard will gi'e me no more bairns. I'll be able to hold my head up now. I'll be able to sleep easy in my bed. Who's going to bury him, but? I have nothing in my purse.'

'Is it my daddy, Maw?' demanded the girl who had distributed the biscuits. 'Is my daddy dead?'

'Aye.' Still Mary McCafferty did not cry. Instead, as the scabby, ragged children gathered around her, she put out a hand and touched them one by one, as if in some kind of benediction.

Mairi scrabbled desperately in her purse and brought out half-a-crown. She beckoned one of the bolder-looking boys towards her.

'Do you know where the chip shop is?' As he nodded, she said, 'And Tina Mackenzie's? She stays open till all hours. Get a shilling's worth of chips, two loaves and a packet each of tea and margarine. Can you remember that?'

'Take wee Joseph with you,' ordered his mother. 'And mind you run all the way back with the chips.'

'I'll see about the funeral,' said Nicol despairingly. But they did not appear to hear him. Their eyes shone in expectation of the food to come.

CHAPTER SIX

Robin Chisholm's big Dalgleish-Gullane stopped in front of the cottage in the Rows, to the evident interest of the women absorbed in lazy gossip on several of the doorsteps further down.

Mairi responded to his knock, her hair falling down from its chignon, for she had been doing the grate, and her hands blackened with their household tasks.

He stood looking at her momentarily without saying anything, unsure of his welcome, for they had not exchanged anything beyond the formalities for a number of years.

'Mr Chisholm,' she said pleasantly at last. 'Please come in. What can I help you with?' It sounded like a stock question for all callers: no doubt it was.

He stepped into the small, friendly room and she excused herself while she washed her hands at the sink. Then she sat down opposite him, giving him all her attention.

'Do you know where I can find Patie? I've been up to Dounhead House, but Nellie wasn't very forthcoming about his whereabouts.'

'Then he must be away at the races.'

'I've got news for him. We've managed to get permission for him to carry out preliminary tests on the car on Calneggie Sands. It means going up to the West Highlands. It's Catriona's doing, really. She brought her charms to bear on Black-Jamieson, the laird of Calneggie. He's also agreed to let the big lodge to us for the summer. Why don't you and the child come up there for a holiday? You'd like to see Patie's trial runs, wouldn't you?'

She looked at him reservedly, even defensively.

'I'm not sure Patie's ready for trials. He gets ahead of himself at times. I would have to see what Nicol thought about the holiday.'

'I expect he could do with one too.'

'He's caught up at the pit. You must have heard things don't look very good there. There might be a closure.'

'I'm sorry. Isn't your husband very happy with the way the Labour government's handling things, then?' He looked at her slyly.

She laughed. 'He says it isn't even a Labour government, as such. Ramsay MacDonald has no intention of upsetting the Liberals. He makes the appropriate noises but he has no cure for the unemployed.'

He nodded his agreement. 'For once I'm in accord with Red Nicol.' She smiled slowly at his use of the nickname, then overcame her mildly defensive reaction and offered him a cup of tea. It was all a long time ago, after all, the contretemps in the Wellington Rooms when he had tried to stop her marrying Nicol. She had shown him and the other doubters that they were capable of making a go of it. She hoped he would not notice how worn the lino was or the paucity of cups on the dresser. After a time of comparative financial ease, things had become rather more stringent over the past year. The weekly paper Nicol had contributed to had gone into temporary (it was hoped) eclipse, due to its editor's fondness for the bottle, and after she had miscarried last year she had cut down her elocution pupils to a minimum. Nicol could never resist a hard luck story and from time to time spent more than he should on whisky. His conscience made him bad-tempered when she asked him for more money. She didn't want Robin Chisholm to know any of this, and in an effort to conceal the strain that had begun, she knew, to show itself on her face, she became lively and talkative over the tea-making.

'What do you think of Patie's car, then? Ugly great beast, isn't it?'

'Ah, but the power!' he said.

'Will he bring the speed record to Scotland?'

'That's the idea. Don't you think he will?'

'I can't see that it matters. When things are so hard economically – '

'That's surely the time we need something to take our minds off things. There has to be a place for the inessential. Besides, Patie's intention is serious. It's to try and bring the car industry alive again up here.'

'He may say that. What it's really about is thrills for Patie. He's a speed maniac. Why is this age so obsessed with speed?'

'And dance marathons and planes flying at two hundred feet! I don't know. It's an anxious old time. We fear the wrath that's been and the wrath to come.'

'Don't say that!' she pleaded. Then, 'What do you mean?'

'Something in my bones. Wars and rumours of wars.'

She shivered and he relented. He was looking at her with that old intentness, making her conscious of the cracks on her hands and the fact that she hadn't changed out of her morning blouse and skirt.

'Are you happy, Mairi Chambers? I've often wondered.'

She gave him the quick, glimmering smile he had been waiting for and said, 'Of course.' She added, 'Reasonably.' Then before he could proceed further shot at him ingenuously: 'Why don't you marry my cousin Catriona? She as good as told Patie she loved you, you know.'

'Ah, well.' He spread his hands, his turn now for embarrassment. 'Maybe I'm waiting for somebody else to change their mind.'

It was half-jocular but she did not let him off the hook.

'She's a grand person.'

'I don't need to be told it.'

'If you're not serious, you should find some way of cutting her off, so that some other man can have a chance.'

'She's coming to Calneggie for the summer. Come too and supervise our romance.'

'Don't be cynical. Catriona doesn't deserve it.'

'Me cynical? Never.' He rose to go, looking suddenly

irresolute and unsure of himself.

'If I see Patie,' she said quickly, 'I'll tell him you were looking for him.'

'It's been nice to speak to you again.' He stopped just inside the door, staring at her. 'I've always had a feeling of being at home with you.'

He saw he had embarrassed her and in place of words put out a hand to move a strand of hair from her cheek to behind her ear.

'No, don't do that,' she said unsmiling.

'Come to Calneggie.'

'It all depends on what my husband says.'

It was eventually agreed that Mairi should go for two, perhaps three weeks, to Calneggie, taking Eleanor and Tina's son, Philip, with her.

Philip was Nicol's idea. The child had suffered a winter of endless colds and bronchitis and was pale and thin. There was no question of Nicol leaving Dounhead himself: pit negotiations over a partial closure were at too delicate a stage. And it was agreed that if the boy went in his place, he would be a companion for Eleanor.

'Will you miss me?' Mairi asked Nicol in bed the night before she was due to set out with the children. She snuggled against the worn soft flannel of his pyjamas, loving his familiarity and suddenly, childlike, hating the thought of losing his presence.

He pulled her to him. 'Don't start, or I'll not let you go. You need the holiday. I've never been able to give you one. Eleanor's going to love the sand and the sea.'

'She's sleeping with her bucket and spade.' She smiled into his kiss. 'It'll be like a different world to her, won't it?'

'And you'll come back all fat and roly-poly.' He pinched her skinny ribs. 'For me to make love to.'

They came together then with a passion and a vigour that had been missing since the miscarriage. He was reluctant to risk another pregnancy as yet and the *coitus interruptus* he practised left her sometimes irritable and unsatisfied. Tonight she would not let him retreat. It was one of those times when physical passion almost entered the realms of the meta-physical and magical: a pledging and a merging, transcending skin and hair and sperm, seeking mouths and binding arms. She said his name when it was over – 'Nicol, Nicol' – like an incantation or the sea running out. In magnificent kingly languor he said, 'You must go away more often,' and she lay against him, shutting out the words, wanting the oneness again, cell on cell, to a killing infinity.

In the morning, their half-rueful smiles slid off each other's faces. She washed, carefully and laboriously, at the kitchen sink, first her neck and face, then the rest of her body, letting down the shoulder-straps of her camisole, and draping the towel, shielding her limbs from the child. She dressed Eleanor with the same scrupulous care she applied to her own toilet and at length, scrubbed, combed, Eleanor's very hair-ribbons stiff with starch, they set off to pick up Philip from the parlour-shop.

He was standing outside waiting for them, with a too-big borrowed cardboard suitcase, his Sunday serge suit shrunk up his arms, his socks held up by broad new hurting garters, his hair sleeked down with water. He was a bright-faced, eager boy, everybody's favourite. Tina's farewell was a little playlet enacted with every shade of feeling from anxious pride to heroic unselfish motherly joy.

But freed at last from the gentle tyranny of her injunctions – not to paddle if the water was cold, to take his cod liver oil – Philip joined Eleanor in the train going north in a puppy-like frenzy of excitement and anticipation.

Neither of thèm had been to the seaside before: all they had to go on was the depiction of holiday fun in their comics like *Rainbow* and *Sunbeam*. Everything that happened there they wanted to happen to them – being cut off by the tide, rescued from sinking rowing-boats or dangerous cliffs. They wanted to throw themselves into anticipation of these imaginary dangers while at the same time extracting every last possibility of enjoyment from the journey.

Before the train there had been the bus and tram journeys to Glasgow, some quick refreshment in a tea-room and all the cobbled, clanging, shabby glamour of the city itself, a rare enough treat. And then fields, hills, mountains, lochs, panorama upon panorama that might have subdued had not the rhythmic clattering urgency of the big steam-train set them off again. Mairi tried to settle them with thin beef sandwiches and a sip of lemonade, but before Calneggie was reached it all had been too much and both had been sick in the train corridor. Pale, seedy, they were led on to the station platform to meet Patie, awaiting them with his car.

It wasn't till next morning that they ran down together to the sands at Calneggie. It was a beautiful morning, one of those that cancelled out all that had gone before by its lambent freshness, all delicate washed blues and pinks and creams. There were miles of sand, sand that looked as though no footprint had ever embedded itself there. The sea was in benevolent mood, small ruffles of waves on a bosom of deep content. On the distant horizon lay the outlines of the western islands, remote and undefined.

'Is this Scotland?' demanded Eleanor precociously.

'Of course.' Philip gave her a lofty but indulgent look.

'It doesn't look like it.'

'Race you to the waves.'

Eleanor looked down at her new white sandshoes. Her mother had told her it did not greatly matter if she got sand on them. They were meant for the holidays and would save her good sandals. They were meant to enjoy yourself in. It was a pity, though. Their white newness was a source of neat, contained joy.

She ran whooping after Philip, the warm sunlight touching nerve upon nerve of bliss. The new white canvas of her shoes became ready sacrifice to this morning like no other morning, when she knew no streets or rows or school or constriction. Philip was already peeling off his socks and running along the creamy foam of the smallest waves.

'Your mammy would kill you,' she said happily, aping him. He looked at her and laughed, not taking in what she was saying. He ran up and down like a wild thing, getting the edges of his trousers wet. Judiciously, she tucked her second-best dress into her knickers.

Afterwards, when they lay exhausted in the sun, their backs against rocks, watching the seagulls, she had no hesitation in agreeing when he said, 'I'll never forget this. Will you?'

'It's beautiful.' Her small sun-warmed face was serious. 'I don't want to go back to Dounhead. Do you?'

'Not ever.' He heaved a large pebble in the water. 'Anyway, we're here for ages. We can do everything. Don't talk yet about going back.'

Big Lodge at Calneggie was a small mansion in itself, creamstoned and baronial in style, with small turreted effusions and window-boxes bearing an outcropping of pink flowers. Mairi thought it the prettiest place she had ever seen from the outside and inside it was just as delightful – polished wood floors, cretonne-covered chairs and sofas, big brass pots filled with massed blooms and on the walls bright, colourful pictures of gipsies, young girls, children, one of them signed 'Augustus John'.

She shared a huge bedroom with Catriona and Eleanor, while Philip had a small room next to the upstairs bathroom and the men, Robin and Patie, were accommodated on the ground floor. Nellie, sleeping under the eaves, had come to housekeep for them, helped by a girl from the village who brought the messages in with her each day – fresh fish and meat and bread when necessary. Nellie liked to 'slip out' – she savoured the vaguely illicit phrase – each evening to stroll along the beach on her own, returning silent but content. 'I wish I had the words,' she told Robin Chisholm surprisingly one day. 'I would like to write a poem about what I feel.' But during the days she was too busy: there was always someone wanting tea or a costume wrung out and her role above all was to be indispensable.

Calneggie – the main place – was more castle than mansion, built among heather and fir to rival the old Queen's Balmoral for romantic hauteur. The Black-Jamiesons had a house-party, some members of which had announced interest in the trials of Patie's racing car. There would be additions later for the grouse-shooting, but meantime the pastimes were hill walking, painting, card games played into the small hours, dancing, flirtations and more serious emotional entanglements. There were besides political arguments, for Colin Black-Jamieson had recently joined the Scottish Nationalists. Although English-reared – the estate had passed to him through an uncle – and Ampleforth- and Oxford-educated, he wore the kilt whenever north of the border (or in North America) and spent part of his not inconsiderable fortune on Scottish philanthropic ventures of an esoteric, not to say eccentric, nature. Nellie had learned one evening from a talk with the head parlour-maid that his recently divorced sister, Camilla, was one of the house-party. 'A funny one,' according to the disapproving servant, given to moods and disappearing to her room with too many cocktail glasses.

'We'll be invited up,' Robin told the others at their first meal together. With a grin round the table he added, 'And you'll all have to be nice to the laird, for we could use some of his spondulicks in the Party. Just remember that!'

Mairi linked arms with Catriona later as they walked along the sands and said, 'I've no intentions of being nice to the laird. It isn't what I came for. But this is!' And she drew in great gulps of air, looking in her cheap cotton dress with its sailor collar like someone just left school. Far along the sands, the children were building an elaborate system of walls and moats.

Patie struck up a friendship with the enigmatic Camilla before the rest of them were introduced to her by the laird. It happened early one morning, when he had taken the car for a spin along the quiet sands and then, in order to think out the problems concerning it, had walked through gorse and heather past a dishevelled tinker encampment near Calneggie village and stopped on the rocky headland to gaze out to sea.

'It seems we are the only two alive in the world,' said a voice behind him. Spinning round, he saw a slight, girlish-looking woman, with short auburn hair, smiling at him tentatively. She wore a heavy, green tweed costume that sat oddly on her elegant bones and heavy leather brogues with fringed tongues. There was a handsome Celtic brooch in her lapel and he thought indulgently that she had tried hard to look the part of Western Highlander but hadn't succeeded any better than most English folks.

'You're the racing driver, aren't you? I watched you from my bedroom window. And then I thought – what an inviting day for a walk before breakfast.' He looked more closely at her and saw strain and fine lines about the eyes. She was older than he had first thought. 'You're Miss – Mrs – ' She laughed infectiously as he blundered about for the correct terminology. 'I'm Camilla Black-Jamieson,' she said easily. 'As my marriage was annulled I revert to my maiden name.'

'I heard you were divorced.' Mairi often told him he had all the conversational finesse of a steam-hammer. He thought she flinched but the look she turned on him was still friendly. 'Then what you heard was wrong. I'm Catholic.'

'I'm not up in these things.' He began to feel more and more uncouth, more and more uncomfortable. Her voice was precise and bell-like. Everything about her was dainty, exquisite, intriguing.

When they had been speaking for a few minutes he realized that there was something about her eyes, a marginal flaw, a tiny cast, perhaps, that made her draw away her gaze self-consciously from time to time. He could have assured her that it didn't matter – the eyes themselves were lovely, almost the colour of her hair, large and perfectly shaped.

109

'Did you see the tinkers?'

'I smelt them!' he joked.

'Squalid,' she agreed. 'But they own the Highlands in a way you and I don't. I almost envy them.'

'Would you like to shove your worldly goods before you in a battered old pram, then? Would you like when it snowed and there were no rabbits to trap or berries to pick?'

She laughed. 'I might. It would be a great æsthetic experience. Waking up to the sky above your head and the smell of wood and earth in your nostrils. I've camped out, you know. I'm very hardy.'

'Would you be so hardy if the farmer set his dogs on you? And you had an old bit of sacking for a roof when the rain poured down? And the dirt got ingrained on your heels and your scabs itched like murder?'

'I could tell fortunes round the doors. Sell pegs and bits of lace and heather and put the fear of death in respectable citizens with my curses.' She was entranced by the fantasy.

The sun had barely warmed the sea-washed rocks but they sat on them anyway. There were long periods when each was locked in their own thoughts and then conversation would burst out between them, spontaneously and agreeably. He found himself explaining to her quite technical problems about the car and she was cagily expressing her feelings about loneliness now she was single again.

'Are you serious about attempting the record?' she asked him. 'Can you seriously compete against the Malcolm Campbells and the Segraves?'

'Not yet! But I've had rally experience, you know. I've been brought up with cars – '

'Yes, but my brother tells me you're doing it on a shoestring. That's why he's so keen to help. And isn't it dangerous?'

He grinned at her then. 'Of course it's dangerous. That's the attraction.' Then his expression changed from teasing to disconsolate. 'Don't worry. I won't be ready for the big stuff for quite a long time. One thing the trials have shown me is the amount of work I still have to do on the engine. It's the engine that counts, you know.'

'Could I drive it one day?'

'Not unless you want to die young.'

'What's it like?'

'You think your eardrums are going to burst. The air's like solid matter and the sand gets in your eyes.'

'Take care.'

'Don't worry. I will.'

'I don't feel I belong anywhere,' she said musingly, as much to herself as to him. 'I'm used to travel but I feel the sudden need to put down roots. To be *useful*.' She said the last word angrily, as though she were reproaching herself, and then laughed. 'Funny, isn't it? How you can sometimes say things to a total stranger you meet – the way you and I have met – that you would never say to your family.'

Here goes, he thought. He had only one way of expressing himself. Not the round-about, hidden, come-at-you-suddenly way of the Highlands, but the direct open attack of the Lowlands.

'Could you not help your brother in the Party?'

'How did you know it? You must be a mind-reader, I think.' She laughed. 'I am totally at one with Colin. I do think Scotland should have Home Rule and that we should go for a kind of imperial federation. But I can't get on with the Left-Wing sympathizers. That's what stops me. The *dreadful* MacDiarmid the poet with his *Caledonian Antisyzygy*. Do you know what he means, for I certainly don't?'

'He means – ' It had been explained to him many times and in the marrow of his bones and the blood in his veins he had the definition precisely. 'It means – contradiction is the life-blood of our nation. It means – chaos is a good thing. It means – don't tie yourself down to definitions. Throw up all the arguments you like, keep alive, keep fizzing. Join the Scots Nationalists and meet a thousand points of view.' The strain of being thus articulate had ben almost too much for him and he collapsed back against the rock, laughing at his own inadequacy. 'I'm a great disciple,' he jeered at himself. 'All I know is, saving your presence, I don't like bowing the knee to the English.'

'I'm half-English,' she confessed, adding impishly, 'Don't tell anyone.'

'It's nothing personal,' he protested lamely.

'Oh, with the likes of MacDonald it is,' she said swiftly. 'He makes no secret of it. And poets are powerful. He hates the English. He thinks them provincial and dull and complacent.'

'He could be right.'

She laughed at his provocation and then said, more seriously, 'Maybe it's understandable. I hate the English myself when I go along the foreshore there and see the grass grow-

111

ing over the ruins of the crofts. Colin says we could re-populate the Highlands. Bring back cottage industries, encourage the arts –'

'No. It would have to be done on a much bigger scale than that. For a start we need a hydro-electric scheme –'

'But then you get people complaining about destroying the beauty and peace of the Highlands.'

They both fell silent, contemplating the scene around them. It backed up her last words, for it had a limned bright freshness that was paradisal.

'I get quite mystical about it,' she said apologetically.

'If you feel that way, then it's simple. Stay.'

The cool, intelligent eyes with their faint hazy squint mocked him a little. 'I'm happy here, I think I've found the answer and then I go back to London and I'm seduced all over again. The parties, the races, the theatres, the gossip. It's as though I'm two people.'

'The Anglo-Caledonian Antisyzygy,' he suggested and was rewarded again by her laughter.

The day had caught up with them. Along the winding sea road a farm cart was slowly making its way to the village with the milk churns. A stray child had wandered from the tinkers' camp and stood in its filthy rags, observing them from the water's edge like some strange ragamuffin sea bird.

She rose a little stiffly and said formally, 'It's been so nice meeting you, Mr Fleming. I expect we shall meet again.'

'Call me Patie,' he said impulsively. She looked at his sun-warm, uncomplicated face. The blond hair had fallen across his brow and when he stood up he towered above her. She smiled her misty, delicate smile. 'Patie, then,' she said.

'What are you going to wear?' Mairi asked Catriona. Colin Black-Jamieson had said they should all come up to the Big Place on Saturday. After consultation with Robin Chisholm he had agreed that it was going to be a rally of sorts, with speeches, but afterwards it would be an open-air party, a picnic, so that the children could run races, have competitions and generally enjoy themselves. There would be as many names from the National Party as he could muster, and a few well-chosen journalists. He had asked MacDiarmid the poet, though it did not look as though he would come. The chairman and secretary, Roland Muirhead and John Mac-Cormick, were engaged elsewhere. Just as well, Camilla had judged tartly. They didn't want too many malcontents from the Independent Labour Party, like these three. She had even suggested there might be advantages in a Right-Wing split, but Colin was cautious. That time might come but at the moment younger membership depended on a certain radical zest.

'I can't make up my mind.' Catriona was listless. She had come with suitcases crammed with new frocks, beach pyjamas, daring shorts which she wore with brassière-like tops and matching coatees. 'This holiday isn't working out the way I wanted it to, at all.'

'Wear your dress with the floaty things,' advised Eleanor, whose white school blouse, above a tartan skirt, was being expertly buttoned up by her mother.

'She means the pink and mauve georgette with the panels,' said Mairi. 'Yes, do wear it, Cat. It makes you look like a precious little piece of Dresden china.'

She was teasing, small revenge for her own meagre wardrobe, and Catriona threw her a reluctant smile. Even after she had donned the dress and carefully combed through her Marcel waves, she was still disgruntled. Vaguely Mairi knew the cause. Ostensibly Catriona and Robin Chisholm were bracketed together as social partners, a pair. They had been swimming and walking together and in the evenings had danced and played cards with a bickering, prickly intimacy. But if Catriona had been waiting for a declaration, it hadn't come. Mairi had played the game straight down the middle. She had not encouraged Robin to talk to her, had made it clear that her role was that of mother to Eleanor and Philip's guardian. Only once or twice in the evening when the talk had been of poetry had she found herself chiming in to agree or disagree with Robin.

He criticized the fashionable MacDiarmid, saying he was a cruel, vain, heartless man who despised his countrymen as dolts and yokels, intellectual bankrupts. She said he had a wonderfully tender side and a sharpness that cut through Kailyard sentimentality like a knife through butter.

He said, jealous of his own classically orientated poems, which he had printed privately, that MacDiarmid would be a seven-day wonder, that he *was* just the Kailyard but a little elevated, and she replied to taunt him that he was the best poet since Burns. One evening she had picked up a slim volume of MacDiarmid's verse and intoned the poem about Scotland being 'the barren fig'.

He had said nothing but she had felt his gaze on her all

evening, wounded and antagonistic. Afterwards Catriona had told her he was angry at her defence of MacDiarmid and had suggested it was better if she didn't get involved in argument with him as he was the academic and knew better than Mairi what was what.

Annoyance over that discussion simmered up again in Mairi's mind and she turned a little defiantly to her own toilet. She had had her fair, maize-coloured hair cut short for the holiday and now she coaxed the curling ends forward on to her cheeks. A tan had enhanced the dark blue of her eyes. All the Rows pallor had gone and she looked – how did she look? Like someone ready for challenges. She wasn't going to kowtow to Robin or anybody else. If there were arguments, she would have her say. She caught herself thinking, 'I am Finn Fleming's daughter, after all,' and then amending it, half-amused, half-ashamed to 'I am Nicol Chambers's wife', until finally the image staring back at her from the mirror made her concede with an inward, assertive smile, 'I am Mairi Chambers and woman enough at that.'

Colin Black-Jamieson and Robin Chisholm had set up a rickety platform of sorts at the far end of the terrace at the Big Place and it was there that the speeches of a hortatory nature were made, calling on the audience to value the beauty of their country, the richness of their heritage, the independence of the Scottish spirit.

Mairi thought it was all very effective in a picture-book, idealistic way, but she found her mind wandering uneasily to the kind of problems she and Nicol had to face all the time, problems of sickness and want and poor housing. It was as though there were two Scotlands, the industrialized belt where the largest number of Scots lived out their lives among pits and steelworks and factories, and this almost mythic Scotland where words like grandeur and beauty and nature were bandied about freely but which struck her as being out of time, an anachronism, if you liked, and certainly a luxury.

The speeches were soon over, Patie's car displayed to enthusiastic small boys and their fathers, races run among the youngsters and a picnic provided on the rolling lawns that peeled gently away from the terraces. The hosts had left the front doors of the Big Place hospitably open and visitors were able to wander in and out at will. In one of the big downstairs rooms someone turned up the gramophone in the late afternoon and there was dancing.

The occupants of the lodge house found themselves seated together under a great cedar tree as the early evening shadows gathered about the Big Place. Only Patie was missing, but he could be seen through the open windows learning dance steps from Camilla.

Deliberately, Catriona turned away from the adults and amused herself playing games with the children. The strange withdrawn mood of earlier in the day had turned into something more hostile. She ignored Robin's attempts to draw her into the conversation, setting herself out instead to charm and please Philip and Eleanor. That was easy enough. She had a fund of silly games and easy jokes and a vein of inconsequential nonsense they found irresistible.

Seated beside Robin, her attention half on the children Mairi tried to explain what she had felt about the speeches. 'They just didn't seem relevant,' she told him.

'You have to remember,' he answered her, 'that the Black-Jamieson brand of Nationalism is founded on a religio-Celtic mysticism. It might seem other-worldly to you, but it's heady fatal stuff to some.'

'I am the practical sort,' she owned.

But as the evening wore on, she had to admit to a sense of being drawn out of time. Calneggie Sands, viewed from terrace and lawns, had never looked more beautiful. There was a magical stillness over everything: out in the sound the water lay like glass and the islands beyond like mirages conjured up in the mind. Cocktails were mixed and handed through the french windows, the children sported tall glasses of lemonade with cherries in it and the gramophone played 'O the moon shines tonight on little Redwing', rackety, banal and sad.

Mairi stood on the terrace with an empty glass in her hand feeling her head spin lightly after one pink gin and Robin came towards her with another, which she resolutely waved away.

'Where are Catriona and the children?'

'She's taken them down to the beach to make sand castles.'

'She's been in a funny mood all day,' he said testily.

'That's what I thought.'

'Do you know why?'

She gazed at him quizzically, responding with another question: 'Don't either of you know what your true feelings are?'

'We're the best of friends.'

'Not enough.'

'I like her. I like her enormously.'

'Still not enough.'

'Mairi. Mairi Fleming,' he said, using her maiden name with great deliberation, 'come and dance with me and I will tell you my secret.' He drew her through the french windows into the room beyond. Everyone else had left it and a record was just running down into great gaping gulps of sound. He wound the machine up again, tightly, and placed the needle on the wax disc. *'The breeze is sighing, the night birds crying.'* He took her up in his arms and they danced with long, dramatic steps round all that free space. She found herself responding in spite of herself. He was strong and had an immaculate sense of rhythm. He had obviously had a lot of practice since that night in the Wellington Rooms when their steps had refused to mesh.

'What is your secret, then?' Getting out of breath, she stopped him summarily. He refused to let go her hand, but led her to one of the small gilt chairs that stood round the room and bowed with exaggerated gallantry as she sat down. Pulling up another chair close, so close he could stare straight into her face, he said, 'I am going to marry her.'

She was stunned by her own reaction. And shocked. She wanted the words unsaid, denied. It was preposterous and disloyal and a hundred other things. But Robin Chisholm held her look, his own gaze unwavering and grim and at last she said in a stranger's small voice, 'Are you sure?'

He put the same record on again and she rose unbidden and went into his arms. Tighter and tighter he held her, till they crashed softly into drawn velour curtains at one darkened window and he tilted her head and kissed her.

He nodded at her. 'I knew how that would be. Did you?'

She shook her head, her hand going automatically to her lips to wipe away his kiss.

'Then you've found out something about yourself.' But his tone, far from being mocking, was tender. 'You've found out you have a greater capacity for living than you ever dreamed of back in the Rows.'

Without hesitating another second she drew her small, hard hand back and slapped his face. Then she stepped back through the french windows and into the sharp evening light. Stick figures on the sand looked up and waved to her. They were a great distance away, like figures in a book. Catriona and the children. She started to walk towards them, feeling her legs tremble, her stomach turn over, knowing it was time now she went back to Nicol.

'Proposals,' said Camilla, 'seem to be in the air. I hear Robin has popped the question to your cousin Catriona.'

Patie was easing himself into the cockpit of the Fleming Flyer and pulling on his leather helmet. He gesticulated, indicating, 'Once I've this on, I can't hear a thing.'

She lifted up one of the flaps and playfully said in his ear, 'I thought he liked your sister.'

Resignedly, he pulled off the helmet and sighed. 'It's no state secret. He's been after her ever since she left school. But she's married to Nicol. My sister doesn't play around.'

She laughed appreciatively. 'Oh, you sure-as-death Presbyterians, you. Armoured to your eyes in righteousness.'

He said uneasily, 'You wouldn't con a man, would you, Camilla?'

'You don't know anything about me,' she challenged.

'I'm willing to change all that.'

'I don't doubt it. Come on. You came down here to test the car, not my moral scruples.' She gazed along the sand to where the marker flags hung, sullen in the evening calm.

'A kiss for luck?'

'A kiss should be for keeps.' But she brushed his brow lightly with her lips.

He adjusted helmet and goggles and revved up the powerful engine. It sent waves of sound crashing through the tranquil air. Quite suddenly the car took off along the deserted sands, throwing itself like a demented mechanical beast against everything it antithesized – the stillness, the perfect pictorial beauty, the ageless calm infinity of the sea and sky. And then it stopped and Camilla began to walk towards it.

He got out and slowly paced the sand in her direction. When he was near enough she saw he was grinning all over his face. She called: 'How fast then?'

'A hundred and thirty, near enough. I felt the flags there were coming up to meet me.'

'That's marvellous.' She was caught up in his spirit of wary triumph. 'What if something had gone wrong, though? You shouldn't do it when the others aren't around.'

'You were around.'

'I was going for a swim, when you stopped me,' she reminded him. She indicated the ruby-coloured towelling robe over her navy and white swimsuit.

'Go now, then.'

'I wish you'd come with me.'

'I'm pooped.' He flopped boneless on the sands. 'Reaction. Holding that bloody car was like taming wild horses. I couldn't even manage a dog-paddle.'

She pulled on a white rubber bathing-cap, decorously folded her robe beside him and ran down the sand and into the sea. He thought how neat and pretty and delicate she was, wrists and ankles no more than the span of his thumb and forefinger. She lay on her back, too far out for his comfort, then would swim perhaps fifty yards in a firm, disciplined stroke and then laze again.

He was impatient for her to come out and stood holding the robe ready to enfold her. 'That was lovely.' Her face was bright. 'Like being born again. Oh, you're right, you know. I should stay here. There's no place like it.'

'I could come up and see you if you did.'

'Are you going back with the others? I thought you said the car was remaining here.'

'I am and it is. I have to go home on business matters but I'll be back whenever I can. Till autumn comes.'

'And then?'

'I might have to take it out to America. Conditions there could be more suitable.'

They were nearing the boathouse and the changing-rooms that Black-Jamieson had had built for his guests. She slipped into one and her voice floated out to him: 'I don't like to think of autumn, do you? The summer's been much too good.'

He pushed the door open and saw her, the perfect little bumps of her spinal column rippling as she stepped out of the soaking woollen costume, the skin of her body an almost luminous blue-white against the golden tan of arms and face. She turned swiftly and he said woodenly, without expression, 'I couldn't help it.'

'Please go.' She snatched up the towel. But he pulled it away, looking down at her breasts and then bringing his lips swiftly down on her shoulder. 'It's salty,' he said. 'Salty and sandy.' She stretched to put her arms round his neck then and he held her close, rubbing the damp skin of her back with his arms and hands, saying, 'There. There. You are wet, wee rabbit, all wet.'

She pulled at his sunbleached hair with her hands and brought his mouth down on her own. 'Patie, bunny,' she said. 'My brave boy, my brave boy.' They fell on to the slatted seat where her robe lay. When they emerged the shadows were lengthening and it was gold and rose and purple along the bay.

CHAPTER SEVEN

Tina's boy, Philip Mackenzie, walked slowly home from school, dreaming as usual. 'Dreaming again, Mackenzie,' the headmaster always quipped when he passed him. But it wasn't really dreaming. It was more imagining, a sort of writing in his head of what he would like to happen and it was an active, dynamic process, not a passive one. He was pondering what his mother would say when he told her he had passed the Qualifying Exam for Bellnoch Academy. He had been expected to pass; Carlie was always giving him books and talking to him about things. She said he was precocious. But it wasn't going to stop his mother looking haunted as well as pleased. 'Where are we going to get the money?' *Aye,* thought Philip, having read the phrase somewhere, *there's the rub.*

He didn't feel particularly cast down. He had been imagining that he lived in the Big Place at Calneggie Sands and that Colin Black-Jamieson was his father. '*You have passed the Qualifying Exam, my boy? I think a motor-boat would be in order.*' It had been great there, last summer. Before he'd gone, his mother had warned him about his table manners. 'If they offer you a second cake at the tea-table, you say, "No, thank you." ' 'Even if I'm hungry?' 'A second cake is just greed.' 'But if I'm *starving*?' Her look had pinned him to the wall. But at Calneggie you helped yourself to anything you liked. Once he'd had seven cakes and had only stopped because Mairi had begun to look at him with mirthful concern. But they had been wee things, the cakes, filled with strange fruit concoctions and cream and coated with chocolate and marzipan. He wore the sandshoes now he had worn then – for the spring day was warm – but a hole was about to burst through the right toe and the heels didn't grip properly because the shoes were really too small. Nearly all the boys wore gumshoes or sandshoes, which passed through various stages of smelly decomposition till they fell apart completely. His were kings to some. That's what his mother said, her face puckered in a way that would reassure no one. She worried about his shoes and darning his jerseys. She shouldn't. He always looked decent and respectable. Two words dear to his mother's heart. Sometimes he 'forgot' to wash his neck but he never left home without running the face flannel round his mouth and under his nose – it was worn and grey in the middle from his efforts.

He knew he would get to the Academy somehow. He would need new trousers and a blazer and *shoes*, not boots. His mother always found some way of providing for him. Again he could hear her voice, totally determined and a little wild – 'We'll manage.' But it was the method of managing that depressed him. They would borrow from Carlie or Mairi and it wasn't that they weren't always kind and ready to help. It was the having to ask. He knew his mother hated it and so now that he was eleven did he. But the day would come when neither of them would have to ask anyone for anything. He would see to that. He was going to provide for them.

Head down, he walked through the wrestling, squabbling ranks of his schoolmates, ignoring them today although normally he was not averse to the usual extra-curricular arguments. They liked him, for dreamy or not, he was good at thinking up games and variations on games. First the Academy, then a move from the Rows. The shop was worse than useless nowadays, for his mother had made the mistake of allowing too much tick during and after the General Strike and now the debtors took their custom to the Co-op and bought only twopenny Woodbines, a quarter-stone of potatoes or Askit powders from her. Tina was no longer able to wheedle supplies on the promise of payment later. As one supplier had said, they'd heard that once too often.

He would explain to his mother about the bursary. It was to be for thirty pounds a year and would pay for his clothes and books. His job, delivering morning rolls for Harvey the baker, brought in half-a-crown and some stale tea-bread. She would start talking again about Alisdair Kilgour, her husband. He didn't like it when she did, for he felt it was supplanting his father. But she said that if she went to him and asked for money, she would get it. 'I only have to ask,' was what she said. But there was always an expression on her face that Philip didn't understand, but which made him profoundly uneasy. If she only 'had to ask' why hadn't she done it before? He knew without being told that asking Alisdair was a last resort. Perhaps not even that. Perhaps a pretence, a falsehood, a whistling in the dark.

He had been waiting for the expression of pleasure on her face and he wasn't disappointed. When she was happy her movements were different, quicker. She brought a bottle of celebratory lemonade from under the counter and poured him a generous helping in a cup.

'I knew you would get there, of course.' She primped her hair and couldn't stop smiling and touching him. 'That'll give them something to think about, won't it? When you get your bursary, you'll get new trousers, a trench coat –'

'What will I wear for the interview?' He had to go that week to discuss what subjects he would take with the rector.

'You can't go in these.' She looked, appalled, at his trousers with the large, other-colour patch over the seat. It didn't matter at Dounhead. It wouldn't do for the Academy. Her face fell, became abstracted, preoccupied, planning.

'I don't want you to ask Carlie or Mairi,' he said. 'For the money.'

She wheedled. 'You could go, son. Tell them you've won the bursary, that we'll pay it back.'

He felt his new pride in his achievement draining away. 'I can't,' he said, desperately. 'I hate it. I hate asking.'

'It's only a loan.'

'They don't meet your eyes when they give you it.' He was suddenly red-faced and defiant. 'No more asking, Mammy. I'll wear what I've got.'

'They'll laugh at you, with a patch on your bottom.'

'Let them,' he said savagely. 'I don't care.'

She sat silently twisting the ring on her finger. He knew it was called a signet ring and that his father had given it to her with both their names engraved on it. Suddenly she drew it off and held it in the hollow of her right hand. 'It'll have to go.' She looked at him straight. 'I've got nothing in my purse, son. I can't buy you trousers with that. But if I get ten shillings for the ring –'

The pawnshop was always a last resort and Tina didn't go to the one in Dounhead. After a scratch meal she tidied herself and they set off to walk to Bellnoch five miles away.

'Remember this,' she said, after they had walked a couple of miles and her stride had slowed down somewhat. 'Remember this is what men like your father fought for.' Her voice was not often bitter, but they had just passed some particularly dirty tenements, with barefoot children, hair matted, running through the foul puddles near by. 'You know they call this place Summerhill? Lovely name, isn't it? And nearly every house is rotten with TB.'

'Don't cry, Mammy.' He could see the prospect of parting with the ring was upsetting her more and more. 'Keep the ring. It doesn't matter about my trousers. God's Honour it doesn't.'

She said nothing. The silent tears ran down her face as they walked on. When the fat privately-run omnibus that ran every hour between Dounhead and Bellnoch passed them, she pretended to be admiring the view over the fields. When they walked on, she had composed her face once again. 'Nearly there,' she said, her voice hardening. 'We should get there before he shuts.'

The pawnshop, bigger and more impressive than Dounhead's, was discreetly placed on a side street and the door entrance was wide and windowed, so that people could pretend to be admiring the wares on display then when the coast was clear could nip in through the swing doors like cats in the night.

'You wait here.' She wouldn't let him come in with her. He didn't argue. He could see she was summoning up all her determination for the task and he could best help by falling in with her wishes.

Once the swing doors had swallowed her up, it was very lonely in the street. He hoped he was inconspicuous. He tried very hard to be. He emptied his mind of all positive, restless thinking and concentrated very hard on not being seen. If anyone he knew came by, he felt he would almost dematerialize just by force of will. But somewhere was the thought of the Academy, the bursary, the day when it would no longer be like this. He looked round the hard, silent, quiet street and thought that it would be good some day to get away from this. From being poor, from borrowing, from living on hope and dreams.

Meantime Tina had accosted the old Polish Jew behind the grille. Despite all her resolution to be hard, to be firm, and demand the highest possible price, she was weeping because in the end giving away Wallace's ring seemed the worst kind of treachery. She had to ignore the tears and the old man's look of strained compassion. 'What will you give me for it? It is solid gold, you know. Eighteen carat.'

He smiled. His face was pink and cherubic, infinitely wise and cynical. 'Everyone say that. I can only give price it worth. No more. Otherwise I go out of business.' He was used, after all, to desperation, but something about this woman, some air of refinement, of having known better things, touched him. He made a rare exception. 'It is worth ten shilling. I give you pound because you have beautiful smile. And don't cry. Nothing is so bad you have to shed a tear, not so?'

She took the redemption ticket and the money, unable to say anything but 'Thank you' and stumbled back into the street.

'What did you get?'

'A pound. Better than I thought. He was a decent old man.' He could feel his spirits rise to match hers.

'You'll get your new trousers.' Now she was all sparkle and flushed triumphant animation. 'I wonder if Waddell the draper's will still be open?' They rushed panting through the last of the late evening shoppers and bought the famous trousers just in time. Tina would not be hurried although the assistants kept looking at the shop clock and yawning behind their hands. In her best *grande dame* manner she sat regally on the shop chair, examining the quality of each price range although both knew very well she would come back to the 4s. 11d. pair. Afterwards she walked round the fashion floor, admiring the dainty cloche hats, the new two-piece suits in marled wool, the crêpe-de-chine blouses, while the money from other last-minute shoppers sped overhead on trolley wires to the plaited-earphoned cashier behind the small castle of the cash desk.

She bought apples and a small pat of fresh butter with a thistle on it from Lipton's, and four dainty cakes in a box tied with mauve string from the baker.

'Would you like an ice-cream?'

He stared at her. Palozzi's parlour with its polished oak banquet seats and glass-topped tables was a treat for very special occasions indeed.

'As a reward,' she said, shining-eyed, 'for being clever and getting the bursary.' She had sponge biscuits with her ice, costing threepence altogether, and he had a double nougat, which was twopence. Always afterwards he was to associate the smooth, sweet perfection of Palozzi's Italian ices with a happiness as rarefied as mountain air. Now he held the cold delicious confection between tongue and palate for as long as he dared before letting it slip down his gullet, all sweetness and chill, while sensation returned slowly to his frozen mouth.

There was no stopping her. When she looked as she did now, carefree and happy, her pale skin warmed to a delicate pink, her dark hair tendrilling down from the small, close-fitting, pudding-basin hat, he loved her with an intensity that made him gruff and silly.

'What about the pictures?'

'What about them?'

'Mickey Mouse is on at the Regal. *Plane Crazy.*'

'Oh, all right.'

He heard her laughter in the dark. It was light and irresistible, the nicest sound he knew, and she gave herself up to it utterly. His own mouth spread in a smile that he felt was fatuous but could do nothing about. For a few days now, there would be a different feeling altogether in the house. She would sing about her work, cleaning windows, washing clothes on the scrubbing-board at the sink, for she refused to use the wash-house, and setting out the table daintily. A little money could make so much difference.

The feature film had John Boles and Dolores del Rio in it. His mother was totally absorbed by the love scenes. When he grew up he wasn't going to go around kissing women's hands, but there were certain attitudes of Boles and others which he felt he might usefully adopt. The right hand stuck inside the outside jacket pocket, negligently. Hair well slicked down – water was usually enough to keep his smooth, but one boy at school said he should try lard or margarine. A certain haughty deliverance of opinions, while looking down an aquiline nose. They wouldn't stand for it at Dounhead Public School, that redstone building where he had stomped in eagerly to many a morning assembly, while old Miss Claverhouse in her lisle stockings and stockinette dress played 'March of the Toreadors' on the Big Hall piano. It had been a good school, the teachers firm but fair. He felt nostalgia for it already, and he hadn't even left.

But just the same this had ended up a special day, knowing he was going on to the Academy and getting the new trousers. She had been sad about the ring, though. As they stood up for 'God Save the King', then trooped out into the dark afterwards, he said in her ear, 'You'll get your ring back, Mammy. And some day I'm going to buy you a real fur coat. What kind would you like?'

On the way to the bus stop (this time they were riding home) they peered into Wilson the furrier's. 'You see that? That's ermine,' Tina whispered. 'That grey one's only rabbit.'

'It looks quite nice,' he volunteered, taken by its comparative cheapness.

'Musquash,' she said. She was looking at a rich, reddish fur coat in the front of the window, with a large price ticket saying £39-19-11. 'With sable cuffs! I can see myself in it, Philip. Can't you?'

It looked a little grand to him, a trifle ostentatious, but if it was what she wanted to dream about, then he was all for playing along.

'You'll have it,' he said brashly. 'I'll get it for you some day.'

She gave him a mischievous, disbelieving smile, but all the way home on the bus her face was dreamy, rapt. He could see them both in the darkling windows – his own face red and serious and disappointingly unlike John Boles; her coat, the navy faded so that it almost had no colour at all, and above it the hat with a threepenny feather she had once bought in Woolworth's, and the dreamy face. It was one of those times he was achingly conscious of being alive, of being both happy and sad.

They got off the bus and in the dark he could hear the heavy-booted men coming up off the night-shift and making for the bright-windowed cottages where fires burned and kettles steamed. From the still-open chip shop came the redolent smell of hot, sizzling fat, curling out into the misty, rain-spattered street, while a distance off at the Co-operative hall, drums and melodeon set the feet of the local youth a-jigging.

He did it unconsciously, as naturally as breathing, the writing in his head, so that when it came to filling pages of composition he was the envy of his friends.

They had had a wonderful day, a strange one, John Boles Mackenzie and his mother Dolores. Now it was over and evening folded its wings about them and the city, while afar off hooted a sleepy owl and a train whistled piercingly as it rushed heedless through the night.

'I haven't come to borrow anything,' said Tina, on Mairi's doorstep.

'I didn't think you had,' Mairi responded. 'Come in. I was

just making a cup of tea.' She watched Tina covertly, trying to judge her mood. She and Carlie were agreed you had to be careful. Tina was touchy, prepared to take offence at anything she imagined to be a slight, to reflect on her poverty. Her chin was perpetually up, her face strained with defiant pride. Mairi admired her for it but tried to cover up her own sense of compassion.

'I want to see Nicol,' said Tina purposefully. 'I've made up my mind. Now that Philip's at the Academy, we're getting out of the Rows. I've been meaning to give up the shop for a long time.'

'I'll tell Nicol,' said Mairi. 'Is it anything I can help with?'

'He once said if I wanted a council house, he would do what he could for me.'

'He does what he can for everybody,' Mairi temporized.

'I don't want one in the slum clearance. There's a two-bedroom in the Auchengingar scheme. Burns Crescent. They're decent folk there.'

'But the rents are higher.' Mairi passed the teacup so carefully it might have been a hand-grenade.

'I've got a job. At the school. Cleaning.' It was Tina's trump card and the hamstrings on her painfully thin neck were drawn up tightly, warding off critical comment.

Bravely Mairi said, 'Will it not be too much for you? Those cold flagged corridors. And the open lavatories.'

'I'm stronger than you think.' Tina shot her a defiant look. She was prone to headaches and 'nerves', periods of depression when she became monosyllabic and hard to talk to, but Mairi had to admit that since Philip had gone to the Academy she had become much more communicative, at times almost cheerful. She tried to imagine what it must have been like for Tina, brought up in a strict but prosperous home, when her marriage broke down and the scandal of an illegitimate child followed. By coming to the Rows it had almost been like punishing herself, like saying, 'This is good enough for me now.' Mairi thought: *it's different for me. Nicol's work is here*, but she was tired of the Rows, too, and would like to be out of them.

Tina said now, her small face beaky with determination, 'The boy has to get his chance. He mustn't suffer for what I've done. He needs a right bedroom, and a bath once a week.'

Mairi nodded and said generously, 'Anything you've done will have been forgiven, long ago.'

'I don't know.' Tina stared into the rosy heart of the fire. 'I did a bad thing to Alisdair. Carlie says he drinks nowadays. What I did comes back to me sometimes. I sometimes think I'll go and see him. Maybe one of those days, I will.'

'Would you go back to him, ever?'

'No.' Tina's answer was immediate, but she sat back a little more relaxedly, as though she welcomed the chance to discuss something on her mind. 'It would never work. It never did. But I feel I have a kind of duty. It niggles away at me . . .' Her voice tailed off. Mairi stared at her, surprised and intrigued at the complexity of people.

'You still go to the kirk, don't you?' Tina said obliquely.

'I was brought up to it,' Mairi answered, a shade defensively. 'Sunday isn't Sunday, without it.' She knew Tina wanted more from her and she went on, 'Nicol's never interfered with me going, although he doesn't believe in it, himself. I suppose it goes back to my great-grandfather. He was the minister here, and Grandma used to polish the lecterns and the pews when she was young. I get a feeling of belonging when I go in there, a feeling I don't get anywhere else.'

'I envy you,' said Tina simply.

'Then why don't you come?'

'Maybe when I get something decent to wear.'

'It shouldn't matter what you wear.'

'Ah, but it does. We both know that. But I still pray –' her voice speeded up with embarrassment – 'and I don't think God has entirely deserted me, though I once did. When I had to go on the parish and the clerk behind the counter said in a loud voice: "And have you *nothing* to live on, Mrs Mackenzie?" I swear I will never go back to *that*.'

Mairi didn't know what to say. It was the kind of statement that challenged her own beliefs and she had doubts all the time. She knew she clung to the Sunday calm and ritual with a kind of desperation, yet there were times when her faith hemmed her in, stopped her from explorations that might lead her away from it. Maybe she was a coward. She only knew that if once she stopped going, that would be that. She would never go back.

Tina looked at the clock and put down her cup and saucer with a clatter. 'I'll have to go. Philip'll be home soon.'

'I'll ask Nicol to see what he can do,' Mairi promised, as she saw her to the door.

'It has to be Auchengingar,' Tina reminded her. 'They've

127

got teachers and a doctor in the houses there. It would be nice for Philip to be among professional people.'

Mairi hid a quick smile. She was tolerant of airs and graces, when they were backed up by so little. She was as good as her word about tackling Nicol and two months later Tina and Philip moved into one of a block of four apartments. They had small trim gardens and all modern amenities.

'Couldn't we move to one?' Mairi asked Nicol. She had known what his answer would be. As a councillor, he had to make sure he didn't take priority over those in greater need. It would soon be thrown in his face if he did. They would maybe manage the rent of a nice little greystone villa like Carlie's anyhow one of those days, if she could find another pupil or two and he only had some lineage . . . She sighed, knowing she had better not proceed or he would accuse her of bourgeois yearnings. She laughed inwardly at that, remembering with an occasional bitter twinge how anxious she had been to take nothing from her father at the time of her marriage and how arrogantly Nicol had accepted the gesture. But it was she who had made the sacrifice . . .

A new era, however, began for Tina and Philip. Although the rooms in the new house were sparsely furnished, everything was clean and cheerful and fresh after the cramped conditions of the Rows.

Once a week in the neat kitchenette (painted in ultra-modern primrose and apple green) Tina stoked the fire to heat the water and ceremoniously first she and then Philip had a bath, emerging quite preternaturally clean and virtuous. Both revelled in the convenience of electric light and an inside lavatory that flushed every time. Although Tina had to count every penny, she miraculously found new linoleum for the living-room and geometric-design curtains for the windows.

It was as though one good thing led to another. The headmaster's wife needed help two mornings a week. Mrs Armstrong was a semi-invalid, saved from pernicious anæmia by the only recently discovered cure of a raw beef liver diet. After she had supervised Tina's dusting and polishing in the parlour, she brought out two glasses and a bottle of tonic wine while she and Tina exchanged confidences of an innocuous and vaguely medical nature. It was not hard work compared to the school and Tina even fell heir to a decent fur coat, now much too small for Mrs Armstrong and 'just a feast for the moths' if left in her wardrobe.

It was after a morning cleaning for Mrs Armstrong that Tina noticed in the paper about the death of Alisdair's father, the old sea captain, Jack Kilgour, at the age of ninety-six. She could not afford a morning paper herself, but often rescued the headmaster's *Glasgow Herald*. Just recently, Philip had wanted to read about the Wall Street crash.

There had been a big turnout for the funeral, with commercial and maritime Glasgow well represented, and there was a lengthy story about Captain Kilgour's mastery of the old sailing ships and the prime seamanship that had taken him on to command of the later steel-boilered steamships. And there alongside the story was a picture of the mourners Sandia and Alisdair, she veiled and scarcely identifiable and he caught by the camera with an expression of lugubrious middle-aged bafflement. He had bared his head and his hair was grey. She could not get the bowed, impotent image out of her mind. The old man had been full of years, they must have been happy to let him go but it would be another gap, another loneliness, for the man on the front page of the *Herald*.

She made up her mind quite precipitately to go and see him. She told no one, not even Philip, but simply said she wanted to spend an afternoon in Glasgow looking at the fashions and bribed him with the promise of tea at Carlie's and a pencil-box from Lewis's.

She took great care over her appearance, washing her hair with green soap and pressing her one good blouse to go with an amber-coloured knitted suit she had bought shop-soiled in a sale. Naturally she wore the fur coat. Only she knew about the moth damage under the collar and right arm. With a neat brown hat and well-polished strap shoes she might have been a prosperous matron from Milngavie or Clarkston.

But she was beginning to feel tired and uncertain by the time she got to Alisdair's West End surgery and apartments. The day had turned out blustery and squally, and apart from having her umbrella blown inside out on the tram platform, she had begun to feel the throb of the varicose veins she denied having and the ache under her ribs that always followed the day she scrubbed the school corridors.

In desperate need of a cup of tea she rang the doorbell and

at first it seemed there was going to be no answer. Then slowly a bolt was drawn back and an old, querulous-looking woman all in black glared at her suspiciously and said, 'Yes. What is it?'

'I would like to see the doctor.'

'The surgery's round the front—'

'This is private business.'

'Who will I say it is?'

'Just say it is a lady who wants to see him. A lady he knows.'

She was smirking slightly from the old termagant's look of baffled curiosity as she was shown into Alisdair's parlour. He gave a perceptible start but waited till the housekeeper had gone before he said her name. 'Christina! What brings you here?'

She pulled off her gloves. 'I was passing. I had the urge to know how you were getting on. I read about your father.' He sat down at a big oak desk, lacing his hands before him, summing her up as he might a patient seeking his verdict on some lung disease, his look measured but not hostile. He had thickened, grown heavy and florid and she had detected the light fumes of whisky on his breath as they shook hands.

'He was an old man. But he wanted to make the century.'

'Yes. That was a pity.'

He had always been awkward in conversation. 'I never expected to see you again,' he said roughly. 'But you're looking better than you did the last time.'

'I've been through hard times. But my boy is at the Academy now. We've a house with the electric light and a garden. What about yourself?'

He didn't answer directly but instead wandered off in search of the housekeeper to tell her to make tea. While he was gone she looked swiftly round the parlour. It was a heavy room like Alisdair himself, with many books, and the grand piano by the window bore silver-framed photographs of his mother, his old father the captain, his sisters and brothers. But none of herself. It wasn't to be expected.

'What do you do with yourself?' she demanded when he came back.

'I spend most afternoons at my club, Sundays I have the kirk and I like sacred music on the gramophone. I have some fine records. Would you like to hear one?' She shook her head.

He pointed to the books. 'I'm also deeply immersed in the

130

history of the kirk and its preachers. One day I might attempt my own book about it.'

'Isn't it lonely?'

'Only sometimes.'

She waited till the old woman had come and gone and she had sipped her first cup of tea before she blurted out, 'I came because I thought we could maybe meet sometimes. Say for a meal at the Corn Exchange. Or a coffee. We should keep in touch. I haven't many friends. Have you? I would like to think life held a bit more for me now than just scrubbing stairs.'

'I'm touched by your concern, but isn't it a bit late in the day?'

She had rehearsed her answer and wasn't going to be put off by heavy sarcasm.

'You can believe it or not,' she said, her face flushed, 'but I'm not proud of what I did to you, that time you came out to see me at Dounhead. It was unforgivable, but I want you to forgive me. I don't like to think of you being maybe lonely. I always have the boy, so I'm different.' He wasn't making it easy for her. 'We could be friends,' she pleaded. 'I don't want anything from you, Alisdair. It's why I've waited till I got on my feet. But friendship would be the Christian thing between us. What do you say?'

'You're suggesting we should meet? How often?'

'Once a month? We could go for a sail down the water in the summer and to a matinée at the theatre in the cold days. I'd pay my way –'

He began to laugh. It was a heavy, grating sound but it had some genuine amusement in it. 'I don't see why not. Platonic friendship between a husband and wife's a new one on me, but if you like.' She could tell that the shock of her visit itself had lifted him, so she had been right to come. She didn't need to ask him. Everything about the house spoke of his loneliness, his solitariness. Poor damaged man, she thought, and caught herself out by the insight.

It had not occurred to him to ask her to remove her coat but now, her purpose declared and accepted, she felt able to do so. She sat back in one of the big moquette armchairs and let him talk, blunderingly at first, about his father. The trophies he'd brought back from his travels. The way his memory of sailing the China clippers had remained needle-sharp to the end. And the talk of his father led on to his mother, how she had accompanied Captain Jack on the big wooden hulk, the *Chancellor*, and how they had both almost been burned, then drowned, when the vessel became a flaming pyre.

The solid mass of his body seemed to ease and soften as he spoke. His face became quite animated and warm. Talking about the family he had a confidence that didn't apply in other areas of his existence and she wondered if perhaps they had all been too necessary to each other, Clemmie, Jack and their closeknit brood, and if Alisdair as the youngest hadn't suffered from this most of all.

When the carriage clock on the mantelpiece gave out a sharp, trilling reminder that it was five o'clock, she rose to go. They had discussed their next meeting and agreed it should be a meal followed by a visit to the theatre.

He gave her an abrasive, analysing stare as she pulled the fur coat about her again. 'You've weathered the storm,' he said slowly. 'I can see that.'

'And so will you, Alisdair,' she said quietly. 'In your own way.'

'Till next month.'

'We'll tell no one,' she said, on a whisper. 'It'll just be between you and me. What do you say?'

He whispered his agreement as he saw her out. The old housekeeper had come out from the kitchen and was hanging about the hall like a suspicious collie. It pleased him to bring the unpredictable into her narrow life. He passed her without meeting her eye on his way back to the parlour and later she could hear him whistling. She shook out her copy of *The Red Letter*, feeling that such bold insouciance must bode no good for either of them.

CHAPTER EIGHT

Carlie Balfour grimly banged shut the door of her house and set out to visit Mairi and Nicol in the Rows. With no children of her own, she was protective and caring with her younger relatives, especially Mairi, and Tina's son, Philip. But this morning it was comfort and diversion for herself she was seeking. It had suddenly become more than she could bear, sitting at home with crisis after crisis happening in the country and Donald kept week after week in London, so that he never got home to see his constituents.

Not that it was in any way a picnic down the Rows. As wife of the local MP she got some bitter looks and dry nods. Well, it didn't matter. It was understandable. With Dounhead Colliery under what was hoped was only temporary closure, but closure just the same, there were more than ever on the dole. Even Nicol Chambers. (And no question of Mairi going to her father for help. The estrangement between Finn and both his children seemed all but complete). She stopped at Harvey's to buy a few bits of tea-bread to take with her. You didn't go anywhere empty-handed in 1931. Even providing a cup of tea strained most budgets.

She passed a man she knew, a kirk elder and skilled workman who had been laid off by the Council. When he raised his hat she saw the once-grey hair he had dyed to help him find another job. It was the kind of subterfuge people had to go in for these days. Since the Wall Street crash of '29, Britain's exports had fallen by half. Half the pits in the area had closed and so the downward spiral went. Other areas seemed better able to weather financial stress, but skinflint, hard-up, patched and darned, on-the-dole and on-the-parish Dounhead never seemed to rise above subsistence level. She spared but a passing glance for the showcases outside the picture-house, with their stills of what was coming next week. Entertainment seemed irrelevant when they were talking about Britain coming off the Gold Standard and cutting the unemployment benefit by ten per cent. What happened then was anybody's guess, but it would be grim.

The Labour Government that had limped and hesitated, hummed and ha-ed under MacDonald would be finished. She didn't think Donald would get in again at the next election. The Unionist, Major Homerton, who had sopped up two hundred of the out-of-work with a newly opened knitwear factory, was much more likely to have the ear of the populace. There was no defence. Labour seemed to have learned little in the Baldwin years. It had been the Lum Hat Government of 1924 all over again, only worse. Donald, Tom Johnston, Jimmy Maxton, Shinwell, had sometimes set the Commons alight with the desperation of their will to bring work to their supporters. Johnston had brought off a six million pound deal with the Russians for engineering tools, with the promise of much more trade to come, but it wasn't a popular project; Donald had pressed for national relief schemes but had been hamstrung when the buck was passed to local authorities. There were times when she had a certain sympathy with the Scottish Nationalists. Maybe, as Robin Chisholm maintained, economics weren't the roots of Scotland's ill. Maybe you had to go deeper, into social and cultural areas, areas where the resistance to change began. Even now, most folk were content to coast along if they had enough for food and drink, a roof over their head and half-decent clothes.

She could hear the children singing at Dounhead Public School as she approached the Rows. Eleanor might be one of the singers:

'All things bright and beautiful
All creatures great and small . . .'

The teacher was beating out the pace, the children would be making their mouths round and careful, but it came out a solid Lowland sound, she thought, not without pleasure. They might well be starting up a dictionary of the vernacular in Edinburgh, an academic work that would take years to finish. It was like locking up the past. But the past wouldn't go. These children sang and spoke in their Lowland brogue. And why shouldn't they? She knew she was looking for a focus for her inward rage this morning and this was just one more target.

She knocked. She began to think Mairi and Nicol must both be out, when the door finally opened and Nicol, drawing his braces up over his rumpled shirt, let her in.

'I'm sorry,' she said, embarrassedly. 'I'm too early.' Looking beyond Nicol, she saw to her surprise that Mairi was still in one of the set-in beds, her pale sleepy gaze apprehending her from under a heap of blankets. As it was eleven o'clock, she decided Mairi must be ill.

'What's the matter?'

Nicol didn't answer. Slowly Mairi sat up. 'I think I've got a chill, I feel all sort of shivery.' But her face told a different story. She had obviously been weeping and not just a few tears, but a great shedding that had left her looking ravaged and ill. Carlie held a cool hand to her brow. 'You're not fevered,' she observed cheerfully, but falling in with the need for deceit. 'You were right to have a long lie. Here, I've brought some cream scones. Will I put the kettle on and make us all a cup of tea?'

Nicol's sullen brow cleared but he was pulling on his

boots, smoothing his unruly dark hair, and still he didn't meet her eyes. An affirmatory 'Aye' rumbled from somewhere between his chin and chest and Mairi sat up, sniffed but looked marginally brighter. Carlie knew a domestic row when one hit her between the eyes but she was past-mistress in the art of tactful conciliation. She said now, determined they should put their private woes, whatever they were, in perspective, 'What's going to happen now, Nicol? The papers say this morning that half the Cabinet refuse to accept the proposed cuts in the economy. The Foreign Secretary's sent Tom Johnston to Paris to try to get to the bottom of these rumours that it's France that's draining our gold. MacDonald can't go on, can he?'

It was like a match to tinder. '*What'll happen?* If they impose this Means Test and cut the dole – '

'They make you sell off what they call non-essential belongings,' said Mairi. 'They'll take the vases I had from Grandma and my spare sheets from the press.'

Nicol ignored her. 'They think the teachers'll take a fifteen per cent cut and the Services ten per cent! The people'll march on Whitehall, that's what. The army'll mutiny. They'll put the gibbets up again at Marble Arch and hang MacDonald strangulated vows and all.'

'So should we come off the Gold Standard?'

'Snowden says it would damage our financial reputation. What reputation? That's what I'd like to know. J. P. Morgan Inc. have us all sewn up. If we don't make cuts, we don't get loans. Tom Johnston had to fight to get us trade with the Russians, yet it's all right to deal with these cut-throats in the States. They'd sell their own grannie if it made them a profit.'

Mairi had hopped out of bed to accept a scone and a cup of tea from Carlie and now she interposed, 'But we could go the same way as Austria, Germany, couldn't we? Our money could end up worthless.'

'What money are you talking about?' Nicol demanded. He gave his wife a surly, bad-tempered glare and said, '*You* know nothing, you mealy-mouthed bitch, so why don't you shut up?'

'Don't talk to her like that,' Carlie reproved mildly.

He turned his aggression on her. 'If your Labour government had had the guts to implement a Labour policy, none of it need have happened.'

'Be fair,' said Carlie, maddeningly calm. 'They depend on

Liberal support. And when the American Stock Market crashed, it affected us too.'

'MacDonald promised he wouldn't cheapen production –'

'MacDonald promised too much.'

'Then we're agreed. He betrayed the working classes –'

Mairi gave him a furious impatient glare and began pulling on her clothes. 'Who works round here? All I see is the bone idle in their dirty mufflers, holding up the street corner or placing bets with the bookie's runner.'

Knowing she was being deliberately provocative, Carlie put herself bodily between the two and said in a quite different voice, 'How about you and me having an outing? Can Nicol's mother look after the bairn after school?'

'Where to?'

'We'll go up the Clydeside and see if we can buy some fruit for jam-making. What do you say?'

'I've no money.'

'My treat this time. I'll need help to carry the fruit.'

Mairi looked uncertainly at Nicol, who said ungraciously, 'Please yourself. You always do.' He pulled on his jacket and without another word let himself out of the door.

Sitting in the fat comfortable bus, passing through Ferniegair and Larkhall on their way to the upper reaches of the Clyde, where the fruit ripened slowly into sweetness, Carlie said carefully, 'Nicol seems to be letting the unemployment situation sour him a bit.'

'He's been like a devil for weeks,' Mairi answered tautly. 'But it's not just the unemployment. It's us. We fight like cat and dog. He'll not let me have an opinion about anything. He puts me down at every turn.'

'He's picked the wrong one, if he thinks he can bully you.'

'He knows that. It's all coming to a head now, what he feels about me having a better education. He can take in the ignorant folk in the Rows, but not me. I can see that all his so-called brotherly love is just to build up the importance of Nicol Chambers. He wants to be somebody. All that ranting and raving at the council is so people'll say what a martyr he is. Him injured in the war, too! His limp gets worse in proportion to the amount of attention he gets. Have you noticed?'

Shocked at Mairi's vehemence, Carlie said nothing at first. Stealing little covert glances at her younger companion, she saw how poverty had altered her. The maize-coloured hair was still striking, and the blue eyes and pretty mouth, but the cheap starchy diet had done to her what it did to so many women, puffed her out and made her look heavy and matronly beyond her years. Her face was blanched of colour and heavy mauve shadows showed under her eyes. It was as though even intelligence dulled after a time. Carlie sighed.

'I thought you two were a love match.'

'Some love match, when a man takes his hand to you.'

'He hit you?'

Mairi looked mildly chastened. 'Well, I bit him first.'

'You *bit* him?'

'I thought he was going to strike me, though he swore he wasn't.'

Carlie gazed out momentarily at the soothing green farm fields before continuing the conversation. 'You don't fight in front of the bairn?'

'How can we help it?'

'It's bad for her.'

'Oh, she's getting to be a hard-necked little madam. She cheeks me up, tells me she'll go and stay with her Auntie Carlie.'

They got off the bus before it reached Lanark and walked past douce whitewashed cottages and picture-postcard gardens till they came to the fruit farm Carlie had in mind. The grower, harassed and taciturn, told them they would have to pick the fruit themselves and armed with baskets they began their task. The late raspberries were dark and full of flavour. At first they sampled as they picked but then, absorbed by the job in hand, were concerned only with reaching the best and juiciest berries, hung like dark glowing lanterns among the aromatic leaves. After the raspberries they picked blackcurrants and the grower, refreshed from his tea and pleased with the quantities they'd gathered, sold them a few of his special Victoria plums, golden and wine-like, to eat there and then.

'Take your baskets down by the river there,' he invited them, showing them a narrow path by the side of his small-holding. 'You'll find a rustic seat where you can picnic.'

Carlie had brought a few hastily-made cheese sandwiches and the grower's shy but hospitable wife sent an elder child down to them with a jug of tea and two tin mugs. A warm golden sun had come up after a damp, glowery morning and now the whole Clyde valley bathed in it, lush, benign and tranquil. It was too much for Mairi. She wept into the mugful of milky tea, stemming the tears with her fruit-stained hands.

'Have a bit cry,' said Carlie gently, and looked the other way. There were small birds she couldn't identify skidding in and out of the river's edge. The soft rush of the water was hypnotic in its murmuring.

'You see,' said Mairi to Carlie's bent listening neck, 'he doesn't love me any more. He just wants – well, pleasure. I want a bairn and he won't hear of it. Says who will put the bread in its mouth –' Her sobs ran accompaniment to the water's threnody.

'If he thinks I'll wait for him to come round,' Mairi's voice was ugly, 'he has another think coming. I can take Eleanor and move up to Patie's. There's always a crust there for me, for us both.'

'It's hard for him, too. Can you not see that?' said Carlie reasonably.

Mairi stared straight ahead, mutinous still but dry-eyed at last.

'He's always ready to help the scabs that come to the door asking for help. "Nicol Chambers'll get you a house." "Nicol Chambers'll put a word in for you for a job." But there's nothing left over for Eleanor or me. He comes in tired and bad-tempered and he tries to write and it'll not fall into place the way he wants it. He gets mad as hell and he takes it out on me.'

'You shouldn't talk about folk as scabs,' said Carlie soberly.

'What would you call some of them?'

'Poor souls down on their luck.'

'Scroungers. Idle, good-for-nothing blackguards some of them are.'

'Mairi!' Carlie reproached her.

'It wouldn't matter what system they lived under, they would be the sort that never managed. Somebody else would always have to pull their chestnuts out the fire.'

'Well, you'll feel better for getting all that spleen out your system.'

'I thought we were going to be *different*.' Mairi's cry came from the heart. 'I've tried. But I must have kindness. I can't live without kindness. I'll not let him into my bed, without kindness.'

Carlie picked up a handful of small stones and plopped them reflectively into the river.

'You know we were talking about MacDonald this morning?'

Mairi nodded.

'I think his number's up. It'll mean an election and Donald won't get back in this time. So I'll have a disconsolate man on my hands as well.'

'Donald always finds something to do. Lectures and so on.'

'For a man who likes argument like my Donald, that'll never be enough.'

'You sound worried.'

'I am. He's not an easy man, either. He gets contentious when he's idle.'

'But it'll be better for his health.'

'If I can persuade him to retire, maybe to the Ayrshire coast, I think that would be best. He could write articles, maybe a book about his life.'

'I'm sorry.' Mairi's warm, rough hand landed on hers and she made a little moue of apology. 'I get to thinking I'm the only one with problems.'

'You always have Eleanor,' Carlie pointed out. 'I wanted Donald's child but it wasn't to be. It's left an ache.' She held her arms over her stomach as though in demonstration.

Mairi stood up decisively. 'Here, we're getting sorry for ourselves. We'll miss the bus if we don't get going. I'll come home with you and help you pick over the fruit.'

'You'll get some of the jam,' Carlie promised. They lifted the heavy baskets and made their way back up the narrow path. At the end they turned. 'It's been peaceful here,' said Mairi regretfully. But she managed a smile. 'Back to Red Nicol, the darling of the Rows.'

'Things'll get better one of these days,' said Carlie. But she didn't sound at all convincing.

She was late getting back from Carlie's. They had stood over the big brass jelly pan, taking turns to stir the sweet bubbling liquid jam, first the raspberry and then the blackcurrant, and she had helped Carlie to lay up the still-warm stone jars in the big cool larder at Tarbert Villas.

Carlie had given her several jars to take home with her, covered with a clean white cloth in a honey-brown basket, and she in turn had parted with one of them to her in-laws when she stopped to pick up a sleepy Eleanor.

When they got back to the cottage in the Rows Nicol had not come home. The fire was out in the dusty grate and the remains of a scratch meal lay on the table. Mairi pushed some firewood between the bars, shook out the dust and ashes with a vigorous pokering and got enough of a fire going to warm some water to wash the grubby child. She was bringing about warmth and order when the door sneck rattled and Nicol came in. Eleanor immediately jumped all over him, full of the indulgences allowed her by her grandparents. 'Grandpa let me take the whippet for a walk. Grandma said I could have an ogie-pogie eye.' This last with a defiant glance towards her mother, who forbade the big slippery round sweets that changed colour as you sucked, ever since one had lodged for an uncomfortably long time in Eleanor's throat.

Low-keyed, silent, Nicol took the child on his knee and let her prattle. Mairi went about her household tasks deliberately, anxious to finish them before the light went.

'Can you not sit down?' he said at last.

'I've work to do,' she said shortly. But she did not extend her tasks unnecessarily and at last sat down on the creaky wickerwork chair opposite him. Soon they would have to light the gas or go to bed.

'Here, give this to your mother.' He took something from his jacket pocket and handed it to Eleanor, who looked at it, then sidled over to Mairi and slipped the object on to her lap.

'What is it?' asked Mairi indifferently.

'Look at it and see.'

'It's Fry's Cream Chocolate. It's tuppence, Mammy. What Daddy always gives you when you have a row.' Eleanor bounced, sanguine, on her mother's knee. 'Can I have a bit? Please.'

'It's not good for you at this time of night.'

'Just one wee square.'

Mairi gave in and said, without undue warmth and extending the chocolate bar towards her husband, 'Would you like some?'

'No, no. It's for you. All of it's for you.'

She pushed it into her pinny pocket and got the excited Eleanor to bed. It was only a matter of minutes before the tired little girl fell into a deep sleep and turning from her, Mairi felt Nicol's hands on her waist, moving her round to face him.

'You smell of sunshine and blackcurrant leaves,' he said

140

huskily. His hands moved on her arms. 'And your arms are all warm still from sunburn. Was it nice up there today?'

'It was hard work,' she said shortly. 'And my back aches from the picking. Excuse me.' She pushed down his arms like barriers and moved to the window, where she stood with her arms folded, looking sightlessly into the dusk.

'Don't sleep with the bairn tonight,' he said. 'Come in the bed with me.'

'You called me a mealy-mouthed bitch.'

He unfastened the strings of her pinny while his mouth sought hers. 'I called you that?' He laughed against her lips. 'I never meant it. You know I never meant it. Come, I'll show you what I mean.'

In the bed she laid her head on his chest and said heart-brokenly, 'You will hurt me once too often, Nicol Chambers.'

'Ah, my love, we hurt each other. And we couldn't do it if we didn't love each other.'

'But there's cruelty in it. You can go out and forget about it, but I have to stay here, brooding on it. And I have to share you all the time.'

'You don't have to share this.' Expertly he caressed her, coaxing her body into response. She said, 'How do I know I don't?'

He reared away from her. 'This is dangerous. We'll be back where we were this morning, before Carlie came.'

'You shared it with others before we were married.'

'Don't,' he pleaded. He would not let her talk. He held her wildly to him, his body hard with the desire for mastery, and he went into her not gently but aggressively, demandingly, brutally. While he moved she lay still, not coming to meet him, an expression of sorrow and non-submission on her face. When he withdrew before the final spasm, as he always did now, to avoid making her pregnant, she turned away from him, a look that was half-triumphant overcoming the passivity on her face.

'Mairi?' He spoke to her back, touching her still, 'Mairi? Love? Did nothing happen to you?'

'No,' she said. 'No, it didn't. No, don't, I am too tired.'

'I love you.' He waited for her response but the darkness reverberated with her rejection, the density of her silent rage.

'Good night.'

'Good night. Good night. Now go to sleep.'

Five shillings lay ostentatiously on the kitchen table as Mairi rose and dressed. Nicol and Eleanor had already breakfasted. He had gone out to buy a morning paper and she to play some long complicated game with her friends down by the Doun burn, as it was school holidays.

Mairi did not touch the money, though her eyes were drawn back to it as she drank tea and scraped some of the recently-made jam on to a heel of bread. There was something challenging about the way it lay there. He hadn't put his hand in his pocket and given it to her in the ordinary way. He hadn't asked her how much she needed. He had placed those two half-crowns there as though he wanted no questions asked, then strategically disappeared for the paper.

'Where did you get it?' she demanded when he returned.

'Get what?'

'The money.'

'Never mind about that. MacDonald's Cabinet has resigned and he's brought in Baldwin, Samuel and Chamberlain for a National government.' He threw down the paper with the shouting headlines.

'I asked: where did you get it?'

'What does it matter? I got it, that's the main thing. I'm going down to the Welfare. The place is humming with talk about a hunger march –'

'Was it from gambling?'

'You know I don't gamble.'

'There has to be a first time. You didn't earn it.'

'You should be thankful I got you something to be going on with. Make it last. When we're on the Means Test they'll take the eye out your head.'

'I'll not touch it. Not till I know where it came from.'

'From Tina Mackenzie, if you must know. She's in work, she offered to help.'

'Take it back.' Stonily.

He sat down opposite her, his dark eyes flashing. 'You stuck-up, stupid besom. Come down to ordinary folks' level for once.'

'Have you been seeing her?'

'I met her in the street, coming out of the Co. The money's not a gift. It's a loan. She knows what it is to have nothing.'

'Take it back to her!' she screeched. 'I'll not have you discussing our private affairs with that woman. You've taken everything else from me, but you'll not take my pride. I still have that. I'll take the bairn and go to my brother. If it's

142

come down to charity, I'll take it from him rather than strangers.'

'Mairi, don't. You knew what it was like when you married me.'

'I didn't know it would be like that.'

'But it's the same for everybody.'

'Well, it's not what I've been used to. I'm used to a cloth on the table, and decent sheets, and cups with handles to them. And I'll not have the dole authorities coming into my home and taking away the last few things I treasure – '

'Go, then,' he said contemptuously. 'What do you give me anyway?'

'And you me? I feel nothing for you. I'm like a stone since I lost the baby – '

'You said it. Stone's the word.'

'I despise you, Nicol Chambers. Away to your Welfare bums and see if you can rustle up a pair of boots between you. A hunger march! All most of them can manage is a march to the street corner to see what's won the three-thirty – '

'You bitch!' Goaded, he raced awkwardly but swiftly round the table and brought the weight of his arm across her face. Sobbing and screaming, she eluded him. 'I'm going! I'm going! Hell mend you, you can die for all I care.' He tried to hold her, pull her into his arms, but she was too strong for him. The paper's headlines forgotten, he collapsed into a chair and watched as she pushed some things into their only case, drew on her coat and snatched a few ornaments off the mantelpiece, wrapping them in dish-cloths and placing them in a basket.

They were both as pale as death. He said tonelessly, 'Don't do this, Mairi. You'll destroy me.'

She placed her face to within an inch of his. 'As you've nearly destroyed me. I'll find the bairn.' She jerked her head in the direction of the two half-crowns still lying where he had placed them on the table. 'You have these. Buy your erstwhile paramour some Phul-Nana face powder with them. I'll not touch them.'

He stared at the coins after she had gone, the phrase about his paramour ringing round in his head like some ghastly joke demanding laughter. But he could neither laugh nor cry. He felt crippled in mind and body and when he rose to stir the fire and absently, almost vacantly, fill the kettle to make some tea, his limp was worse than it had ever been and his leg ached as though the shrapnel had freshly gaped it open. The pain was everywhere.

'I told you what he was like,' said Nellie Chambers remorselessly.

It was the next day at Dounhead House and Mairi had begun to feel a chastening of the spirit. Yesterday she had been caught up in a wild swirl of emotion that had been almost exhilarating while it lasted. There had been a deep wounding satisfaction in hurting Nicol, in defying the watchful faces in the Rows, in retailing the drama first to Nellie and then to Patie. But now the full realization of what she had done was coming home to her. Eleanor was mooning about in the garden, sulky, pale and asking when she could go to see her daddy. And Mairi was beginning to think that although she had left one intolerable situation behind, and would not go back to it, another might be shaping up here.

One drawback was that Nellie had been established as housekeeper for so long now that she behaved as though Dounhead House was hers. Quietly but firmly, she would have to be put in her place. It would be a battle for supremacy and it would have to be fought with the small, the delicate armoury, for she did not want to antagonize Nellie. She wanted her uncritical support and friendship. She needed all the allies she could get.

So why was her reaction now one of defence on Nicol's behalf? In the circumstances it was ridiculous, but she felt Nellie should observe the family loyalties.

'It wasn't him I left, so much as the house,' she said evasively. 'It was getting like the rest there, scruffy, dirty, smelly. I couldn't even afford rubbing-stone for the step.'

'There's a wildness in him.' It was as though Nellie hadn't heard her. 'I know he's my own brother, but he's not like anybody else I know. Nicol Chambers could never take any pleasure out of things as they were. He had to change them. He tried to make you into someone else, someone you weren't.'

Mairi stared at her in bewilderment. '*I* went to *him*.'

'Aye, but you were a young, idealistic lass, and he took advantage of it. You weren't cut out for the Rows. You don't have the hardness bred in you that you need to survive down there. I know. I've seen both sides of the picture.'

'Don't blame Nicol.' Mairi felt a swelling ache inside her, for it was all coming back to her, the night she had run away from Catriona's dance in Glasgow and come out in the snow and ice to look for the man she was determined to marry. *He* had been the one to give then, for with her father out of her life, her mother dead, she had been like a starveling, dying for want of love.

She didn't know what had happened, but maybe Nellie was right. Maybe the will to make a success of something wasn't enough. Maybe what was determined by your birth, your family, your upbringing was stronger. Predestination. She felt chilled, as if layer after layer of her pretensions, evasions, aspirations were being stripped away and she stood buffeted in the slipstream of eternity, knowing her function as well as the last leaf on a wind-slaughtered winter tree.

Shivering, she handed over the cake she was creaming to Nellie and said, 'I think I'll go down to the sheds and see Patie. He seemed subdued last night. Is the car giving problems?'

'Doesn't it always? No, his problem has a painted face and a big fox fur. She's called Camilla Black-Jamieson.'

Mairi stared at Nellie, wondering whether she should encourage her to say more, or whether this was a good occasion to indicate by her own discretion there were boundaries Nellie ought to keep. She decided on the latter. She would hear it best from Patie. Walking down towards the car sheds, it felt a bit like being fourteen again, herself and Patie against the rest. Whatever emotional problem he had, she would try to help him, back him up. It would be a relief from her own worries.

He was grimy-faced and overalled, working on a large bench at what looked like the engine of the Fleming Flyer, while a younger assistant whistled and hammered over his labour further down the building. He looked up absently, acknowledging her only with a sketchy wave of the hand, and she stood silently watching him until at last he wiped his hands on an oily rag and said, a little less than welcoming, 'What brings you over?'

'Curiosity.'

'You've never shown any before.'

'Not about the engine. About you.'

'Has Big Nellie been shooting off her mouth, then?' The epithet was savagely disparaging.

'She inferred something about the woman you tig-togged with at Calneggie.'

'The *lady*.'

145

'Woman. Lady. Camilla Thingummy-bob.'

He threw down the rag as if he had come to a summary decision.

'How would you like a trip to Bellnoch? Too many listening ears here.' And with the merest shift of his head he indicated his young assistant, who had stopped whistling and was making no bones about finding the newcomer's conversation – what he could catch of it – more fascinating than work.

'All right.' She went back to the house for her navy edge-to-edge coat but wearing it over her one decent rayon dress she felt shabby and ill-at-ease beside Patie in his dapper plus-fours and Fair Isle pullover. In the car, an early commercial Flyer which he kept in immaculate condition, he said, 'I'll give you some money to spend on yourself after we've had some lunch. You could do with some smarter clothes.'

'No, I can't take it,' she protested. Curiosity overcame her and she said, 'You seem flush.'

'Had a win at the races. You might as well spend some of it. It'll only get back to the bookie in the end.' And he gave her a big ingratiating grin that stifled any further argument.

They went to the Royal Hotel at Bellnoch and she sat smoothing the beautifully laundered white cloth with her rough fingers and feeling the weight of the heavy silver cutlery. The soup was piping hot, the Angus beef rare but tender, and the light creamy trifle melted in the mouth.

'I'm not letting you go back to him, you know,' he said, when they were sipping the strong, sweet coffee.

'We've been over all that.' The night before she had had to restrain Patie from going down the Rows to assault Nicol, when she had told them about him striking her. She felt she could face no more strong emotion, no more attitudinizing. 'I want to hear about your lady-love. I thought it was just a passing affair, that summer at Calneggie. You've played it close to your chest, haven't you?'

It was difficult for Patie's broad, open features to look cagey but that was the only description for them now.

'Camilla didn't want us talked about.'

'I can understand that. She's nearly old enough to be your mother – '

'And yet you asked me why I played it close to my chest.' His face had reddened with hasty anger.

'No, wait a minute,' she said placatingly. 'I liked her. I

146

could see what attracted you to her. But I thought it was just a young man's fling – you know, before you settled down with somebody your own age.'

'Who? You'd think to hear you talk that Dounhead was full of eligible maidens who understood about racing cars and politics.'

'Oh, you love her for her mind, then?'

'Well – ' He began to relax, be more expansive. 'When you've been with somebody you don't need to explain things to, who just naturally cottons on to the way you think, going back to the Dounhead beauties is like swopping a Rolls-Royce for a Model-T Ford.'

'And she's rich.'

He didn't flinch, but admitted half-ruefully, 'She is. And it helps.'

She smiled at him. Her affection for him had always been direct, uncomplicated and maternal. 'Don't get hurt, that's all.'

He waved to the waitress to bring them a second cup of coffee. He took a cigarette from a monogrammed silver case (she didn't ask whether Camilla had given him it but thought it likely she had), lit it and smoked it with a fierce concentration. She pretended interest in the red-faced farmers and their plump, sweating wives, tucking in heartily at the other tables, and waited.

'I want to marry her.' He looked past her, addressing the cruet. 'But of course she's a Pape and I'm a Prod, she's twelve years older, she's had one bad marriage – '

'Did she tell you about it?'

'I can't discuss it, Mairi. He was – look, you've heard of Oscar Wilde, that sort of thing?'

She looked bewildered but he rushed on, 'But the big stumbling block is her brother. Before she met me, there was some stuffy Catholic academic from Glasgow and Black-Jamieson sees him as a good match for her. He's one of those talking about setting up a new Scottish Party, a lot more Right-Wing than ours, and Camilla's sympathies lie in that direction.'

'What does *she* want?'

'She wants to use her life properly, she says. But if we get married, it would mean – it would mean I would have to turn Catholic. That's the stipulation she makes.'

She felt as though the breath had been knocked out of her.

'Oh no! You'll not give up the kirk?'

'I don't go to church, the way you do –'

'But you were christened into it, brought up in it.'

'It doesn't matter to me, the way it does to you. It's Camilla that matters.'

'Do you think the Pope'll think Camilla a good enough reason? Look, you have to think this thing out. You have to want to be Catholic for its own sake –'

'I'm aware of that.' He had never looked more stiffly, more solidly Presbyterian.

'There are too many obstacles.'

The closed, stubborn look she knew was sometimes mirrored in her own expression took over, maddening her while forcing her to admit they could be two of a kind. She began, delicately, to steer the conversation away from this one compulsive direction to another. She got him talking about the time he'd taken the Flyer to Utah, the phenomenal speeds it had achieved there before some vital part of the engine split: and led him on to Brooklands and his description of the public-school mad-heads, ex-Service eccentrics and hooray-Henry devotees who threw themselves round the track there in the ever-increasing search for speed records.

She hadn't wanted to ask him about the Monte Carlo Rally, which he had entered from John o' Groats with Camilla, knowing that when they'd reached their destination he had caught up with Catriona and her husband, Robin Chisholm, in the bar of the Metropole Hotel there. Somehow, she never wanted to talk about them. She had gone to the wedding, of course, Catriona having provided her matron of honour's dress and the bridal attendant's dress for Eleanor. She had even danced with the groom, for it would have looked odd if she hadn't. But the marriage made her uncomfortable and the house the newly-weds had built near Robin's mother had filled her with unaccountable disgust and envy.

Patie reported that Catriona had been the belle of the Monte Carlo ball. She was certainly bent on spending some of the money her father Dandy had left her when he died. She had been wearing a Molyneux gown she had bought in Paris and hadn't wanted for partners, one of whom Patie had heard refer to her as the Glasgow Cake Queen. As for Robin, he had stood about looking a shade out-of-place and had piloted Patie into a corner to talk politics and whether Beaverbrook would help the Home Rule cause now his paper, the *Scottish Daily Express*, had taken up the cudgels.

'Did they look happy?' She forced herself to ask the question.

'I don't think they're a match for each other,' said Patie candidly. He mistook the look that crossed her face for one of impatience or boredom, not hurt, and said, 'I'll get the bill.' He pushed a small wad of notes across the table at her. 'You go now and get yourself a smart rig-out. To please me.'

Later, when she had bought a coat with a small shoulder cape, and two dresses, a navy one and a multi-patterned crêpe-de-chine, and a Robin Hood hat with a feather in it, she thought how embarrassing it had been, hiding the state of her underwear from the beady-eyed shop assistants, and finished off Patie's money by buying some new vests, knickers and bright pink, ugly corsets. She could bear then to think of Catriona on holiday in the South of France, and of her Molyneux gown, but she tried not to think of Robin Chisholm. Every time she did, she was filled with the hurt of abilities not realized, of newly-roused tentative wishes to assert herself, to grow out of the cocoon that was the Rows and poverty. He had warned her it would be like this. And it was painful to acknowledge the truth.

CHAPTER NINE

'Uncle Patie,' said Eleanor from across the dinner table, fork poised precariously near the edge of her plate, 'why do you like racing cars?'

Patie glanced irritably at Mairi. 'Can you not shut that kid up at mealtimes?' He was bolting his pudding, followed by a scalding cup of tea, so that he could get back to the sheds. He had mounted the aero engines on a common crank case with a single shaft, fitted the huge front wheels with their expensive tyres and placed the driving-seat as far forward in the streamlined nose as he dared. The Flyer was unbearably near to being finished and he was hamstrung, bedevilled by lack of funds. Somehow he had to get it back up to Calneggie Sands for the trials which would reveal whether it was fit for the big circuits. With the wind in the right direction and all the gods smiling he might just do 250 in it. With the big names going for 300 it wasn't going to be enough but it would prove the machine was worthy of further refinement. He knew he was difficult to live with at the moment and uncharacteristically sharp with his niece. She was not put down by his irascibility. She had a way of pursuing an argument, a train of thought, that was as logical and unrelenting as Nellie unpicking a seam. Now she swallowed the meat on the end of the fork, having chewed it nine times as Nellie had instructed and protested, 'I am not a goat, Uncle Patie. A kid is a baby goat. Why *do* you like racing cars so much? It's just speed for speed's sake, isn't it?' She'd heard this in a grown-up conversation and the phraseology had appealed to her.

'You heard what your uncle said.' Mairi gave a forbidding nod in her daughter's direction. 'Get on with your food.' She turned the barrage of her disapproval on Patie. 'You'll get an ulcer, bolting your meals the way you do.'

Patie rose, beating his chest. 'Me? Never!' Pulling Eleanor's pigtails as he passed, he made a clattering exit from the room, leaving in his wake an explosion of exasperated sighs from the womenfolk.

Mairi escaped to what her grandmother had always referred to as the morning parlour, leaving Nellie to clear up. In half an hour she had a pupil coming for an elocution lesson and in the meantime she wanted to finish a dress she was making for Eleanor. As she picked up the bright, balloon-printed cotton, she decided rightly that Eleanor was in one of her contrary moods. She knew the symptoms – the persistent questions, the small face growing closed and a little sullen, almost as though inviting rebuke. She was missing her father again and Mairi was unsurprised when the child came into the parlour after her and, sitting on the edge of a chair opposite, fixed her with an accusatory stare, her toe tracing the flowers on the thinning Axminster carpet, and in her hands a copy of the evening paper.

'Mam? What are rickets?'

'Rickets? You should know. You've seen children with bowly legs. That's rickets. It comes from poor feeding –'

'It says here "Councillor says rickets on increase". That was Daddy, Mam. And further down –' she began to read carefully – 'it says, "The councillor added that the Means Test must be abolished and schemes started to bring relief work to the Dounhead area. Dounhead colliers were prepared to go on hunger march to make their protest, but he doubted if they would reach London before their strength gave out. There were shouts of 'Rubbish' and the councillor leapt across the chamber and tore up the notes lying on the chairman's desk, throwing them in his face." '

'Your father up to his capers again.' Mairi's face was grim as she held out her hand for the paper. 'You read that well,' she said absently. 'Red' Nicol Chambers stared back at her from the front page and all her ease and equanimity from the good meal, the clean, well-furnished surroundings went up in the air like the chairman's notes. He was wearing a shabby, once white raincoat someone must have given him and the ends of his collar had begun to turn up from wear. He hadn't had a haircut and, Maxton-like, a dark lock fell over his brow, while his eyes burned out from his starved, wild face.

Her legs were shaking as she got up, all thoughts of the lesson she was about to give fled. She caught sight of herself in the big oval mirror between the parlour windows and she looked the person she wanted to be – trim, well-shod, in a smart, unstained skirt with a freshly-ironed blouse and a plum-coloured cardigan, but the face had become tense and questioning, unbearably strained.

'Do you not like him much?' demanded Eleanor miserably.

'It's not a question of liking, or not liking.'

'Then can we not go back and stay with him?'

'You know we haven't got a house of our own any more. The Rows are being knocked down and your daddy lives with Grandma and Grandpa.'

'Is it because they live in the slum clearance?'

'Not just that. Your daddy can't provide for you –'

'But I love him,' said Eleanor irrefutably. 'I like you and I like Uncle Patie and Nellie and everybody, but I love my daddy. Can I go and see him? While you're teaching?'

Mairi sighed and gave in. In the year or more she had been at Dounhead House, she had seen Nicol no more than twice, each time traumatically, but she allowed Eleanor to visit her grandparents freely so that she could see her father.

Blindly she went down to the kitchen now and, cutting three huge slices from a still-hot cloutie dumpling, scattered them with sugar as Nicol liked them and wrapped the spicy, fruity mass in a clean cloth. She put the dumpling and some jam with a bottle of Nellie's homemade wine in a basket and carefully wrapped eight half-crowns in a piece of paper, instructing Eleanor to give these to her grandmother. 'Go straight there,' she warned, 'and tell your daddy I'll turn his collars for him if he likes to send them to me.'

Eleanor put on her school blazer and wiped the sleeve across her mouth in a hasty toilet. She looked into the basket like a little miser, but its contents must have pleased her for she gave her mother an absent-minded but approving grin.

When she had gone Mairi tried to compose herself before her pupil arrived, for the twenty-five shillings a quarter from her and the others were all she and Eleanor had to live on. It was enough but only because she paid no rent and because with hens and garden produce the household was almost self-supporting.

She was glad when the session with the grocer's round-faced daughter was over. For once there had been no satisfaction in teaching the music of the vowel sounds, the importance of correct breathing and proper projection, in trying to open narrow, careful minds to the beauty of poetry. She kept seeing Nicol's lost, wild face in her mind's eye, so that it seemed she almost conjured up his physical presence. With the utmost clarity she was remembering things like the shape and fineness of his hands, how white and good his teeth were although the years of inadequate feeding when young had left him scrawny of limb and trunk. For a year now she had schooled herself not to miss the sexual side of her marriage, for it seemed to her everything had gone wrong after she had miscarried and he had refused to try for another child. She had resented him for that and it had made her cold at times. He had borne her rejection and her moodiness patiently on the whole, but he had not been able to understand how bad it had been, losing the baby. No one had been able to understand that or how she still felt less than whole because of it.

She shook herself mentally. Perhaps Patie's present moodiness contributed to her restlessness. He hadn't seen Camilla for several months: she had been in London enjoying the social whirl and he was worried in case the car would not be ready for its trials when she returned to Calneggie.

She picked up the little dress again and finished putting a hem on it, half-watching the wag-at-the-wa' clock and worrying about Eleanor getting back before it was too late. Nicol would bring her to the drive and wait at the gates till she got to the door. Tonight it was all she could do to stop herself going to the gates for a glimpse of him. Only the thought of what Patie might say prevented her.

That was Eleanor now. She rose precipitately and saw

that her husband's shadow waited on the back step while Eleanor came running in, calling out loudly in an important but half-frightened way, 'Mammy, Daddy wants to see you. He says to come to the door.'

'Well, Nicol.' She kept her voice level and friendly, although her eyes were all over him, seeking for change. He was still the same shabby, put-together figure, just this side of respectability and cleanliness, somebody else's jacket sitting, as always, uneasily on his narrow shoulders, but the navy knitted tie well-knotted, with a pin behind, and the eyes shrewd, lively, dark, those speaking eyes.

'I brought the bairn. And these.' He handed over a paper bag with half a dozen grubby collars. 'Eleanor said you'd turn them for me. I came to say thanks.'

'How are you keeping?' She could not keep the eager concern out of her voice.

'Fit.'

'Will you come in?'

'I'll not,' he said, decisively. 'I just came to say – thanks.' He smiled at Eleanor, standing by her mother's side, her arms around her waist, and ruffled the child's hair. 'Away you to your bed now. Be a good girl for Mammy.'

She made a great show of washing Eleanor and putting her to bed, teaching her *Green Glass Beads*, the poem that shaped rough and childish Dounhead vowels into something else, then listening to her prayer:

> 'Gentle Jesus, meek and mild
> Look upon a little child,
> Pity my simplicity,
> Suffer me to come to thee.

God bless Mammy and Daddy and Uncle Patie and Nellie and Grandma and Grandpa and all my relations and friends, And make me a good girl, Amen.'

Going downstairs, she was halfway between elation and tears. He had spoken to her without bitterness tonight, there had been no shouting or threats. Almost as though he knew she had been thinking about him. Strange, that, and oddly comforting.

'Don't jump.' But she did, going into the kitchen and seeing the figure materialize from the direction of the pantry. The room was all dusk and subtle shadows and she had been on her way to put on the light.

'Nicol!'

'Nellie's night for the pictures?'

'Yes. It is.'

'Good.'

'But she'll be back soon.'

'No matter. I had to see you again, once Eleanor was in bed.'

'Why?'

'I don't know why. You told me once – I'm not a rational man.'

'Well, there's no harm in us talking. Sit down and I'll make us a cup of tea.'

He moved swiftly before she could put on the light and drew her into his arms. She felt his mouth on hers and her lips parting, her whole body opening immediately to him, like a tight, slow bud eased and warmed into instant flowering by a miraculous sun. 'No,' she said harshly. 'Nicol Chambers, no.' She cast round wildly for self-possession. 'Nellie will be back any minute – '

He dragged her into the pantry. It was deep and cool with a stone floor and smelled of scones, spiced ham and apples. His hands were touching skin somehow, he was murmuring into her hair and neck. 'Oh, lassie, lassie, let me feel you, Mairi, be kind.' She put her hands to his head and forced his mouth down to her mouth, exultation filling her so that when a saucer was pushed and fell to the floor, splintering into pieces, she merely laughed softly and whispered his name, identifying this madness, this joy, this undoing that swept through her as she had thought it would never do again: 'Nicol. Nicol Chambers.' The Italian ice-cream man, going home through the waning light in his little yellow cart, blew his whistle for the last time. A bluebottle buzzed against the netted pantry window. She straightened her clothes, pushing him away, suddenly aghast and urgent: 'Nellie's coming. You'll have to go.'

He put his cheek to hers. 'Come back to me.' She knew it for a command.

'We'll see. We'll see.' She pushed him out of the door and closed it swiftly behind him. Then before Nellie returned she ran up to her room, standing at the window for a long time before she undressed. In the warm evening even the birds did not seem to want to go to their rest. She heard them calling down by the grassy banks that fell away from

154

Dounhead pit, and all the musky scents from the fields came to her on the evening breeze.

'All I'm saying is: I have a job.'

Nicol was sitting, awkward and out-of-place, in the big parlour which only that morning Nellie had swept and polished. Rich and dark, the furniture gleamed and sparkled from years of careful waxing. Brass curb and fire-irons sent out small suns of their own from the bright fire which had been lit because the morning was cold and wet. In a crystal vase Mairi had arranged sweet peas and gypsophila. Now, her face taut and watchful, she sat between her husband and her brother Patie, Eleanor having been spirited away to the kitchen by Nellie so that the present conversation could take place.

'What bloody clown thought digging founds a right job for a lame man?' demanded Patie.

'It's all there was.'

'Can you get nothing better?' This was Mairi.

Nicol shook his head.

'What does it pay?'

'Thirty shillings a week.'

Patie's expostulation rattled the engineered calm of the occasion.

'Thirty bob! You want Mairi to come back to you on that! Have some sense, man. I've told her – it's tantamount to giving up her health and strength if she does. It all but killed her before –'

'I'm getting her a house in the Auchengingar scheme. What she always wanted.'

'Pity you didn't do it sooner. She used to plead with you but would you listen? I don't think it will be any different this time.' Patie made a valiant but unsuccessful effort to sound impartial. 'It's the kind of man you are, Nicol. Public affairs come before your wife and wean. And my sister is too good to be put to the bottom of your list of priorities –'

'Patie!' Mairi's tone was more harshly peremptory than she had meant it to be, and she softened it swiftly. 'Don't go digging up what's past. I've said Nicol could come here to talk things over. If we could get a house –'

'What would you furnish it with?'

'We still have some sticks left. I could take some stuff from here –'

Patie refused to take the scowl from his face. 'Does he

155

know you hadn't a rag to your back when you came here?'

Nicol rose. 'I'm sorry I troubled you. In future, I'll see my wife elsewhere.'

Mairi said agitatedly, 'Sit down, Nicol, and be quiet, Patie. So far you've both been a bit too ready to have your say. Now let me have mine.' To Nicol she said, 'It's too early to say, Nicol. When you hear tell of a house –'

'I want your commitment,' he said doggedly.

'And you heard what *she* said.' Patie placed his large frame between them. More propitiatingly he said to Nicol, 'I have no objection to you visiting, but you have to have something to offer my sister before I'll let her leave my roof.' As Nellie and the little girl came back, big-eyed, into the room, he said commandingly, 'Bring out the sherry, Nellie.' He was looking directly at Mairi as he said, 'Nicol knows the score. There'll be no hard feelings on my part if he takes up his full responsibility as husband and father.'

With this part-reconciliation Mairi and Nicol had to be content for the time being. They took to meeting once a week to go to the pictures in Bellnoch and sometimes if funds allowed they had a modest meal of mutton pie and chips in a tea-room beforehand. Mairi got ready for these occasions with a sense of excitement and pleasure, like a young girl dating her first boy-friend.

She always wore her best dress and a little perfume, perhaps Californian Poppy, behind her ears, and in the dark he held her hand while they watched the newsreels of hunger marches; dog-racing; children drinking free school milk; the man Adolf Hitler, newly come to power in Germany; pundits explaining what Cockcroft and Rutherford were up to, splitting the atom, and the huge liner called the '534', eventually the *Queen Mary*, sluggishly a-building on the Clyde.

Nicol had been in and out of work during the winter, sometimes because he was ill and sometimes because of the hard weather, so when the colliery started up again after new export agreements with Canada, Ireland and Scandinavia, it was with much relief that he took up his old job of pit agent. This coincided with the availability of a three-rooms and kitchen in the Auchengingar scheme, and with predictions of disaster from Patie ringing in her ears, Mairi moved back to her husband and into a period of comparative calm and happiness.

Something had changed and hardened in her, however. She

had learned the emotional devastation that could come from relying on one other person solely for fulfilment. She still loved Nicol but could be more detached from and accepting of his feelings. Eleanor was growing into an interesting, strong-minded girl and took up some of the emotional slack caused by Nicol's public involvements. But apart from all that, Mairi began to exist as an adult in her own right, with interests in drama and public affairs, and with more elocution pupils, began to put on small concerts to raise money for charities. In a funny way, whenever she proved herself she thought of Robin Chisholm and the desire to vindicate her chosen life was strong. She would not go under. Never, never. Poverty would not make her less than she was.

In the new year, Nicol was one of a party of industrialists and trade unionists invited to visit Russia. With the memory of six British engineers from Metropolitan Vickers recently tried as spies, Mairi had grave doubts about the wisdom of him accepting, but public interest in what went on in Russia was insatiable and intellectual 'long hairs' from the English universities painted intriguing pictures of how society was being changed there.

'Ask them what happened to the Kulaks,' said Donald Balfour grimly when he heard about the trip. No longer an MP, he was testing his wife Carlie's patience to the limit as he spent his new-found leisure fighting old battles with a bitterness that threatened to sour their whole existence. He felt betrayed and disillusioned by the MacDonald government, with nothing to put in the place of old ideals.

'All that's behind them now,' Nicol replied.

'Don't you believe it.' Donald's tone was rancorous. 'Stalin is just biding his time. There'll be more purges. You can't run a Communist state without eliminating the opposition.'

'I'll go with an open mind.'

'And you'll see what they want you to see.'

Carlie and Mairi exchanged patient glances. There were times when the contemporary obsession with all things Russian got a bit too much. Everyone knew who 'Big Joe' was; shopkeepers joked about him, pitmen threatened recalcitrant bosses with him. Stalin was far enough away to be a safe cult-figure, while Ramsay MacDonald dwindled into history as the arch-betrayer of the British Left.

Nicol returned with stories of the Hermitage and its treasures in Leningrad; of low rents and crêches in Moscow, free false teeth and glasses and the ease with which Communists could get divorced or married. It took him weeks, months even, to sort out the myriad impressions in his mind. Nothing was simple. He had been appalled to hear that the child mortality rate was sixteen per cent and discovered that this was partly due to lack of milk and meat because the threatened Kulaks had killed off most of their livestock. Mairi in turn was aghast to hear how women in Moscow could have their babies aborted for the asking.

His description of the Comradely Courts which placarded details of the cleanest and dirtiest rooms in the Moscow tenements went down well with tenants of the Auchengingar scheme, bothered as they were by the tearaway exigencies of the nearby slum clearances. But all in all, in that way in which wives train themselves to catch subliminal messages husbands aren't always aware of sending, Mairi judged he had been bewildered, perhaps sobered, by what he saw. Once in an unguarded moment he described a ragged old priest to whom he had given a few coins. 'He had no food card, you see. Officially he ceased to exist. He wasn't regarded as a citizen.' Another time, he told her of barefoot beggars on the outskirts of the capital and the near-rotten herrings and cucumbers peasants brought into town to try to sell.

Well, better minds than Nicol's were bewildered by what was happening, not only in Russia but elsewhere. Germany was openly re-arming, Mussolini strutted absurdly across the Italian scene and in India Gandhi's civil disobediences were forcing Britain to give Indians a small share in the government of their country. Perhaps people had never been so politically conscious as they were now, but passions and polarities ran strong, the need for answers more desperate, it seemed, than ever before. As though in a spasm of atavistic fear, the electorate of 1935 put the Tories in under the reassuring father-figure of Stanley Baldwin. Too much was happening too quickly. Carlie assured Mairi this was exactly how she had felt before the First World War. Her face darkened by Donald's catching pessimism, she was sure there was soon going to be a Second.

'Hitler is harmless enough,' said Catriona. 'He just wants to look after his own. Isn't that what the Scottish National Party wants too?'

She and her cousin Patie were sitting out on the terrace of the Big Place at Calneggie, on one of those bright pearly mornings that seemed like the start of all creation. She was being deliberately provocative, silly even, because Robin, her husband, and Colin Black-Jamieson were in conclave about the future of the now conjoined Scottish and National Parties – yet again – and Camilla, with whom she had struck up a close friendship over the years, had still not put in an appearance.

Patie looked at her dispassionately. The engaging girlish need to be *au fait* with the latest fashions had hardened into a brittle sophistication, but he still treated her with a cousinly latitude.

'I used to think you were a sensible wee soul. That you had something in your upper storey.' He tapped his head. 'Now I think all that travel abroad must have softened your brain.' She had been all over Europe and America on the late Dandy's money. 'Look, Hitler is about as harmless as a cobra. The French should never have let him send his troops into the demilitarized zone in the Rhineland. It was a direct breach of the Versailles Treaty. Do you really think he'll stop there?'

'He just wants more room to breathe – '

'No, you're goading me, and I'll not let you.'

'Robin says the Party will oppose conscription if there *is* a war, unless carried out by a Scottish government. You'd have to refuse to fight – '

'You're enjoying this, aren't you?'

'Well, would you? Refuse to fight? Unless for a free Scotland? Robin says we lost a disproportionately large number of men last time – far more than England.'

'I don't know how I'd react.' Patie's face was suddenly brooding, but he slapped his knee, jumped up and said resolutely, 'Come and see the Flyer. I think I have her nearly ready. All we need is for the weather to keep up – '

'You haven't asked the papers this time?'

He gave her a sideways glance. 'Weren't exactly kind last time, were they? If you're not Malcolm Campbell they don't want to know.'

'I wasn't here. What did they say?'

'Referred to it as the Tinpot Flyer, the Jamjar and sundry other less than respectful names. They think I'm some kind of harmless eccentric building from a Meccano set and string.'

Catriona laughed. 'And aren't you?'

'Nearly,' he said ruefully. 'Money's been bloody tight.

159

My father could have helped but he's turned his coat good and proper. He's met up with some English widow with nearly as much money as he has. I think they'll get married.'

They walked along the silvery-gold Calneggie Sands, seagulls wheeling and keening high above their heads, and at the far end stood the Flyer, solid on its broad tyres, faintly menacing and incongruous. Ned Allan, Patie's engineer, raised a flushed face from work on the dashboard and gave them both an absent-minded greeting.

Patie patted the machine as though it were some great resting animal, and after describing its latest refinements to Catriona walked her out of Ned's earshot.

'What do you think?' His eyes watched her face closely.

'I'm impressed.'

'Really?'

'Yes, really.'

He grabbed her arm. 'Then I'll tell you something. I think I can go over the three hundred mark on her.'

'Three hundred miles an hour?'

He nodded. 'When we've finished testing her, I must get the money to take her to Utah. Try to get Camilla on my side, will you? She wavers about financing me. She'd get it all back if I broke the record –'

'It's your safety she worries about. Not the money.' Catriona's voice was upbraiding, but she softened it as she pushed her arm through Patie's and they directed their steps back towards the house. 'She's so very fond of you, Patie. What's the future going to be for the pair of you?'

He didn't answer and she went on cajolingly, 'She would marry you in a register office, you know, quite happily. It wouldn't please her brother but he'd come round in the end.'

'It's not a satisfactory solution. Her church matters to her.'

'Well, what is? The pair of you have dragged on for years.'

'Maybe it would be better if I broke it off.'

'Do you want to?'

He looked away from her probing gaze. 'Sometimes I think it would cause less pain. I can't give up my driving and she gets more and more nervous about it.'

'Yes.' Catriona stopped, troubled eyes raking his face. 'Her nerves are bad. She told me it's why she sleeps in of a morning. She can't get over for ages. She gets up in the night and paces about.'

'You make me feel guilty. But I didn't destroy her nerves.

That was her first marriage. That was what brought her back to Calneggie.'

'She takes cocaine.'

The words seemed to swoop and dive about the clear morning air. He looked up and about him helplessly as though for interpretation. Catriona kept on walking with small, deliberate steps. He raced after her and drew her furiously to a stop.

'How do you know?'

'She told me.'

'She never told me. I don't believe it. I would know. You're lying.'

'No.' She shook her head sorrowfully. 'She's kept it from you, darling. Not all that hard. She says you're naïve, ingenuous. It's what she likes about you. The doctor's trying to break her of the habit. But easy it is not.'

'Why did you tell me?'

'I don't know. It slipped out. No, it didn't. You two shouldn't have those kind of secrets. You've got to level with each other, sort things out. I want to help you.'

'You know your trouble. You've too much time on your hands.'

'Oh yes? My husband's a public figure. But wives of public figures become ciphers. Did you know that?' It was Catriona's turn now for bitterness.

'I warned you not to marry him.'

'I had no option. I loved him.'

'And do you still?'

She shrugged her shoulders, but managed a smile. 'Daddy's money softens a lot. I've got loads of girl-friends. Like Camilla. Like myself. We know how to have a good time.'

'You haven't answered my question. But don't bother.' His face had become almost savage. 'You I don't give a damn about at the moment. What about her?' He jerked his head towards the drawn curtains in an upstairs room of the house they were approaching. 'She's an addict, isn't she? All that feyness, as I thought – it was drugs. Dope.'

'Don't,' Catriona ordered. 'She's still Camilla. Don't distort things. You think it's easy to have her kind of money, her kind of inheritance? It's not, you know. It gives you too many options. But she came back here and tried to make reparations. What about the cottage industries she's subsidized and fought for? The crofts she's rescued? The youngsters she's trained in pottery and weaving? Money doesn't necessarily give you the answers, you know. You need to have concern first, and that she has.'

He couldn't speak. Instead, he left her summarily once they got inside the house and raced up the stairs, knocking loudly and peremptorily on Camilla's bedroom door and sending a small chambermaid scuttling downstairs in alarm.

There was a momentary pause then Camilla called, 'Come in.' She was sitting up in bed in a cream swansdown jacket, toying with the remains of her breakfast. He could see how pale she was, and how there were hollows in her cheeks and at the base of her neck. Her frailness still disarmed him. He approached her bedside slowly, the anger draining out of him.

'What's the matter?' She sat up in fright at his expression.

'Why didn't you tell me?' He took the tray away from her, laying it on top of the tallboy. Out in Calneggie Sound he could see a small yacht becalmed, and beyond that, a fishing smack.

'Tell you what?' Her voice was breathless.

'That you're addicted to cocaine.'

'Not addicted, dear boy,' she said, evenly. 'Not totally. Not completely. Just a little more reliant on it than I choose to be.' Her breath came and went quickly. 'Did Catriona tell you, then?'

He nodded. 'I'd rather not have heard it from her.'

'It's my business.'

His rage overpowered him again and he brought his big fist crashing down on the eiderdown. '*Our* business. *Our* business.'

'Baby!' Her arms went out to him and she cradled him to her. 'Darling bunny baby. I wanted to give this up on my own. Keep it away from you. Not worry you when you were driving.'

He lay back on her lace-edged pillows, the scent of her in his head like a madness that wouldn't go away. She was so giving, she made him feel like a king in bed. Yet he had grown tired of being treated like some kind of a toy, like some kind of a child, like some kind of sexual treat. Maybe in the beginning he'd wanted it, the smile that was a little like his mother's smile, the worldliness and the tenderness. But the gap was there in their ages, and the guilt, and the knowledge that he couldn't conquer her, that she could always slip away, into that feyness, that mysterious past, that gap of years, in which he had no part. Plenty had warned him of the dangers.

Playfully, contrivingly, she lifted his forearm and bit it. 'Would you like me to help you to go to Utah? I have been thinking. It's what you want to do and though I'm terrified for you, I should let you do it.' He saw the big amber eyes fill with tears. 'You can have the money. All you need.'

'I don't want it.' He pushed her away from him and sat up, his thick blond hair awry. 'I've finished with you, Camilla. Catriona's made me see it. If we'd been going to marry, we would have done it long ago. I'm not staying on to be some kind of gigolo.' He saw his face in the old-fashioned wardrobe mirror, lop-sided with self-disgust.

'Is that how you see it?' She made no pretence at coquetry now.

'It is.'

'No real love? You never missed me when I was in London? I never missed you when you were driving abroad? Who ran down the platform at Calneggie Station this very holiday and picked me out of the train into his arms?'

'No.' He denied all of it. 'It's a disease we're better off without. I don't know you. You're just a body in the bed. Your secrets you choose to keep. Well, keep them.'

'Get out.' She shook with a sudden storm of anger.

'*You should have told me.*'

'Get out! Do I stink in your Presbyterian nostrils? I thought so. I knew it wouldn't last. Get out! I don't want to see you again.' She had begun to sob, fiddling ineffectually under her pillows for a handkerchief.

He could never remember afterwards what had happened immediately after. He must have left her room, eaten lunch, spoken to Ned about the state of the car and of the weather. What he did remember was the need to get into the Flyer seat, to feel the throbbing power of the engines start under him, to know that this obsession at least was safe. He would make the Flyer beat the world. He had not intended a trial run: he would not do that without Ned to time him. But the car had almost flown along the sands of its own volition. The air pressed against him like an iron blanket, his hands shook with the need to keep the machine on course and there it was, the glorious, the marvellous realization of male power and conquest. Afterwards they said there must have been a bump in the sand. The Flyer took off, literally, into the air, somersaulting before landing and breaking its back. He saw the world turn upside down, splinter, fall apart. Then all was darkness.

CHAPTER TEN

They brought Patie home to Dourhead House. At first he
had been taken to the cottage hospital at Calneggie and then
to the infirmary in Glasgow. He had broken bones and skull
and a weaker or an older man would not have survived.
But once over the shock and bruising and immediate pain,
it was a matter of waiting for bones to knit and unused
muscles to strengthen again. Nellie could not wait to have
him under her care and pushed beef tea and calves' foot
jelly down his throat relentlessly.

He cared more about the car than about himself. At first
he could not bear to talk about it. All that work, all that
money, all that waiting and preparation, gone for nothing.

'Not for nothing,' Mairi tried to assure him. At last the
Flyer had caught the imagination of the newspapers and the
public. There had been various offers of help to rebuild. But
beyond saying that he would go on with it, as the weeks
went by Patie refused to get down to practicalities. It was
an attitude Mairi felt inclined to encourage, except that
behind her brother's singular lack of enthusiasm she sensed
some further worry. Delicate probing elicited nothing. Whatever it was, Patie-like he was playing it close to his chest. But
three months after the accident, all became clear.

Mairi was in alone, having allowed Eleanor to go to see
Shirley Temple at the pictures with a friend on the night
Nicol was occupied at the British Legion. The big chauffeur-
driven Daimler drew up outside the gate and out stepped a
neat, be-furred figure she recognized as Camilla Black-
Jamieson.

Mairi opened the door cautiously at first, then wide as she
saw that Camilla was agitated. The chauffeur drove away.
'I've told him to come back in an hour,' said Camilla. 'Mairi,
I have to talk to you.'

Automatically, Mairi put the kettle on and watched as
Camilla lit a cigarette with fingers that shook. Calm but
intrigued, Mairi at last demanded, 'What is it, then? What do
you want to talk about?'

'How is Patie?'

'Better than we have any right to expect.'

'Oh, thank God.' Camilla exhaled the smoke, her relief transparent. 'I have been longing to come, longing to see him. But he won't answer my letters. I – I've been ill myself. I had to go into a nursing-home –'

'I'm sorry.'

'No, don't be. Not for me. It's Patie who matters. I came to you to ask – do you think he is well enough for a visitor? Will you come with me to Dounhead House? Please, Mairi. You're so steady and wise.'

'I – I don't know.'

'I won't upset him. I promise.' The beautiful amber eyes swam, the lips trembled. Beside this small, finely-formed woman, so exquisitely dressed and made-up, Mairi felt her four-square Scottishness awkward and raw-boned.

When the chauffeur returned on the hour they went together to Dounhead House. Mairi went first into the parlour where Patie still lay on his day-bed, surrounded by newspapers, six-penny Penguin books and racing sheets.

'I don't want to see her.'

'How can I send her away? It's too brutal.'

'You don't understand.'

'No,' Mairi answered shortly. 'For you haven't bothered to explain.' She went to the door, anyhow, and showed Camilla in. Leaving them to it, she joined Nellie in the kitchen.

Camilla walked carefully across the faded Brussels carpet and sat down on a straight-backed chair by the window. 'You shouldn't be here, you know,' she said, in a conversational tone. 'You should be with me at Calneggie where I can look after you. You have put me through hell, not answering my letters.'

He didn't reply at first. He folded his arms and looked at her. Then he said, 'You had a bloody nerve. Coming here.'

'I know.'

'Have you got the bloody nerve to marry me? Never mind what anybody says.'

'Yes. I have.' Her voice wavered but her gaze did not.

'I'm not changing my religion. It'll be register office or nothing. And you do as I say, keep off drink and that other filthy stuff. Understand?'

She rose then and came over, putting her hand into his stiffly upraised one. She smiled for the first time. 'Understood. Tell me you're glad I came.'

He said nothing, merely drew her into his arms and held her there, feeling the terrible tension drain out of her till finally she shuddered and melted against him. Their lips met in a chaste and gentle kiss.

Although she and Nicol agreed to be witnesses at the ceremony Mairi felt disturbed for days after her brother's marriage and departure for Calneggie. The rich, cushioned, slightly eccentric life led by the Black-Jamiesons in their Highland keep, their myth-ridden and romanticized view of the country, went against everything she saw and knew around her in the Lowlands. Patie would be caught up in their Nationalist excesses, their dreams of a free Scotland that had no basis in the practical exigencies of life. But when she tried to explain this to Nicol, he brought her up short by saying, 'It's natural you should miss him. Some other woman is ordering his life for him now, as you did for so long.' He softened the statement with a teasing smile, but there was enough truth in it to silence her. Keeping an eye on Patie had become a habit and she hadn't outgrown the proprietorial attitude that stemmed from their orphaned days together. She still ached with feelings of concern and possibly, she acknowledged, jealousy. But there was nothing she could do about it. Faced with disapprobation at every turn, Patie had made his choice.

To take her mind off things, she agreed to join Nicol in a borrowed lorry going round the housing schemes and remaining pit rows to pick up tinned food to send to Spain. Franco had led a military revolt from Morocco against the Spanish Republican government. Without going all the way with the Communists and the ILP, who wanted to send direct aid to the Republicans, Mairi could go along some of the way with Nicol in his dislike of Franco.

As with every other political issue of the day, people held strong views and Carlie and Donald were wary of any kind of temporary alliance with the Communists. The Labour Party had, after all, expelled Stafford Cripps because he supported the idea of a Popular Front government in Britain (so did Lloyd George), one which would make no bones about fighting Franco.

Democratic socialism had to oppose Communism, Carlie insisted, for Communism was a dictatorship just like Fascism. But for once, Mairi waived her scruples and helped Nicol collect the soup, the baked beans and pork, the fruit and meat, which when all was said and done was for empty, hungry stomachs and therefore an act of simple humanity.

The lorries run by Nicol and others, with their placards and loudspeakers and, in one case, a gramophone, brought a strange frightening whiff of gunsmoke and shrapnel into the streets of Dounhead. Coupled with the rifle range on the town's outskirts, where the Army practised rigorously, and the newsreels and headlines full of the unholy alliance between Hitler and Mussolini and Franco, it was enough to keep arguments about the likelihood of another war spinning across table and counter and back again. Nobody wanted it. Everybody feared it. Maybe the tins people brought out from their sparsely-lined shelves were a kind of propitiation to the great god War. Maybe the meat that someone would do without for supper would keep those grey-flowering explosions on the cinema screen and away from Dounhead.

They were coming to the end of an evening run, the dilapidated lorry rattling like castanets with its load of cheap tins, when a large woman approached them from a battered house in the slum clearance.

'Here, Red Nicol,' she temporized, placing herself before the revving car bonnet, 'I want a word with you. Get up to the McCafferty hoose there and see where some of your tins are ending up. They're no' going to Spain, that's for sure.'

Mairi was inclined to dismiss the tale as malicious. The McCaffertys, the family she had done her best to help after their father's death on the ship back from Canada, now had one or two 'grown-up' members – that was to say over-fourteens – in work. There were curtains at the windows and the children had shoes of sorts. Eddie, married at sixteen and already a father, had volunteered to help on one of the lorries. But he was an open-faced, likeable lad, old and philosophical beyond his years. Mairi would not contemplate the likelihood of him stealing.

Nicol wore the set look of a man who has known the bleak side of human nature. When he had taken Mairi back home, he made the desultory journey back to the slum clearance which the obligatory local wags had christened Up the Amazon, so wild and jungly had it become that it looked like the site of a permanent earthquake.

Eddie at first denied the story of the tins. But Mrs McCafferty, her mouth full of wobbly new false teeth, reddened and then broke down. 'Gi'e the man back the cache,' she sobbed. A big-eyed child went out to the scullery and came back with a pathetic cardboard box holding a dozen small tins of baked beans. 'You'll no' get the polis, will you, Mr Chambers, sir? It'll no' happen again. I'll see to it. It was with his wife having the wean and him wanting the extra nourishment for her.' Mrs McCafferty had become expert over the years in the cringing soft soap.

'What nourishment's in these?' Nicol demanded. 'Get your wife some fresh eggs and milk, Eddie. I'll have to take these back. You shouldn't have done it. But I'm giving you a chance, providing you give me your word it will never happen again. I'll replace the tins and hush the matter up. For your mother's sake. Do you understand? Don't give her more to grieve over. She's had enough.'

'Thank you, sir.' Mrs McCafferty, bursting with relief and gratitude, showed Nicol to the door. She wore a clean print dress and the younger children were in a more sanitary state than when he'd last seen them. Mrs McCafferty, if still somewhat short of the ideal, had been making what for her must have been a gargantuan effort. He put a hand on her shoulder, patting it. 'May God bless you, Mr Chambers, sir,' she responded. 'And Mrs Chambers. And your braw wee lassie. You're a good man, Mr Chambers. That's what I tell them. I'll no' let anybody say a word against Red Nicol. Will I?' she appealed to the surrounding faces, and the little girl who had brought in the box of beans responded obediently, 'No, Maw.'

'Sorry, like.' Eddie shuffled at the back of the crowd, his wife and runny-nosed baby beside him. 'It'll never happen again, Mr Chambers, sir. God's Honour it'll no'.'

Nicol put the incident behind him. It was impossible to be hard on the McCaffertys. That Eddie had grown up with even a modicum of social responsibility was a miracle. That the family were poking their heads up like dusty, determined gladioli in that physical and spiritual wasteland was another. Who had written 'how beautiful are the children of the poor'? Some long-forgotten Victorian philanthropist, probably. But it was true. The McCaffertys in their indomitable, dirty togetherness struck chords of unbearable poignancy. If he had not married someone like Mairi; if he had gone for some free and ignorant lassie in his early teens, he could see how easily his life could have turned out like that. When they had all been small, his own mother had let things go during periods of illness or apathy: he remembered dirt, smells, crying and hunger. They were no strangers.

Nicol put the incident behind him, but the affair was not

to finish there. At a council meeting the next week when he was making a speech about teachers who were less than tactful about schoolchildren who had to wear 'parish' boots and clothing, he was astonished to be the recipient of a red-faced attack by his Unionist opposite number, Major Jack Halliday.

'What kind of a whited sepulchre is this man,' Halliday demanded, 'who stands there taking up the council's time with his tales of woe of children being shamed and embarrassed in front of their peers? The same kind of man, I am saying, who will go round the same Rows these children came from, taking the food out of their mouths for the doubtful privilege of sending it to the Communist Spanish, and then refusing to be accountable for that food when it comes to the final reckoning.'

Nicol was on his feet in a flash, demanding what Halliday meant by his innuendoes. The Major began back-tracking, saying he was not making any actual personal accusations, but that it was a fact that food had gone missing from lorries going round the town.

The two men were enemies of old, for all their differences of status and opinions not unalike in temperament. Halliday was a landowner, who rode to hounds, fished and hunted with the best, a brave ex-soldier who had been awarded the MC. He was a man guilty of a thousand hasty kindnesses who still never forgot a grudge. Nicol had roasted him many times in the council chamber and he was not prepared to let the occasion pass now.

'Will the honourable Major retract?' Nicol demanded, dangerously.

'What is there to retract? I want to get to the bottom of a lamentable situation.' Halliday took his eyes off his opponent to appeal to the Chair and the next moment Nicol had sprung across the room and had him by the throat. Chairs overturned and water-glasses spilled as the remaining councillors sprang to their feet to try and separate the protagonists, but the place was in uproar and Halliday and Nicol so tightly locked in a tossing struggle it was impossible to lay hands on them.

'Order! Order!' cried the Chairman, banging his gavel till it looked as though he would bring it crashing down through the lectern in front of him. At last two senior Labour men laid hold of Nicol. 'Take him out of here. I await his apology to the Chair.' Straightening his wool knitted tie, Halliday gave a dangerous smirk as Nicol was dragged past him.

'I'll get you for this!' Nicol gritted it through clenched teeth. Before the meeting had been wound up, someone had brought him a double whisky in to the ante-room in a mistaken effort to calm him. He broke away from the well-meaning men urging caution on him and approached Jack Halliday as he was about to enter his chauffeur-driven car. Knowing what was coming, Halliday stepped nimbly back, but not nimbly enough to avoid Nicol's pile-driver of a right hook on his jaw. He fell into the gutter, striking his head again, but got up only for another punch direct to his stomach. Then, seeing blood pouring from his forehead, Nicol at last stepped back. Two Glasgow bobbies were bearing down on the scene as fast as their boots would carry them. 'Let him go,' said Halliday contemptuously. His shaky hand held a spotless handkerchief to his head. 'I'm sorry, it's no' for you to say, sir,' said one of the policemen. 'This man has whisky on his breath. I am taking him in for his own good.'

Halliday looked irresolutely at Nicol, then without another word turned and stumbled into his car. By evening it was all over the *Times*, *News* and *Citizen*. 'COUNCILLOR ARRESTED FOLLOWING FRACAS.' 'ALLEGATION OF STOLEN GOODS.' 'WAR HERO ATTACKED IN CHAMBERS.'

It was Mairi who had to scrape the money together for Nicol's bail. The union helped and so did the councillors who had tried to keep Nicol out of trouble. One of them said to Mairi seriously, 'Try to make him calm down, Mrs Chambers. He has to learn to keep his fists to himself, or he'll leave himself friendless.'

'Not among the folk he represents. He'll never be friendless there.' She would not allow a word of criticism of him in public, but when he came back home, released on bail and pale and subdued, she said to him, 'Why attack Jack Halliday? He's straight and honest, not like some. And he must have had word about the McCafferty business – '

'He implicated me. That was below the belt.' He took the cup of tea she pushed across the table, his hand shaking. 'I'll get thirty days for it. How are you going to manage?'

'Won't you get the option of a fine?'

'It doesn't matter. How could I raise fifty quid?'

'I'll get it somehow. I'll write to Patie.'

'You'll not.'

'Why not?'

'I'll take my punishment like a man. *My* punishment. Why should you be involved?'

'You know why.'

He took a great, juddering breath. 'I wouldn't blame you if you left me.'

'Well, I won't.'

She was desperately worried when after the court appearance he still refused to countenance trying to raise the fine. As he had expected, he was given the option of paying fifty pounds or thirty days' imprisonment and the beaky Glasgow baillie cut short his speech about the impossibility of someone like him raising that kind of money.

When she went to see him in his cell she found him defiant and euphoric. 'I'll show the bastards,' he kept saying.

'What bastards?' she demanded wearily. She could not get him to sit down and face her. 'Nicol,' she said distractedly. 'Do this for Eleanor and for me. Let me try and get money for the fine.'

He was in no mood to listen to reason. 'I'll not take the money if you get it. Tell Eleanor not to be ashamed of her daddy. All he ever did was try to protect those who can't protect themselves.'

She felt bone weary as she made her way back to the house in the Auchengingar scheme which had come to mean so much to her. The carefully furnished sitting-room, its Rexine suite brightened with hand-worked cushions, its cheap furniture and lino polished with pride and pleasure, everything about it neat and welcoming and clean, no longer seemed to her a desirable place to be. She wanted to run away and hide, to forget the fact that her husband languished in jail like some common criminal caught up in a public brawl. But Nicol's growing violence of spirit was something she couldn't deny. More and more his desperation took on physical manifestation. Like the time he had struck her before she left him. Like the brouhaha, the violence he seemed to create now every time he was involved in argument in the council chamber. He was becoming so extreme no one would take him seriously. At base she felt she knew that and it was why he lashed out. Going to Russia hadn't helped. Perhaps in some juvenile, immature fashion he had expected to see Utopia there, not people caught up in doubts and shambles and experiment.

And then there were the half-written stories and poems, stuck into drawers because he hadn't the words to encompass what he wanted to say. Maybe if just once he had finished something . . .

The winter digging founds had not done his physical health any good and he had a rasping cough that shook him when he was tired, but he wouldn't go to the doctor. But it wasn't just his health that worried her. It was the intransigence of his attitudes. Given the threatening, ranting pose he had taken up lately in the council, especially if he had been drinking before the meeting, the incident that had landed him in jail had been almost inevitable.

She had to prepare Eleanor for the jeers of 'jailbird' she knew would come from the rougher children. But Eleanor's indignation crowded out any humiliation. She was totally on her father's side, even down to his obtuse reasoning over the fine. When Mairi finally broke down and cried one evening it was Eleanor who stood beside her, hard-eyed, stroking her hair. 'Put on your lipstick, Mammy. For Daddy's sake. He says we have to stick by him. We have to show we're not ashamed.' Shaken by her stoicism and shamed by her loyalty, Mairi determined it would be the last time she wept. But ceaselessly in her mind she went over ways of getting Nicol released. She thought of going to Robin Chisholm and asking him to help, but time and again, though desperate, drew back from the brink of action.

Perhaps she was not altogether surprised when she saw him on the doorstep. He had chosen a time of day when Eleanor was at school. He came straight to the point. 'We have to get him out of that jail. I can arrange it so that he won't know who pays the fine. It isn't my doing, by the way. The offer has come from a quarter that will surprise you.'

'Come in,' she said belatedly, suddenly weak-kneed with relief. Occasionally she saw him at the Academy, when attending some event like a prize-giving or a concert. He was head of the classics department and deputy rector, which no doubt explained why he was able to get away in the middle of the school day.

He sat down without waiting to be asked and said, 'Halliday came to me and asked me to act as intermediary. He says that even if Nicol couldn't be seen to get away with the assault, he still hoped he wouldn't go to jail. Both ex-soldiers, you see. There's a sort of bond. Even if Nicol has the wrong end of the stick, as Halliday sees it, in the political sense, he says he still did his bit for the country and got small thanks for it.'

'He said that?' Mairi ran her tongue around dry lips. 'It was decent of him.'

'He says it's all going to happen again. War with Germany. And that neither Red Nicol nor he need have bothered last time. Nor all those other poor blighters lying under the sod.' She found herself saying fearfully, 'I'm sure it won't come to war this time.'

'The Jews in Germany would not agree with you.'

'Nicol would never take his charity.'

'But he need never know. I want you to let me do this. For *you*.' Robin looked at her as though to reassure himself she was all right and saw the trembling hands being pushed down into her lap. He crossed to the settee and put his arm around her, kissing her temple. Soberly he said, 'It will all work out, Mairi. Your friends are behind you.'

Suddenly she burst into tears and put her head on his shoulder. He held her till the weeping had subsided, providing her with his handkerchief, and then he kissed her again on both cheeks. 'You little know the funny pleasure it gives me to be here with you,' he said ruefully. 'All these years and my feelings haven't changed. It seems we never learn.'

'Oh, Robin!' She half-smiled, reproaching him. 'You're making it up. You and Catriona are happy enough, are you not?'

'Happy enough? My wife runs after other men. What's more, I let her. Would you call that "happy enough"?'

She put his hands away from her. 'I don't think we're behaving right,' she said remorsefully. 'And you have to know, Robin, I have no intention of being disloyal to Nicol.'

'I can't see any harm in us meeting occasionally. Would you not let me take you for a run in the car? Down into Ayrshire, for a quiet meal?'

'No.'

'Don't you have any feelings for me, then?'

'You know I have.'

'What are they?'

'Mixed.'

'But you'll not challenge convention, will you? Break the code? Nicol Chambers has made you tired before your time. I can see what he's doing to your spirit. You're humble, self-effacing, in case they say, "Who does she think she is?" If you were just yourself, they would think you were giving yourself airs. I see how even now you keep a bit of yourself apart from it all, the politicking and do-gooding and being the councillor's wife. "She is not here, she is away." Mairi, wake up before it's too late and see what he's doing to you.'

'I love him.'

'Love him? Christ,' he said vehemently, 'you don't know what the word means. You use it as a destructive force. You "love" him so you push down everything in you that aspires to better things. You cut yourself off from people like me, poets, musicians, writers, actors, painters, because you want to do yourself over in his image. You know what happens, don't you? "Too long a sacrifice makes a stone of the heart", as Yeats said. You'll find out it's true. You'll hate him, as sometimes I hate you.'

'I can't do it, Robin.'

'Then admit it's because you're a moral coward, not because you love him.'

'I shall do no such thing.'

'Listen to yourself. You're so cut off from your feelings you're talking jargon. Where's the girl who sat in my car and quoted Byron? I can still hear you. I can see you turn your head towards me, laughing and bonnie.'

'No,' she said sharply. 'While we're talking like this, he is in that smelly, awful cell. Get him out for me, Robin. That's all I ask of you. And tell Jack Halliday I will never forget his kindness, to my dying day.'

'What thanks do I get?'

She touched his wavy hair that had begun to grey at the temples. 'I don't know how to thank you.'

'I think we should see more of each other. Come up and see Catriona. Bring Eleanor. Bring Nicol, too.'

'Nicol among Catriona's rich friends? Can you see it?'

'It's you I'm thinking of. You mustn't let what's happened send you into your shell.'

He must have lost no time. Whatever strings needed to be pulled were pulled and Nicol was released next day. He returned home knowing only that his fine had been paid by 'a well-wisher', on whose identity he speculated endlessly. He would not have accepted the offer, he said, but the cell had been unbearably claustrophobic and had made him ill. Indeed, he didn't look well.

'Nicol,' said Mairi at their first meal together, wanting to talk of anything but his incarceration, 'do you think maybe the country's on the road to war again?'

'Why do you ask?'

She did not answer, but saw clearly in her mind's eye the stringy military figure of Major Halliday with his medal ribbons up. Nicol's kicked about in a deep drawer in the dresser, like so many others up and down the land.

It was unusual for Tina Mackenzie to have people to tea on Sunday. Mostly she went to church (in her fur coat) in the morning and was glad to take it easy the rest of the day, for her cleaning jobs took an increasing toll on her energies.

But today she had forsworn church, given the room she called the lounge a merciless polish and by two o'clock had the table already set with a lace cloth, doylies, paper serviettes, and flowered china painstakingly gathered an item at a time from Woolworth's. The three-tiered cake-stand held scones, pancakes, Paris buns and on the lowest plate delicate chocolate cups filled with sponge and apricot and topped with cream. Philip's favourites. And since Philip was going away, anything that would please him was in order.

Rough tears had gathered with the saliva at the back of Tina's throat, but she ignored them, bustling about in desperation to make sure everything was as it should be, a cause for pride. There was no going back now in any case. She had paid into a club to buy the big fibre suitcase with its expanding locks and at the Co-op had selected with Philip three pairs of underpants and three vests, a pair of fine grey flannel trousers, two white shirts and a sports jacket. His school raincoat would have to do. Money would only stretch so far. He had been impatient with her insistence that he should have things 'nice'. She suspected that when out of her sight he wouldn't polish his shoes every day. God only knew what he would do when out of her sight.

She had made Joe Grant the butcher cut the gammon razor-thin and now on each larger plate she arranged two slices per person, with two slices of tomato and a curl of lettuce. She stood back for a second, lulled out of her feverish pain by the attractive sight of the laden table. Surely he wouldn't forget all this in a hurry? She wanted his memories of home to be good ones, of things like a fire well-lit and drawing brightly, a table graciously laid. And herself tidy and neat, hair freshly washed with soft green soap, brightened with camomile, beads at the neck of her best blue dress.

'Still a pretty woman,' Alisdair her estranged husband had said last time they had met for tea in Glasgow. He had been stolid, puffy, unwell but denying it had any more significance than the fact he was now over sixty. And she into her fifties, she had pointed out. It was then he had said it. 'Still a pretty woman.' The point of the dart had pierced through layers of guilt and shame till it struck the bedrock of her rejection of him all those years ago. 'Still a pretty woman,' he had insisted heavily. 'Don't be silly,' she had answered brusquely, refusing him even the pleasure of a compliment. But she hadn't time to think about him now. Tomorrow, after she had seen Philip off, she would go and see him. She would have to find some corner where she could unburden her desperation. She had thought all along of Alisdair's place, with its echoing quiet, sepia photographs, castor oil plants and Bibles. It would be appropriate.

'You've gone to too much trouble.' Philip eyed the table with a mixture of approbation and exasperation. 'You'll wear yourself out.' He extended a hand and deftly snipped a piece of gammon from the plate he knew would be his. Absently, Tina covered the ragged end with a piece of lettuce. 'Let me look at you,' she demanded. He was wearing his new clothes, his dark hair well slicked down with brilliantine. For a year, since leaving school, he had been working in a Glasgow shipping office. It had proved unbearably dull and poorly-paid. Now by a persistent letter-writing he had found himself a job with a London magazine. Lowly paid, also, but with prospects. Nervously he shifted from one foot to another, full of contained energy. 'This time tomorrow I'll be on my way. About Derby, I should think. Or Crewe. London, here I come!'

'Maybe the new King and Queen'll be there to meet you,' she said drily.

'I can thank them for my Coronation mug.'

'Be sure to do that. Bring in the two kitchen chairs, will you, Philip? And the one from my bedroom.'

Donald and Carlie were the first to arrive. Since losing his seat in Parliament, Donald's health had deteriorated. It was as though all these years he had needed the constant injections of stress and argument to keep him going but was now paying the price. But Carlie had spruced him up and as they came in the gate arm-in-arm they looked cheerful, ready to enjoy their afternoon out. Shortly afterwards they were followed by the Chambers family, Mairi looking Sunday-smart in a light coat, Nicol wearing the dingy raincoat and wide-brimmed Fedora that made him a kenspeckle, instantly recognizable sight in the Dounhead streets, and the long-limbed Eleanor looking self-conscious in the roomy new blazer bought at the start of her third year at Bellnoch Academy. All over Dounhead gates clicked and doors opened as similar Sunday visits took place in all their formality. Quiet, pressed-down Sabbatarianism still held sway, even if the churches were emptying.

Donald made the point as they were ushered to their seats at the table. 'You'll find London quite different on a Sunday, Philip,' he said. 'Cafés open, speeches in Hyde Park. Here in Dounhead you'd think the world had closed down, wouldn't you? Even the dogs lie quietly at their gates, frightened to bark.' Suddenly catching sight of the apprehension on Tina's face, he said reassuringly, 'He will be all right, Tina, never fear. London's a great place for a young man on the make.'

'You'll be able to eat cheaply, too,' Carlie interjected. 'There's Lyons and the ABC and Express Dairy and you'll get a meal at any of them for one and threepence.'

They tucked into the boiled ham while Tina went round the table, delicately pouring tea into cups. 'What made you want to be a journalist?' Nicol demanded heavily.

'I'm not one yet!'

'Oh, never fear. You'll soon be telling us lesser mortals how the aeroplane was born. Or how to go up the Ganges in an orange box. That's the sort of stuff your paper does, isn't it?'

'You're against popular education, then?'

Nicol smiled. 'Not me! Just hang on to a bit of integrity, though. Fleet Street's a jungle, from what I hear of it.'

They were kind to him. They reminisced over his childhood, holding up this or that sign of his precocity as a writer, delicately indicating that in their communal judgment the way was open to him to the editor's chair of *The Times* itself. It was as though by their affection they could put an extra skin around him, a magical one that would ward off any evils.

And when the tea was over and the dishes washed and put away they brought out their gifts. Carlie and Donald had bought him an etymological dictionary, Mairi and Nicol a leather case with hairbrushes.

'You're not saying much.' When the discussion was no longer centred on him and his departure, but had taken a general turn, Philip sat down beside Eleanor and gave her shoulder-length hair a tug. She turned a Sunday-sullen face towards him. 'What is there to say?'

'Eleanor!' Her mother reproached her.

'I hate London!'

'But it's not you who's going there,' he humoured her.

'As if I would. If everybody goes there for jobs what happens here?'

They sat back and smiled at her indulgently. She had after all grown up with polemic. 'She's a bit of a Scottish National-ist, like her Uncle Patie,' said Mairi half-apologetically.

'Not everybody has to go to London for jobs,' said Carlie. 'Ask your Uncle Donald here. The work he and others did in Parliament is bearing fruit. What about the Hillington industrial estate and the orders coming to the Clyde?'

'Armaments,' said Nicol, briefly.

'What would your prescription be?' demanded Carlie angrily.

'Is it right? That you're a wee Scot Nat, with a Glen-garry bonnet on your head and a fly on your nose?' Philip tried to joke with Eleanor but she would have none of it. 'Did nobody tell you writers were different? They have to drink from different cups.' She merely glared at him and would make no further contribution to the afternoon's chat. When Tina had made a farewelling cup of tea and coats had been gathered and last good wishes pressed upon him by the others, Philip turned in vain towards Eleanor for an expres-sion of goodwill.

She slipped a hard, cold, small hand into his at her mother's urging. 'What about a kiss?' he teased her. For answer, she suddenly tightened her grip, bending his arm upwards and twisting it almost as an invitation to struggle.

'You wee besom!' He winced with not altogether-pretended pain. But she was making off up the garden path behind her parents, smiling at last.

'Goodbye, Philip darling!' she called, in mock-English tones of ridiculing gentility. Once outside the gate she turned and screwed up her face at him. Finally she stuck out her tongue.

'They'll have trouble with that one,' said Tina grimly.

She sat opposite Philip as they ate their lunch in Lewis's, the department store in Glasgow's Argyle Street, the next day. An early lunch, before he caught his train. A treat, to preclude sighs and tears and last-minute clinging.

'Eleanor? I don't pay any attention to her.'

'Mairi did say she has been upset since Nicol and that jail business. He made a right fool of himself. Eleanor puts on a hard front, but she'll get it all cast up to her. You know what children are like.'

'There's something in what she says. Something rotten in the state of Scotland.'

'Somebody once said all it needs is an umbrella.' It had been raining as they came into Glasgow. 'I'm being flippant.' She attacked her rhubarb tart purposefully to show the moment had passed.

'I remember,' he said, looking round the plum-faced matrons in crêpe-de-chine and pearls, the men in blue suits attacking their three-course meals in respectful silence – 'I remember coming here with Mairi and Eleanor, the time we were going north to Calneggie. I'd never been in a restaurant – not a proper one – before, and when Eleanor and I saw there was an orchestra we thought we had landed up in a Hollywood film. Mairi warned us we were to tell the waitress we had had our dinner – which was a lie – and just wanted tea and a cake. She said if Eleanor took two cakes she'd kill her – and the wee besom nearly did. Her hand hovered over the cake-stand like a greedy wee buzzard. Finally Mairi took her out to the ladies and she came back talking about the liquid soap. She couldn't get over it.' He smiled at Tina. 'I made up my mind at Calneggie, you know. That I would get a share of the honey. And so will you. When I've made it.'

She kept thinking of it afterwards, when he'd gone, and the sooty smell from the train was still in her nostrils. *A share of the honey.* He had been bony and awkward in her embrace, unable to keep the eager excitement from his eyes, his voice. She had suddenly remembered Wallace going off from the same place and loathed the station for all the partings it had witnessed. She could not wait to get out of it, bumping into aggrieved travellers in her sightless exit. She hadn't been able to afford any of the extras for him, the school trips to the continent for twenty pounds, the theatre visits, the bicycles and tennis racquets. Now she mourned it. He had seen himself through school to the attainment of his 'Highers' on a shoestring, never complaining, and in the year of the tholed office job had patiently taught himself shorthand and sat among girls at night school to learn typing. Why was it she saw the last few years with him with the clarity of a documentary film? Even the books he borrowed or brought home from the library. The latter were treated with scant respect in some of the homes they entered. He had taken out a D. H. Lawrence with a slice of bacon in it for a book-mark. *Cooked* bacon. You needed a strong stomach as well as a literary cast of mind. *Decline and Fall*, *Essays of Elia*, *The Master Builder*. In among the rubbish. He said you had to be catholic in your tastes. *A share of the honey*. She had known she would have to let him go. *A promising lad*. For a long time, she'd known it. *Pays no attention to lessons which don't interest him*. The streets looked different. Hope Street! What a misnomer, surely. *But writes an uncanny, polished prose*. This from the Rector. But he was her son, whose food she had put on the table for so long, whose clothes she had washed, whose mud she had shaken from the mat. *Should go far*. Too far. London was too far.

When she got to Alisdair's house she was beyond tears and even managed a pale, composed smile for the old house-keeper, Mrs Penicuik.

'He's in his bed,' said the latter, without preamble. 'He said would you go in, madam.'

'What's the matter?'

'He'll be telling you himself.' Mrs Penicuik opened the bedroom door and nodded at Tina drily.

She sat on the old-fashioned chair by his bedside and took one of his big, dry hands. It had been an unwritten law of their meetings that they never touched. Now it seemed easy, even natural.

'Alisdair, what have you been doing to yourself?'

He looked more rested, healthier than the last time she had seen him. But there was something.

'I've been prescribing myself a rest, that's all. I'm feeling the better for it already.'

'That's all it is? Over-tired?'

'Certainly. I've been working on my church history. Time I had it finished. But I'll lay it to one side for a while.'

'Mind you do.'

'You've seen that boy of yours off? I must ask you not to fret for him. He'll be a credit to you. I have come to the conclusion as an erstwhile student of modern psychology that it is not good for a man to be too mother-dominated. As I was.'

She felt strangely, strangely comforted. Mrs Penicuik kicked the door open with a smart jerk of her ancient house-shoe and pushed in a trolley laid for tea. They ate in a companionable silence and the hot, sweet tea brought her out of the shock of parting, back to the practicalities. 'I've told him to send me home his washing week by week.' 'A good idea.' 'And of course, he'll write.' 'I should certainly hope so.' 'He'll be home for Ne'erday.' 'Of course he will.'

'Isn't it funny, Alisdair,' she said at last, 'how we've got on with each other these last few years? To an outsider, it must seem daft. Two folk that can't live with each other, still managing to be friends.'

'I've found life a lot more various than you might expect.'

'I can't make up to you. For what I've never been.'

'Now don't distress yourself.' She looked up sharply at the strength of his plea. At something in his eyes that filled her momentarily with a wild, nameless distress. 'We'll see this out between us. In kindness. As friends. Would there be a spot more tea left, do you think?'

When she sat in the tram afterwards, it came to her that she would not be making the journey to see him much longer. Of course he had been confident of pulling the wool over her eyes. In that case, he should have removed the medicines from the side-table. He had not been able to do anything about the look under his eyes. It had been there a long time. And there must have been a question in hers, for the old dame, with whom she had never been able to strike a chord of amity, had briefly nodded at her as she went out. Confirming.

She would keep going to see him. He would tell her in his own time. The hurts had become so familiar they were no longer hurts. Would Philip be in London now, rattling through those miles of suburbs to the dusty, clanging heart of the capital? She got off the tram, seeing fading posters of the Coronation peeling from a hoarding. The little princesses, Elizabeth and Margaret Rose. One day they might pass up the Strand in the Royal car and see a lad in a jacket from the Dounhead Co-op. Eye might light to eye, but each remain a mystery to the other. Was it not the same for everybody?

Walking up Fleet Street in the dusk, Philip looked up at the names of the newspapers. How imposing they looked. How jealous of their secrets, their command over the printed word. The newsstands bore more newspapers and periodicals than he had ever known existed, some even in French and other languages.

181

He was in the land of Bloomsbury and Bath buns, Orwell and *The Strand Magazine*. He was a stone's throw from Conan Doyle's Baker Street and Dickens's wharves and law courts; tomorrow he could stroll past the Café Royal. Down by the Embankment there were tramps on the benches and in the Ritz and the Savoy somebody must be playing Coward on a piano. The light above St Paul's was blue and golden and he had already written his impressions of a provincial lad's arrival in his head. He felt quite absurdly happy. He bought his first packet of Abdullah cigarettes and as he drank a cup of tea brought him by a Nippy in Lyons he wrote on a postcard of the House of Commons: 'Dear Mater, I am here at last and all is well.'

Part Three

CHAPTER ELEVEN

'Heavens, I think we're just going to get there in time. Whether we'll ever get out again is anybody's guess. When it snows at Calneggie, it really snows.'

The speaker was Catriona Chisholm, driving the big Daimler along the lonely moorland road bordering the Sound, her husband reluctantly having swopped seats with her half an hour ago. With petrol severely rationed, driving was an occasional treat Catriona insisted on sharing. But she was a somewhat erratic chauffeuse, as the expressions of at least two of her passengers in the back seat showed. Mairi and Nicol sat with Eleanor between them, clinging to each other's knees as Catriona flashily turned a snow-covered bend, coming perilously close to the water's edge and almost landing them all in the slate-grey sullen deep.

'I *love* the snow.' Eleanor wasn't intimidated by Catriona's recklessness. All the way up from Dounhead she had been marvelling a little at the luck of the Academy closing down early for want of coal to heat the classrooms. She had never been away from home for Christmas before and even if everyone kept reminding each other, 'There *is* a war on,' she was determined to make the most of this unexpected adventure. What it was that had so upset Aunt Camilla that the holiday invitation bore more the marks of a summons she wasn't sure. Something to do with Uncle Patie. And then because Robin Chisholm was out of a teaching job, too, there had been this great scrounge round for petrol, organized mainly by her mother and Catriona, and *voilà*! Snow on the moors and the mountains and the promise of greater thrills to come.

Eleanor let her mind wander pleasantly over the possibility of meeting a vaguely Tyrone Power-ish figure in the romantic Highland setting. She was only half-listening to what the others were talking about.

'I think Patie feels uncomfortable about being in a reserved occupation,' Mairi speculated. 'I know Calneggie's producing food but farming isn't really his work. The farm could go on without him.'

'And you think he wants to fly?'

'Why else would Camilla send me the advertisement from the *Scotsman*? She wrote: "This is what he pores over, day after day." ' Mairi took the cutting from her handbag for the umpteenth time and read it aloud:

'Join the Champions of the Air. From their Fortress, flying in the sub-stratosphere, Britain's Knights of the Air rain down destruction a thousand times more deadly than the boulders and boiling oil that fell on mediæval aggressors. All men who fly with the RAF must be young, must be fit, must be full of fight; for RAF Air Crews are the spearhead of Britain's attack. The time to book YOUR seat for Berlin is NOW. (Accepted as pilot if you are 17¼ but not yet 31. Observers up to 33, or in special cases up to 41.)' When she had finished quoting, Mairi said, 'It's the last bit Camilla has underlined. About the observers.'

'She doesn't want to let him go,' said Catriona. 'I don't blame her.'

Robin made an expostulatory sound. 'What she feels is irrelevant.'

'No, it's not.' Catriona shot him a hostile glance. 'She's nursed him back to health after that awful crash. Why should she send him up in a plane to get shot at?'

Mairi said, her face strained, 'She's a Douglas Young supporter. She'd like to see Patie come out like Young and refuse to have anything to do with the war.'

'I regard Young as a loonie. Doesn't everybody?' Robin's voice was clipped. 'Anyone that tries to say we're not all in this together – '

'What he says is, Scotland should negotiate a separate peace,' Nicol interjected. 'I suppose *he* would have talked to Hess. Hess must have thought *somebody* would, or he would never have landed. But you can't write Young off entirely. He's a poet and scholar like yourself, Robin – '

'Well, I'm no conscientious objector,' said Robin angrily. 'If they'd release me from the Academy, I'd go into war work. I'd join the Army, if I could.'

'You did your bit last time,' said Catriona shortly. 'With your eyesight, you'd be picking off your own men.'

Perching forward on his seat, Nicol observed, 'The Scot Nats would be as well to give up the ghost while the war lasts. Young is just bringing the movement into disrepute with his legal palaver.'

'People like Camilla and her brother don't see why we shouldn't exploit the war.' This from Mairi.

'Exploit it? Who says we'll survive it? Anyway,' Nicol insisted, 'Churchill has virtually given Scotland Home Rule for the duration. We've got our own Whitehall now at St Andrew's House and what's the Scottish Council about, if it's not about legislating in Scotland. Tom Johnston is in a position to get anything concerning Scotland passed through Parliament *tout de suite*.'

'It's funny to hear you talk well of Churchill,' said Robin slyly. 'I suppose it's because you're hoping for a Second Front to help your beleaguered friends in Russia.'

'You read what the TUC thinks? That the Allies hope Russia and Germany will knock hell out of each other?'

'Can you blame them?'

'We've got to have a Second Front. We could finish Germany off in no time if we had.'

Eleanor let the voices flow in and out of her consciousness. Nobody ever talked about anything but the war, how many clothing coupons for a dress or a suit, the carrot-stuffed Woolton Pie you got to eat in the British Restaurants. At least no one thought now that Hitler would invade Britain at any minute, as they had done after France fell. That had been what truly frightened her most, from the day she had been hanging her coat up in the school cloakroom and a girl had rushed in crying hysterically, 'German planes are bombing Poland. It's war! It's war!'

But you never knew. The poor Scots evacuees on the sunken *Athenia* doubtless thought they'd make Canada. The pilots who'd died in the Battle of Britain and the people in the blitzes on London and Clydebank – no doubt individually they'd thought they would come through unscathed. No one ever thought death would come to them. It was funny. If it happened to her before she had the chance to fall in love, her ghost or her spirit or whatever was left would be very angry indeed. She supposed that made her a trivial kind of person. But it was true.

Watching the intensity on her father's face and Robin's as they argued, she remembered how, like death, the possibility of the war had been something no one would properly face up to. Right up to the last everyone had hoped against hope it wouldn't happen. The *Daily Express* had kept on repeating 'There will be no war this year' and with the big Empire Exhibition she had so loved just wound up at Bellahouston, Glasgow, people had convinced themselves that if only war could be kept at bay, trade might look up and things improve for everybody. She'd had the evidence of her eyes that in Dounhead things were just the same. Well, they'd had to pull down Tait's Tower, intended to be a permanent memorial to her lovely Exhibition, because it gave navigational help to the enemy. Just the way they'd had to pull down all the mad fabrications about Hitler being satisfied after annexing Czechoslovakia.

Her father was talking now about Scotland being in a strong bargaining position because the Clyde was so important in wartime, taking care, he reckoned, of eighty per cent of the merchant shipping. He'd gone a bit Scot Nat since they'd started seeing more of Robin Chisholm and Aunt Catriona, after he'd been released from prison. He had not been well since then – she had become used to the wheezy creaking of his lungs, the herbal smell of Potter's Asthma Cure – and the present holiday was partly because he had recently been ill with pneumonia. The Chisholms had been very kind, supporting her mother, helping her unobtrusively, but there were times when Eleanor felt Robin thought too much of her mother. Although he never said anything, she knew her father didn't like it, but put up with it because her mother needed friends. Mairi got sad and depressed, worried about her father, worried about Uncle Patie, worried about the war. It came to Eleanor that her mother should have nice things like Catriona, not always have to scrape along, make do and mend. She'd had too much of being poor, that was the truth of it. It showed in the paperiness of her skin and the way she laughed embarrassedly but took the small packets of unrationed fresh butter or Black Market tea that Catriona brought and in the kind of desperate animation she showed on a trip like this, as though treats had become necessary to counter-balance the nights she'd sat up with Nicol. Once when he'd been very bad she'd surprised them holding hands and looking into each other's faces. She had felt she shouldn't be there. Looking out at the delicate, dancing snow, aware that the talk around her had faded into anxious silence as visibility lessened and darkness fell, she thought forcefully: *I want someone for myself.* Someone to be close to, to look at me as though I mattered more than anything.

At the Academy there were nice boys she partnered at the school dances, but you didn't get to know each other outside school. They maybe respected you too much, while the Dounhead boys who'd left school at fourteen to go into pit or foundry didn't really respect you enough, or teased you for being a swot and 'going on'.

Soon she would have her Highers and then she would have the office job she craved. Till she was called up. It didn't please her parents or teachers that she wouldn't consider going on to teachers' college or university, but then they weren't really being practical about where the money was to come from. She wanted to help out at home, to have a little to herself to buy shampoo and clothes and go to the pictures. The discipline and orderliness of an office somehow appealed to her. Maybe then she would meet . . . Her best schoolfriend Janet and she had agreed they wanted someone who looked a little bit like Ronald Reagan while speaking like Charles Boyer, although they had also cut out pictures of the air ace 'Screwball' Beurling to pin up beside their favourite film stars.

To the passengers' patent relief, Catriona at last brought the car safely within sight of Big Lodge, which Camilla and Patie had taken over on their marriage. Calneggie itself had been requisitioned as billets for the Army, with Colin Black-Jamieson as laird accorded a couple of rooms only for his own use. Maybe there would be some handsome young soldier . . . Eleanor, like her friend Janet, agreed that uniforms did something for a man. They had a photograph at home of Philip Mackenzie, already an officer, sharp-eyed and smiling under his cap. He had survived Dunkirk. It would be pleasant to report back to her friend some little romantic skirmish, some meeting of eyes, some promise of passion . . .

'I said, we're here, Eleanor.' Her mother's finger prodded her knee. Stiffly, groaning with cold, they spilled out on to the snow, moving arms and legs to restore feeling, laughing with relief to have the last, hazardous part of the journey behind them. The cold Highland air nearly took Eleanor's breath away. She was aware of forest, sea and night and the big amorphous bulk of Calneggie itself, dark keep of military souls.

'Chocolate!' gloated Catriona after the evening meal. 'I thought it was only for the war workers.' She bit sinfully into a section of Fry's Cream. 'Where did you get it?'

'Oh, the soldiers up at the Big Place give me it,' said Camilla. 'I arrange dances, parties, entertainments for them. They're very appreciative.'

'Are there any – very handsome ones?' Eleanor could not

forbear to ask the question

The others laughed at her. Even Camilla, who had been a little restrained all evening, smiled reluctantly and said, 'I should think at least a hundred. I'll take you to the dance at the week-end. I'm sure you won't want for partners.'

Eleanor sat back pinkly. Patie looked at her with evident good nature and said, 'So even my niece is falling for the uniform. Do you think I would suit a uniform, Eleanor? Air Force blue, perhaps?'

'Not tonight, Patie,' said Camilla quickly. 'They're all tired.'

'All I'm doing is tossing the idea about a bit.'

Camilla rose so precipitately that the khaki sock she was knitting fell to the floor. A quick anxious glance passed between her and Nellie, now resident housekeeper at Big Lodge and busy clearing the dinner plates on to a tray.

'I think I might be excused,' said Camilla quietly. 'I'm sorry. I think I might have a cold coming on.'

'As you like, dear.' Patie rose and kissed his wife. Against her fragile, china-doll figure he looked big, protective – and young. In the hush that followed her departure everyone was very aware of him crossing back to his chair, settling uncomfortably, lighting his pipe with deliberate movements and finally puffing it with a not very convincing calm.

It was Mairi who finally brought herself to break the silence.

'What is all this, then?' she demanded. 'Why can't you be content, Patie, to stay on the ground? They need you here at Calneggie and the farm is war work, if it's your conscience that troubles you.'

'They need pilots more. And observers.'

'They wouldn't let you fly planes, would they?'

'I could. I have. Privately. You're not telling me that if Paterson Fleming the racing-driver offered his services they'd turn me down. But I'll train for observer if need be.'

'They might. Turn you down. What about the medical?'

Patie got up and looked moodily into the depths of the big open log fire.

'I'm all right. It's Camilla who keeps looking for things to go wrong with me. She wants me here. I can understand it; it would be hard for her, lonely too.'

'But her view is that a United Kingdom government can't conscript a Scottish subject or it violates the Act of Union.' This was Robin.

'It wouldn't be conscription! I want to offer of my own free will.'

'Then if you feel so strongly, do it,' said Catriona decisively. 'It's no time to play domestic politics, of whatever sort.'

Patie looked imploringly at Mairi. 'Would you and Nicol — and Eleanor — move here for the duration? If she had company, it would be different. She'd come to terms with the idea, in time.'

Nicol laughed, a chesty sound that turned into a rattle of coughing. 'We don't belong here, Patie. I've nothing against Mairi and Eleanor coming up from time to time —'

'It would be safer than Dounhead —'

'Dounhead's safe enough.'

'It isn't a safety zone.' He concentrated his entreaty on Mairi. 'Please, Mairi, think about it. She can't be left alone. She — she's nervous.'

Catriona said hardly, 'So are a lot of other women, and they just have to get on with it.'

'You know what I mean. She goes to pieces, almost literally, if I'm not around.'

'Then take advice from her doctor.'

'I have. He supports me.'

If they all had their views on what Patie's course of action should be, they kept them to themselves for the rest of the evening. Deliberately, Patie tuned in to the Home Service and Billy Ternent and his Dance Orchestra, while they chatted quietly about domestic trivia. Nellie brought in cocoa and joined them in reminiscences about old times before they took their steps upstairs towards the bedrooms. The one shared by Mairi and Nicol was the only one heated; the others had to be content with hot-water bottles and mounds of blankets. It was still snowing lightly and a moon was up, setting off a landscape of unearthly silvery-white beauty.

Mairi looked round the big, cosy room with its polished floor and skin rugs. Nicol had climbed into the massive, carved bed and was sipping the nightcap toddy prescribed by Nellie for his cough. She felt suddenly strange and shy.

'We've never been away together,' she said. 'I've never seen what you look like. Away from Dounhead.'

'Same as I do there.' He laughed, indulgent but puzzled.

'No.' She leapt in beside him, chittering as the cold parts of the sheets struck her body. 'You don't understand what

I mean. I feel as though I've got you – *you* – to myself at last. Nobody can come knocking on the door saying: where's Red Nicol, I want a house, I want him to mend my broken heart or my leaking roof.'

'That's poetry. Nearly.'

'Nicol.'

'Lovie, what is it?'

'Don't you feel it too?'

He put down the toddy glass and snicked out the light. She felt his arms go around her and the easeful scent of whisky from his lips. It had been a long time, since before his illness. Their bodies had become so attuned to each other's needs it was like playing a well-rehearsed tune. Except that some nights the music could be banal, on others muffled or merely adequate, and once or twice the perfection you sought on every other occasion. Tonight nothing was mechanical, but all heart and feeling, a coming home of the spirit, a harbouring. She had brought him here to nurture him, blatantly, on Patie's comparatively lavish board. If only she could get him built up, could get some flesh on his bones. But she knew the strength was beginning to ebb from his body, slowly and irrevocably. All that was Nicol was increasingly focused in his face and in his eyes. Those kindling eyes that had never changed, that still had the power to claim and soothe her, reiterate who she was and where she belonged.

He was sleeping before she was. It was so magnificently warm and snug in the great bed that she lay watching the last shadows cast by the dying fire, thinking idly of the night she'd run away to marry Nicol and ended up behind his mother's massive form in the set-in bed, watching shadows just like these.

She put her hand forward and touched him again. Nicol, Nicol, she said in her mind. And did not care if she was crying.

Eleanor got up the next morning and looked in the bevelled mirror of the dressing-table. 'Good morning, my darleeng,' she said to herself, in the tones of Charles Boyer, and then waited till her face took on the expression of someone thus addressed: one of long-suffering ecstasy. 'I weell wait for you for ever, if necess-airy,' she said, in the Boyer accent, and in the mirror watched herself lift her chin and purse her lips for the kiss that would be her passport to paradise. Meanwhile, part of her was calculatingly assessing how she looked. It was very difficult to analyse yourself: that was why her friend Janet was so helpful. And Janet thought she had arresting eyes. They were dark, like her father's. She had her mother's good teeth and firm mouth. She practised looking pretty, alluring, breathless. The kind of girl Micky Rooney would like in the Andy Hardy films. Or the kind of girl Ginger Rogers had played in *Kitty Foyle*. The kind of girl who would stand on the edge of airfields or in troop-crowded stations, waiting for the man she loved. Oh God! She suddenly became impatient with herself, fed up with all the mystery of her feelings. From her room she could see Calneggie, the Big Place, and troop cars and soldiers were already on the move from there like so many snow ants and their encumbrances.

She pulled on warm tan-coloured corduroy slacks and a pale blue polo-neck jumper. Now she was so nearly seventeen it was a relief to be out of school uniform whenever possible. Downstairs Nellie had set breakfast in the kitchen, for warmth, and her parents were eating their boiled eggs with a kind of apologetic, working-class self-consciousness that irked Eleanor more than it amused her.

Robin Chisholm felt no such inhibitions about sitting tidily at the table. He was moodily supping his porridge over by the window and looking out at the snow-covered kitchen garden. Beautifully groomed, in pale green tweeds, twin-set and pearls, Catriona was having Melba toast and tea. At a query from her mother, Nellie announced that Patie had already eaten and gone out and Camilla was breakfasting in bed.

'What's the news?' Eleanor demanded brightly. She was determined to make it clear she was not going to be overwhelmed by the evidence of grand living like starched napkins and silver coffee-pots.

'The papers haven't come,' said Robin gloomily. 'Apparently the village "boy" has been called up. Someone'll have to go down for them.'

'I will.' Eleanor was delighted to have the chance of exploring the village, remembering it only vaguely from her visit as a child. She would have to pass the Big Place and would be able to see the soldiers. She did not ask her mother if it was all right to wear her best coat, the one that had taken all those coupons, rather than her standby school

191

navy trench coat. She buttoned herself guiltily into the fawn one upstairs, feeling the softness of its brushed pile fabric against her neck. Calneggie had already begun to affect her, making her reject second-best. How easy it would be to be haughty like Catriona, languid like Camilla!

Running downhill in the dazzling, snow-reflected sunshine, she rejected such notions for the base pretensions they were. She wouldn't really change places with anyone. She felt in possession of the future in a way the older women could never know again. Everything was going to happen to *her*. Beautiful (perhaps), knowing and waiting, she was ready for it. She ran her Fair Isle gloves over snowy railings and observed the melting, diamond granules on her woollen fingertips with a kind of wonder.

The village had quietly and treasonably changed while she had been away. There was a baker's with a tea-room, an Italian ice-cream and sweet shop, even a draper selling heather-coloured capes and ghillie's stockings. There was far more activity than she had believed possible. Soldiers walking purposefully down from the Big Place, stopping to chat to each other and the local inhabitants. Officers with canes under their arms, stamping booted feet before going into the Calneggie Arms Hotel for morning coffee. When she stopped to look in the draper's window, a small Polish soldier (Nellie had told her they were part of the village garrison) came up and offered her chocolate, doing his best to get a conversation going in fractured English. She could only make out the word 'walk' and she gave him an abashed but upbraiding smile before hurrying on to the newsagent's. Still, it was an anecdote for Janet! A conquest made so early proved something.

The newspaper headline didn't at first make much sense to her. All through 1941, the big type had been used for headlines announcing the bomber raids on Düsseldorf and Cologne, Berlin and Hamburg; for the siege of Leningrad and the Churchill-Roosevelt meeting in mid-Atlantic. 'Japs Bomb Pearl Harbor.' She had never heard of Pearl Harbor.

An Army corporal was talking to the elderly newsagent. 'Roosevelt's going to find it out now, isn't he? You can't save freedom with words.'

'We'll be expected to take on the Japs too,' said the old man with a smouldering anger. 'They'll be after Singapore; see if I'm not right.'

It explained the busy-ness and the febrility. Everybody wanted to come out and talk about it. Eleanor lost no time in rushing back to the lodge house. In the bustle of their arrival, no one had been listening to the news bulletins on the wireless. Patie had come back now from the farm to change out of cold water-logged boots; Camilla, maquillage of rouge, lipstick and eyebrow pencil masking her underlying pallor, was making shivering noises by the fire and her mother was pouring coffee while Catriona offered round cigarettes and fitted one into a long amber holder for herself.

'The Americans have been attacked by the Japanese.' Eleanor stood on the kitchen threshold enunciating the words with dramatic clarity and holding up the newspaper so that the headlines were clear to all. 'They've sunk ships at a place called Pearl Harbor.'

When the babble of words had died down it was Patie who took the paper away and sat down with it by the deep window-ledge, reading the lead story word for careful word. Eleanor was conscious of her Aunt Camilla rubbing the tops of her arms, a brisk, constant movement as though she could get no feeling through to them.

'Well, you know what this means,' said Patie at last. They all looked at him, even Nellie who had been working to loosen dead ashes from the fire and build it up with damp slack and potato peelings. 'It means I am going down to Glasgow to offer my services.'

He looked over to Camilla as though she had spoken, but she had said nothing. Merely rubbed, rubbed at her arms.

'I can't look at myself any longer in the mirror.' He addressed Camilla as though none of the others existed and placed himself squarely in front of her. His voice was unexpectedly tender. 'I'm sorry, darling, but there it is.'

'Go, then.' It was a thin, small sound of infinite pathos. Camilla had stopped rubbing and sat as still as a statue, except for her carefully lipsticked mouth which worked and stretched and puckered.

'God, this house is like a morgue.' Catriona came into Mairi's bedroom and closed the door behind her with exaggerated caution. 'I can't get Camilla to come to the dance. Please come, Mairi! It would do you good to get away from Nicol for a night.'

'He wouldn't like it.' Catriona and Eleanor, who was carefully pulling on a precious pair of silk stockings, glared at her in twin exasperation.

'Robin won't come either,' said Catriona. 'Ah well, that leaves you and me, Eleanor my girl, holding the fort. I've promised Camilla I'll keep an eye on things, liaise with the officers, make sure nobody's sick in the stairwell, that sort of thing. Come on. Let's do our bit for Britain, eh? Keep up the morale of the troops?'

All this was said with such a mocking, Betty Grable-ish ogling, pouting and sticking-out of bottom and bosom that even Mairi brightened and laughed. 'I've nothing to wear,' she said.

'No excuse,' said Catriona sternly. 'You could borrow something of mine.' She let the matter drop, seeing Mairi's mulish expression. 'Don't you think Eleanor looks stunning in my pink chiffon?'

Mairi looked at her daughter consideringly. The pink had set off Eleanor's complexion to perfection. The girl had brushed her soft brown hair up in front and at the sides and let it fall softly to the padded dress shoulders. An artificial damask rose at the dress's yoke somehow emphasized the youth, the bloom of the wearer. With satisfaction Eleanor looked down at the cheap, patent shoes with butterfly bows she had talked her mother into buying her and up again, still and smiling, into her mother's face.

'She looks all right,' Mairi conceded, with pretended diffidence. 'Away you go, the pair of you, and have a nice time. Don't do anything I wouldn't do.'

Walking towards Calneggie with her arm through Catriona's, Eleanor remembered the wistful note in her mother's voice. She was in danger of making a career out of other people's worries. Not only did she worry incessantly about Nicol, her father: she had also now taken on the worry of Patie's wailing, woeful wife. She had suggested Camilla coming to live with them at Dounhead, if Patie came back with word he had been accepted. Camilla in a council house! They had tried to laugh her out of it but in the end she had persuaded them it might not be so unthinkable. The war had broken down a lot of barriers and Camilla might be happier with their company than immured alone with Nellie at Calneggie Lodge.

'Might as well enjoy ourselves.' Catriona hugged her arm, a little guiltily. 'We're a long time dead.'

Eleanor followed Catriona into the cheerful maze of

sound and music in the big hall at Calneggie. One of the old pantries had been converted into the ladies' cloakroom and they handed in their coats and scarves. Eleanor was secretly pleased to be with Catriona, with her social verve, her gaiety, her assurance that she would be welcome and looked after. Catriona introduced herself, as Camilla's stand-in, to the two moustached senior officers in charge of operations. With a less confident feeling and a pasted-on smile Eleanor watched as one of the officers immediately swept Catriona off to dance. The other older officer said in a deep, embarrassed wuffle, 'Damned awful weather, I would say, wouldn't you?' 'Yes,' said Eleanor thinly. A couple jitterbugged unfeelingly in front of her.

She didn't know what she was supposed to do. At school the girls lined up at one side of the gymnasium, the boys at the other, and as the dances were announced, the boys slid and slithered across the floor to the girls of their choice, making invitatory noises deep in their throats. Left behind and you were a wallflower, which was what she was rapidly becoming now.

The wuffling officer had gone off in search of a drink and she was alone and terror-stricken. The hall seemed full of very large soldiers and red-faced girls from the village and surrounding countryside. The orchestra, if you could call it that, was making a confounded din that was mainly tympany – *crash, bang, wallop!* – and bore no resemblance whatsoever to Geraldo or Carroll Gibbons. '*Oh, Johnny, oh Johnny, how you can love . . .*'

'*Please,*' she appealed to a nameless deity, under her breath. She could see Catriona waving at her reassuringly from under her partner's moustache. It didn't help. The pink dress was too old for her, too big. The shoes were all wrong. Tarty, cheap, as her mother had said. Longing for the straight-forward concern over who partnered you for the supper-dance at the Academy overwhelmed her. Once, at fourteen, it had been a boy in short trousers, but that was as nothing to this.

'*May I have the pleasure of this dance?*'

Eleanor felt she was being shot through her tautened skin as the words sounded in her ear. From the paternal direction of the moustached wuffler a young Army officer had appeared and now moved in front of her, bowing shyly.

'Er, yes, what is it?'

'A foxtrot.'

195

'Yes, I can do it.'

Gauchely trembling, she moved into his arms. 'Introductions will be effected later,' he said. 'For the moment, do you mind if we concentrate on the steps?' As though to underline the necessity for this, his large right brown boot came over her unguarded left instep, causing her to bend and squeak with anguish. As her head rose again, his concerned face took a mouthful of her piled front hair. His spluttering apology had a muffled sound. They had meanwhile bumped into an unmollifiable sergeant and his partner, but at last pain and desperation had dimmed social anxiety sufficiently for a modicum of common sense to return.

Looking up into the sweating, embarrassed face above her, Eleanor said with more reassurance than she felt, 'Look, let's start again, shall we?' They waited for the beat of the music and this time took off with comparative ease. But they were both tense, afraid of making more mistakes and when the dance ended he gave a small grimace of relief and said, 'Sorry about that.'

He led her towards the wallflowers, male and female, and went on, 'I don't seem to have what it takes to make a ballroom dancer. I'm not instinctive enough. I know up here–' he tapped his head–'what I ought to do, but my body's always half a beat behind the message.'

She laughed. At last his worried expression resolved and he said, 'Geoffrey Benson's the name.'

'Eleanor Chambers,' she returned. 'Are you a lieutenant, then?' She indicated the one pip on his shoulder. 'Just promoted.' He couldn't hide the note of pride in his voice. His accent was plummy, London-y, she would have thought a little affected. But she liked his face. It was thin and mobile and there was no mistaking the look of interest and pleasure in his dark eyes. There was still enough of the boy in him to make him less intimidating than, as an English officer, he might have been. She felt a revving inside her, a tide carrying her forward to further delights of the evening. When the music started again, he held out his arms and she glided into them.

'*That certain night, the night we met.*' This time, they were more deliberate. His arms and body were already a little familiar, so that she could trust herself to them. '*And a nightingale sang in Berkeley Square.*' How supple and responsive her own body felt, more so than ever before. At the Academy, the boys had been all tweed elbows and hot palms. But his grip tightened possessively as their steps matched more and more precisely. He looked down at her with a grin of happy achievement and said, 'As they say in the films – "Hey, look, Mom, I'm dancing!" You have a natural sense of rhythm, you know. You must be passing it on to me. I'm not usually this good.'

'*I know 'cos I was there, that night in Berkeley Square.*'

As though on cue, he stumbled then and trod all over her lightly-protected toes. 'Ooooh,' she said, and 'Ahhhh.' She began to laugh and he held her again, ashamed and apologetic, but delighted with her, laughing too. 'Eleanor,' he said, 'it's a pretty name. Do you work in the village here, or on a farm?'

'Do I look as though I do?'

'No, I thought not.'

She felt a desperate need to impress him. 'I shall be seventeen soon. I shall leave school once I've taken my Highers. I mean to make something of my life.'

'Such as?'

'I don't know yet. Travel. Meet people.'

'Do you read much?'

'Oh yes.'

'What?'

'Well . . . poetry. And *Anne of Green Gables. The Girl of the Limberlost.*'

'*The Girl of the* what?'

'*Limberlost.*'

'Tripe. Tripe and onions. Haven't you got on to any proper authors? Hardy, James?'

'I've read some Ibsen. And Shaw. I have to read what I can get.'

'I'll have to lend you something decent.'

'All right,' she said meekly.

'Can I see you home later?'

'I'm with my mother's cousin.'

'The flirtatious red-head?'

'Yes.'

'Must you go back with her?'

'Yes, I must.'

The music had stopped once again and this time Catriona ploughed her way determinedly through the dancers with a new partner in tow.

'The next dance is a Dashing White Sergeant,' she explained. 'Eleanor, come and make up the threesome.' She smiled beguilingly but dismissively at the young lieutenant. 'Over there.' She pointed. 'They need a man to make up their set.'

CHAPTER TWELVE

Eleanor had been hurrying home from Calneggie village with medicine prescribed for her father's cough and had not paid much attention to the muffled soldier, who like several others was striding in the opposite direction towards his billets.

It came to her that it might have been Geoffrey Benson, whom she had not seen since the night of the dance. She looked round in any case, as much out of longing that it might be him as from any real conviction, and saw that the figure had stopped also and was gazing after her.

Something rose in her throat, almost suffocating her. She should not have turned round: it had been a silly, forward thing to do. And so maybe she should turn at once and go home. But her steps were carrying her back towards the soldier, and he was coming towards her, grinning above a great hand-knitted khaki muffler.

'I thought it was you –'

'I've been to the shops –'

'I wasn't sure. Last time you wore a pink dress, after all –'

Damn, damn, damn, she thought. To be wearing the dreaded school Burberry. 'How are you?' she demanded lamely.

'I'm well. If frozen. And you?'

'Me, too.'

Their feet shuffled in the powdery snow. Their faces glowed with cold and awkwardness. Yes, she thought, I was right about his eyes. A kind of hazel brown. And the one tooth that overlaps. And the keen, shy way of looking.

'Will you be going to the next dance?'

'I might be.'

'Couldn't I see you before then? Would you like to come for a walk?'

'When?'

'This afternoon. About three? Meet at the War Memorial?'

'Yes, all right.' She said it on a rush. She scarcely dared look at him, lest all her uncertainties about how to proceed showed in her face. She had never been out with a boy before and wasn't at all sure her mother would go along with the idea of her meeting a soldier. So she wouldn't tell them. She would simply let them think she was going out on her own . . .

He was standing by the War Memorial, looking down towards the Sound road which they took without a word. She wore her good coat and a blue pixie hood and, because the snow was hard and impacted, the silly, impractical shoes. It had turned out one of those orange-bright, invigorating winter days, with a big marigold sun burnishing a spotless, cerulean sky. To their left, dark ploughed earth showed patchily through the icy anæsthetic white and gulls shouted their hunger amidst heavy, interweaving, unceasing parabolas. She thought she had never seen a day so bright or perfect. Even the big boulders on the sea-washed sand had been specially limned to declare their glossy perfection, the blue-green-glistening irregularities set off against the sky in a grandly casual act of creation.

When they were out of sight of the village he took her hand and pulled her down to walk along the beach. Taking a book from his greatcoat pocket, he said, 'I've brought you Gerard Manley Hopkins and marked in the index the poems you should read first.'

'Thank you.' She took the book obediently.

'You've heard of Hopkins?'

'Didn't he write "Adelstrop"?' She grabbed at the first vague option she could remember from her Palgrave's *Golden Treasury*. Falling apart, because school books were scarce. *Didn't he know there was a war on?*

'No.' He placed himself in front of her, grinning his exasperation. 'That was Thomas.'

'I like it, anyway,' she said.

'Yes, of course, it's not bad. But Hopkins is my favourite. He went up to my college, Balliol, at Oxford. I had a scholarship at seventeen . . .'

'You mean you have a degree?'

'Yes. I took it just before the war broke out, summer of '39.'

She looked at him with a hint of respect. 'They wanted me to go to university.'

'Well, of course, you should.'

'Can't afford to.' She was turning the pages of the book and began to quote:

> 'I caught this morning morning's minion,
>   Kingdom of daylight's dauphin,
>   dapple-dawn-drawn Falcon.'

He caught the book and her hands, gazing at her appreciatively. 'That was nice.'

'My mother teaches elocution. When she can get the pupils.'

'Yes,' he said, 'I knew it. You're a bit different from the rest, aren't you?'

'I wish I knew more,' she said soberly. 'I would like to get drunk on knowing more.'

He looked with a great intense earnestness into her eyes and said, 'There was the Oxford Movement, you see, when Hopkins went up to Balliol. Religion and innocence. Hopkins became a Jesuit, a priest, and all he felt about love and beauty was sublimated into his poetry, though it broke him as a man.'

They sat down on a flat boulder. 'I can understand because although I'm Anglo I sometimes want to go all the way and be Catholic. I had this tutor who almost convinced me.' He covered her gloved hand with his. 'You don't understand what I'm getting at, do you?'

She shook her head.

'I feel it's important to have some sort of philosophy. I mean, the war might take me anywhere and anything can happen. I'm so unprepared.'

'Don't talk like that,' she said huskily. 'I'll pray for you if you like. But it'll be Church of Scotland prayers.'

'It's a kind of agony for me, being where I am. I'd got used to other things. Matthew Arnold now, he said the true soul of man dwells apart from the tumult! But tell that to the Army. It's discipline and orders from morning till night. And crude simple minds. Crude dirty soldiers' minds.'

'What will you do, afterwards?'

'Go into the Civil Service. Family tradition.'

'Do you like things like that? Tradition and so on?'

'Yes, perhaps so. Institutions. They help my insecurity.'

She pushed the book of poems into the big, saddle-stitched pocket of her coat. 'I promise to read them. Carefully.' She got up and started to run along the beach. 'Come on,' she called, 'I'll race you to the headland. Last man there's a donkey.'

He caught up behind her just as she reached the big rocks. Panting and laughing, she jumped on to the narrow road beyond the shore, scraping snow from the grass verge till she had enough for a small, hard snowball. Taking accurate aim, she hit him in the chest, then ran back on to the beach and dodged behind the rocks. He caught her eventually, his breath coming in great rough gasps, and trickled grains of sandy snow down the back of her collar, so that she yelled fiercely with the shock.

She saw that his face had changed from troubled introspection to sheer boyish enjoyment. His somewhat pale, sallow skin was tinged with pink on the cheekbones and laughter spilled over as he caught her and held her, pausing before dropping a brief kiss on the side of her nose.

'Yell!' she cried exultantly. 'Shout! Nobody can hear you. Down with the Army! Up with Gerard Manley Hopkins! Poets are important! Geoffrey Benson says so.'

'Walter Pater!' he shouted at the seagulls. 'John Ruskin! Matthew Arnold!'

'Rabbie Burns!' Eleanor called to the cold sky. 'Hugh MacDiarmid. Even Robin Chisholm.'

'Donne and Marvell and poor John Clare!'

'Tommy Morgan.'

'Who's he?'

'A Glasgow comic.'

She paused for breath, her cheeks rosy and her eyes sparkling. 'You're mad, you know,' she informed him, laughing. 'The seagulls are never going to listen to you.'

He stood fronting the sea, his legs straddled, his slender figure buffeted by a growing wind. He raised his arms and flapped them, drawing in great exaggerated breaths.

'Are you happy?' she shouted. She was off along the beach again, heading towards the village, dancing and turning like a seven-year-old, her scarf ends flapping in the wind.

He followed behind more slowly. He was reluctant to leave the shore. But as she dwindled from sight, he began to race after her, holding on to his officer's cap. 'Yes, I think I am.' He did not think she heard what he had said.

'An Englishman!' they teased her. 'We never thought our Eleanor would fall for an Englishman!'

'He looks a bit of a delicate plant,' said her Uncle Patie,

ebullient over his acceptance by the RAF. Camilla had looked at him reprovingly. 'He's a genus unknown to you,' she said scathingly. 'An intellectual.' She went on like that now, day after day, scratchingly attacking him over everything and anything, unable to dent the new, brash persona. Always he smiled at her. Always she looked away, in a kind of despair.

Eleanor was waiting for it to be like what she and Janet had known it would be like, for him to say 'I love you', and when it did not happen despite the warm bear hugs and sweet, sharp kisses, she took the situation forward, one night on the way home after a dance. 'I love you,' she said. 'I have to tell you, Geoffrey. You haven't said it, and you don't need to, but I want to say it. Or I'll burst.' There was a kind of shame in her. Had she been forcing the issue before going home, so that it would tally with the romantic notions she and Janet had picked up in a generation of picture-going? Even as she said it, she knew it could have been Myrna Loy talking to Clark Gable. She didn't want Hollywood banalities mixed up in this priceless, precious situation they were in. She was churned up and frightened – above all frightened of having destroyed something – and still he walked along with her arm in his, saying nothing.

It was the narrow, uphill road towards the lodge they were on and there was a glimmering, silvery light from the Sound. He stopped by the sea wall and said quietly, 'How can you be sure?'

'I just am. I'm so happy, so different, when I'm with you, it must be love.'

'You know where that might take you?'

'No, I don't.'

This time when he kissed her there was nothing sharp or sweet. He held her lips, moving slowly forward with her and when they got to a break in the wall, half-staggering, he pulled her down on to the sand. He opened her dress and cupped and kissed her breasts; he pushed his hands between her legs and touched her inside her body. He took her hand and, having unbuttoned his trousers, put it against moving skin. All the while their lips clung, they fell about helplessly on the sand. She felt something wet and sticky pulse against her hand and at the same time her own world expanded endlessly, so that she was caught up in the sea and sky and endless beauty of the night. She gasped and sighed and cried his name in a kind of terror. 'Geoffrey!'

'Oh, my sweet pretty one. Oh, my Eleanor!' He sounded

as though he had run a race. She buttoned them both up again carefully, she combed the sand from her hair. Shakily they both stood up and then moved together again. 'Say it,' she said against his chest. 'Please say it.'

'I love you, Eleanor.'

She stumbled against him, her feet sinking in the sand. 'I knew you did. I knew you must.'

His face looked down on hers. 'You look transported by joy.'

She brushed sand from her face. 'I am flying apart with it.'

'I think we may be on the move, after Christmas. But say to no one I've told you.'

'Where to?'

'Even if I knew, I couldn't tell you.'

'You'll write?'

'Of course.'

'I'll write to you every day.'

'But you'll be back at school, studying for your Highers. Don't muck that up.'

'I won't. I just want to get it over with. Then when you come back, we'll get married.'

He laughed. 'You've got it all sorted out.'

'Don't you want to marry me?'

'You should know I won't tempt Fate. And you're still terribly young. Let me get the war over. If I don't come back, you've to stay in one piece and marry someone else. Understood?'

She said nothing, chastened. After that, she wouldn't allow him to talk about going away. She insisted they live entirely in the present.

At Christmas, he gave her an expensive powder compact.

'I've never had a present like it before,' she told him. 'We don't give each other big things. Just little ones.'

'I want you to have it.'

'But I've only got gloves for you. That I knitted myself. And something went wrong with the thumb join. I'm sorry.'

He told her he thought the gloves were wonderful and wore them although the fingers were about half as long again as they needed to be.

After Christmas, her mother followed her into her bedroom one night and asked, 'Eleanor, are you and Geoffrey Benson going further than you ought?'

White-faced she demanded, 'Why do you ask that?'

'There was glit on your clothes.'

'Glit?' She was near to tears.

'Semen.' Not looking at her, her mother went on: 'You know what I mean. I don't think you should go on seeing him.'

She gave a cry and threw herself down on the bed. 'He could be going away at any moment. I *will* go on seeing him, you can't stop me.'

'Wait a minute.' Mairi sat on the bed and put a hand on her shoulder. 'Stop making such a row. I'm merely warning you what will happen, if you go on as you are doing. There will be a baby. You know Dounhead is full of babies without daddies. So-called blitz babies. Would you like that to happen to you?'

'Could it?' She sat up, tear-stained and full of remorse.

'You know it could.'

'I don't know much. You've never told me.'

'Then I am telling you now.'

'Please let me go on seeing him. We're going home soon, he's going away, I might never see him again.'

'Then will you be careful?' said Mairi forcefully. 'Your daddy's so worried he's talking of going to Geoffrey's commanding officer.'

'I'll never forgive him if he does. But I'll not have a baby. I promise you, Mum. Trust me.'

'You see,' said Mairi, 'it can happen so easily. And it would be such a tragedy.' She kissed her daughter. 'You have to come straight home after the pictures or dances, now. I am going to tell Geoffrey the same.'

There was a Hogmanay party at the lodge and the day before Geoffrey was told his platoon would be on the move on 1 January. Eleanor pleaded that he be allowed to stay the night and as several other officers were being put up after the jollifications, Camilla and her parents agreed.

As she had known and prayed he would, he came to her room in the middle of the night. He had not removed his uniform and he lay beside her on top of the bedclothes, with just the eiderdown covering him. They were both terrified of starting something neither would be able to stop. In the days since Mairi's warning they had argued ceaselessly about whether they should, in fact, become total lovers. Her own reaction had been to shy away in terror from the idea of a child out of wedlock. His had been bewilderment and then worry as to how he could accomplish the act, if they decided on it, with a protective sheath, such as he had never used before. And this notion was bedevilled in both their minds by the moral justification for using such an item, or for making love before they married.

But now he simply lay in his uniform beside her and it was strange and almost tranquil, the physical propinquity enough. In her mind she tried to go with him wherever the New Year would take him: across submarine-ridden seas to strange enemy shores. She knew what it would be like. In this war there were newsreels and everyone could see. 'I will think about you every day at one o'clock, and you must think then of me,' she said. 'That way we will be close.' She had read it somewhere.

At dawn he rose quietly and left her and after breakfast she put her arms round him for the last time before he left. Then she did not know how to go back to being as she was before. She was a different person.

Camilla went back with them to Dounhead but she did not stay long. She took them to see *Blithe Spirit* and *Flare Path* in blacked-out Glasgow and they met up with Catriona once or twice for carefully-regulated wartime restaurant meals. Then she took off for Kent where it seemed Patie was going to be stationed, but when he began going out on missions the strain and young wives were more than she could bear and she went back to Calneggie and its old Celtic church and the quiet. Her hope that they might have kept him on the ground because of his age was not fulfilled. They needed all the bomber pilots they could get and he had a solid nerve that was valuable when transmitted to the younger men. He had glamour value, too. The papers spoke of 'racing ace' and 'pilot hero' and it was all good propaganda these days when everybody wondered when the Army would go into Europe and the Air Force, the 'Brylcreem Boys', satisfied some atavistic need for action-worship.

As Eleanor began sitting her exams, Patie went out on the first thousand-bomber raids over Germany. He was one of the Pathfinders who marked out the target areas in advance. He came home on leave whenever he could, hyped up on action, whisky and nicotine and sometimes Camilla tried going back with him until once more it became too much and she retreated to the Highlands. A pattern was set that was to continue right up to the airborne landings in Sicily.

News came that Philip Mackenzie, who had taken part in

the commando raids on France that were the rehearsal for invasion, had been wounded and later had been invalided out because an arm and an eye had been affected. He went back to journalism, not this time to the squeezed-thin wartime version of the pulp magazine he had previously worked on, but to a national newspaper where, because of shortage of manpower, he was soon in a position of some seniority. He had met a Scots girl, Elizabeth, while on active service, she being in the ATS and when he went back to 'Civvie Street' they married and set up home in the leafy 'queen of the London suburbs', a depredated autumnal Ealing. Tina pleaded with him, in vain, to return to Scotland. On a brief visit home after the wedding he pointed out 'Greek' Thomson's lovely St George's Church, destroyed at Queen's Park in Glasgow, saying the risk was the same everywhere. He was not to know it was the last raid Glasgow would experience, while rocket bombs were still to wreak their peculiar whining devastation on London and the south.

When Eleanor left school, having done well in her Highers, she went into an office for a short time, then, knowing she would be called up soon in any case, elected to work in a well-paid munitions job so that she could save some money. She had become mature, settled, almost as though she were a married woman already. Before going into the WRNS her friend Janet still dragged her to dances with her and they were giggling and confidential in the way of best friends, but, still hoping for Mr Right, Janet respected the depth of feeling, the life experience, that had come to her friend through Geoffrey, whose somewhat mysterious, unsmiling face was pinned in several guises behind Eleanor's bedroom door. He reminded her, she said, of Tyrone Power, though without the mischief or the turned-up mouth. And he was thinner, more like Franchot Tone perhaps or Ronald Reagan, when you thought about it.

They had established in many hours of careful, protracted analysis that this was the Real Thing. Why else, every day, no matter what happened, would Eleanor sit down to write the careful letters in purple ink on lavender paper and why else did the thin airmails arrive from North Africa, if not so frequently, at least often enough to prevent despair?

Prickly and aware of her reserve, her better education, the girls in the munitions factory were prepared to prevent Eleanor from being a 'swagger', by reminding her she was Red Nicol's daughter but she quickly learned the tricks and formalities that made social intercourse easy. Some of them were quicker on the practical uptake than she was and she learned to defer to them. They were nice girls, mainly, their teeth and hair betraying the poverty of their childhoods and the gallus older women, with their turbans, endless cigarettes and fancy earrings, made tedious repetitive work bearable by their jokes and their sense of fun.

'Heard from Geoffrey?' they would say. Quite a lot of them had met English servicemen, Poles, Czechs, Frenchmen and, more recently, prized nylon-bearing Americans. It was all right, but a little dull, to be going with a Scotsman, unless he was in the Air Force or had sailed with the Navy to Murmansk.

In order to make sure that the rigidly husbanded food supplies went where most needed, the authorities had begun serving schoolchildren with midday meals, the first many Dounhead youngsters had seen of anything as sophisticated as a home-made soup or pudding. Mairi took a job at the school canteen and her other war work was through the church, organizing 'comforts', knitted scarves, socks, gloves and balaclavas, as well as sundry extras like soap and Penguin books, for the Services, and running concerts to raise the necessary funds.

Since his bout of pneumonia, Nicol had entered the category of near-chronic invalid. His lungs, never the same since the First War, worked with only erratic efficiency, so it was just as well that although he remained pit agent, trade union activity had slowed down and any disputes there were quickly settled by the National Arbitration Tribunal. Nobody wanted strikes or hold-ups with a war on.

True to his promise of support, Robin Chisholm made a point of frequent visits, bringing Mairi fresh eggs from the hens his mother kept and occasional Black Market tea or sugar which Catriona unscrupulously scrounged from hard-up large families only too ready to part with the necessary food coupons for money. He and Nicol would then embark on lengthy arguments about the Beveridge Report, the possibilities of a decline in national backbone if the State took over with 'cradle to grave' Welfare care and provided a 'free' National Health Service. Mairi knew that these visits were partly out of marital loneliness. Catriona was involved with Red Cross war work that took her into Glasgow most days and at week-ends there were always officers – American ones now – being entertained at their home.

On a day that had been warm and clear enough for Nicol to attend a Second Front meeting with other Left-Wing sympathizers, Robin arrived on a visit as Mairi was baking scones and pancakes on the old iron griddle she had inherited from Great-Grannie Kate. He sat on a chair of the new Utility three-piece suite Eleanor had helped her mother to buy and watched the domestic scene with a sort of wistful relish.

'You shall have some,' Mairi promised. 'As soon as I've made these, I'll put the kettle on.'

He settled back in the chair. 'You'll not shift me,' he averred. 'It's too comfortable here.' As she shot him a brief, preoccupied smile, he went on, 'You and Nicol have a good existence together. I can see that. The things you've had to put up with have brought you closer.'

She saw his words as a preamble to something else and met him halfway. 'Don't you think Catriona's too caught up in her voluntary work? She should be at home more. I'll tell her so, if you want me to.'

He moved his bony hands together with a rasping sound. 'Anything you say will be too late.'

'What do you mean?' A scone burned, sending up a little blue wisp of smoke, as she waited for his answer.

'She's met somebody else. Somebody she wants to leave me for. A Yank.'

'Robin! You never told me. How long have you known?'

'Long enough.' His laconic tone belied the spaniel misery of his eyes.

Mairi whipped the griddle off the flames, carrying it into the kitchenette, removing her floury apron, before coming to sit opposite him by the fire.

'I don't know what to say. Does she want a divorce? Will you give her one?'

'She says she'll go, whether I agree to a divorce or not. So in the circumstances, I have no option.'

'I'll make the tea.' Mairi rose in a flurry. 'I'll talk sense into her, Robin. See if I don't.'

He caught her hand as she passed him. She stood there, looking down at him, bewilderment and anger and sorrow chasing across her face. Slowly he raised her hand to his mouth and kissed it.

'You wanted Robin badly enough. How do you know you'll not tire of this one as you've done of him?'

Mairi sat with Catriona in the near-deserted tea-room

in Bellnoch, having met her by accident the day after Robin's disclosure.

Catriona stubbed out her cigarette for longer than was necessary. Her shining red hair, always her best feature, had been elaborately permed and set into a mass of curls on top and was drawn into a curly chignon at the back and secured with narrow black velvet ribbon. Another band of narrow velvet was round her throat. Her lipstick was a vivid scarlet slash. She had lost her youthful plumpness, was all flashing, hard sophistication, in contrast to Mairi's well-worn tweed suit and simple blouse.

'I'd expect you to be on his side,' she said hardly. 'Don't think I don't know what's been between you two.'

'Nothing,' said Mairi hotly.

'Well, he wanted you.' Catriona looked suddenly weary of the whole thing. 'It doesn't matter. But I'll tell you something, Mairi: I know what it is to be moved by a man for the first time. Haydon means more to me than life itself. And he's rich, too, so I know he's not after my money.'

'You're not suggesting Robin was?'

'It was useful to him, wasn't it? He couldn't have indulged his politics on his pay, or had his poems printed. Where has it got him? He sits in that study worrying whether Macbeth was as black as he was painted, or reading Catullus.'

'Don't be so bitter. It doesn't become you.'

'I've told him I am going back with Haydon when the war's over. I am going to have his child no matter what.'

Suddenly everything about her softened and Mairi at last felt she had the answer to all the questions churning through her mind. This was no whim, no desperate answer to Catriona's endless search for amusement and gratification.

Catriona's emotion came over as a palpable thing. She took a photograph from her handbag and pushed it across the table to Mairi. It showed an American Army colonel with a frank gaze, big ears and a boyish smile. Catriona took it back after her cousin's scrutiny. Her small frame shook with seriousness. 'I've found him, Mairi,' she said. 'And so everything's different.'

When Patie Fleming took his bomber on its last flight over Sicily, softening up for the airborne landings and commando bridgeheads which were to follow, his mood was a strange mixture of anger, regret, euphoria and even nostalgia.

They were going to make a desk-wallah of him. He had

taken part in so many bombing raids he had lost count and awed juniors were claiming there was a magical aura about him that saved him from harm. Not altogether, he pointed out. Once he had bailed out over the drink and another time got back against all the odds with a wing on fire. Camilla would be pleased. But the veiled hint that he was over the top, too old, slow in his reflexes annoyed him, scratching at his self-esteem like a dog with fleas.

His crew had watched him climb into his seat with that louche swagger they all tried, unsuccessfully, to emulate. There was nobody like The Old Man, The Boss, The Guv'nor. He gave them that chocolate-box smile. Anyone but him would have to have had the long fair hair cut short. Already they were privy to the party planned for him on his return in the Officers' Mess. The Old Man would put it away in style, they thought. Even when flying there was the whisky flask. But it never affected his composure.

They smiled, taut, preoccupied, wary smiles, as his voice rose in song over the Channel.

> 'Speed, bonnie plane, like a bird on the wing
> Over the Eyties' shore
> Carry the bombs that will make them all sing
> Don't comma here-a no more!'

Ebullient. He was always ebullient, stinking with bravado, in the air. The rear-gunner, remembering the snorts, the little whining helpless cries of his new-born son at home, thought so. His co-pilot, in that state of suspended animation which took over every time he flew nowadays, thought so. But they tuned in to his courage, and it bolstered them, making more bearable the eerie flak-traced night, the heavy aircraft smell, the gold-rimmed purple cumuli in their heavenly beauty, the throb and thrust of the engines, like a separate, interminable pulse. He hadn't failed to take them home yet and they were proving their manhood once again, even if their bowels turned to water and their terror crushed their chests.

'Frank Sinatra, his forebears came from Sicily,' said the gunner.

'He'll never be the equal of Crosby. Or Al Bowly.'

'He's the king of the crooners, Frank Sinatra.'

'He's a big stick of macaroni.'

'Bombs away!'

210

He always felt a sense of great release, of personal lightening.

'That- reminds me, chaps!' he cried. 'Have your bowels moved today?' They were heading for home. 'We've crapped on them for the last time. Now it's over to the poor bloody infantry.'

There was the familiar homeward throb. Different, they swore, from the outward sound. The crump-crump of anti-aircraft guns. And the enemy fighters, somewhere in the dark. They crouched like timid animals in the carapace of their skins. With an unbearable certainty their consciousness denied, they knew this would be the night they finally bought it. This would be the night the engines would pack up, the tail be shot off, the wings crumble to ash and they would spiral, dizzy, top-like, to the uncharitable earth or the swallowing sea.

'England.' Even Patie was silent as the bomber crossed the shoreline. The darkened countryside was rolled up like a length of cloth, the landing ground came up to meet them like a warm blanket of relief. 'Perfect,' acknowledged the co-pilot. The gunner remembered again the sweet-sour smell of his first-born. The air was sweet and damp.

The sense of anti-climax burned in him as he went to the celebration party. He had wanted Camilla to come, but full of Highland superstition she would have no talk of celebrating before the last journey was over. He wanted her there, in her classy frock with the pearls, with that quick, loving look that turned to stillness, calming him at the centre.

When they began to sing, late on in the night, 'There'll always be an England', it was Camilla and Calneggie he was thinking of, with a hazy, drunken concentration.

'There'll always be a *Scotland*,' he contradicted them, getting laboriously on top of one of the mess tables to emphasize it.

'Good old Fleming,' they were saying. 'Attaboy, Ace, you tell them.'

'There'll always be an England, as long as Scotland stands.' Diplomatically, they helped him down before he fell down. One of the faces peering into his own belonged to the station commander. Although as suffused with whisky as his own, it looked owlish, disagreeable and Wykehamist. An ulcer was throbbing.

'By *England*, old chap,' said the commander, 'we mean,

you see, *all* of Britain. I would not make the point on your night of deification but you see you're in on a kind of colonial basis, I'm afraid. Ask anyone. You say England they know you mean Britain. Ask the Yankees. Ask the Frogs. Fifty million to five. Makes an odds, old boy.'

It was the whisky, they said. The Guv'nor had put away a skinful and an elephant's skin at that. They had not been able to get near him as he systematically tore up the mess. There were six broken chairs and four wounded tables. The commander was cut under the eye and a batman gashed his hand picking up broken glass. It was one of those nights that happened when a man was suddenly released from intolerable strain. A fuss over nothing at all.

The fighting in Italy took longer than everyone expected. Even when the King took over from Mussolini and surrendered unconditionally, a year's hard struggle lay ahead of the troops. The savage battle of Cassino was to test the Allied nerve.

It was at Cassino that Geoffrey Benson was taken prisoner and it was then that Eleanor, finding it harder and harder to recall his physical presence, his Tyrone Power-without-the-smile look, felt that the war was going to go on for ever.

CHAPTER THIRTEEN

Eleanor had tucked herself into the corner of the compartment and for the first few hours she had scarcely moved. Her mother had cried when she saw her off and she herself had been fighting back tears, all the way to the Scottish Borders. Once into England, it had been different. Every heavy thwackety-thwack that the wheels made took her nearer London and Geoffrey. She tried not to think of her father, sitting up in the bed they'd put up for him in the living-room because he could no longer manage the stairs. So gaunt and white and willing himself to smile at her jauntily. No, she'd better not think of that.

Even if her father was frail, he had survived the war. She had to remind herself of the thousands who hadn't. Mostly young. And in the concentration camps and at Hiroshima and Nagasaki, thousands more. Being alive now was a bit like coming out of the dark tunnel, where you'd lived so long your legs and your confidence had gone wobbly. You kept wanting to take great gulps of air, to cherish the sunlight, to look around and reassure yourself it was possible to plan freely once again. Well, more or less freely. There would be rationing for a long time yet, and scarcity and a dire shortage of places to live. But living was the thing. She realized she was literally holding herself together, unable to relax in case this moment she had looked forward to for so long escaped into the post-war air with her very next breath.

She had come to London just once before, when Geoffrey had been brought home from the prison camp. She thought she would probably never get out of her mind that image of him, shaven-headed, pale, his uniform, even his very boots, looking too big for him and his eyes full of the haunting of the extermination camps which he had seen on his way home.

She had been nearly twenty hours in the train, stiff, sore and soot-marked and they had met on the platform like two uneasy ghosts from the carefree days at Calneggie nearly five years before.

But now she was coming to London for good. She had a job in a Holborn insurance office at seven pounds a week and on the third finger of her left hand was the small twist of diamonds that showed she and Geoffrey were officially engaged. One thing that had made it easier for the parents to agree she should come was that Philip Mackenzie and his wife had offered her digs in the house they had just started to buy at Ealing. But they should know she was well able to take care of herself now. In her grey tailored suit with the frilly nylon blouse and her good wedge-heeled Joyce shoes she was meant to look the picture of competence. And did. But it took her those hours from leaving Glasgow Central Station and the atmosphere of wartime stress and partings that still clung to it like a damp slimy weed to stop herself shrinking into her corner, to allow herself to take out the sandwiches Mairi had made her and to permit her to take part in friendly if desultory conversation with the other occupants of the carriage.

They were all going to live and work in London or to visit relatives already there. Like herself, they were doing their best to refine their Lowland speech into something that would be acceptable in the south. It always made her feel half-sad, half like laughing out loud. But there was no help for it.

Later on, she slept or pretended to sleep, the years since Calneggie slipping between her eyelids like a ceaseless febrile newsreel . . . the see-saw of fighting in North Africa, the Germans pushed back at Stalingrad, the Yanks pouring into Glasgow in their thousands, Geoffrey taken prisoner, the emotional release of D-Day and the rain of V-2 rockets on London.

She kept remembering the St Crispin's Day speech from Henry V which they'd studied in her last year at school:

> He that outlives this day and comes safe home
> Will stand a tip-toe when this day is named.

The speech and Geoffrey were as one in her mind. So English. And here was she, who had jeered at Philip Mackenzie when he went to Fleet Street before the war – she well remembered how rude and beastly she had been to him – here was she coming south to marry her Englishman, in a bit, when they had saved enough. 'Cry "God for Harry! England and St George!"' She mocked herself, yet the ache was there. You could not lay aside loyalty to Scotland as thought it were a book.

He was waiting for her in his grey, pin-striped demob suit and grey felt, soft-brimmed hat. It was in some ways like looking at a total stranger: the uniform had given him a presence that the ill-fitting civvy clothes did not. He looked slighter, smaller. Yet the smile he gave her was greatly reassuring and when he took her arm after finding a porter to look after her suitcase the whole bewildering experience fell into place like pieces in a jigsaw. London made sense because Geoffrey was there. It was as simple as that.

In the days to come there was so much to adjust to that she found it difficult to find time to write home. But she had promised and no matter how weary she was, even if it meant sitting up in bed before going to sleep, she scrawled the swift pages that would reassure her parents. And there was so much to tell!

Ealing where she lived with Philip and Elizabeth was a leafy, pleasant place, but it was the bombed and scarred landscape around her office in Holborn that laid siege to her imagination.

Poor capital! It had been one thing to read about the raids that devastated it at the beginning and end of the war. It was another thing to see the rose-bay willow herb grow over the blackened ruins of what had once been proud citadels of commerce, banking, publishing and journalism. Here there might have been a block of flats, whose occupants crept defiantly through the blackout, smacking into the sandbags, to see *While the Sun Shines* or Olivier and Richardson in *Peer Gynt*. This might have been a little shop where typists bought their polka-dot dresses, and that a restaurant where poor Bloomsbury writers met for a meal before going to the pictures to hear Bing Crosby sing 'White Christmas' in *Holiday Inn*.

The small serve-yourself restaurant where she met Geoffrey most days for lunch was all that remained of a larger building and was surrounded by the jagged ugly teeth of ruins. An old woman stood at the door selling matches and boot-laces. She did not look ill-fed or -clothed and Eleanor wondered if she did it more from eccentricity than need. Another old woman, wrapped in stained coats, daily fed the scraggy lost cats that swarmed over the bomb sites. In London even more than at home the populace in general had the look of occupants of a burrow just recently come up for air and warmed and gladdened by the light and the absence of attackers. But the old looked stunned and lost like animals who had come up in another part of the forest for which they had no instinct, no scent, no terms of reference. Uniforms had begun to look obscene. It was as though the secretaries in the frilly blouses and the shopkeepers who stuck up their bright, new, striped blinds were the ones who knew the way ahead. It was too soon for the dead to be properly buried. Their going was mirrored everywhere, in the sharp, burning stare of women who charred and men who held out the newspapers. London was Austerity Town, a no-man's-land between the war and the future.

Geoffrey had given up notions of the Civil Service and had opted instead for a lowly job in publishing, with prospects. It meant their offices were near each other; it meant they could meet after work to go to the theatre or the pictures, for a quick snack in a Lyons Corner House or a walk in the park.

He lived with his parents. Sometimes at week-ends she was invited to Stanmore, taking what rations she could scrape together to eke out the restricted meals of shepherd's pie or toad-in-the-hole. It took her a while to sum up his parents but she decided in the end his father had not quite attained the station in life he wanted and that his mother, out of a wish to formalize everything, down to the minute they sat down to their meals, had allowed a gentle spirit to atrophy into anxious vacuity.

They were worried about Geoffrey and how little he had told them about his war experiences. Eleanor asked his mother as they were washing up one evening, 'Have you *asked* him to tell you?' 'Oh no,' said Mrs Benson, looking shocked. 'We don't force confidences in this family.' Eleanor thought how at home everything was dragged out into the daylight and your pain became family, if not public, property. But the English, she had discovered, were reserved, oblique, tentative, the soul of discretion and the heirs of a bleak, sometimes sour, sense of humour. She thought they were sometimes guilty of the very sins they most often accused the Scots of: stinginess, meanness, a lack of generosity. Worse, they were never spontaneous but offered a minimum of hospitality at a strictly stated time. Of course, the Bensons were suburban, their lounge furnished with pale green Maple damask, lit by mock candles, inexpressibly decent and dull. Maybe it was different in the smart flats, the Chelsea terraces, and places like Hampstead and Earl's Court.

She had thought money, the middle-class way of life, would confer freedom and gaiety on their devotees, but the people she saw were more shackled than the poor in Dounhead, who knew how to enjoy new clothes or a night at the pictures or the prospect of a wedding.

She tried to convey some of her reservations, with a newfound delicacy, to Geoffrey, but he would not discuss his parents and pointed out that he only stayed at home so that he could save towards their marriage. This usually brought the protestation from her that they could marry anyhow, and save together, but he did not think that a good idea, and realizing in an unformulated way that he had the right to find his intellectual and emotional bearings, she did not push the matter. She did not push anything, for fear of losing the marvellous ideal she had carried inside herself for five years of the life they would eventually lead together. But she was sad that their love-making, though ardent, had to be perfunctory, unfulfilling. It was like a physical pain, a central emptiness, which all the innovations and new horizons of her London life did nothing to mend.

It was more than fortuitous she had the Mackenzies. Their hard-edged, thrusting vitality was just what she needed to take her mind off the perplexities of her relationship with

Geoffrey and the demands of her job. They had a strident, lovable two-year-old called Timothy whom she bathed sometimes and put sentimentally to bed. The house vibrated with phone calls from Philip's office and Philip's voice in turn delivering threats, cajolements and encouragment to his staff.

He had the air of a man who knew exactly where he was going and fuelled by the adrenalin of getting there. Generally capable and good-natured, Elizabeth was behind him, smoothing his path, offering encouragement, keeping her lipstick bright. 'He's going to be the editor of the *Clarion*,' she told Eleanor, displaying by the rigidity of her neck tendons one of her few moments of tension.

'Was it Barrie who said there were few sights as impressive as a Scotsman on the make?' Geoffrey asked Eleanor. He regarded Philip as ruthless and unprincipled while Eleanor saw him as a sort of latterday buccaneer, whose exposés sensationally attacked the fiddling and dishonesty that had become a post-war way of life. But it was more than that. Philip was living and enjoying life while Geoffrey hesitated and pondered it. She could feel her sensibility vibrate between the two polarities, like a buzz-saw in a breeze.

When the winter cold came to the scarred and convalescent capital, like a new underground movement parties erupted all over the place, despite rations, gas-fires capable of no more than a candle's peep and bath-water restricted to a few inches. The young men in their pale suède shoes and the girls in their lengthening dresses met to dance and talk and listen to T. S. Eliot on the gramophone. His broken, measured tones, those of a man who had seen and suffered too much, seemed right for the times, just as the cheapened emotionalism of the Warsaw Concerto on the radio brought back the celluloid engulfing flames of war many had been lucky enough to experience only on a cinema screen, though that had also been enough, and sometimes too much.

When Philip and Elizabeth gave a party, Eleanor met a fellow Scot called Tom Wishart who was a reporter on the *Clarion*. Nodding over his second whisky at Geoffrey on the other side of the room, he said in couthy unmistakable Lanarkshire tones, 'What are you doing caught up with yon weedy Nihilist?'

She moved away from him. But sitting on the big settee under the Topolski print of Churchill and Attlee, she eavesdropped shamelessly on Geoffrey and the two other intense-looking young men with whom he was deep in discussion.

She could not follow all that they were saying. They were talking about Nuremberg and the burdens of guilt and reparation. She heard him describe what the death camps had been like, how the Germans there had behaved, what his thoughts were about a Christianity that had allowed such a fate to befall the Jews.

Afterwards, he dropped on to the settee beside her and she said in a low voice, 'You never told me any of that.'

His eyes were very bright. 'Why should I?'

'Because I love you,' she said, 'and I want to understand.'

He gave her a quick, uncomprehending smile and patted her hand, leaping up as his former listeners brought another man into their circle and beckoned him to join them again.

Tom Wishart returned to her side. He was in a thick green tweed suit and you could see where his braces went through the loops in his underpants. Somebody, surely his mother, had knitted him an execrable Fair Isle pullover.

'For each man kills the thing he loves,
By each let this be heard,
Some do it with a bitter look,
Some with a flattering word.'

He quoted the Wilde impeccably, then said, 'You just killed him with a look. What did he say? Ditch him anyhow and come with me to the Casbah.'

She managed a strained smile and he said encouragingly, 'That's better. You shouldnae go around with your heart on your sleeve, you know. Wee bits of it get chipped off and it becomes very painful, especially for folk who bump into you.'

'How would you know?'

'Oh, I know.' She met his eyes. They were honest, intelligent eyes and despite the mass of crinkly, wavy hair and big head she always associated with clever laddies, top of the class and the dux medal, she warmed to him a little more. They became embroiled in a fairly heated argument about whether living in Scotland was tolerable any more.

Scenting sparks, Philip joined them.

'You know it's all parish pump and Kailyard,' he insisted provocatively. 'Whether we like it or not, Scotland's England's annexe. There's no cultural life, no political dynamism and the journalism's all about "silvery salmon slipping up the stream", hog-tied to a kind of pictorial fairyland that doesn't

218

exist for the folk in Motherwell or Glasgow or wherever.'

'Tom Johnston,' Wishart argued. 'He exists. The best we've ever had. I wish he'd stuck to his notion of trying to get all top brass to stick together and refuse to travel south to conduct Scottish business.'

'What does *his* vision amount to? He wants to turn the country into a tourist paradise, feed the trippers on herring and oatmeal and cover the bogland with trees for pit props that nobody's going to want in a few years anyhow.'

'Be fair,' Wishart insisted. 'Since the Scottish Council on Industry started in 1942, something like seven hundred new industries have been started up. That's work for an awful lot of people. Something like ninety thousand. And he's made the banks more alive to Scottish industrial interests – '

'It'll never be enough. You'll see, the Yanks'll leap into the breach and colonize the country – '

'But once he gets the Hydro-Electric Scheme going in the Highlands, think of the difference that's going to make.'

'Most folk think it'll end up providing cheap water power for England.'

Wishart's argumentative force dissipated into a still sort of truculence. 'Have you no vision, man?' he asked, half-despairingly, half-mockingly. ' "Without vision, the people perish." '

'*You* go back,' Philip joked. 'I'm staying here, where the money's better.'

'I might,' Wishart answered. 'Next time somebody says "Pardon" when I ask for a Tube ticket, or refuses to take a Scottish pound note, I'll take my cultural dirk from my stocking and declare war.'

Eleanor retired from the argument, feeling it was all beside the point. If she ever went back – and until that moment the thought had not surfaced in her consciousness – but if she ever did go back it would be because of the small, scarcely legitimate reasons, like wanting to hear the kindly intonation of a voice, the unguarded response on children's faces when you met them in the street, the recognition that there should be time to be kind to a stranger. That was not much evident in London. When the party was ending, she pressed Wishart's hand swiftly before she went to look for Geoffrey.

The next time she was on her own with Geoffrey, she had to drag the conversation back towards the substance of the party. More and more as they circulated that winter, she had noticed his animation in talk with young publishers and journalists. And it was talk from which she felt more and more deliberately excluded. She tried to make him see this.

'You're beautiful,' he said irrelevantly, kissing her. And it was true. She had a robust, fine-skinned, full-bosomed beauty that turned lorry-drivers' heads. But she edged away from the compliment in a sort of disgust. 'Faugh! Don't say that. You mean I'm bound for the role of little wife and mother. Don't worry! I've noticed it. I'll end up like your mater, with never a word to say for myself.'

'I'd rather we didn't discuss her. My mother.'

She laughed at his comically priggish expression. 'I won't be excluded, Geoffrey. I know I haven't been to Oxford or Cambridge, but there's nothing wrong with my intellectual functioning. Don't shut me out.'

His look was more direct than any for a long time. 'There are gaps and longueurs,' he said, 'as there would be with most women.'

She was too furiously angry to reply. As they had been sitting on the deserted top of a bus and were now alighting, it was not the time, in any case. But she stumped silently along beside him after that, the feeling of alienation which she had already acknowledged growing and growing till it filled her whole mind. Englishwomen were different. They kowtowed to the men. Well, she came from a long line of females who had always had their say. Madame Butterfly she was not.

Now she could not bear it when he pulled her up for some variance in grammatical usage. Now she would not listen when he embarked on some long exposition of a philosophical point. She was certain he did not regard her as an equal but as some charming northern savage who had to be tamed and educated gradually. She would not ask him again about marriage. Twice when Tom Wishart came to the Mackenzies' she went out with him instead, because he made her laugh with his Clydeside brand of iconoclastic lunacy.

The trouble was she was in love with a stranger. And the love persisted and would not go away, for either of them. She remembered when it had all been uncomplicated, when in the snow and sand of Calneggie they had been bound together like lovers out of time. And still in his patient eye she saw the truth of what he felt, while in his voice she heard the truth of what he was. Cold grass in Regent's Park and warm seats in the Classic at Marble Arch, common denominators because in both places their love at first had been so urgent and secure, came back to haunt and torment her. In the end she was almost pleading with him to let her go from the scenes and anger and reproaches. And afterwards if a dark head turned in the street, or a pair of narrow shoulders moved ahead of her into the Tube, she prayed for it to be him, though it never was.

So in the end she went back to Scotland and Tom Wishart did, too, because he said he'd had enough. Quite quickly she agreed to marry him because the heart on his sleeve had been chipped too and because though he was a sharp, needling man she saw he had no wish to antagonize people the way he did, but that she could help him. And while she smartened him up and found a Glasgow flat for them, and cooked him things he liked and started his baby indecently soon, he made her laugh and loved her enough for both of them and thought it was just a novelettish girlish whim which made her call the boy Crispin, for Tom was, after all, though short and serviceable, a little bit everyday, it had to be admitted.

'He's frail, Robin,' said Mairi, answering the unspoken words in the caller's eyes. She took him into the shining living-room where, with a small bright fire burning, Nicol sat up in bed, pullover on top of spotless pyjamas.

'Ach, you have the best of it, man,' Robin addressed the invalid. 'It's cold enough out there to freeze your eyeballs. How are you?'

'The streptomycin's wonderful,' Mairi answered for her husband. 'Clears up the coughing and the temperature. But he's still weak. Naturally.'

Robin sat down on the chair he had begun to think of as his, so often now was he a visitor. With his mother dead and his divorce from Catriona completed, he could not pretend he was other than a lonely man. But there were things he could do to help here, and they were appreciated. It was as though the three of them had grown closer out of the urge for survival: a kind of atavistic, psychological huddling together, generating enough warmth to keep them ticking over.

This time, Nicol had almost slipped away. There had been one night Robin had not gone home at all, but had sat with Mairi while a curious, rhythmic struggle for breath and life took place in the corner bed. From each attack of illness Nicol emerged yet thinner, yet frailer, but burning with a kind of heroic, spirited will to live that affected the other two deeply. Now Robin could see that rest and Mairi's careful cooking had done the near-impossible: Nicol had put on a little weight. He was sitting up bright-eyed and smiling, ready for chat.

'You're on the mend. I can see that,' Robin pronounced and was rewarded by Mairi's quick, grateful smile that acknowledged his kindnesses. He always came armed with papers, books, a few scrounged delicacies. But more, he kept Nicol's interest in politics alive.

They loved to argue about the new constitution that Robin's party had adopted. Robin was deeply scornful of it. 'A lot of idealistic hot air,' he growled, while teasingly Nicol was prepared to give credence to its populist and social credit policies while insisting that its wish to de-centralize power, to 'think small', was a commendable and humane conception.

Robin knew well enough that by rejecting all contemporary and current modes of political thought, the Party was in danger of becoming yet more exclusive and rarefied. It was unlikely that the zealot's notion of putting independence first – getting a majority of SNP members returned to Westminster, then withdrawing to found their own 'Dail' like the Irish Sinn Feiners – would ever come to pass. It was a dream, a fantasy, that had no basis in reality. And what he saw happening was a split between Left and Right that would leave the Party so divided as to be almost non-existent.

Today, however, as Mairi busied herself making tea for them, he seemed a little distant and preoccupied after the initial rejoinders, not rising to Nicol's bait as the latter read out from his rustling newspaper the news that a National Assembly was being mooted for Glasgow. The organizers were the Scottish Convention which had been set up by a Scots National dissident, John McCormick.

'What would that be about?' Nicol speculated. 'Another battlecry for Home Rule?'

'It's the one that should have been held in September 1939 and would have been, but for the war. And there is something I want to discuss with you about that,' said Robin heavily. 'But later. I have something else on my mind at the moment.'

'Do you want to tell us what it is?' This from Mairi, handing him his teacup and studying him under level brows.

He fumbled in the pocket of his tweed jacket and brought

out a letter. 'I had this, this morning. Go on. Read it.'

She turned it over in her hands, recognizing the handwriting. 'It's from Catriona.' She gave it back. 'I don't want to, Robin. It's between the two of you.'

'There's nothing intimate there. Just telling me she sails for America next week. The GI bride! Ye gods, sailing with a lot of eighteen-year-olds! Had she told you, Mairi?'

Mairi shook her head. She still saw her cousin and in the intermediary stage of the divorce had given what practical help she could to them both. But she had been too busy recently nursing Nicol to meet Catriona in Glasgow for as much as a quick cup of tea at the Corn Exchange. She told Robin as much.

'Why upset yourself?' she demanded bluntly. She had seen his long fingers tremble as they replaced the letter in his pocket. 'You knew she was going some day. Now it's up to you to make a new start, too.'

With bitterness, he said, 'Think of the archetypal GI bride, and you have her. All she cares about is clothes, nylons, red paint for her fingernails.'

'You sound just like John Knox,' said Mairi, daring to smile.

'All I can see is the years I've wasted. When I wanted to work, the house was full of cackling women, supposed to be on war work but in reality talking about their fur coats or looking for men.'

'You're too hard on her,' said Mairi lightly. 'She wasn't brought up to seriousness. Aunt Sandia and Uncle Dandy had her late in life – and all she knew was being spoiled and pampered.'

'Dear God!' he said savagely. 'Think of her in the bride ship – '

'I read once,' Nicol interposed diplomatically, 'that ninety per cent of all the American servicemen landed up in Scotland at some time or another. So it's no wonder some lasses fell for them.'

'She was no lassie. That is precisely the point.'

'You're crushing a butterfly with a brick,' said Mairi. She held Robin's bruised and angry gaze till he was the first to look away.

'Ah, well,' he said at last, his voice shaking with contained anger but also with resignation, 'it's departure time for me too. I'm leaving the school, I'm selling the house. I'm going over to Scottish Convention.' He looked sharply, a shade sourly triumphant, at Nicol. 'You didn't think I had it in me, did you?'

'Just so long as you're aware what moves you,' said Nicol quietly.

'What do you mean?'

'The politician should always be asking himself: what do I do it for? Are you doing it for Scotland? Or for Robin Chisholm whose heart is sore because his wife's away with the Yankees?'

Mairi moved quickly and instinctively to put two protective hands on Robin's shoulder.

'Don't, Nicol,' she upbraided. 'You have no right to speak to him like that. Robin's impulses are always kind ones. Look how good he's been to us. No brother could have done more.'

She could feel the anger go out of him; knew, just from looking at the back of his head, that she had comforted. He patted her hand and, turning his head, smiled at her. 'I should have had a wife like you. I love her, you know, Nicol. You're not the only one who does.'

He could not have made that statement, however lightly, a year or even six months ago. But now there was a tacit, almost comfortable assumption of his feelings for her between the three of them.

'Aye, but you can't have her,' said Nicol, smiling at Mairi. 'She's the best wife I've got, and I'm sticking to her.'

Mairi bade Robin stay for supper and went into the kitchen to prepare the food, leaving them to their arguments about the wisdom of Robin leaving the Party. When they ate, the discussion moved on to where he should live, once he'd sold the house, and what he should do, when he gave up teaching. They came to no firm conclusions but it was clear that money was not going to be a problem. He would have what he described as 'a fair bit' behind him and hoped to augment that by writing as newsprint became easier.

Robin demolished one of Mairi's home-made scones. 'It would be useful,' he averred, 'if I could take your brother Patie with me when I join the Convention. A war hero. A household name. His wife, too. Do you think he would listen to argument?'

Mairi was so pleased at the good meal Nicol had taken that she was in a receptive frame of mind.

'I tell you what,' she suggested. 'When the weather'

warmer, why don't we all go up to Calneggie and see them?'
She suddenly wanted very much to see Patie out of uniform
again, almost to reassure herself he had come through his
dangerous war unscathed.

'I'll drive us there,' Robin promised.

Mairi rose and drew the curtains, putting another careful
lump of coal on the fire. Robin had brought a small bottle
of precious whisky and she poured the men a measure each,
but abstained herself, protesting that drink was wasted on
her, especially when so scarce. She was thinking of the
Highlands, of Calneggie, of space and air and sunlight. It was
suddenly possible to do so again, because Nicol's breath was
easy and he had eaten everything on his plate.

She had crossed the big scarf over his chest and tucked it
in under his waistcoat. The soft hat that set him apart as
councillor from the rest of cloth-capped Dounhead sat
almost jauntily atop his gaunt, lantern-jawed features, making
him look like the sheriff in some grainy Roy Rogers film.
But he looked eager and happy, so much so that as Mairi
settled the travelling rug over her husband's knees she could
feel the sick constriction of tears at the back of her throat.

'It's good of you to take us,' she said to Robin's neck.

'It was all my idea,' he boasted. 'And look at the day we've
picked.'

It was indeed a spring jewel of a day, the first of its kind
that year. They rattled over the tramlines and cobbles of a
busy morning Glasgow, seeing the inescapable warnings of
'Export or Die' on posters everywhere, alongside invitations
to the evangelical meetings that were like a rash all over the
city, as though in a sort of guilty reflex to the late war.

When they were halfway to Calneggie they stopped on
the banks of a small loch to eat their sandwiches and drink
hot tea from their flasks. All was quiet, theirs was the only
car on the road and when they heard the distant plaint of
sheep in the hills they smiled like exiles on their way back to
paradise.

Camilla, in a full-skirted New Look dress, and Patie, sport-
ing an enormous 'Flying Officer Kite' handlebar moustache,
gave them the warmest of greetings, but Mairi thought she
detected something strained and urgent in their demeanour
and after the welcome meal, it all came tumbling out.

Patie was willing enough to talk politics with Robin, eventually, but there was a more urgent matter in hand. The

damned Hydro-Electric Scheme that Tom Johnston was determined would disfigure the Highlands was going to encompass Calneggie.

Raging, a whisky in his hand following the meal, Patie drew them over to the back windows of the big dining-room. 'There,' he said, a sweep of his arm indicating yellowing wintry hills, a distant glint of loch and river, dark clusters of fir, '*there* is where they are going to put their bloody pylons and turn the country into a fun fair.'

'Wait a minute,' Nicol objected. 'You don't want to believe all those panicky letters in the *Glasgow Herald*. The Board isn't out to destroy the Highlands, merely bring light and work and power where it's needed.'

Camilla intervened. 'And we all know the kind of work, don't we? Electro-metallurgical plants which the poor Highlanders will have to subsidize by paying higher costs. The people in the crofts will be the last to be considered – '

'I don't think it's a diabolical capitalist plan to destroy the north,' put in Robin, but his jocular tone drew furious putting-down glares from Patie and Camilla.

'No consideration has been given to the people who already live here,' argued Camilla. 'They came here for the scenery, to get away from so-called civilization. Why shouldn't there be parts of the world where time can have a halt?'

'Because,' said Nicol, 'with due respect, *you* can generate your own power here, but the farmers up in the hills there have to make do with oil lamps and burn water.'

'Johnston can't have it both ways,' said Patie. 'If he wants the Highlands for tourism, he can't disfigure them with industry. Let him modernize the shipyards on the Clyde with the money. But I'll tell you something: there are no pylons going up at Calneggie.'

'I don't see how you can stop them,' said Mairi mildly.

'Aha.' Patie gave a grunt of pure satisfaction. 'That is where you are wrong, my dear sister. You've just turned up in time to see one of the great rearguard actions of all time. If we can't stop them, we can bally well make it as hard as possible.'

Noting with a grim pleasure the bewilderment on his visitors' faces, Patie at last led them through to the sitting-room and the big log fire and when they were seated, with many a conspiratorial exchange of looks between himself and Camilla, set out his explanation.

'You remember the Army camp set up in the valley during the war? Well, a little bird has brought us the information that it is going to be derequisitioned and handed over to the Hydro-Electric battalions. They can't get timber for new hutments, you see, so they're on the scrounge for what they can get. What they don't need here they'll take elsewhere and my information is they sometimes lift the camps before official permission has come through. Bloody larceny, on top of everything else.

'Well, they ain't going to do it here. There will be no hamesucken if I can help it. I'd rather let the tinkers take the baths and the doors and anything else they can get their hands on, and sell them, even use the wood for their fires —'

'Because they've been in the Highlands for longer than the planners,' added Camilla. 'Just think,' she added, 'of us getting up of a summer morning and looking out at a forest of big steel pylons and electric cables.'

'You'd get used to it,' said Nicol flatly. 'I've got used to getting up and looking out at my neighbours' drawers and rabbit hutch.'

'How you stand it,' said Camilla faintly, 'I'll never know. Dounhead is the last outpost of civilization, to my way of thinking. Like something from the Klondyke during the gold rush.'

'Well, I'll tell you one thing,' said Mairi tartly. 'You are not going to involve us in any of your illegal activities.' She ignored Camilla but gave Patie a hard look. 'Dounhead was good enough for you once. What's made you think you should become a sort of King Canute of Calneggie?'

She saw Nicol and Robin break into slow smiles but Camilla silenced the answer on Patie's lips with a wave of her hand.

'While my brother is away, Patie *is* the laird here. Because I say so. And it's no use looking shocked because we stick to paternalistic notions —'

'Feudal, you mean,' interjected Nicol.

'Call them what you like. People have been happy here, that's what matters. They like having the laird to go to with their problems. They like the feeling someone is looking after their interests. And we're going to look after our own. Ask anybody in the village and they'll tell you they're in full agreement with us. Nobody wants the pylons. Nobody wants industry.'

'Don't they want electricity in their cottages?' demanded Mairi. 'They've got so used to kowtowing they don't know anything else. But it isn't good to treat people as children.

However are they going to learn to stand on their own feet?'

'Things that apply elsewhere don't apply here,' said Patie slowly. 'The folk in Calneggie are the least materialistic people I've ever known. And it's not out of ignorance. Their shelves are full of books, they're great readers. It's as though fresh air and freedom are what matter to them; what sort of roof goes over them when they sleep, they're not all that concerned about.'

'I think,' said Nicol sourly, 'that there's something grovelling about the Highland nature.'

Camilla looked from face to disapprobatory face and gave a forgiving if dismissive smile. 'Don't worry. You don't have to engage in our sabotage if you don't want to. But we had to warn you: tomorrow's D-Day, the day the tinkers arrive. Patie got word through to their head – an old matriarch called Black Meg. I suggest you stay up here and play patience if you don't want to join in the fun.'

The next day it was of course impossible for any of them to stay indoors. As though by a sort of magnet they were drawn along the coast road to the camp site which was from early morning the scene of frenetic activity.

Someone Mairi recognized from the old days as the village plumber and builder had brought his dilapidated lorry and was loading rainwater pipes and wash-basins on to it till it began to groan like a veritable beast of burden. A woman who ran a small boarding-house staggered under the load of a large zinc bath and an old man calmly dismembered a small hut that had once been an office and loaded the timber on to a handcart to take away, as he explained, for fencing.

And then, about eleven o'clock, the tinkers appeared, pushing their hoodless prams and carts, the children barefoot and scabby, all of them looking as though they had never washed in all their history or taken a comb to their hair. Mairi gazed on them with pity and a kind of horror. Camilla had spoken truer than she knew when she said they had been part of the Highlands for longer than the planners. Surely they came from some Godforsaken sect who had been left behind after some internecine massacre. They looked as though they had risen from bracken, spume and bog, been dug out of ditches or resurrected from the turnip heap, a sub-species halfway between inert matter and life, between the quick and the dead.

They said little, but fell on the camp and cannibalized it of anything of worth. Two poor old horses, pulling separate carts, dragged off perilous loads of wash-basins and timber. As a surreal touch, Mairi noticed a disconnected telephone on top of one pile. The tinker children gathered up timber that had been broken or splintered and made a huge fire. At one o'clock, Patie and Camilla delivered a load of food, a bottle of whisky for Black Meg and a month's sweet ration for the children. By nightfall, little was left but white ash from the bonfire, a tin mug and the skeleton of an old filing cabinet, without the drawers.

Patie said then he was ready to talk about going over to Scottish Convention. Anything that would bring Home Rule nearer. He was prepared to sign any declaration. So was Camilla.

Robin said soberly, 'If we want devolution, we have to know the road we'll take. After what happened today, I can't say I have any faith in anything you might come up with, Patie.'

'No, but by heavens, it was fun!'

'It isn't fun to put hardship on folk who need the light and power.'

'I took bombers over Europe till my aircraft was coming apart at the seams.' Lifting his head along with his whisky glass, Patie's gaze wavered towards his wife. 'I fought to keep Scotland beautiful.'

'They won't come here with the bulldozers,' said Camilla, with finality.

'But it's *privilege*,' protested Nicol. 'You can't command the vista. It belongs to the people.'

'Oh, save that for Stalin,' said Camilla angrily. 'The people here want a champion, and that's what they've got.'

'I think,' said Mairi, 'we should leave politics alone. I came to see my brother. And you, Camilla. We've just put a war behind us. Isn't that enough? Let us not fall out.'

Rumbles of temperament died away in the days to come as Calneggie exercised its old magic and calm. One day they saw what looked like a Ministry car drive along to where the camp had been. A small neat man in a raincoat, and carrying a rolled umbrella, got out and walked over the site, before slowly and thoughtfully driving away.

CHAPTER FOURTEEN

The wind scourged down the main street of Dounhead and Mairi, busy putting up her coat collar, had jogged her wicker shopping basket against Robin Chisholm's arm before she recognized him. He steadied her and they both laughed.

'Come to my cottage and have a hot drink,' he said instantly. 'I want to ask your advice about curtains for the living-room. Folk-weave, do you think? Or whatever?' It had taken him almost three years from the word to the deed and he had only recently moved into a double-fronted, solid stone cottage on the outskirts, near the one that Carlie and Donald had once inhabited before they had moved to Arran and retirement.

To Mairi Dounhead had not somehow been the same since they left. She missed Carlie's motherly warmth and instant caring, the endearing way Donald had increasingly turned every chance encounter into a quasi-philosophical discussion, acknowledging with a satirical gleam his elderly penchant for playing the oracle.

She looked quickly away from Robin now, saying, 'Thanks for the idea, but I can't spare the time. Eleanor's with Nicol. I'll get you some snippets of samples from the Co-op, if you like, and drop them off next time I'm passing.'

'Would you?' He looked helpless and relieved. 'I can't go in and pick *curtains*, you see.' He made it sound nefarious, even dangerous, and she smiled again, but like someone out of practice.

'Is he much the same?'

'Oh yes.' Her bright blue eyes watered only minimally from the chafing wind. 'No better, no worse. Just the same.'

'You have to acknowledge, Mairi,' he said carefully, 'that no one could have done more.'

'I can't acknowledge anything. Only his spirit. Anyone else but Nicol would have been gone long ago.'

It had not been his intention to push her to the edge of her control, as he saw he was doing now. So he touched her arm briefly and said, 'Send for me if you need me. You know I'll come.'

'Thank you.' She managed the formality gratefully and

turned to carry out her final errand, at the post office. Then she hurried through the battering wind back to the scheme. It was a day when not many were about. The wind blew the feathery feet of an old Clydesdale pulling a cart for the rag-and-bone man. Patched sheets flew like mainsails from back gardens and mittened toddlers turned a bluey-pink as they fought over tricycles. She wondered if she had been too brisk with Robin. In these recent days she had discouraged even him from calling, wanting Nicol entirely to herself. She had had this feeling of haste, of urgency, of things to complete, and when she asked herself what things there was no answer.

She let herself in at the back door now and saw that her grandchild, Crispin, was playing in the kitchen with an old Meccano set a neighbour had given him. The thoughtful kindness of people overwhelmed her again as she took the little boy up and kissed him. 'I make a car,' he said and briefly she remembered Patie with his cotton-reel and treacle-tin engines. Before that Finn, her father, and before that, old Paterson Fleming the engineer himself. Curious, how qualities were handed on. She sometimes thought that what steadiness she had, she possessed from Grandma Honoria and maybe the legendary Great-Grannie Kate, though she felt they must have been stronger, more resilient, less given to reflection and doubt.

She took a breath now and went through to the living-room where Nicol sat in the big chair by the fire, a blanket over his knees. His head went up in that familiar gesture, seeking air for starved lungs. She saw Eleanor turn, was aware of the wistfulness in her smile. Tom Wishart had gone home to his mother, leaving Eleanor spinning holding-off yarns about his absence to friends and neighbours. Mairi knew he was not altogether to blame. They might or they might not salvage matters. Eleanor had been difficult, prickly, unreasonable, unable to define what ailed her except that looking after little Crispin in an old cold-water flat was not what she wanted out of life. Her shoulders looked hunched, defeated. *Not now, lovie*, Mairi addressed her silently. *Can't you see he's going? What will we do when he's gone?*

Nicol said, marshalling each syllable, stretching the oxygen, 'Come and get warm.' She took out the tea-bread she had bought, gave the little boy a biscuit, made a pot of tea and put her rationed sugar into Nicol's cup. He liked it when Eleanor came, and watched the little boy, his grandson, with a look compounded of pride and something keener than

231

joy. But she was jealous of the demands they made on his strength and concerned that Eleanor should keep her own problems from him as much as possible. When Eleanor and Crispin went, she could feel strain run weakly out of her. She put him to bed, gave him his medicine and a hot-water bottle, sat near him so that if he felt like talking, she would be there. She turned the pages of the *Woman's Pictorial* Eleanor had brought her, seeing the same print over again, not taking it in.

He slept for a while and when it grew dark she drew the curtains, built up the fire and then on a strange whimsical impulse took her best dress out from the wardrobe and put it on. Once she had been quite plump but now her clothes hung on her. She liked the dress, however. It was of a dark chocolate brown rayon, with bands of grosgrain sewn horizontally across the bodice, and a neat cream satin collar with an orange velvet bow. She pushed her feet into her best court shoes, hearing the times he'd praised the neatness of her ankle, turning her foot about to make sure the compliment wasn't misplaced.

Then she did her hair. She still wore it in the pageboy style that had grown popular during the war, taken up in one deep wave at the front then turned in at the sides and back. It suited the peculiar, silky heaviness of her thick, two-toned locks, still maizey-fair on top and dun as a sparrow's wing beneath.

Lipstick. A little judicious rouge, *pace* Grandma Honoria. She went stumbling through the dark lobby and into the room where he lay with only the firelight for illumination. She did not want harsh light. She sat down and took his hand.

'Eleanor gone?' She nodded. He had forgotten the parting kisses, then. Just as well, for Eleanor's face had crumpled. 'Would you like a wee toddy?' He nodded, and she brought him it in an egg cup, holding it to his lips.

'You're looking very perjink,' he told her.

'Just felt like it.' She put her hand up to her hair in an ineffably feminine gesture that made him smile.

'All for me, is it?'

'No,' she teased. 'It's for Santa Claus. Crispin says he'll be coming soon, down the lum, with a fire-engine for him.'

'It's nice without the light on. I'm lying here looking at you and thinking of the time you came down the pit to tell me you were going to marry me.'

'Not in so many words.'

'No, words were a shade superfluous. And the funny thing is, I had known you would come back.'

'You always had a big opinion of yourself.'

'I wish I had it all over again, Mairi. I would do it different.'

'In what way?' She had brought her face very close to his, so that he would spend the least possible energy on the words.

'I don't know.' To her alarm, his breathing became laboured, distressed, but he pushed himself up on his pillow and said, 'I only know I made a botch of it.'

'I don't know what you mean,' she said falteringly.

'I wanted to write. I hadn't the words. I wanted to make things better for the folk of Dounhead and I hadn't it in me.'

'You tried. Surely that's what counts.'

'I should have gone back down the pit.'

'Not you,' she said. 'Besides, you're talking as though it's all over. When you're better, maybe you should start that book you always wanted to write.'

He fell back on his pillows, his breathing shallow but easier. 'I wish I could type,' he said, almost petulantly.

'I'll learn to type. I'll go to night school. You write it and I'll type it.' She was past mistress of the nourishing promise.

'We'll see. You never know.' He smiled at her. 'Your hair is bonnie, Mairi. Have I not always said you have bonnie hair?'

She laid her cheek next to his. 'You always have. But I think we've talked enough. You try and have a wee rest and I'll just work about.'

She felt a curious peace fall about her as she carried out the mundane evening tasks. She was aware he sometimes slept and sometimes watched. She wanted to cry out to him *We've been happy together*, but it didn't need saying. There had been a perfect rapport between them for a long time.

That night she chose not to go to bed. She sat up in the big chair watching the fire sink lower and lower and at one point she rose and put her heavy tweed coat around her. It seemed she felt neither discomfort nor cold.

She did not know exactly when he left her. At about daybreak she got stiffly up and went over to the bed. He looked very peaceful and still. She felt his hand and it was cold. She sank to her knees and stayed with him, dry of tears, until the morning.

'The best way,' said Eleanor hardly, 'is to get up and do something. Put on your coat and come out with me. Robin says we must get more signatures.'

'What would I be doing, working for Scottish Convention?' said Mairi irritably.

'Well, even the Church of Scotland backs the signing of the Covenant,' Eleanor pointed out. 'All it wants is a consensus on home rule. Dad would have gone along with that. Come on, Mum. It cuts across parties this time and besides, you know you've always had a sneaking regard for the Scot Nats.'

'A bunch of cranks.' Mairi hoisted Crispin on to her knee and kissed him.

'What? Robin Chisholm? Uncle Patie and Aunt Camilla, maybe, up there in their Highland keep. But Robin's always been consistent. And he wouldn't have filled Dad's old place in the council if people weren't ready to listen to him. Come on, Mum, we mustn't give up.' She pointed her finger dramatically and Crispin giggled, enjoying the dramatics. 'Your country needs you.'

Mairi did as she was told. In some ways it was easier if you just flowed with the tide. In the six months since Nicol had died she had grown very close to her daughter. Eleanor had seized the chance to give up the flat in Glasgow and come and live with her, bringing Crispin.

There had been stormy, intransigent meetings with Tom Wishart, who came to stay occasional week-ends, but the marriage did not look as if it could be mended. Mairi could not put her finger on quite why she felt sorrier for Tom than she did for Eleanor, but perhaps it was because she saw him at some deep unconscious level as the injured party. There was some gaping hurt in him that made him vicious and wild in his accusations, like a little boy hurling charges of not being loved at his mother. Eleanor was always preternaturally calm in her determination not to set up home with him again as yet.

'Do you know what it was like,' she had charged him, 'living in a place where nobody knows you with only a baby to talk to?'

'It would have got better,' Mairi had intervened. 'Babies grow. You get to know people.'

'Not the po-faced lot up our close, arguing about washing stairs and leaving pram marks.' And Eleanor had crossed long elegant legs dismissively, her face set as hard as granite.

Mairi was in favour of letting time pass, of giving both young people time to lick their wounds and reflect. It was unthinkable that they should contemplate divorce, as both had hinted, when they had been together for such a short time. And there was little Crispin to think of, the effect it would have on him if he saw little of his father. Divorce was only something to enter into as a last resort. Although it was painful for her, she tried to share her own experiences with Eleanor, of the time she and Nicol had lived apart, only to find when they came together again their emotional commitment had survived stronger than ever.

One evening when Robin Chisholm had called Eleanor's veneer of harshness had cracked and she had brought up the name of Geoffrey Benson. It had been during a discussion of English attitudes towards Scotland and she had brought forth some of Geoffrey's minor prejudices with what seemed to Mairi an untoward bitterness.

Clumsily Robin had said, 'It sounds as though there wasn't a lot of love lost between you and your Englishman!'

'No,' Eleanor had contradicted him, 'on the contrary, I did love him. Too well, as it turns out.'

'You left him,' Mairi had pointed out.

'Yes. Notice the pattern?'

Into the awkward silence that had followed, while Eleanor's fingers flew like demons over her knitting, Robin had quoted:
' "I hate and love, don't ask me to explain the contradiction." '

'Catullus.' Eleanor's eyes had been bright and hard. 'You didn't know I'd read him, did you? "I only know the pain." Oh, Geoffrey taught me that, too. He liked Catullus, especially the dirty bits about boys in bed with older men.'

'Eleanor!' Mairi had been shocked. So clear had her disapprobation been that quite quickly Robin had shuffled up the books he had been lending and gone home. Afterwards, Mairi had been unable to stop herself commenting on the unsuitability of the conversation.

Eleanor had faced her squarely, half-laughing. 'Ma,' she said, using the appellation she kept for when she was being angry or facetious, 'we've all got to learn to be a lot less repressed. You know that's what's wrong with this country, don't you? We go around ignoring how things are, stating what we think they should be. We're needing to develop our critical faculties and that means being honest with ourselves. Not mealy-mouthed.'

That had hurt, the mealy-mouthed bit, as Mairi painfully

remembered Nicol had used the same expression. But it acted as a sort of bracer now, as she stepped out down the street with Eleanor and Crispin, the latter protesting in stentorian tones against the indignity of his push-chair. But it was convenient because there was a carrier between the handles which held the pages of the Covenant.

Because she was Nicol's widow and still in black, she was received in a kindly fashion wherever she called, though not everyone wished to sign, by any means. There was still a good deal of resistance to what were seen in the main as eccentric and unpractical notions. Although support for the post-war Labour government was on the wane throughout the country, in Dounhead it was still strong, and Conservative voters, while making occasional sympathetic noises, saw the Covenant as an irrelevancy in the present situation. But Robin was quite a popular councillor and those who liked him signed the Covenant, indulgently. After nearly three hours, Mairi and Eleanor were ready to take the signatures to Robin's cottage, where he welcomed them in, providing hot coffee and biscuits and milk for Crispin.

The exercise and argument had enlivened rather than tired the women and the evening turned out a happy one. Robin even had the temerity to ask Mairi's help once more with the curtains he still had not bought for the living-room and she laughingly agreed, saying she would also make them up and hang them for him, otherwise the job would never get done.

Going home in the pleasant dusk, with Crispin falling soundly asleep in his push-chair, Eleanor said, 'You and he will get together one day, and no bad thing.' Then she added, 'He's got a strange, sleeping sort of look to him at times. Like a man under an anæsthetic.'

'Mind your tongue,' her mother snapped at her. Even as she loosened the sleeping child from his pram straps, Mairi's face remained forbidding and thundery and after one or two further attempts at conversation, Eleanor finally gave up. The next day Mairi said the house needed a clean from top to bottom.

'You go to the Co-op and get Robin Chisholm's curtain material,' she ordered. 'He needs twelve yards of the fawn and brown stuff I showed you the other day.' And when she had made the curtains up, it was Eleanor she insisted take them to Robin.

'I haven't time to spend on that man's house,' she defined

the situation unequivocally enough. 'I have enough to do in my own home and I might as well make it clear to him.'

Eleanor listened to it all as calmly as she could and decided it was wisest to say no more on the matter. In any case, she thought it was time to take up office work, if not in Glasgow then in Bellnoch, and her mother would have to look after Crispin till he was old enough to go to school.

Sometimes she saw a look of chill bewilderment on her mother's face that she learned to overcome with little gestures like making tea or asking for help with a sewing pattern. But mostly her mother set about proving herself right about the demands of her own housework and although Eleanor took up some more work for Scottish Convention, Mairi declared herself uninterested and wore her No Trespassers look whenever Robin's name was mentioned or he himself called by.

'If Christmas at Calneggie is what you want, Eleanor, I'll go along with it,' said Tom Wishart reasonably. Whenever he came to see his wife and the boy now he was like a man walking on egg crates, Mairi thought; terrified he put his foot in it, yet watching his wife's reactions so scrupulously he didn't always see where he was going, and then it was crunch! splat! and yolk on his face.

'Mother and I are going, and Crispin. Whether you come or not is up to you,' said Eleanor carelessly.

'Don't you want me to come?'

'It's all the same to me.'

'Maybe Crispin should have both of us, for Christmas at least.'

So they went on, in the marital dance she had come to know so well, thought Mairi. She was sometimes amused and sometimes exasperated and occasionally fearful. Since she had started going out to work again and become financially independent, Eleanor had become quite overtly aggressive all round. She was playing some complicated psychological game with Tom in which he was being forced into the subservient role, whether he knew it or not. When she tried to redress the balance, Mairi was mercilessly put in place by her daughter. 'Keep out of it,' said Eleanor fiercely. 'This is no concern of yours, Ma.'

Mairi at least was glad to be getting away to Calneggie when Christmas Eve came round. She had not seen Patie nor Camilla since Nicol's funeral and the letter urging them all to come for Christmas had been warm and urgent. Robin was taking them, of course, for he was the one with the car and the petrol. He had been determined to go in any case, with or without passengers. There was some matter concerning the Convention between him and Patie which he would not talk about idly in the car. Mairi thought, not for the first time, that men played politics like little boys playing with cigarette cards. 'I have more inside information/cigarette cards than you have.' 'I won the last game, so I start this one.' 'Look at my standing in the Party/the pile of cards I've won.' Robin was being deliberately mysterious about something, but whether it was a bid for attention (the small boy again) or some genuine preoccupation, she could not be sure. It lent a sort of spice to the journey. If it weren't for people worrying about the Korean War escalating into something much worse, this Christmas could have had the best feeling about it of any year since 1939.

She was thinking in terms of other people, of course. Not of herself, for tearing at any carefully woven threads of complacency or pleasure was the loss of Nicol, a raw and burning edge that was irreducibly there. There had been the times when his name had broken from her in a cracked involuntary cry, and the tears had streamed down her face even as she went about her normal, everyday duties. And that one occasion when she had willed him back so strongly she had been afraid to turn round in case he was actually there, as she felt him to be. These days were behind her now, but there was still the raw edge, like a place where a limb had been wrenched away, part of her own being.

But it was good to see Eleanor and her husband sitting next to each other, smiling conjointly at Crispin's excited Christmas babble. And she was pleased to see Robin's cheerfulness, for despite his public busy-ness there must be times when he felt oppressively alone in the stone cottage. She felt it a matter for congratulation that she had been able to keep a slight distance between them in the past year without hurt or indifference creeping in.

People they raced past in the car looked more animated, too. The English habit of a lit tree in the window was catching on and the shops in all the little towns made a brave display with reindeer and cotton-wool snow and cheerful Santas.

'My God,' said Tom Wishart nervously as they neared Calneggie. 'Nobody warned me what the roads would be like.'

'Never mind the roads. Look up the valley there at the houses. All with electric light.' Robin took a hand from the steering-wheel to point.

'But where's the sign of industry? I thought the Hydro-Electric Scheme was going to be another Tennessee Valley wonder. They would have been better to spend the money on accessible roads, wouldn't they?'

Robin laughed. 'Patie wouldn't agree with you. They like being inaccessible.'

Eleanor interjected drily, 'And I suppose the Calneggie villagers are quite happy to pop down to the post office for their National Assistance and Family Allowances, wearing their free National Health specs and jiggling their free National Health teeth. They'll be quite happy to drink themselves into happy obscurity, jobless but blissful.'

'It isn't as bad as that,' said Mairi.

'No, but it could be.'

'That's the scenario for post-war Britain,' said Tom, uncomfortably aware as he did so that he was trying to hand down journalistic cliché as holy writ.

The lodge house was bursting with light and music and conviviality, like a great surprise parcel. 'Baby, It's Cold Outside' blaring from a radio seemed appropriate to the travellers as they hurled their stiff and frozen forms over the threshold at a solid wall of heat from the big log fires.

Surprisingly, there were other house guests, two young kilted men and their wives and what turned out to be an overspill from the laird's party at the Big Place. People of all ages were drinking and laughing and talking loudly. Whatever the rationing stringencies elsewhere, there seemed to be no shortage of meats laid out on the big banqueting table; hams, venison, hare and fowl.

Mairi could feel herself withdraw from such overpowering conviviality and went in search of Nellie. In the kitchen, they held each other wordlessly for a long moment. Then Nellie turned back to her pots and oven, her face, as she described it, 'fair bursilt' with heat and exertion.

'They're making a night of it tonight,' she said resignedly.

Mairi picked daintily at a broken crust from a mince pie.

'Are they happy, Nellie, do you think? Patie and Camilla? I never thought they would be.'

'He's not interested in other women, if that's what you mean.'

'The age difference doesn't seem to count. That's good.'

'They've made the Highlands into their bairn, as it were. Always some new scheme for home industries – '

'But it'll never be enough, will it?'

'How should I know?' Nellie brought out a huge fish pie from the oven, redolent with Finnan haddie, and scattered it with dried parsley and chopped hard-boiled egg. 'He's started on the cars again. Some Scots-Americans are putting up the money. Wants to try out a new engine. She moans about the expense, but she lets him go ahead.'

Mairi sighed. 'I'd hoped he'd left his speed mania behind him.'

'He has to be best,' Nellie pronounced. 'He's one of those — what do you call them? — chauvinists. One of those who has to have Scotland best at everything.'

'There are a lot of them about.'

Nellie smiled grimly. 'Aye, but it gets wearying. It wouldn't be so bad if there was some truth in it. But that crowd down there are nothing but a bunch of dreamers.'

'And you were always practical, Nellie.'

'I believe in getting on with it. Here.' Nellie handed her a covered dish with mashed potato and turnip in it. 'Even if you are a guest, you can make yourself useful. And make sure Eleanor and her man get first go of this lot, before the other gannets settle round.'

Mairi saw little of Patie or Camilla that evening. They were always part of some laughing, chattering group. Both came up to her to push food or drink at her and reassure her there would be more time for family talk later. She tried hard to be part of the hectic festivities but she was glad when she could finally slip away to bed. Even then, she could hear the beat of music and dancing and the high-pitched laughter of people with no thought of going home in their minds.

The next morning, Mairi had been convinced that only little Crispin would be ready for the excitements of Christmas Day itself. At six o'clock the rattle of a drum and a shriek of triumph heralded fulfilment of all his expectations and the drum was beaten till a chorus of adult voices pleaded with him to desist. But contrary to Mairi's forecast, everyone turned up for breakfast, a little bleary-eyed and shaggy-haired, perhaps, but filled with anticipation. Christmas in the Lowlands had always been a fairly low-key affair. Perhaps the Highlands were different.

There was no lunch, just a huge tureen of soup and a selection of titbits, for dinner was going to be early and Camilla promised that Christmas Eve would have nothing on the *ceilidh* there would be on Christmas Night.

By one o'clock, hiatus had set in by common consent. Eleanor had taken Crispin to his room for a rest and the others were quietly reading or dozing or turning over presents. Mairi, looking out at the hard, dour day, nevertheless thought it might be pleasant to stroll along the sea road. She tightened the belt of her elderly tweed coat and wrapped a big camel-coloured scarf about her ears and neck. The inhospitable cold almost made her recant, but after a little it did not seem so bad. She stood on the edge of the sands, watching the gulls, allowing her mind to empty. The quiet and space loosened knots of tension in her, so that after a pause she walked further, her steps springy and energetic and the pink of exercise creeping up her cheeks.

A little guiltily, after half an hour, she started back. She should be helping Nellie, talking to Camilla, being sociable. She was more ready for the hurly-burly now, even looking forward to it.

Rounding the rocks at the point, she saw Robin coming in her direction. Up here, his kilt and Ulster greatcoat seemed less of an affectation. He was beaming hugely as he saw her, beating his arms to get warm.

'You're mad, leaving a log fire for this!'

'It did me good.'

He looked at her pink face. 'I can see that. Now let's get back to warmth and comfort.' He drew her arm through his. 'I wouldn't have come after anyone but you.'

'There was no need to follow me. I'm a big girl.'

'But there was. I wanted to.'

They both stopped, she in fright and aggravation, he in a stubborn determination.

'Robin – '

'Let me speak! Let me speak! You can't go on fending me off for ever. I'll tell you what I want, and I ask you to listen. Will you do me the honour?' The formal words were almost peremptory.

She pursed up her lips. 'Very well.'

'First of all, I want to tell you that my feelings haven't changed. Next, that I want you to marry me. I want you to come and live at the cottage and turn it into a home. Even allowing for your mourning of Nicol, it is time you gave some thought to me.'

She laughed. She had not meant it to be as heartless as it sounded, but it had been totally involuntary. 'You can't come out here and *bludgeon* me into marrying you. I like you as a friend.'

'No.' His face, brought close to hers, was suddenly as dour as the day itself. The expression darkened and twisted till she was suddenly afraid. He put his arms about her, so that her own were pinioned, and he kissed her roughly and angrily.

She made a joke of it. 'Robin! Desist!'

He was rubbing his cheek against hers, as though to raise a spark of responsive emotion in her. He took her hands and chafed them. He held her by the hair and scarf, kissing her face again. Then, as he got no response, he threw himself away from her. 'Jesus!' he cried, 'but you're a cold-hearted bitch. What does a man have to do to melt you?'

To her horror, she saw that he was almost weeping, his mouth twisted in self-disgust, all his previous bravado melted.

In conciliation, she said, 'I don't want any man after Nicol, Robin.'

'No, I know that,' he said doggedly. 'You have this fixed, misbegotten notion you're capable of love for only him.' He gave her a savage, unforgiving look. 'I could teach you to love me. I could bring you out of yourself in a way he never did. I'm too old now to cast around for somebody else.'

'I wouldn't say that.'

He made a dismissive movement of his hand. 'I'll not ask you again, you know. You have to the end of this day to let me know. If you'll not come a little of the way towards me, you can remain where you are till you're as dry as an old husk. And I'll damn you, Mairi Fleming, the way you've damned me.'

'Christmas Day, nineteen-fifty,' said Patie, rising from his seat at the head of the dinner table and holding up his glass of whisky. 'We drink to Christmas Day, Camilla and I, and to all our good friends and family who are with us today.'

He looked down at the twin rows of guests in their paper hats and smiled a triumphant, teasing smile. It had been the best meal any of them had tasted since the war, and it showed in glazed eyes and replete expressions. He kept holding the glass up and at the foot of the table Camilla's was held up towards him. She wore a black dress of faille satin with long black evening gloves and a silver Celtic cross at her neck. The effect was bold and dramatic. There was something between them, some current, some vibration and still the glasses remained aloft while their smiles grew broader and a seething burst of speculation rose from the diners.

'I have to tell you,' said Patie, with dramatic deliberation, 'that this historic day the Scottish Coronation Stone has been successfully abstracted from Westminster Abbey and brought back to Scotland where it belongs.'

Chairs fell back as the men leapt to their feet and shook hands with each other and the hubbub was deafening. How many of them had known about the plot, Mairi could not judge, but she was sure it had been this that had made Robin so determined to be present at Calneggie on Christmas Day.

The noise rose to a crescendo and a few minutes later the iron bell at the door announced more jubilant Convention supporters with the laird at their head.

'What do you think of it?' Robin confronted Mairi as she tried to find her way through the mêlée in the dining-hall, to a less crowded scene in the outer parlour.

'Will it do anything?' she demanded. 'It's a fine bit of Highland fun and games, but it's just storybook nonsense, is it not?' She was trembling a little, not able to look at him directly after what had happened earlier in the day.

He took her elbow and steered her into the quieter room. 'You helped to get signatures for the Covenant,' he reminded her. 'And two million people took the trouble to put their names to it. But as long as Labour's in power, the devolutionists aren't going to get a hearing. It comes from our horse-trading with the other parties. Well, we have to show them we mean business. We *will* be listened to.'

'It'll be jail for whoever did it.'

'They'll never find it, nor the men who did it.'

'Do you and Patie know who did it?'

'If we did, do you think we'd admit it?' He gave a slow, ingratiating smile. 'Even at the level, as you see it, of a bit of Highland fun, can you not join in the celebrations? We've trumped the English for once and made Attlee choke on his turkey.'

He began to rumble with laughter and Mairi found herself joining in. Thereafter the evening became a wild charivari, with bagpipes played for the dancing of reels, Gaelic songs and mouth-music and a ferocious gaiety.

In the small hours more food was brought in and Mairi helped Nellie serve coffee to those who wanted it. Although the younger guests were still dancing, the rest settled down to more sober speculation as to what the stealing of the Stone of Scone might spark off.

It was Robin who came up with the most practical answers. An awakening of the national consciousness was the best that could perhaps be hoped for: but it was such an imaginative stroke that its consequences would reverberate into the unforeseeable future. It would rattle the complacent and frighten the recalcitrant, like the Scottish Secretary, Arthur Woodburn, who had after all been sympathetic to devolution during the war, then turned his coat afterwards.

Discussions as to how the country might develop economically and culturally if independence ever came were tending towards argument and confusion when one of the young kilted firebrands broke in.

'We've decided to elect a monarch,' he announced. 'Now that we've got the Coronation Stone, we need a king to sit on it.'

'Or a queen,' somebody suggested.

After strong lobbying by the women, it was decided it should be a queen, picked from the company. The crown would go to the person who came up with the best suggestion as to what she would do if chosen.

There were a number of wild and ribald suggestions, from libbing the Cabinet as the English had castrated poor William Wallace, to sending Arthur Woodburn on a slow boat to China. Mairi alone refused to come up with a suggestion, but when two of the men brought in a great carved oak chair from the outer hall, Eleanor and Tom placed a yellow paper hat, serrated like a crown, on Mairi's head and Camilla dragged a fringed shawl from the grand piano and draped it about her shoulders. Robin led her up to the seat and held her hand while she stood abashedly smiling, only half entering into the nonsense and play-acting.

And it was then as though some inspired spirit of mischief entered her. She began passing down the ranks, doing a wickedly accurate imitation of George VI's spouse, the little, winsome Queen Elizabeth, handing out an imaginary flower here, accepting a gracious compliment there, waving a delicate hand at the crowds.

It was so funny and touching people laughed till the tears came. Afterwards, the dancing started up again, this time not the traditional dances but foxtrots and quicksteps and the rumba, and in her plain blouse and tweed skirt Mairi was no longer like some self-chosen outcast, but part of the spirit of midwinter festival that trailed through the lodge rooms, a joyous *ceilidh* the like of which, certainly, the southern parliamentarians seeking the trail of the Stone would never know, for you had to be Scottish and preferably of Highland blood to be part of it.

It was Robin who danced the last waltz with Mairi at five o'clock in the morning. Leaving the formalities aside, younger guests were bringing bacon and eggs in from the kitchen and eating them on the stairs. After this, Patie announced, there would be no more music and they must all go to bed.

'It's been good to see you enjoying yourself,' said Robin. 'And they were right to make you queen.'

He could feel her body, still surprisingly young and firm, suddenly slump tiredly against him, and he held her so close it was like an intimate embrace. He said against her ear, 'I still want your answer.'

She did not move away from him. He could feel her allowing herself to flow into him, a giving and an acquiescence that came in the end so suddenly he was shaken.

'Mairi?'

Her smile and her nod were faint yet had a curious, dream-like intensity. He felt suddenly ashamed that he might have used the occasion to his advantage. But the grasp of her hand on his was warm, womanly, sweetly strange, and he knew with an utter conviction as they walked off the floor, she no more wanted to relinquish it than he did.

Undressing to get into bed before daybreak, Eleanor pulled aside the heavy velvet curtains and looked out at snow just beginning. Gazing towards the big heap of white stone that was Calneggie, her mind peopled the landscape with soldiers. One bent to pick up snow and turned his face to smile at her, showing an overlapping tooth . . . She sighed and turned away.

'What did you think of it?' she asked her husband.

'The *ceilidh*? It was a revelation to me.' They climbed into bed, whispering, drawing up the blankets against the nipping cold. 'I thought it was tremendous. All that singing and play-acting. And did you ever see such dancing? The men even. Where did the rest of the world get the idea we're a nation of po-faced Sabbatarians? It was like going away back into the past, into a kind of pre-Christian era when pleasure came first and you worked at it.'

'I asked for your comment, sir,' said Eleanor. 'Not a dissertation on Highland man.'

He put his arm around her, as though absent-mindedly. 'It caught your mother up in it, whatever magic it was. She turned into a different person before our eyes.'

'I can remember, when I was wee, she liked to sing and dance,' said Eleanor thoughtfully. 'But then it was all sickness and poverty with my dad.'

'Don't be sad.'

She turned with a deliberate gesture and pushed her head into his broad chest. 'But what did you really think, Tom-Tom? They were so jubilant about the Stone you'd think they'd solved all Scotland's problems, straight off.'

'"It's a poor heart that never rejoices." That's what my dear old mum says.'

'They're mostly folk with money or land.'

'How do you deduce that?'

'Only the folk who are sure of their identity, their worth, wear the kilt the way these young men did tonight. One of them, I know for a fact, owns so much land he doesn't know what to do with it.'

'Where is this taking us? Can we not lie down and I can come on top of you?'

She hit him irritably. 'Don't be so crude! I suppose I'm trying to say they don't take our problems seriously. Uncle Patie and Camilla, for example. They see themselves as sort of gladiators, fighting for their romantic notion of Scotland. But there's no romance where we come from. Is there?'

'If you're asking me, I have to say no to that. Not much romance growing up in Glasgow beside the River Cart, with its delectable tin cans and dead cats. Not a lot of romance about my schooldays, either.' He leaned up again on one elbow. '*Pish-tunk, pish-tunk, pish-tunk.* That was the noise the big steam hammers made at Weirs and you heard it all the time you were in the playgie – *pish-tunk, pish-tunk, pish-tunk.* The men came out of there with tin ears and that look folk have who've just missed the gist of your last sentence.'

'Jelly pieces,' said Eleanor, 'that's what I was brought up on. A big doorstep of bread and jam when you were hungry –'

'My mother used to wrap mine up and throw it down into the yard from the third floor of our tenement.'

He held her, rolled her over and placed his full weight on top of her.

'A gentleman takes the weight on his elbows,' she protested.

'Not tonight he doesn't.' He covered her mouth with his

while his member found its own way between her legs and she curled round him like a mewling kitten.

'What bloody nonsense,' he said later, 'to think that we can live apart.'

'It was the drink and the music.'

'Say you don't mean that.'

'I'm thinking of Dounhead and Cathcart and Motherwell and everywhere and the wind that whistles up the dirty closes. It's still jelly pieces, isn't it?'

'Shall we try again?'

'Do you think we should?'

Part Four

CHAPTER FIFTEEN

The little boy in the shabby kilt, open-necked shirt and brown sandshoes raced along the sea road towards Calneggie, face white under its liberal sprinkling of freckles. Twice he had fallen in the heavy bracken coming down the hill and scratched himself, and now he needed to do number one but dared not stop even for that.

There was a man lying bleeding to death up there on the hill road that led to the hamlet of Kilnor, just next to the postbox set in a wall where Crispin had been about to post a card to his best friend Ian, back in Glasgow. Well, the postbox *had* been set in the wall. Now it lay with bits of jagged bricks stuck to it, face forward on the grass verge. The man had been lying sprawled at the wayside, just as though he had been drunk, but his right hand had been such a gory mess that Crispin, no faintheart when it came to cut knees or bloody foreheads, had not been able to look at it for too long.

The man had been groaning and when, greatly daring, Crispin had gone reluctantly up to him to ask 'Can I do anything, mister?' had said the one word, 'Help!' which Crispin felt now, running his heart out, was just how you imagined it would sound when you saw it in a comic, a big balloon above somebody's head. 'HELP!' He hoped the man wasn't dead yet. He was running as fast as he could. Nobody could have run faster, not even Ian, who was an inch and a half taller. And even as he ran, his brain had been functioning with unusual, crystal clarity, not at all in that dreamy way that so exasperated his mother.

Would he go and tell her first? She would be busy at this time laying the tables in the dining-room for lunch in the waitress uniform he didn't much care for but which she said was all right as a kind of joke. She was making Good Money helping Uncle Patie and Aunt Camilla this summer. Dad's face always went a bit sour when she said that but there were his own school fees and the new suite she wanted for their house in Clarkston. She liked keeping up with the Joneses, whoever they were, and Crispin certainly had no objections to spending the summer at Calneggie. It was his notion of heaven on earth.

Once Aunt Camilla's brother had owned the Big Place, but then he had died and left it to her and it had been decided because of Debts to turn Calneggie into a hotel. Uncle Patie supervised it but Aunt Camilla had the estate cottages to see to. She wore a tartan cape and a bonnet with a cairngorm brooch with a real eagle feather in it. Crispin's private view was that she could have gone straight into his *Beano* comic, but he liked her. She was teaching him the Gaelic.

He had a terrible pain in his side as he reached the hotel gates and the alternative plan that had been formulating as he ran seemed suddenly the better one. He would go to the big barn where Uncle Patie might be working on the car and tell *him*. If the jeep was there, they could take the coast loop to Kilnor and get the man to a hospital. If he wasn't dead. Crispin suddenly felt very weak at the knees, as though the Last Ounce of Strength was Ebbing from his Body. This holiday, so many things were happening just like they were out of books. Heroes or treks across sand or ice, giving their All. Now him. He staggered into Patie's workshop, holding his side dramatically.

'There's a man dying. Up the hill at Kilnor. Hurry up and come!'

Patie dropped the piece of metal he was holding and it made a clanging, reverberating sound on the stone floor. But the next minute the jeep was through the gates and his great-uncle was quizzing him. 'What did he look like? Was he young or old?' His face had gone all pinched and white under the big moustache that Crispin always felt the urge to play with.

'He was – youngish. Well, maybe – oldish.' Crispin was aware he was not distinguishing himself under interrogation but it was difficult for him to know ages once you got over about fourteen. Up to fourteen, he was sound. He could bet anybody that up to fourteen he could guess anybody's age. If it was a boy, that is. Girls were different.

'Can't you be more specific?' Patie demanded with an intense irritability. 'Had he a shotgun? Could he have been shooting rabbits?'

'For the myxomatosis?' asked Crispin. He was pleased with the way he got his tongue round this big word that had defeated Ian back in Glasgow. Ian had said the disease would wipe out every rabbit that ever lived, including his pet white one called Bonnie, but Mr Know-All hadn't been able to pronounce the word. 'Myxomatosis,' said Crispin now, with satisfaction. 'Do you know, Uncle, Ian Ferguson can't even say myxomatosis?'

What with holding on for dear life and thinking about rabbits Crispin had momentarily forgotten the injured man. But the jeep jolted now over rough ground and halted near the Kilnor postbox and the man was still there, moving his head slightly but lolling like a badly-stuffed toy. Crispin was suddenly aware of how bright and hot the sun was, sparkling like diamonds out on the Sound. And how quiet the air was, save for the sound of a peewit, disconsolate over a field of corn.

'Hamish, man!' said Uncle Patie, kneeling. 'What went wrong?'

If he pulled himself down very low in the big chair that was turned to the window, they might not even see he was there. He knew his mother would be furious if she knew he was eavesdropping, but the need to Find Out had become paramount. He held the jotter and pencil carefully in front of him. If discovery came, he could always say he had been drawing and unaware of anyone else being in the room. *A lie. A lie. A palpable lie.* He scrunched himself up into an even smaller ball. There was a certain amount of delicious terror in defiance.

Aunt Camilla's voice. 'When the sergeant came to the hospital, did you tell him the same thing? That his hand had been caught in a game trap?'

'Yes.'

'And he believed you?'

'No more than Sister McCallum. But he can't prove otherwise.'

'It's bound to be in the papers.' His mother's voice. 'Tom's been on the phone to me, but I didn't let on I knew anything. They're sending somebody up for a picture of the postbox.'

'Good girl.' Uncle Patie.

'All very well for you to say "Good Girl", Uncle Patie.' His mother's voice was low and furious. 'The child saw that man with his hand half blown off. He must have been scared to death. What you get up to with the loonie fringe is your affair, but don't count too much on any more family loyalty. I don't happen to care two hoots whether the new Queen is Elizabeth One or Two in Scotland. Does it really matter what insignia postboxes carry?'

'Yes, it matters.' Aunt Camilla.

'If Hamish had obeyed instructions, there would have been no danger. He couldn't have understood the importance of the timing device.'

'Will they save the hand?'

'I doubt it.'

He heard his mother's breath explode in a sharp burst of exasperation and the click of her black patent shoes going away over the polished wood floor. In a little, in softly cajoling but more normal tones, his Aunt Camilla said: 'Maybe you should suspend operations for a bit, Patie. I'm afraid for what might happen to us.'

'Why should they connect us with what happened? Hamish is as close as a clam.'

They got up then and went out also, still arguing but in carefully muted voices. Crispin stretched and climbed out through the big sash window, dropping on to the flower-bed beneath and guiltily hiding a broken dahlia stem before going off to the summer-house in the grounds for a think.

He began to write into the jotter: 'There was this band of men who did not want the Queen of England for there queen.' Should it be 'there' or 'their', he wondered? He still made mistakes in that direction. Probably 'their'. He changed it. 'They were led by a tall, fair, youngish' – or should it be 'oldish'? – 'man with a handelbar' (cross out) 'largish moosetash.' 'Moosetash' looked impressive but he was sure it wasn't right. He got fed up worrying about spelling, a poor pastime for the holidays, tore out the page and stuffed it in his sporran, then edged round to the back of the house where there was an old bicycle he had been forbidden to play on. He didn't see why – it was rusty and it wobbled, but he could ride it. He took it down the drive and on to the coast road, whistling and happy, for the moment laying all burdensome surmises to one side. He fancied a paddle and he had twopence in his sporran, enough to buy an ice-cream wafer afterwards from Antonio in the village.

He was getting good at detecting. He had trailed a couple of guests from Calneggie this morning, pretending he was just learning to ride the bike. He thought they might be smugglers or something. They had negotiated the hire of a boat and claimed they were going fishing. It was possible they were taking treasures from Calneggie in that big wicker basket, to be delivered to confederates when they rounded the point.

Good word, confederates.

He lost interest a little when one of them rounded on him and said sharply, 'Don't hang about, boy.' He hadn't been hanging about. Hanging about suggested a person who had nothing better to do and it should have been obvious he was a fee-paying pupil up from Glasgow, top in his class for sums and a shrewd detective brain into the bargain. Someone who knew Secrets That Must Not Be Disclosed.

He would never reveal what had happened to Hamish. They could give him the Chinese Water Torture and he still wouldn't tell them anything. His mother had been worried last night in case the police would question him, but Uncle Patie had said he'd fixed that. What was annoying, of course, was that Uncle Patie wasn't letting him in on what was really happening. It was maddening for a boy who had organized his own secret society at home with Ian Ferguson and Billy Anderson. It was rotten only half-knowing things. You felt left out and unable to concentrate on building things like rafts down on the beach.

He wasn't allowed in his uncle's workshop, either. That was another drawback. The design of the new car was supposed to be top secret and there was supposed to be a gas turbine engine that could possibly go over the four hundred. Crispin knew a lot about engines. He and Ian Ferguson had made their own go-kart at home. He might have been able to give Uncle Patie some advice. There might have been some small point everybody else had overlooked that he would spot. He was very quick on the uptake. Everybody said so.

He picked a large, round stone to kick all the way to the workshop. Other people were allowed in there, all day long people like Big Jock Campbell from the farm, and Hector Talbot, the teacher, who knew less about cars than Crispin did. Sometimes the big doors stood wide open, to let the light in: and sometimes, as on this still, quiet evening, with the midges biting, they were closed.

Some of the people who came, of course, were on hotel business, irritated that Uncle Patie wasn't behind the big desk in the reception hall, and others came to pay their cottage rents or just to gossip. Crispin thought he had seen Talbot and Campbell go towards the workshop earlier and it irked him that he had not seen them coming out again. If the doors were closed, could they still be in there? It would be as well to stop kicking the stone, go round the blind side and by standing on an old rusty plough peer through a crack in one of the high, dust-caked windows. Nobody would ever have thought of doing that but him, because there were shoulder-high nettles and thistles that stung and tore. But he had discovered that if you strode purposefully enough into the nettles, they bent away from you and like an Indian fakir you could ignore the pain from minor blisters. Good job he had trained himself as a scout, up in the heather. It would take keen ears to detect him.

It was harder than he thought, getting a balance on the plough and remaining steady long enough to peer through the crack. But what he saw then made his jaw drop open and his heart begin to thump like a steam-hammer. For there were two, four, six, eight men and his Uncle Patie, all of them except one with guns – rifles, that was – at their shoulders. The man without a gun – Crispin recognized him as Jock Campbell's son Fergus who delivered the milk – had a broom handle. Crispin thought that was so funny he nearly fell off the plough.

Very faintly he could hear his Uncle Patie giving the orders, and the men wheeled and turned and marched in a very orderly, resolute fashion. Each of them had a green tartan rosette pinned to jacket or pullover. They pulled in their chins and thrust out their chests. They wore soft old shoes that made little sound on the workshop floor.

When the drilling had finished they gathered at the far end of the workshop near the car, but greatly to Crispin's chagrin he could hear nothing of what they discussed. It seemed to be very serious, even heated at times, and papers like plans were brought out and laid along the car bonnet, pointed at then folded away and stuck between the back and seat of the car's cockpit.

Crispin waited till the meeting had ended and everyone had gone. Several melted from a small door on the other side of the workshop that he hadn't even known existed and the rest, one at a time, headed for the hotel or the village.

Crispin could not wait to try the secret side door. To his exasperation it didn't give way to his push, and there was a padlock on the big front doors. There was nothing for it but to try the windows by climbing back up on the plough. After much pushing and shoving he got one to open, stiffly, shedding rusty dust and he wriggled through and dropped to the floor. He drew the papers out from the car seat, opening them up on the bonnet the way he'd seen the others do.

They were plans, maps, beautifully drawn and illustrated so that he had no difficulty in recognizing the reservoir in one, the Hydro-Electric pylons in another and the railway line to the north in a third. Drawings of spruce and fir trunks laid horizontally indicated road blocks and drawings of rifles showed gun caches hidden in the heather and at river banks. Crispin began to shiver with excitement and that kind of scary overwhelmed feeling you got when your understanding didn't quite encompass what was happening.

Somebody was at the big doors! He scrabbled the papers together and pushed them back down the car seat, but two had fallen and he picked them up as he ran and stuffed them down his shirt-front.

He had barely time to hide under a trestle-table when Uncle Patie came in, lifted a deerstalker hat off a hook near the door, and went out again. Crispin heard the key grate in the padlock with a sigh of resignation. He would have to get out through the window and it would be harder from the inside than from out. But he managed it. In a way he was quite glad he had brought two of the papers with him. It would be something to show Ian Ferguson when he got back, otherwise he'd never believe any of it. He would have to swear him to secrecy, of course, and no one else should know. It eased him a little to think of telling Ian, his friend. It eased the weightiness and the guilt and the thought that was coming back to him of Hamish's gory hand. If only he could tell his mother!

Good job there was no one around to see he had been crying. But coming off the bike on to that bit of badly macadamed road had been right sore. He'd skinned both knees and an elbow. And the blooming bike wouldn't go now, not even if he pushed it. He would have to carry it all the way back to Calneggie and he would be late for his tea. He wouldn't half catch it for that from his mother.

'What's up, sonny?' He'd been so busy saving spit to clean the more badly grazed knee that he hadn't heard Sergeant MacFadyen come along the road on *his* bike. Instantly, he was on the alert like a red deer in the heather.

'Nothing.' He clamped his hands over his sporran and the shaking began inside him, so bad on top of the fall that the tears started again.

'Oh, come away there. You're the wee fella from the hotel, aren't you?' The sergeant came and sat beside him, offering him a peppermint from a crumpled paper bag. 'Fall off your bike, did you? Dinna greet, there's a wee man.'

'I'm not crying,' he said furiously.

'Of course you're no'. Not a big chap like you.' The sergeant gave him his handkerchief for his knee and kept up a soothing flow of chatter and Crispin began to feel better.

'I expect you help your auntie and uncle at the hotel,' said Sergeant MacFadyen. 'A big laddie like you.'

'Sometimes.'

'Run messages and the like?'

'Sometimes.'

'Does your uncle get you to take messages for him? To the likes of Big Jock Campbell or Hamish MacLintock, that hurt his hand the other day?'

'No. He doesn't.'

'Have you got a message or something in your sporran there?'

'No!'

'Just let me see, laddie.'

He had been about to scrabble up and run but the big firm hand held him. Sergeant MacFadyen smoothed out the page from Crispin's jotter first of all and began to read: 'There was this band of men who did not want the Queen of England for their queen.' His thin-lipped mouth spread in a smile of grim satisfaction.

'A child's vivid imagination, Sergeant,' said Patie. He had persuaded MacFadyen to come up to his office at the hotel. The raid on the workshop had gone off at half-cock: the men had got away through the side door while the sergeant and his constable were conducting the formalities at the front. But MacFadyen had found the maps and guns and a small quantity of explosive.

'The maps are nobody's imagination,' MacFadyen insisted. 'And the bairn must have seen or heard something. I can question him again.'

Camilla had come quietly in and sat down. Now she judged the time had come to intervene.

'I don't have to remind you, Sergeant, do I, that my husband has an illustrious war record?'

'No,' said the sergeant, with a stubborn look, 'I don't need reminding.'

'Is it likely he would engage in the sort of activity you're accusing him of?'

'Not likely. But possible. I ask you again, sir: what were those men doing in your shed?'

'They're interested in the Fleming Flyer.'

'All of them?'

'All of them. Do you find that so strange? You know I'm going to America soon to attack the record?'

The sergeant looked discomfited for the first time. 'There's them that doubt you'll ever do it.'

'That's their privilege. The guns are easily explained. They were for the Twelfth. We always have a shooting party then.'

'Aye, but the maps and tartan rosettes.'

'A bit of innocent fun.'

'Aye, and I was born yesterday.'

'I'm sure my husband would have no difficulty in putting things right with your Chief Inspector,' said Camilla. 'He's rather a friend. We're on the committee together for the Calneggie Games.'

'I must warn –'

'I hear you have a daughter getting married soon, Sergeant,' Camilla went on smoothly. 'What about holding her reception at the hotel? Just by way of apology for all the trouble you've been put to.'

'One of the cottages will be becoming vacant, too,' said Patie. 'Nice little place. All mod. con.'

'See here, sir,' said Sergeant MacFadyen. 'I might confess to a certain sympathy wi' some of your ideas. But no' to the extent of blowing up postboxes and starting tartan armies. Do you get my meaning?'

'Entirely. But I am innocent.'

'I am confiscating the explosive. Good job it's a small amount.'

'From the time we wanted to dam the stream higher up,' said Patie blandly.

'Aye. Pigs might fly. Now see here.' The sergeant became suddenly fierce and threatening. 'I know every man jack involved in your bloody stupid operations. You can be sure I've got my eye on you. Drop it. It's only fooling about, anyhow: dreams fit for a wean.'

'The reception, Sergeant,' said Camilla. 'How many should we expect?'

'I'll let you know,' he said surlily.

Camilla poured him a tot of whisky, then one each for herself and Patie. Holding hers up, she kept the sergeant's eye and smiled. ' "We are the image makers, we are the dreamers of dreams," ' she quoted softly.

The sergeant plonked down his glass. 'Aye,' he said irately. 'You're the kind to look out for. And don't forget. I will.'

Eleanor came down the stairs of the small, neat, semi-detached house in the Clarkston suburb of Glasgow, wearing a thoughtfully disturbed expression. Dumping herself down on the settee next to Tom in the carefully furnished, formal, small room they called the lounge she said: 'He still has nightmares about Calneggie. Maybe I should take him to the doctor.'

'They'll fade,' said Tom easily. He shifted himself to indicate mild irritation at being disturbed when he was reading his paper.

'I hope he'll go over now,' said Eleanor, barely hearing Tom's answering 'Hmm'. She was still seeing Crispin's fretful, anxious face. The whole summer at Calneggie had been a bit traumatic for him. In some ways she felt it was a pity they had ever gone. But at the same time it had allowed her to save something, to buy the suite and carpet for the room they were sitting in now. Putting down a mortgage deposit of £150 for the £1500 house had been a big struggle when she and Tom had finally made up their minds to live together again. And she had been determined to have everything nice. The furniture was a mixture of Utility and carefully scrutinized second-hand. She had scraped, painted, varnished, upholstered, sewn, half-amused at her own determination to get away from the shabby backcloth of her growing-up.

And it was doubly amusing – or ironic – whichever view you chose to take – to regard her own efforts in the light of the home her mother had now with Robin Chisholm. Her step-father was determined that Mairi should have everything she wished for and if that meant velvet curtains and damask-covered chairs, no matter. Eleanor felt the house at Dounhead was in danger of becoming overstuffed, just as her mother's figure was being padded out by Robin's indulgence of her taste for chocolates and restaurant meals. She didn't want a Clarkston version of the Tuileries for herself. She wanted to lay her own stamp on each small room, colours blending, furniture in proportion, pelmets erected so that they did not have that shaky, impermanent look, and the kitchen a model of practicability and labour-saving.

Her little house should be a work of art where friends who came for coffee would not be able to hide their admiration. She felt now, however, she had almost accomplished what she had set out to do. In the beginning, there had been challenge and fun and a sense of achievement. But lately the rooms had begun to mock her as if to say: what does it all amount to? She had to be honest and admit that there was not all that much difference between her home and those of her neighbours. Her friends were all skilled home-makers, good cooks and perfect mothers. So what? What now? What next?

She threw down the magazine she had been staring at with a sharp intake of breath to indicate the extent of her boredom.

'What's up now?' Tom peered at her over the top of his spectacles. He wore the wary look of a man who dreaded the answer to his question.

'You know.'

'How should I know?'

'Same old thing. I don't really like being a housewife.'

'Then get a job.'

'What about Crispin?'

'Get a woman in to keep an eye on him.'

'It would have to be the right woman. I would have to pay her fares, for you wouldn't get anybody about here doing it.'

'What worries you,' said Tom, sitting bolt upright, 'is what they would say about here if you worked. That you would then be accused of being less than the perfect wife and mother. The hell with them. Make up your own mind.'

Eleanor took a nail file from her handbag and began to rub over the top of her nails. Thoughtfully she said, 'During the war it was all right for women to go out to work. Their kids didn't come to much harm, did they? Now we're being shoved back into our little boxes. I'm not the only one who feels it, Tom. There's a lot of discontent seething around under the apparent calm. Bad nerves. Too many sherries. Mona up the road gets these trembling fits and Sandra Bateman takes pheno-barbitone tablets.'

Warming to her theme, Eleanor said, 'I mean, it's as though people have suddenly started worrying about what a mother should be like. Saying she should be this, and that. That a child needs her there all the time. What happened in the old days when there were big families? The mothers were too tired to bring up the later ones: it was the big sisters who did that. You used to see them in Dounhead, wee trauchled souls of eight or nine dragging the babies around wherever they went. And why should society suddenly start laying down rules for mothers when everybody else can do what they like?'

'It's the Bulge,' Tom pointed out, unwrapping a caramel with meticulous care and poking it into his cheek, pleased he had done so without getting thumb and forefinger sticky. 'Nature's way of replenishing the stock after the war. Nature is saying to you: Eleanor Wishart, it's time you had another baby.'

'But nothing's happened, has it? I half want it to, and I half don't.'

'Then take a bloody job!' Tom's voice rose on a testy note. 'I'm beginning to know this script off by heart. I could sell it to MGM.'

'But what job?'

'Typing.'

'Boring.'

'Shop assistant.'

'Even more damned boring.'

'Paper girl. Mendicant. Gipsy going round the doors selling clothes-pegs.'

'I wish I'd gone to university.'

'Come in, the violins.'

'Do you think I'd make a journalist?'

'Too old.'

'Thank you very much.'

'You know what I mean. The profession is over-subscribed. It doesn't need a neurotic refugee from the stew-pot and nylon queue.'

'So I'm neurotic?'

'Verging. You said it yourself. You're all neurotic. Half in and half out of the kitchen. Half in and half out of the nursery. You're going to have to make up your collective tiny minds one of these days.'

Eleanor was not exactly sulking. The arguments had covered familiar territory, the heat had gone out of them. But she spent the rest of the evening in an abstracted reverie and once they were in bed lay looking at the ceiling, at once patient and stunned.

Unable to bear it any longer, Tom cast around for anodynes and came up with the suggestion that they should have a sail to Arran the next day, which happened to be a Saturday, so that they could visit Carlie, not long since widowed. Donald had gone to a Glasgow Labour Party rally, come home worn out and protesting his disillusion and the next morning had failed to wake up. At the funeral, Carlie had said he had longed for the old days, when people like Jimmy Maxton were prepared to get up in the House and shout 'Murderers!' when they cut the health grant when thousands were dying of TB. He thought the heart had gone out of the Labour Party, that it had been taken over by the bureaucrats and grey men.

On the steamer going over to the island, Eleanor admitted the day out had been a good idea. The hard, racing wind blowing through her hair seemed to clear her head of cobwebs. When she saw Tom coming up on deck after he and Crispin had been to see the engines, a ritual observed by small boys and their fathers since the steamship had been invented, she felt a sharp familiar pang, a gratitude that they were hers. Slipping his arms round her, Tom saw she had been lifted out of her recent mood and gave her a hard, joyful hug.

The big, elderly man standing near them at the steamer's rail smiled down at Crispin and said in an American accent: 'Your little boy been down to see the engines, has he?' When Tom said he had, the man gave a slow, reminiscing smile and said, 'I used to do the same, at his age.'

'But you're a Scot no longer, sir,' said Tom.

'Once a Scot, always a Scot.'

'Yes,' said Tom. 'They tell me nostalgia for the old country's quite an industry out West.'

The man turned heavily towards the ship's rail, looking out over the waves. When later, by accident, Tom found himself next to him again, he took up the conversation where it had been left off.

'I come back, whenever I can. Nobody left now in the old country, though. My brothers all emigrated, too. What option had we? And now I see it all happening again. It made me sad, passing the shipyards earlier on.'

'They were busy enough. Twelve per cent of the world's orders is not to be sneezed at.'

'You'll pardon me,' said the man, with New World politeness. 'Ships are my business and in the States we are building for the twentieth century, not the nineteenth. Container ships, supertankers, vehicle ferries. Not mammoth liners that are going to be out of date as soon as they're built. They tell me the same thing is happening with your railway engineering: they still persist in making steam when the future lies with diesels and electrics.'

'But we have the finest shipbuilders in the world.' Eleanor had been listening and could not forbear making the comment.

The man shook his head. 'You've failed to modernize. You'll pay the penalty. No, the old country's dying. Done for. Leave it to the whaups and the peewits.'

'Then what do you come back for?'

'For this.' Eleanor thought there might have been tears in the man's eyes. He indicated the sunlit water and Arran hoving into view.

'Beautiful, isn't it?' she said softly. She had been wounded by his criticism and now wanted his commendation, as though she and her country were one. He nodded. They stood with their faces into the wind as the ship nosed steadily towards Brodick Pier. Soon ropes were thrown, faces smiled upwards from the quay and standing off from the crowd, resolutely smiling, they saw the solitary figure of Carlie.

'Don't you get lonely?' The question Eleanor had bitten back several times already would no longer remain unasked, as she and Carlie sat on a large rock by the water's edge and watched Tom and Crispin row out into the bay to fish with a hired line.

Carlie drew her light coat more closely about her. In old age her face had grown sweet of expression, and placid, yet there was a glint of the old firebrand Suffragette behind the gold-rimmed glasses.

'No time to be lonely.' She stirred the little white West Highland terrier sitting in front of her with her foot. 'Dougal here takes me for walks. My housework keeps me busy.'

Eleanor tried again. 'You know what I mean. Is it bad without him?'

Carlie gave her a piercing look. 'We were so close. I don't feel he has gone away from me entirely. I often turn and say, "What do you think, Donald? Shall we have a haddie to our tea?" ' She smiled. 'I just feel he's there. I can't explain it. But it's a comfort to me.'

'Would you not come back to the mainland? You would be nearer the rest of us: we could see more of you.'

'I've thought of it. But I'll see my time out here.'

'It shouldn't be like that. Seeing your time out. You were so good to all of us – Philip Mackenzie, Mother and me. Whatever we were short of it was: see if Carlie can spare us.' Eleanor smiled at her companion with open affection. 'What would we have done without you?'

Carlie patted her hand. 'Now, now. I can always look forward to seeing you in the summer. And seeing Crispin today has cheered me up no end. That bright wee freckled face, bursting with curiosity and intelligence! He has a look of your Grannie Kitty about him. That's one rewarding thing about growing old, the way you can trace family likenesses back over the generations.'

'I don't think of you as *old* old.'

'Well, I'm getting on!'

'And what are the other rewards?'

'Well.' Carlie considered. 'Nature. I don't mean examining plants and flowers. I've never had green fingers. I mean wind, rain, sun. Being out in them. Part of the elements. When I'm up to it I like to climb the hills and see the brown water chatter down over the rocks and feel the rough branches of heather brush against my legs.' She laughed at Eleanor's look of surprise. 'Quite the little Emily Brontë, me. I like to think of Arran as being Scotland in miniature. I think it's the beauty of the scenery that's made us into a nation of romantics.'

Eleanor picked up a pebble and drew a heart with an arrow through it on the wet sand. 'Philip Mackenzie's gone into television. Did you know? According to his mother, he's earning more than the Prime Minister.'

'He wrote me a very nice letter when Donald died.'

'He's done all right, hasn't he?'

Carlie looked at her in some perplexity. There had been a note, not of jealousy or resentment, but more of a wistful nature, in her voice.

'What's the matter?' she asked quietly.

'I don't know.' Moodily Eleanor threw down the stone, stood up, held out a helping hand to Carlie and said, 'Come on, I'll buy you a cup of tea at the tea-rooms. These two will be out there for a while yet.'

Over the familiar three-tier cake-stand in the little restaurant, she said, 'Carlie, I feel I'm wasting my life.'

Carlie said nothing. Instead she cut her potato scone into four pieces, and waited.

'It's not Tom. Not this time. We've settled down and I think he's the right man for me.'

'Then you'd like another child?'

'Not terribly.'

'That's honest, at least.'

'No. Academic. It doesn't look as though I *can* have another. I don't mind. I want out of the house.'

'A job? Why not? Does Tom raise objections?'

'Far from it. He backs me up.' Eleanor trickled the sugar over the sugar-bowl. 'It's me. I've lost all confidence. I've grown timorous as a mouse. I defer to Tom in almost everything. I'm hypersensitive. If people are critical of me, even in a constructive way, I just curl up and die.'

Carlie eyed her noncommittally. 'You're in a bad way!'

'Don't laugh! I am. Your generation seemed to have more backbone. Look at how you went out and got the vote. And now we've got it, what do we do with it? Ask our husbands how we should think. They're the ones out in the world, after all.'

'I didn't think you were this bitter. Have you asked your mother what she thinks?'

Eleanor's face was carefully blank. 'Well, she married Robin and she's his wife now. I don't have her to myself any more.'

'I see.' Carlie patted Eleanor's hand sympathetically. 'Life's just one adjustment after another, isn't it? And here was I thinking I was the only one who had to get used to new ways. Well, if you ask me what I think, I think you should get out of the house somehow. If you don't want to take a full-time job, take a part-time one.'

'Selling ribbons?' Eleanor was scornful.

'Have you thought of going into politics?'

'Not seriously.' Eleanor's hand relinquished the sugar spoon and lay still on the table top.

'Why not seriously?'

'We've had enough politicians in the family, I should have thought. My father's politics dominated our life.'

'But you're not a Communist, like him.'

'Nor even a Socialist, like you, Carlie.'

'What are you, then?'

'I am, as they say, a bit of a Scottish Nationalist.'

'Like Patie.'

'I'm no activist.'

'Is he?'

'He mixes with a number of hotheads on the fringe of the movement. I think it's more talk than anything nowadays.'

'But it's a waste of time!'

'Not any more.' Eleanor wasn't conscious of it, but her

face was showing its first real spark of animation that afternoon. 'There's a kind of – of groundswell of opinion in the direction of independence. Ask Tom. He says so, too. People can't go on leaving the country at the rate they do, but they will if we don't somehow make it important to stay at home.'

Carlie nodded. 'Donald's mind sometimes ran on those lines.'

'How could it not? I would like to get into the thick of the fray and ask some questions. Do you think a woman could do it, Carlie?'

Carlie rattled down her teacup and pushed back her shoulders, reminding Eleanor of the old photographs taken of her in her heyday.

'A woman can do anything she sets her mind to.'

'You really think so?'

'Yes. Disregard the collywobbles. Forget about the sniping. Confidence comes with practice.'

Suddenly all was rush as they had to change Crispin's wet socks, gather up the day's trophies and make for the evening steamer. Eleanor felt very glad they had come, for Carlie had lost that forlorn air of their first glimpse of her and was almost her old, bright self. They waved to her and the little dog Dougal till their arms ached.

The elderly man in the big American hat was on the return trip also. He sat on one of the damp, slatted benches with a bunch of white heather on his lap.

Eleanor and Tom sat beside him while Crispin, with inexhaustible energy, roamed the ship and spent the last of his pocket-money in its little shop, eating rock till he grew pale and seedy.

The sail was tranquil, with no one saying very much. But when it was over and they rose to disembark, Eleanor impulsively put her hand on the old man's arm.

'Scotland's not ready to disappear into the mist just yet.' She smiled at him. 'It'll still be here next time you come back.'

'Is that a promise?'

'Yes,' she said. 'It is.'

CHAPTER SIXTEEN

Mairi Chisholm put the telephone back on its cradle in the hall and entered her husband's study with a half-thoughtful, half-excited air.

'What was it?' He held out his hand for her, drawing her towards him as he sat at his desk.

'It was Camilla.' She perched on the desk-top. 'She's just had one of her more outlandish bright ideas. She wants Eleanor and me to go to the States with Patie.'

'She's not going with him, then?'

'She says she isn't up to it. That it needs someone young and sharp like Eleanor to deal with the publicity side and that I could look after Patie's socks and shirts and see he gets his meals on time.'

Robin permitted himself an unamused smile. 'She has a nerve! What is supposed to happen to your husband while you're looking after hers? Or to Eleanor's husband, for that matter, and the boy?'

'She's got that all worked out. You are to stay at Calneggie, finish your book there. All meals cooked by Nellie. Lovely walks to jog your inspiration.'

'And Tom?'

'Tom could stay with his mother. She would be only too ready to look after both him and Crispin.'

He studied her pink face. 'It's not on, is it?' he demanded carefully. 'You don't want to go, do you? You hate everything to do with Patie's motor-racing. It would be a nightmare for you.'

There was an infinitesimal pause and then she moved away from him and said, 'No, of course not. I told Camilla it wasn't possible. But you know how persuasive she is – she went on and on. First we had the hearts and flowers bit about her health and then how I was the only person apart from her that Patie could turn to when he was worked up and needed calming down.'

'Is her health so bad?'

'It's difficult to tell with Camilla. But she certainly sounds – weary. That's the only word for it.'

'Look,' he said, laying down his pen, 'if Patie is determined at his age to go chasing a will-o'-the-wisp like the land speed record, that's his affair. I won't have you involved in his sweaty death-wish preoccupations.' He looked at her almost supplicatingly. 'This book's important to *me*. And you've made it possible, just because you're you and you're here with me.'

She came over and kissed his brow. 'I know,' she said lightly. 'I'll bring you in your coffee soon. Now forget I've ever been in here. Back to the treadmill!'

At lunch, he skirted round a series of other topics before coming back to the phone call from Camilla.

'All things being equal – I mean, no strain on Patie's part and no book on mine – would you have liked to go to America?'

She smiled at him, vigorously cutting up her salad. 'I never went anywhere as Nicol's wife. I suppose now life has opened up so much for me in many respects, things I never thought could happen to me are suddenly feasible.'

'That was below the belt.'

'In what way?'

'In your roundabout, sleekit, feminine way you're trying to tell me that as my wife you have *carte blanche* to do what you like.'

'It's *your* reasoning that's tortuous.'

'Go, then.' He wiped his mouth and threw down the crisply laundered napkin. 'Never let it be said I held you back from experience. I'll go to Calneggie and listen to Camilla's endless Celtic fairy tales and eat Nellie's prodigious meals. The book will very likely go to pot like my digestion – and at this late stage, too.'

She shook her head. 'I don't want to go.'

'How long would it be for?'

'Six, eight weeks. Not more. It's all carefully planned and scheduled. The attempt on the record will be tied up with all kinds of promotion for Scottish exports. As Camilla puts it, it could bring in millions of pounds' worth of overseas orders. It's the reason Patie wants to do it, to help the country. And, of course, Utah is better than Calneggie or the Pendine Sands in Wales. They'll have pipers to see them off, tartans and woollens to wear, propaganda to help American firms think along investment lines in this country.'

'A kind of three-ring, Wild West circus in reverse?'

'Well, yes.'

'Has Camilla asked Eleanor yet?'

'No. She wanted to consult me first.'

'And do you think Eleanor would play ball?'

Mairi's face shadowed slightly. She did not answer for a moment or two, then said restrainedly, 'It's the main reason I might have gone. She would take Camilla's line about it being a great promotion for Scotland. It would do her no harm politically now that she's hoping for adoption as a Scot Nat candidate. It would give us a chance to be together – her and me – for I feel we've grown apart recently.'

He rose from his seat and came and put his arms round her, his expression contrite. He kissed her, then looked straight into her eyes.

'You go. I'm being a selfish brute. I know I'm possessive of you. I would cut you off from brother and daughter and everybody if I had my way. But you must stand up to me, for my own good.'

'Robin, do you think I should?' she asked, almost fearfully.

'Everybody should go to America at least once. I've been there. Now you go. And when you come back, the book will be finished and we'll go away somewhere for a quiet little holiday. Just the two of us.'

She put her arms round his neck and held him tightly. She knew as well as he the tendency to be sufficient unto themselves.

Since the Convention had broken up, splintering into secret factions, he had come back once more to the more formal constraints of the Scottish National Party. But he attended few meetings. With his domestic life on an even keel he had reverted to his studies and his writing, finding an enjoyment and a discipline in them he had once thought had deserted him for ever. Although Mairi had not his breadth of scholarship, she was able to listen constructively, as he put it, and to offer comments and criticisms that homed in unerringly on the mark. With Nicol, she had had to tune in to a mind that throbbed with the compassionate ideal, but which seldom found relief in perfect expression. Robin was different: he had no sooner found access to an idea than he was able to articulate it. She did not hold one up above the other, but her own natural inclination of mind was more towards Robin's.

'Yes,' she said now. 'If you finish the book, then when I come back we'll go off with free minds and just be on our own. All obligations discharged.'

'Do you still feel some obligation towards Patie?' he asked wonderingly.

'I suppose in a way I do. I've always felt the need to protect him from himself, from his wilder impulses.'

'Do you think you have been very successful?' he asked, straight-faced.

She laughed at him but her eyes were serious. 'I don't suppose I have!'

The Flyer had been hoisted aboard ship, safely stowed away in the hold, the last reporter had gone ashore with the last answer to the last question in his notebook. The piper who was coming with them to Utah had laid aside his bagpipes like some tired, groaning animal and gone to his cabin for a lie-down.

It had been a mammoth send-off, the kind the Clyde was good at, with music, civic speeches and a back-slapping, participatory public crowd shouting 'Good luck the Flyer!' and, 'You show 'em, Patie son.'

Now they had met in the bar – the suède-shoed, natty PR man, Gordon Watson; Patie; his engineer Alec; Eleanor, who wore a smart, red, A-line suit, and Mairi, shivering with nerves inside the warm fur coat Camilla had insisted on lending her.

Eleanor turned away from the men and confronted her mother.

'Are you all right?'

'Right as rain.'

'You look nervous.'

'Aren't you?'

Eleanor gave an exaggerated series of nods and pushed her arm through her mother's, hugging her, and suddenly it was better for both of them.

It was a smooth, uneventful crossing. Some of the plans for the itinerary across America had still to be worked out and Eleanor was kept busy typing notes and letters for Gordon Watson. Mairi seized whatever chance she could to be with Patie. She could see he was tensed up, worried as to whether the car would get to Utah on time for the trial runs that would precede the actual attempt. She who, as Robin had said, hated every aspect of Patie's motor-racing, now put all her guile and energy towards reassuring her brother, building up his confidence, keeping him cheerful and calm and well looked-after. It was what she had promised Camilla but it came naturally in any case. It was as though all the fierce, protective love she had felt towards Patie when they had been together as children welled up in her again after all these years, making her want success for this trip because it mattered so much to him. And it did matter. Until they had been thrown into close contact during the sea trip she had not realized the strength of his will to break the record. No wonder Camilla had been under strain in recent months. People with such obsessive ambitions could crush the life from those around them.

Camilla had been strained, distraught, her sentences disjointed, when Mairi and she had met before the embarkation. 'You won't let anything happen to him, will you?' she kept saying. Her behaviour had veered from the wildly brittle and gay to the abstracted and even sad. Mairi felt it would have been better had she been able to summon up the courage to come. As it was, she was stuck at home worrying about all the things that could go wrong.

It became clear as the crossing proceeded that having Eleanor in the party was a great advantage. She was developing gifts for getting on with people and she milked the passenger list shamelessly for the entertaining and useful, while getting rid of bores without making them feel they had been insulted or ignored.

She also kept the emphasis on the exploitative side of the expedition, taking Patie's mind off useless, repetitive speculations as to what awaited them at Utah. They had contacted all the influential Scots-Americans they could think of, as well as clan and Caledonian societies in the cities they would pass through. As Gordon Watson pointed out, Scots in America were more diffuse and scattered than say, the Germans or Irish, but someone who had taken the trouble to study the census papers had once pointed out that 166 out of every 100,000 people in the USA bore the name of Campbell, which meant at least half a million well-wishers from one clan only!

It was Eleanor who got them arguing fiercely in the small hours about the way Scotland might be developed in the future: this despite Gordon Watson's entrenched scepticism as to whether the natives possessed or deserved any identity worth saving.

A good-looking, dedicated paterfamilias who had been educated at Glasgow University, his contempt for the 'keelies' among his countrymen – the heavy drinkers, gamblers, razor-slashers, street gangs and corner-boys – was total, as was his hatred of the empty chauvinists, the boasters and music-hall stereotypes who by their vacuous behaviour lowered the name of Scotland at home and abroad.

At the same time, he could be equally merciless about the 'cruse London-Scotties, wi' their braw shirt fronts' that MacDiarmid the poet had attacked, and the others began to suspect that under his bluff, deprecatory manner there burned a concern for Scotland as deep as their own.

They were determined that the image they would present in America would be restrained, informed, dignified; that they would not overdo the tartan but would present as up-to-date and contemporary a picture as was possible.

Patie had a lot of fun upsetting the apple-cart whenever he could, threatening to get drunk and sing rude bothy songs, or go into his skilled interpretation of a Glasgow dance-hall Lothario asking a partner to dance. But at least the back-chat counteracted the tension and by the time the little team reached New York they knew they were working together smoothly and Patie was bolstered by the warmth and spirit of their support.

When they got to Utah, there was no avoiding for any of them the real purpose of the trip. On the way there they had been fussed and fêted and treated with great kindliness and hospitality. But now the pressure began to build inexorably. The tyre and engineering firms backing the attempt sent their representatives to make sure all was well. Patie had not previously been admitted to the front-ranking names of motor-racing like Cobb and Campbell, but interest sprouted everywhere now for this 'challenging oldster' as one American paper referred to him. The national press both in Scotland and England flew in reporters, who passed the time until the attempt on the record by writing about the new cults of hot-rod and dragster racing which threatened to outdo anything with driven wheels.

When Patie was conducting his trials, Mairi found herself standing on the sidelines gazing at the Flyer with mingled hatred and awe. There was no doubt it was impressive. She could not cope with the technicalities but she knew it was structurally unconventional, with the engines mounted at odd angles and the driver's seat pushed as far up into the streamlined nose as functioning would permit. It was painted a dark, metallic, forest green, its huge wheels a glittering silver padded with the tyres that made it look like some strange monster about to go on the prowl. She loathed it. She hated it. She did not want to see it yet she came back time and again to look at it, as though by doing so she could put some kind of safety hex on it that would protect Patie from all harm.

One night in their hotel she dreamed they were back in Dounhead House and she was running endlessly down the long drive telling Patie not to take the wheel of Peter Frensham's car. When she woke that memory of the incident that had happened when he was twelve years old was as fresh as though it had just occurred and she put up a shaking hand to wipe sweat from her forehead. She began to see why Camilla had avoided coming at all costs. She thought of Parry Thomas killed on Pendine Sands, Cobb and Segrave both dead carrying their lust for speed from land to water, as though determined to seek death somewhere. She was sick with apprehension, yet each morning she had to go down to breakfast and smile and wisecrack as though nothing troubled her. She wanted to plead with Patie not to go through with the attempt, and yet she knew there was no way she could ever dissuade him. She began to find excuses to go to her room to rest in the afternoons, in case she should give away her feelings to some ferreting journalist, or worse, disturb the equilibrium of the party.

She knew Patie himself wasn't free of nerves. Contrary to his shipboard worries, the Flyer itself presented few technical problems, and Alec in his silent, gritty way coped with these admirably. It was just the inevitable stress that built up with any challenge. The jokes were becoming a little febrile, the temptation to stay a little later at the bar each evening stronger. Sometimes Patie looked like his own doppelgänger, his face haggard in its seriousness and his eyes sunken from the sleep that had not come.

The trials, cloaked in secrecy, went well on the whole. While they were taking place, Mairi and Eleanor did some sight-seeing and sent home letters and postcards. Mairi spoke to Camilla on the phone and was so anxious to reassure her all was well she managed to dissipate some of her own anxiety at the same time.

The night before the record attempt was deliberately low-key, with dinner in Patie's suite at the hotel. Mairi and he found themselves reminiscing about their childhood in Glasgow, the Christmas their Grandpa Fleming had found a precious train-set for Patie, the parties their mother Kitty had been so fond of giving. When they looked back now, that seemed like a golden time, before the deaths and departures and the unhealable rift with their father. When Finn's name was mentioned even now, Patie got up and prowled off, beetle-browed, in search of a whisky. Hastily Mairi changed the subject, talking optimistically of the interest their trip had aroused in Scotland and of Camilla's pride in her husband and urgency to have him back with her at Calneggie for their walks in the hills and of the big *ceilidh* that would surely follow on his return.

The day was bright, hard, hot, throwing the sun's rays back from the sand grains in a long, harsh, white strip. Patie breakfasted off orange juice and toast and climbed into the Flyer almost to the second stated. To Mairi and Eleanor the earnest activity of his helpers seemed distanced, of another dimension a great way off. All they could focus on was the helmet and goggles that represented Patie. When the Flyer's engines revved into a crescendo of ear-splitting sound, they put their hands up to their heads like automatons but their eyes never wavered.

The newspaper headlines in the hotel lobby that morning had screamed CAN SCOT FLYER TOP 400? How can he, Mairi thought, with sick dread. Certainly Cobb had done 394 mph, but going over the 400 was superhuman. And it was her kin, her brother, in that shining, bullet-like missile down there. A gasp that was more like a moan escaped her and Eleanor touched her arm, pity and horror in her face.

In order to clinch the record, the trip had to be carried out both ways. The Flyer had no sooner revved its engines than it seemed to shoot like a stone from a catapult. Its aim was direct, unerring, in its way beautiful, and endless. Mairi felt as though time were being twisted out of joint as she watched the car fly along the sands. Flyer indeed. No artifact had ever earned so fit a name. Just as suddenly it stopped and then the air seemed full of jubilant sounds and swimming with triumphant faces.

'He's topped four hundred.' It was Gordon Watson's voice. 'Now see what he does on the way back!'

Time had begun its strange twisted dance again. This time Mairi could not bear to look. A dread so powerful had taken hold of her she pushed her face into her daughter's shoulder and hung on to Eleanor as though to life itself. She had begun screaming before the others did, before the peculiar loud whining sound took place, followed by a thud and a juddering, terrible silence.

When she looked, the great metal bird lay broken-backed and skew-whiff a great distance off-course. They were running down to get Patie but she knew before they told her he was dead. She had known it all along and so had Camilla. That was why she had not come. People were screaming but she thought: you have left it too late. The time for that was before. She remembered the car going round the drive at Dounhead House. 'Patie! Patie!' she cried. She had not thought herself capable of such lamentation. She wanted to stop the shouting but she could not. The bright day came up and burned all before it.

The water lapped in the Sound, slapping up against the rocks and the crumbling sea wall, eddying back over the polished pebbles, sighing over the sand. In the village, the shops had all closed, drawing their blinds or putting up their shutters. It was like the Sabbath, with no children at play, not even a sniffing dog to be seen.

Patie had been laid to rest in Calneggie churchyard almost two years before. It had taken a long time to choose the obelisk, to have it made and decide on the site. Camilla hadn't rushed matters because the memorial of polished marble had been the only balm her frantic sorrowing mind could find. She wanted it placed at the headland where it would be seen from all over the village and from ships in the Sound. She agonized over the form of lettering and the words of the inscription, taking advice from no one. In the end she had merely put Patie's name and dates and the words 'Killed on a mission for his country, which he loved above all else'. She would not be persuaded even to consider any alternatives. Now after the little service she stood alone at the foot of the memorial, a small, slight, greying figure all in black. When she turned to join the others, her head went up automatically with that proud tilt it had never relinquished. The hazel eyes with their soft, light cast held no hint of tears. On this beautiful day it was almost imperative to believe that death would have no dominion.

As the party moved off, walking slowly back towards the hotel, the piper who had accompanied the tragic mission to America remained on the grassy knoll, playing Celtic airs. The sound followed the mourners like a disembodied spirit from the hills, as though mist and sunlight had taken on musical form. Jock Campbell, his son Fergus, and Talbot the teacher, paid heavy-eyed respect to Camilla and left to go back to work.

Automatically, the walkers seemed to feel the need to be close to each other, to link arms. Mairi and Robin parted to take Camilla between them, and Eleanor walked close to Tom and Nellie, stumbling sometimes on the uneven road, while Crispin came behind, a teenager looking for somewhere to belong. The village mourners, dressed out of respect in their best clothes, stood silently by the roadside, returning Camilla's looks of acknowledgment with awkward, compassionate nods. Still the threnody of the pipes went on, till as they reached the hotel they had to strain through the susurrus of the firs to hear it and unconsciously keep in step.

The journey home after the accident two years before had not been without its trauma. Mairi had had to be sedated all the way, Patie's engineer had been driven to the edge of breakdown thinking some omission of his might have cost Patie's life. In the end it had proved to be metal fatigue at a speed Patie had never taken the Flyer to before; not, as the papers had speculated, a burst tyre or a bump in the sand.

Mairi had gone at once to a Camilla strangely calm and tearless. It had been the latter who had shown unexpected strength. 'There was nothing anybody could do to stop Patie from doing what he did.' She had repeated the words till Mairi had put away her handkerchiefs and accepted that it was so. She and Patie's widow had then been able to sit down together and put Patie's life into perspective.

Mairi acknowledged that he had always had a wild, ungovernable streak, which she traced back to their mother's sudden death and what looked like their father's desertion of them. Camilla did not think that these happenings had all that much relevance. 'We have the seeds of our own destiny within us from the start,' she insisted. 'It was his wildness that drew me to him. I would not have changed a hair of his head.'

Already, in the surrounding countryside, legends were growing up about Patie and, like all legends, feeding on each other till it was difficult to separate truth from fiction. In these hills, after all, there were people who still talked about Bonnie Prince Charlie as though they half-expected to see him materialize one day among the heather. Patie's exploits for the Nationalist cause were remembered and embroidered upon and any comments about foolhardiness squashed by the Highland necessity to tell a good tale.

Once inside the hotel, the few guests Camilla had invited outside the family were looked after with her customary hospitality, but soon disappeared to catch trains or drive home before nightfall. Perhaps some tension within the family made this seem like a good idea. Robin and Mairi did their best to converse but topics died away, still-born, and Tom and Eleanor sat by a window, occasionally looking in the direction of their elders but saying nothing.

When it was almost dusk, Nellie took Crispin for a walk along the coast road to watch for fishing-boats coming in while the others gathered formally in the little sitting-room which Camilla had made her own next to her office.

'You know why we're here,' she said, without preamble. 'You know I want to get out of looking after the hotel. It is too much for me without Patie and I feel I would be happier back in the lodge house. You know what my offer is to Eleanor and Tom. Patie and I had no children but Eleanor was dear to his heart and I want Eleanor and her husband to have Calneggie. Somehow it seems right and proper to me. But I want to hear what the rest of you think.'

Mairi ran her tongue round suddenly dry lips and said obliquely, 'What would happen to the hotel if – if Eleanor and Tom refuse?'

'I don't know, to be honest. It could make a museum. In a way I wouldn't mind that. I like to think of it as a reposi-tory for all sorts of Highland lore. But the organizational side would be taxing and the money might not be forthcoming.'

'Tom wants to accept.' Eleanor's voice broke sharply across her aunt's tentative speculations. 'He thinks we could make a go of it and he's disenchanted at the moment with the news-paper scene.'

Tom stood up, suddenly animated. 'I don't think this part of the country has even begun to scratch the tourist market,' he said, excitedly. With an apologetic look at Camilla, he went on, 'I know you've kept up the traditional attractions, but with things like a heated swimming-pool, television in the bedrooms, conference tariffs and so on, we could really make the world take notice of Calneggie.'

'There's a snag, though, isn't there?' said Camilla quietly.

'Yes. Me.' Eleanor looked down at her hands. 'I don't want to be side-tracked from my political career.' At a swift, half-ironic glance from Tom, she burst out angrily, 'Yes, I know.

"What political career?" Here's this female with the temerity to say she wants to be a Scot Nat candidate at the next election.' She looked around, red-faced, at the others. 'My husband thinks I've taken leave of my senses. Two years ago, before I went to America, I would have agreed with him. But you learn from things. You learn how short life can be, how unwise it is to dodge your options.'

'I don't think you've gone out of your tiny mind.' Tom held his wife's look, his voice growing heavy with overpowering irritation. 'I think you can be a candidate here as well as in Dounhead.'

'Why Dounhead?' Camilla's question was sharp, and it was Mairi who answered it, her voice soft but brooking no interruption. 'She wants to stand in Dounhead because that's where she started in the movement, working for Robin here. And it's where we have family connections – both Donald Balfour and Duncan Fleming stood for Dounhead. Nicol was a councillor there. They know our name. It's a question of roots.'

Camilla assumed a look of bewilderment. 'Surely politics are politics? Does it matter *where* you work for your ideals? Patie laid down support for the Nationalist movement here, all the years he lived at Calneggie. Doesn't that mean anything to you?'

'I am embarrassed,' said Eleanor, quietly. 'Embarrassed because you've always heaped kindnesses on us, Camilla, and I must look now like a heathen ingrate.'

'Well, *tell her*,' Tom demanded, angrily. 'Put your cards on the table.' When Eleanor glared at him but remained silent, he went on: 'She doesn't regard the likes of Calneggie as worth fighting for.'

'It's not true.' Eleanor struggled for control. 'I just want to get away from this Highland image, this picture of Scotland as a heather-filled bog decorated with leaping red deer with charming eccentrics pushing the lost cause of independence. Well, it is that, too, but really, Dounhead and Glasgow are what really matter. That's where most Scots live, and they've never seen a red deer in their lives or even worn the tartan.'

Suddenly Camilla smiled in spite of everything. 'She's just like Patie,' she admitted. 'This one's got the bit between her teeth, too, and she's off.' She laughed nervously at Tom's thunderous face.

'Come on,' he invited Robin, who until then had been sitting with a quietly guarded expression, drawing gently on his pipe. 'Tell her how many members your cause has – yours and hers?'

Robin took his pipe from his mouth and answered, 'Two thousand. Something like that.'

'You hear that?' Tom laughed in Eleanor's face. 'Two thousand, and you call it a movement!'

'Our time is coming.'

The door opened and Nellie came in with a loaded supper trolley. 'The wee fella's gone up to bed. He's got a book to read,' she announced. No one answered her, although Mairi and Camilla gave her somewhat absent-minded smiles. With a look of exasperation she withdrew.

Tom bit into a ham sandwich, watching moodily as Eleanor took round the cups and offered milk and sugar. His gaze as it lingered on his wife was suddenly vulnerable, readable. More quietly he said, 'I want us to come here because I would like us to have more children. I think it could all be different here, a different pace of life. She says I'm disenchanted with my work. It's more with myself. I know what's wrong with Scottish journalism but I don't know how to put it right. I want out, out, out. I want to call my soul my own. Who in his right mind wants to stay in Glasgow now?'

'That's it,' said Eleanor triumphantly. 'You've admitted it. Defeat. The men are giving up all over the place. Well, the women won't. I won't. I hope I can always come to Calneggie.' She shivered suddenly, thinking of snow, knowing at subliminal level that the place still held the pain of being young here and meeting Geoffrey Benson, surprised all over again at the strength of memory. 'But I won't live here. I'll live among the snot and grot and if Tom doesn't like it, he knows what he can do.'

In their bedroom later, Mairi said to her husband, 'Do you think they could make a go of it here?'

He watched her undress, suddenly hungry to touch her. 'I don't know. It would only work if they were both determined it should.'

'Camilla would give them all the help she could.'

He put his hands on her waist before she could remove her silky blue underskirt, unmanned by her soft warm flesh. He put his lips in the hollow between her breasts. 'You see what you do to me. Come between the sheets. I want you.'

She did as she was bid, her nyloned legs slipping deliciously

277

against his bare ones.

'You never deny me,' he said exultantly. 'You have a body made for love. Did you know that?'

She kissed his chest. 'I suspected it a little. From the attentions you give me.'

'You like it too. Don't deny it.'

She pushed her chin into his shoulder. 'I don't. Deny it, I mean. Eleanor's different, isn't she? My generation were taught they had to subjugate themselves, make themselves available to the lord and master.'

'Who taught them?'

'Books and things. Public attitudes. Your parents. Something you absorbed. The woman was – available. To her husband. Her children.'

'It doesn't lie in your construction, then? It wasn't all arranged by your Maker?'

She felt her flesh warm and relax under his hands. 'When we went to America together, I got closer to her. I got the feeling that sex for her wasn't a giving up of her whole personality – '

'As it is with you – '

'Yes, as it is with me,' she agreed, turning to him and submitting herself wholly to his embrace.

Later she said, 'I have the feeling that with them it is more – detached. Eleanor told me Tom had been with other women before they married. He used to carry a little suède leather pouch in his waistcoat pocket with a Woolworth wedding ring in it, and when he picked up a girl at a party they went to a hotel for the night. As Mr and Mrs. This was in London.'

He lay grinning in the dark at the notion of a young man's compromise between lust and respectability. 'He seems a loyal enough husband.'

'Yes. He loves her. He's more in love with her than she with him. But I think it's because she's a challenge. She hasn't given all of herself. You can tell from the way he talks about coming to Calneggie. It's so that he can have her to himself, so that she won't develop her notions of independence. For I think he feels one day they will go too far and take her away from him entirely.'

'Poor chap.'

'Yes, in a way. But poor Eleanor too, trying to find her way. You know this Pill they are talking about? It will mean a lot of Eleanors kicking over the traces, won't it?'

'I think you overstate it. They will sort things out between them. We can't interfere.'

'I know that,' she said, forlornly. He gathered her close to him, so that they lay together like spoons in a box. He could enjoy her delicate womanly scents, her musky warmth, and he sank into secure contentment as though into a great feather mattress.

In their bedroom neither Eleanor nor Tom had undressed. She stood fiddling with the catch of her necklace and when he came over to help her she moved away from him, rejecting him.

'Did you have to drink so much?' she demanded coldly.

'I am not drunk.'

'I did not say you were.'

'You inferred as much.'

'Oh, go to bed. You bore me.'

'I should think you made that clear to everyone downstairs.'

She sat patiently on the edge of the bed, her look more weary than puzzled, and raised her eyebrows ironically.

'You suggested I was running away from the job.'

'And aren't you?'

He suddenly pushed her back on the bed and leaned over her, his breath coming quickly. 'You bitch! You know how I feel, being sent out day after day to the courts. Nothing to get my teeth into.'

'Why should I be a slave to your fantasies?' She pushed him away, sat up, caught his protesting arm and wrestled with him with a fierce strength. 'You have no time for mine. For what I want.'

'We could make a mint. It would be hard work to start with –'

'I won't do it!'

He rose and began undressing with a swift, competent rage. She did the same and they got into bed and lay back to back. When he turned and put a tentative hand on her arm she shook him off, but he tried again and eventually turned her round so that their breaths mingled, as if they were still struggling.

'Eleanor?' His voice was sober.

'No.'

She could not move away from him. 'But I say yes, yes, yes.'

CHAPTER SEVENTEEN

Tom Wishart was beginning to wish he had not had that last whisky and possibly, even the one before that. Eleanor was wavering up and down as he gazed at her from his stance at the back of the hall, the colours of her blue and green dress running into each other, her face a pink blur. Even her voice was distorted by the microphone in front of her. He cursed all party hacks and helpers who did not make sure the platform equipment was working properly before they subjected their candidates to public scrutiny. But at a deeper level it was himself he was despising. What was the male equivalent of camp follower? For that was all he was, traipsing from one draughty platform after another, listening to Eleanor put across her particular brand of folksy, gutsy common sense, that she hoped this time was going to take her to Westminster. (And his feet were frozen.) Sometimes he thought of Calneggie and the hotel that could once have been his: now it mouldered away, empty, neglected, for Camilla had not achieved her wish to turn it into a museum.

He turned to the slender, saturnine man in the tweed safari jacket next to him and managed the glimmer of a reassuring smile. 'She'll not be long now.' The man bent his head forward to catch the whisper. 'We get the bit about being content to be second-class, second-rate no longer and that's usually it.'

Tom Wishart's companion had attracted a number of curious glances that evening. Among the mixed bag of politically-aware Dounhead citizens, with their decent hard-wearing coats, their caps and headscarves, his cosmopolitan ease, verging on the disdainful, had been instantly apparent.

The onlookers were careful, of course, not to allow their interest to appear too overt. Anyone with an English accent – or even an 'Englified' one – required careful watching. If it was someone out to patronize or talk down, hackles rose immediately. Defensiveness – no, something more, an angry, dour intransigence – spread across every face till it was like a solid wall and it would be a brave man who tried to breach it. Tom they thought they knew. He put a good face on it, did not seem to mind his wife's increasing public recognition.

He held her coat and got her drinks and opened car doors for her and threatened 'heavies' who got out of hand at her meetings. He talked about 'we' when everyone knew it was Eleanor who was the dominating one, the one who made the papers. But they quite admired the way he kept his dignity and if he was fond of a dram, it was a human enough failing. He never got quarrelsome on it, just a bit red-faced and silent, and on those occasions it was Eleanor who took the wheel of the family car.

'My God,' said the man beside Tom, as the meeting finished as predicted and the audience filed past them. 'It hasn't changed. "As it was in the beginning." The same stolid burghers. It would take a steam-hammer to make an impression on some of them.'

Tom hurried him round to the changing-rooms of the Dounhead Co-operative Hall, in time to catch Eleanor with her platform party and abstract her before she got caught up in the evening's post-mortems. Eleanor turned to her companions and said, 'I want you to meet Philip Mackenzie. My forty-second cousin, or something like that. Anyway, we're related. He's doing a programme on Scotland for the BBC.' She gave a mannered, fluting laugh. 'He might even do a wee bit about me, now that the word's getting about down in London that we mean business.'

She and Philip kissed, while the others looked embarrassed.

'Went off quite well, I thought,' said one man, touching Eleanor's arm briefly before moving off.

'See you at the committee meeting Monday, Ian,' she called after him. She smiled at the rest, who stood around uncertainly. 'And thank you all. I think we were getting across to them tonight.' One or two looked as though they'd like to stay and argue, but she put her arm through Philip's. 'Where are we going? You promised me a nice red steak. I could do with it.'

The car speeding towards Glasgow and its bright lights was permeated by Eleanor's perfume. The freelance work offered her after the American trip by the publicist Gordon Watson was enough to keep her well-dressed, well-groomed. Headlights from other cars gleamed on her carefully tinted blonde hair, back-combed on the crown in one of the new, high hairstyles. Her full-skirted dress, though demure, had been carefully chosen to show off her neat waist, just as her pointed shoes with their high narrow heels set off her trim ankles. She worked hard at her image, which she hoped inspired confidence in her as someone practical, up-to-the-minute, quietly and acceptably sexy, yet as down-to-earth and approachable as a favourite aunt. It was a difficult feat to bring off, but it seemed to be working. She had polled twenty per cent of the vote in a by-election and she was taking on all three major parties in the coming battle. Anything could happen this time. The Profumo scandal of '63 had weakened the 'never had it so good' Tories who had shelved Macmillan for Douglas-Home.

'Have you seen your mother?' she asked Philip Mackenzie now, turning her profile slightly from the driving-seat for his backseat reply.

'Yep.' The answer was depressed, monochrome.

'And?'

There was no response for a matter of seconds. Then the words came in a vehement torrent, drowning the classless accent: 'I can't bear it. Not her: the house. Everything so obsessively neat and clean. I left the tea-caddy an inch out of place and she was fussing behind me, putting it right. I came down after nine for my breakfast and her brow was like thunder.'

'You have to make allowances. She's getting on.'

'I suppose so,' he conceded. 'Don't get me wrong. I love her. When I look back on what she did, how she survived, I am filled with an admiration that verges on reverence. But I hate being back. That little house –' Philip's voice shook – 'it brings back memories that shred me into little pieces. Indignities, like not having money for the school lunch. Like going to the pawn. Like drinking water to put down hunger. We weren't the only ones. I know that now. But by God, it felt like it.'

'Well, that's what I'm trying to put right,' said Eleanor matter-of-factly. 'That's what I say in my speeches. We've come to accept that if you want to eat or work or learn, even things like the social graces, you go to London – well, England – to do it. And why should it be? We once had all the brains and natural resources, all the leaders and the scholars we needed. What happened to them?'

'Philip knows what happened to them,' Tom put in pointedly. 'They all bought big houses in Ealing.'

Philip laughed. They were going up Hope Street in Glasgow in search of one of the few restaurants that would still be open. The city seemed dead, except for a trickle of people from the bingo halls.

'Where are the trams?' demanded Philip, outraged.

'They went in '62. Didn't you know? We got Polaris instead.'

'Nobody told me! It isn't Glasgow without the trams.'

'Wait till the planners are finished with it,' said Eleanor. 'Fewer folk have cars in Glasgow than practically any other place you care to mention, but the word is everything is going to be sacrificed to the great urban motorway.'

'I've read the Buchanan Report,' said Philip grimly. 'That's what you mean, isn't it? They're going the right way about killing what little industry there is left in the city. But they'll never get away with carving up Edinburgh in the same way. There's enough of the old guard left there to fight them off, and thank God for it.'

Tom made a noise of mingled disgust and aversion. 'Once they've stacked the Glasgow folk neatly away in thirty-storey blocks, or housing schemes with all the social amenities of Sing-Sing –'

'Or carted them off willy-nilly to the windy new towns,' interjected Eleanor.

'– once they've done all that, it'll be really great. You'll be able to drive right through Glasgow at tremendous speed on your way to Kirkintilloch. Or wherever. And wave to your grannie on her thirtieth-floor flat when the lift's stuck.'

They parked the car in the street outside a discreetly lit restaurant. Against its new plate-glass windows a drunk in a muffler was being sick while at the same time trying to undo his flies for a pee.

'That's Glasgow to me,' said Philip, shuddering. 'Drink and vomit.'

Eleanor pushed open the restaurant door hurriedly, her expression showing a guilty distaste. Inside all was soft lights and pleasant music. A deferential Italian head waiter approached them and led them to a pink-covered table.

When they had eaten scampi and steaks and ordered the sweet and coffee, Eleanor sat back with a sigh of contentment. 'That's better. First decent bite I've had today.' She put her hands together in a businesslike pose and said to Philip, 'And when are your production team coming up, then?'

'Not till nearer the election. I'd like to cover one of your meetings. But tell me honestly: you don't think you'll get in, do you? The happy burghers of Dounhead didn't look too ecstatic about what you said.'

'Perhaps not this time,' Eleanor admitted reluctantly. 'I'll be content if I push up the percentage and get my face known. We've got some good people in the SNP now, you know – people like William Wolfe and Ian Macdonald, who're busy sweeping away all the old cobwebs.'

'They've a well-oiled publicity machine,' Philip admitted, 'and they seem to be getting themselves organized with a nice old-fashioned Presbyterian thoroughness!'

'But what about you?' Eleanor changed the subject, putting a hand out and touching Philip's while at the same time casting a critical glance at Tom, who was finishing off the second bottle of Chianti. 'You haven't told us much about the family. Is it,' she finished up shrewdly, 'because there's something you don't want to talk about?'

'Eleanor!' protested Tom.

'I'm allowed to quiz him.' She waited for a reply without taking her eyes from Philip's face. There was a look of disillusion – no, it was something more than that, something deeper – about him. Allowing for the fact that he was in a disillusioning profession, that he trod regularly and heavily all over feet of clay, his demeanour was more than the assumed, world-weary, know-it-all attitude of the media man. Something more human and painful underlay it, she was sure.

Philip adopted a heavy Western drawl. 'Where do the cowboys go now for a bit of fun in this one-horse town?' he demanded evasively, his gaze slipping away from Eleanor's. 'What about Barrowland or the Palais or, wait, I have it! the Plaza! Where, as I remember it, a violinist called Benny Loban moved among the dancers playing excerpts from *The Lilac Domino* and *Lilac Time*? I feel in need of such refreshment for the soul.'

'Elizabeth,' said Eleanor tenaciously, 'is all right, isn't she? I haven't heard you mention her once.'

'Hardly likely, since she's no longer with me.'

'No longer *what*?'

'She's vamoosed. Scarpered. Toddled off. With a big sulky scenic designer who wants to give her one before it's too late.'

'Give her one?' said Eleanor bewilderedly. 'Do you mean – ?'

'Would you mind finishing your sentences?' said Philip. He looked at a glazed Tom and smiled without heat. 'She should finish her sentences, shouldn't she, old man?'

'Who are you calling an old man?' asked Tom belligerently.

'Don't mess about.' Eleanor was firm. 'Do you mean give her a child?'

'Pardon my patois. Comes of giving up your heritage and pissing off south.'

Eleanor took away the third bottle of wine and put it out of reach of both men.

'We're going home,' she said. 'Come on. Crispin will be waiting up to meet you, Philip.'

In the back of the car, Tom fell asleep and Philip sang as he looked out at the silent, moonlit suburbs:

> 'Oh-hon! for somebody!
> Oh-hey! for somebody!
> I wad do – what wad I not?
> For the sake o' somebody!'

'Has she gone off with him for good?' Eleanor persisted.

'How can any man tell how long love will last?' demanded Philip in stentorian tones of reproval. 'I fear she is already in the pudding club, *enceinte,* up the spout. Somewhere off Parliament Hill Fields, or Kentish Town, where they carry sheaves of drooping dandelions to the courts of: you remember your Betjeman, don't you?' He put his feet up on the back of the driving-seat and let forth once again:

> 'My heart is sair, I dare na tell,
> My heart is said for somebody:
> I could wake a winter night,
> For the sake o' somebody!
> Oh-hon! for somebody!
> Oh-hey! for –'

'For Christ's sake, shut up!' said Eleanor. 'It isn't a laughing matter. What about Timothy?'

'He's up at Cambridge, learning the noble art of cutting the parent down to size while sponging on him for foreign holidays.'

'Don't be bitter,' she pleaded. 'It doesn't become you. Crispin has started to grow his hair. Long. I could get in a state about it. But I don't.'

Going up the close and stairs of the red-brick tenement Eleanor and Tom had moved to after Clarkston, Philip shouted outrageously, 'I smell Glasgow! What is it? That unforgettable aroma of urine, strong disinfectant and something else? What is the mystery ingredient? Soot? Rain? Ignorance? Bigotry?'

'This is a respectable tenement,' said Eleanor savagely. She pushed Philip and then Tom through the heavy front door.

A thin, tense-looking boy with hunched shoulders came into the spacious lobby to greet them. He wore his thick hair in a long version of the pudding cut made fashionable by the Beatles, and glared at the unsteady figure of his father from under a heavy fringe. 'Is he canned again?' he demanded.

'Not exactly canned, Crispin,' said Philip, putting out his hand. 'Tiddley, foozled, inebriated, but not canned. At least not totally.'

'I would have thought he was,' said Crispin curtly. He shook the proffered hand in perfunctory fashion. To his mother he complained, 'There were no eggs in the fridge. I had to have toasted cheese.'

'You'll survive. Come on.' As Tom seemed in danger of sagging into sleep on the hall carpet, she grabbed his arm and indicated to Crispin to take the other. 'We'll put him to bed.' They entered one of the rooms off the hall while Philip gazed owlishly through the open door as they divested him of coat, jacket and shoes and then laid him on top of the blankets with an eiderdown tucked round him. 'Best place for him,' said Eleanor regretfully, smiling at Philip. 'We'll hear no more of him till morning. If you hear someone howling like a banshee for the Alka-Seltzer, it'll be him!'

She looked at her pale, untidy son, and her voice softened. 'I'm sorry about the eggs, lovie. I'll do the shopping in the morning.' She led the way into the big sitting-room where a gas-fire hissed at full power. Crispin's books and papers for his university studies were scattered about the chairs and settee. A radiogram emitted the powerful grating voice of John Lennon singing 'I Want To Hold Your Hand'.

Eleanor cleared a space on the settee so that Philip could receive the full warmth of the fire. To Crispin she said, more relaxedly, 'Have you said hello properly to Philip? I can't quite work out what the relationship is – call him Uncle if you like.'

'Hello properly,' said Crispin. 'I'll call you Philip.'

'Are you annoyed?' said Eleanor.

'What about?'

'The eggs.'

'Of course not.' Crispin dropped to the hearthrug and pulled plimsolled feet under him, surveying Philip with a candid irritable gaze. 'Have you come up to portray the natives, then? Don't forget the usual stereotypes. One, the incoherent football fan, preferably fisting a broken bottle. Two, the ignorant bigot or Scots chauvinist, loudly protesting in ungrammatical English that we're the best in the world. Where was I? Oh yes, three, the singing kiltie, born up a close in the Gorbals, with knees like knots in string singing of his Highland hame when he's never been further north than Govan. Shall I go on?'

'If that's the way television portrays you, that's how you must seem to the outsider,' said Philip mischievously.

'It's easier that way, isn't it?' Crispin argued. 'Saves you having to make up your own mind about the way we are. Just go to the file marked Scotsmen and draw out the same old lies and shibboleths.'

'Here,' said Philip admiringly. 'He's inherited the family gift of the gab. But just remember I'm as Scots as you are. They haven't taken away my passport yet! What are you going to be, young fellow? When you grow up?'

'Honest,' said Crispin. 'I hope.'

'Then let me tell you a story.' Philip smiled at Eleanor, who was listening to them both with sleepy amusement. 'Did you hear about the great international conference that was held somewhere in Africa? The Swedes came back from it and wrote a paper about the extinction of the African elephant. The French wrote about – shall we say? – polygamy among the pygmies, the English about the influence of the eighteenth-century novel among the Beri-Beri. And the Scots? Well, they turned in a paper headed "Scots on Scotland".'

Eleanor laughed first. 'I know. Gazing at the belly-button is a national preoccupation – '

'But if you're in danger of extinction, like the African elephant, then you need to go in for what I believe you telly pundits call agonizing reappraisal,' said Crispin. 'I would rather find out first of all what it is to be a human being before I find out what it is to be a Scot. But we're a threatened species. That's the truth. We could end up in the Regent's Park Zoo marked the only remaining example of our kind.'

'So what do you think I should concentrate on in these programmes, Your Worship?'

'Ask why we've still got a loony economy. Why thirty per

cent of the jobs here are created by America. Why the High
land hydro-electric scheme works at less than thirty per cen
of its capacity. Why the kirk still exerts repression. Why ou
university chairs go to Englishmen. Why – '

'Have you finished your essay?' Eleanor interjected.

'Not exactly.'

'Do you not think you should take it to your room and do
that small thing, then? Your eyes are like holes burnt in a
blanket.'

Crispin got to his feet reluctantly. 'I'll maybe see you in
the morning,' he said to Philip.

'That one,' said his mother, when he had gone, 'would
talk the hind legs off a donkey. He should make a good
lawyer. But I wanted to talk about Elizabeth before we go
to bed. Would you like some coffee?'

'No, thanks. There's not much to tell.'

'Is there someone else for you?'

'Of course not.' She turned towards him on the settee and
saw that his eyes were bright with hurt and the reluctance
to discuss things. She looked away quickly.

Philip said with a slow deliberation, his fatigue after a
long day catching up with him, 'It was simply the old business
of career versus domesticity. I worked all the hours that
God sent and she got fed up with it. She had jobs with
Marriage Guidance and the Citizens' Advice Bureau and then
this somewhat attenuated affair with George Carradine –
that's his name, her lover. I had to go to Kenya for the
independence celebrations and when I came back she had
bolted.'

Eleanor moved along the settee and took his hand.

'I'm sorry. I wondered why she had never written. I liked
– I like Elizabeth.'

'So do I.'

She leaned against him. 'Oh God, Philip, I am so sorry. I
do understand. If it's any comfort, Tom and I haven't had it
all sunshine either. He doesn't particularly care for being
drawn into the political scene, he'd rather have run the old
hotel at Calneggie that was once Uncle Patie's.'

'Why didn't he?'

'I wouldn't go along with it.'

He held her off with both arms, surveying her ironically
'That was brave of you.'

'Do you think I *should* have gone along with him?'

'I'm not saying that.'

'I suffer agonies of guilt. But I think it would just have been a soft option. I would have ended up doing all the organizing and he would have been away fishing.'

'Don't rationalize. You had your own call to answer –'

'But women do feel guilty.'

'They'll get over that. If Elizabeth had had her own row to hoe, we might have survived.' He caught her hand and squeezed it. 'This isn't bad. Lovely and warm! That Dounhead hall was freezing tonight. Maybe I'll change my mind about that coffee. What do you think?'

She plugged in an electric kettle on the hearth and brought two mugs containing instant coffee powder from the kitchen, and a tin with biscuits. She had slipped her feet from her shoes and held her curling toes out to the leaping gas jets.

'I arranged this assignment,' said Philip, sipping, 'so that I could judge whether I could ever come back.'

'You might, then?' she said, surprised. As she looked, his face seemed full of lines and regrets. 'Hasn't worldly success been all it's cracked up to be, then?'

'Worldly success?' He smiled ruefully at the phrase with its overtones of Presbyterian stricture. 'Oh, I still get a kick from a good story. Maybe I should have stayed a newspaperman, but television seemed a good idea at the time. No, I'm starting to go over old ground. Everything I do, I seem to have done before. The thrill's gone out of it. I suppose I came back –' He stopped, as if searching for the right words.

'Yes, go on.'

'I suppose I came back to see if there was a space I could fill. But I doubt it. Despite youngsters like your Crispin there, life still seems – I don't know – constricting and narrow. Minds close down and faces turn away. You get the feeling that since the Scottish Office started expanding there might have been nepotism, favouritism, maybe even, when you come down to it, jiggery-pokery and nest-feathering. Maybe there's an excuse for the officials of a poor nation, but ain't it sad? Ain't it sobering? No room for comets, for what they used to call "the uncanny Scot".'

'Yes, and you *have* been a comet,' said Eleanor warmly. 'I think you should come back. It's all going to be different –'

'I suppose,' he said, 'I carry enough clout now to wangle a job up here if I want one. See? I'm no different from the folk I criticize! If I stay in London they want me to go over to the admin side, become a sort of grey eminence.' He shook his head. 'I don't know. I don't know. I'm at the cross-roads, I know that. Without Elizabeth.'

Eleanor stared into her mug.

'Talking of *éminences grises*,' said Philip suddenly, 'I bumped into that old boy-friend of yours – what was his name? Geoffrey Benson, was it? – in Whitehall. He's one – one of your important faceless ones now. Left publishing after all and went into the Civil Service.'

She could feel her heart pound suddenly and wildly and smiled at the betrayal, determined to give it no credence now after all this time.

'Geoffrey?' she said steadily. 'How is he doing?'

'Married. Got the customary two point four kids, I think.'

'I wonder who?'

'Didn't say.'

'And how old are the children? Are they boys or girls?'

'Probably,' said Philip kindly. He grinned at her omnisciently. 'He asked me how you were. Quite pointedly for him. Did it hurt, at the time?'

She nodded, then her tightened, folded arms relaxed and she laughed, as though with a shaky relief. 'I'm very married to Tom now. The rest are blotted out. Have you ever . . . apart from Elizabeth?'

'I won't say I haven't been attracted – '

'Me too. I quite fancy Gordon Watson, the man I work for. But . . . all the times you go to sleep with someone, and all the times you wake up, they make a difference, don't they?'

She put up a hand to her cheeks and found they were wet. He moved up to her and put his arm around her.

'What's the matter, pet? Tell me.'

'Tom. The drinking.' She had meant it to come out quietly and matter-of-factly and it turned into a sobbing wail. She turned her face into his shoulder and wept without constraint while he patted her awkwardly, like a man out of practice at such things. In a few moments she drew away shame-facedly and dried her eyes with a handkerchief that was slightly grubby. He noticed an absurd embroidered cartoon cat in one corner.

'The occupational hazard,' he offered.

'Do you mean for Scots? Or journalists?'

'Maybe both?'

She nodded ruefully. 'You can say that again!'

'How bad is it? Do you want to tell me?'

'Bad enough for him to flake out quite often, as he did tonight. Bad enough for him to be sent home from the office in a taxi. Bad enough for him to hide bottles –'

He let his breath out on a low whistle.

'You're going to have to take advice about him. Get him treatment. Medical treatment.'

'I'm right, then? He is an alcoholic?'

He said carefully. 'Who am I to stick a label on him? Would you like me to talk to him?'

'No,' she said quickly, protectively. 'I'll do it. My poor Tom-Tom!' She gave him a watery smile. 'I am responsible for him, after all. But thanks for the offer.'

'And so, with Labour now in power, although with the slenderest of majorities, and Harold Wilson the new Prime Minister, we can look at Scotland's future and predict that it will be the focus of unprecedented planning to rid it of its worst, long-standing problems. Can we now look forward to the lowering of the country's traditionally high rates of emigration and unemployment through the direction of industry and perhaps preferential grants? Can the Scottish workman now expect to be paid wages on a par with his English counterpart?

'One thing is clear. For Mrs Eleanor Wishart, the Scottish Nationalist candidate who pushed the Liberals out of third place in the Dounhead constituency, the time is not yet. Although the Scot Nats claim a new spirit and a sizeable share of local government wins, the electorate are not yet ready this year of 1964 to return them to Westminster.'

Under the harsh studio lights, Philip Mackenzie turned towards Eleanor. 'Mrs Wishart, in a word, can the planners do for Scotland what the industrialists failed to do?'

'No, they cannot,' said Eleanor vigorously. 'I am not impressed by the calibre of the new Government, nor the prospect of a new Scottish Secretary doling out endless jobs for the bureaucratic boys.'

'Thank you, Mrs Wishart,' said Philip decisively. 'That is all we have time for and this is Philip Mackenzie bidding you a good "Good night" from Central Scotland and returning you to London.'

CHAPTER EIGHTEEN

Philip Mackenzie walked along the main street of Dounhead, trying to remember what Eliot had written about arriving back where you started and knowing the place for the first time. Scuffed doors, fading paint round the windows, shops whose window displays owed nothing to modernity or the hard sell. The pubs bleak and battered, cardboard stuck carelessly over jagged, broken windows. An old pitman, huddled in familiar defensive stance at the street corner, gathering his spit to aim at the gutter. The same bright-eyed, curious, argumentative children hurrying back to school after the lunch-hour, underprivilege written all over them. Badly fed. Poorly clothed. But lively, by God! The carefully nurtured little automata stepping from cars in the soft south seemed like stookies by comparison. Define stookie: a shock of sheaves; a rigid, unimaginative person. He felt his heart lift against all the odds. Some freedom was abroad in these shabby streets. Some certainty. Some joy. And how could it be? Was it just empathy with those unputdownable cheeky kids running to school? Did he suddenly remember how once because your fancy and imagination were unfettered there were worlds to conquer, seas to cross?

The euphoria passed, but a balmful, comforting, mild optimism remained, even though as he walked he saw the modest, unexciting shops, the stretches of council houses, as his lately dead mother Tina must have seen them, stultifying by their sameness. Until she was over eighty, she had liked to take a bus right into Glasgow to boost her spirits, to walk round Lewis's and have her tea in Buchanan Street.

She hadn't liked the new Glasgow, though. Once he had taken her to Edinburgh at Festival time, in the days when he and Elizabeth had still been married. She had loved the cosmopolitan atmosphere, the variety of tongues in the streets, but like a true Glaswegian she had argued it was nothing like her own city in its heyday. She had been very content with her ordered life in later years. Her husband Alisdair had left her several hundred pounds. That had brought her great peace of mind.

What novelist could convince about the strange, platonic

relationship she had had with the man she had married? She had spoken of his own father with a wild and yearning look he only understood now that he was older. As a child he had not liked it: it had threatened him, gnawed at the attentive love he felt should be his alone. Elizabeth had said he had remained a selfish, demanding child. Never mind what Elizabeth had said.

He turned into the wide windswept street where no trees grew. That was the big difference between the south and here. He had not been prepared for all the trees turning Ealing into a kind of suburban Sherwood Forest. Strange southern folk. He liked, he realized, a certain bleakness of townscape, just as he liked cold, even rain, better than heat. How pleasant to agree with Mr Eliot. All these places in his mind he was acknowledging as for the first time.

He opened a creaky iron gate and walked up a short path to the glass-fronted vestibule door of a small, greystone, semi-detached cottage. It must be, he reflected, some seventy-odd years old, and efforts had been made at modernization. So this was where Eleanor had finished up since last he saw her. When things had started going badly wrong her mother and step-father had helped her to buy it. They lived a bare street's length away.

He was unprepared for the gaunt-faced, barely smiling woman who opened the door to him. Eleanor had always smiled easily: her insouciant bravado, her ability to fight her own corner, had always been the most attractive thing about her. You forgot she could bleed like the rest.

'Come in.' She turned on her heel and led him up a small, white-painted hall into a pleasant, unambitiously furnished living-room. She was wearing mules and the hem of her short tweed skirt dipped slightly where stitches had come undone in the hem. How he hated the mini-skirt, especially on older women.

Overnight in 1967 the country had turned itself into a nation of sluts. He could hear his mother's sharp, derisive tones in his own mental criticism. Scottish knees, besides, were too plump, and Scottish thighs too hefty. The mini-skirt was made for slender public-school Dianas, just as a lot of the male clothing seemed to be designed for the shilpit. Definition of shilpit: bottle-shouldered, skinny, undersized. But as men were growing their hair and beginning to dress like lasses, with their flowered shirts and what-have-you, maybe it didn't matter anyhow.

'Sit down.' Eleanor's tone was peremptory. She picked up a half-finished cigarette from an ashtray, took a hard chair in order to give him a qualifying stare and said, 'Want a cup of tea?'

'Anything stronger?'

She began to laugh, a harsh, angry sound. 'You have a nerve! After what drink's done to this family! No, tea it'll have to be.'

'Tea's great. How is he, Eleanor? Can I go and see him?'

She shrugged her shoulders indifferently. 'If you like. You'll see a difference.'

'I'm sorry I couldn't be more precise about when I was coming – '

'That's all right. Going to milk us for another telly programme? Don't you get fed up, sitting on the fence? The observer. The voyeur.'

'It's the nature of the beast.'

'But don't you hate it?'

'Sometimes.'

'I thought you were maybe coming back.'

'I do come back. Quite a lot now. It's all happening up here now.'

'What do you mean?' she demanded, in the same harsh, unwelcoming way. 'All happening?'

'Well, the eastern ports are filling up with tenders for oil-rigs out in the North Sea. It's going to be a big oil bonanza, isn't it? Scotland's going to be incredibly rich. At last you're going to get the "one thing needful", aren't you? Independence. Isn't that the word?'

'I'll believe it when I see it.'

'I'm sure you're right to be sceptical.'

He was trying so hard to be ingratiating, placatory, that she finally gave a small, capitulatory smile and jumped up to put the kettle on. He followed her into the tiny kitchen, noting the bare tidiness of the food shelves behind the glass doors of the cabinet. She poured milk carefully into a chipped jug and set some biscuits out neatly on a plate.

'Tell me about Tom,' he insisted. 'Why are they keeping him in hospital? And why aren't you doing a Winnie Ewing? If she can get in for the Nats, why can't you? It's like I said: suddenly it's all happening. The impossible dream – '

She held the tea-cosy to her bosom. 'It was marvellous about Winnie! They put on a special train to take her to London, the way they hadn't done since the Clydesiders went to Westminster. It was a tremendous shot in the arm – '

'But you said in your letter *you* were thinking of giving it all up? Why now? When the tide is beginning to turn? When the Nats have the largest party membership in Scotland – '

'Well, isn't it obvious?'

'But Tom will get better – '

She gave him an unreadable, almost hostile look. 'What makes you think that? In any case, why should I worry about carrying the can? My son is opting out now, too, just like his father. The one chooses drink, the other's a hippy going on about peace and love. Why should I be the one to fight on?'

Philip deliberated, unwilling to look at the alarming naked misery breaking up her face. Then he said slowly and carefully, 'Because you're one of the gladiators, that's why. Someone once told me we're a nation of gladiators. Hats in the ring. Professional combatants. You can pick us full of holes but one thing we don't do is give up. Do we?'

'Crispin has.' He felt her desolation seep round the edges of his own mind.

'But all the young ones are influenced by Flower Power. Timothy too. I'm sure he smoked pot at university.'

'Pot? If only it stopped at that. Besides, your Tim has a job.'

'Hasn't Crispin? He graduated, didn't he?'

'Only just.'

'And where is he now?'

'How should I know? He told me he was taking the golden road to Samarkand. He sold everything he possessed – his record-player, camera, books and he went off with what he stood up in – an old pair of jeans and a duffle-coat. He was scruffy, dirty, long-haired, smelly. He proposed to hitch to wherever it is he's going. He says the journey isn't just outward, but into the self. I don't profess to know what he's on about.'

'You should try,' he suggested mildly.

'Well, of course I do!' She turned on him furiously and he was unreasonably glad to see a spark of the old, proud spirit.

'I've read R. D. Laing as well as he has. They idealize that wee man whenever he comes up to the universities. I know what a constricting society can do. Do you not think the hurt is twice compounded when you're a woman?'

'It's a time of great change, great upheaval. Historians are going to marvel at how well we've withstood it.'

'Have we?' She shivered. 'You speak for yourself. All I know is that I'm barely holding together.'

When he had confessed hunger and she had toasted him some strong cheese on a slice of Scottish batch bread, she went off to change. He was pleased that the blue dress she wore with a matching jacket was a little longer than the tweed skirt with the drooping hem, and that she still had an adept way of doing her hair that was smooth and sophisticated, without being hard. He put his lips to her temple and kissed her. She acknowledged the gesture with a bleak little nod.

Tom had been taken to the alcoholic ward of a large psychiatric hospital in the heart of Lanarkshire. Since Eleanor no longer ran a car they took a bus, reminding Philip of the times he'd gone to Bellnoch with his mother when a child, walking one way, then riding back because she'd pawned something and had money in her purse. He seemed to see that small, valiant figure in her cracked strap shoes and grey lisle stockings trudging that same road. He told Eleanor about it and her face relaxed into a tremulous soft receptiveness he liked better than her previous hard mask. He saw he had eased the way into asking what he wanted to know about Tom.

'Did he collapse? I mean, was it a dramatic thing, or did you just know gradually – ?'

'Oh, he collapsed all right. All over the place. He kept swearing he was going to stop drinking and he tried. Really he did try. But after a couple of days it would be worse than ever.'

'And the doctor thought hospitalization was best?'

'The only answer. He felt it would bring him up with a jolt. It would also help if he could face up to some of the reasons he got drunk.'

'And what do you think they were?'

She sighed, looking through the steamed-up bus window at rusty hedges, sad cows. 'He's a sensitive man. All quivering nerve-ends. The artistic type without the artistic ability. Or without having that – that dedication I imagine you have to possess if you want to be a writer, a creative sort of journalist. He caved in.'

'The wound without the bow? Commoner than you might think.'

'I don't quite get the classical allusion, but you're in the ght speculative area. He has one of those massive, matri-rchal types for a mother. Her Tom was going to show the orld, and especially the folk in her street.'

'Another gladiator?'

'Aye, but this one ended up with a cut knee. If we're going for the imagery of childhood. Which is, so I'm told, here it all begins.'

'I'm glad,' he said relievedly, 'that you don't blame your-lf.'

'Who says I don't? Poor Tom. He needed two assertive males like a hole in the head.'

The hospital was set in peaceful countryside with a long rive and formal gardens, round which a few patients were king the air, huddled into their coats and scarves, for the ay was cold.

The ward that Tom was in was long, bare, functional, ith several empty beds because the patients were attend-g therapy. In the other beds, men slept, read or waited for sitors. Tom had hoped to be up and dressed but had been ept in bed because he had had a cold and a temperature. e looked, thought Philip, like something that had lain on e sea-shore for years, for æons, till he was washed clean f everything but basic bone.

Even his eyeballs looked scraped, scoured. He felt a jolt f superstitious pity and fear.

But Tom, smiling and taking Philip's bag of grapes with a rateful 'Thanks', spoke in a normal, pleased-to-see-you voice at the others found reassuring. The cold had been nothing, e said: he was over it. He could contain himself no longer. e grabbed Eleanor's hand and said, 'I'm coming home. The uack wants to see you.'

She kissed him. 'Are you sure? They said it would take nger.'

'Ask the doc,' he urged her jubilantly. 'I'll have to come ack and see him from time to time. But he says if you can ope, he thinks I might be able to. I'm not going back to the b, Eleanor. He says no work for a while, then maybe local urnalism. Slow and steady.'

She put her arms round him, hugging him. 'Where do I see im?' He pointed to an office at the end of the ward. 'Down ere.'

He grinned at Philip. 'Philip and I will have a blether while ou're away.' He wrapped his arms around his body as though he were cold, or naked. 'Would you like to do a programme on what booze does to the personality? If so I'm your man.'

'Trouble is,' said Philip, 'it's been done, old son. Too many times.'

When she finally saw the doctor, Eleanor came straight out with her worries. 'Isn't it too soon? He still seems so frail.'

The rotund, balding man bursting out of his fraying white coat gave her a measuring, not unkindly stare. 'Your husband *is* frail, Mrs Wishart. You can't assault your body and mind with alcohol and not pay the price. But we've dried him out. He's an intelligent man. He has a certain amount of insight into *why* he drinks. His *amour propre* has taken a battering, but you, I think, are particularly well placed to rebuild his confidence. I think it can be done. With love and patience.'

'I'll try,' she said sombrely. 'I *have* tried.'

'What about your own parliamentary ambitions? Your husband tells me you are thinking of laying these aside?'

'Certainly. Tom comes first.'

'Don't be too hasty.' He fiddled with a blotter on the desk in front of him. He had the appearance of a man looking for words to say, finding them and then rejecting their utterance. Eleanor felt a flutter of disquiet and the psychiatrist's blue eyes, wary and equivocal, met hers. He smiled then, briskly and professionally, betraying an underlying sadness and doubt more bitingly than if he had shouted them out loud. In the silence of the room Eleanor was aware of the scraping back of her chair like something scraping on the uneasy unconscious depths of her mind.

'What you must remember,' said the doctor, 'is that no one can be a hundred per cent responsible for anyone else. Not if there's free will. We have to allow the possibility of setbacks. We have to allow options.'

'Yes,' she said woodenly. 'Yes, doctor. Thank you. I understand.'

Going home in the bus, Philip drew her out of her reverie by saying briskly, 'You'll have to help me, you know. You're my political correspondent. The oil tenders at Aberdeen are going to look good on the new colour tellies, but I have to have some decent background info to make another piece by me about Scotland stick.'

She gave him an abstracted look. 'Dr Ewart said – well, suggested – I shouldn't let my political interests flag. Why ould he want to say that?'

'Because as a sensible man he's a feminist. What sensible man would be otherwise these days?' He grinned at her teasingly, trying to lighten her spirit.

She shook her head, as though denying his interpretation, but after lapsing into reflection for several minutes, the need to talk politics was too strong.

'You remember what I told you three years ago?' The tone was lecturing.

'You told me a lot of things then.'

'What I said about Labour and planning? I was right! What a dog's breakfast they've made of Scotland! You know what they say about Labour these days? To get on in the Party you need to be a kind of charismatic numbskull – no, I didn't coin the phrase, it was one of their own Left-Wingers. But it's true. They've had committees and enquiries, commissions and development bodies. Like a dog chasing its own tail. Harold Wilson has closed his mind to devolution, never mind independence. It's madness, as even the Tories know. Their numbers may be going down but they've got the sense to set up a study group on the subject. And wait and see. Labour will be forced to do a turn-about. They haven't the nous to see they are strengthening the Scot Nats' hand, in the meantime, but when the penny drops they'll have to come up with something.'

'Would you, personally, be pleased with devolution? It seems to be becoming the respectable answer, the darling of the intellectuals.'

'Only inasmuch as I think it would eventually lead to total independence followed by a federation of British states.'

Philip sighed. 'It's a pipe-dream. Confess. That's all it is.'

'Well, what about the 1320 Club?'

'Never heard of it.'

'It's true what they say about the media, isn't it? They know a little about everything and nothing very much about anything!'

'Spare me the character assassination! What is this famous club?'

'I'll be fair to you. It *has* just been founded and the name comes from the date of the Declaration of Arbroath. All the oldies have joined it – Wendy Wood, Hugh MacDiarmid, Douglas Young. And, of course, Aunt Camilla.'

'And what about the youngies?'

'Some of them too. The romantics. But the SNP has slapped

an interdict on it, thank God. We have to live in the present.
'So it's not important?'
'I didn't say that. It's a symptom: a digging-in of heels.'
'Will you come on the programme and say that?'
'If you like.'

She had been reading about *The Forsyte Saga* in the *Daily Record*. Wondering why, like everybody else, she looked forward to Sunday nights on the black-and-white box and the convoluted relationships of Galsworthy's middle-class English family. Like most women, she was half in love with horrid Soames, just as most men were with frigid Irene. But as the front gate clicked, she whipped the paper down on a chair and rose to open the door for Tom, the fictional family instantly forgotten. She was a little ashamed of her recent addiction to soap opera, however high-toned. It was as though the literary solution of human problems spread a kind of easy gauze over her own. Was it bad or dangerous? She didn't know. Why should it be? It was probably merely her hairshirt of a conscience, putting down anything labelled innocent pleasure.

'How did it go?' She tried to keep her voice light, blasé. Tried not to meet his eye.

He hung up his coat on the hall rack, while she attempted to judge his mood from the set of his shoulders. He was taking a long time. Her heart began its familiar, slow, inexorable sinking, like a tired old basement-bound lift. 'Tom,' she urged, before the lift hit rock-bottom. 'Tell me. What happened? Any luck?'

He turned, holding out towards her a half-pound box of Black Magic chocolates. 'For you.' She took them, scarcely aware of her actions. She thought how painfully drained and thin he still was, like something out of a refugee camp. But the shoulders were all right. Jaunty. He had something to report.

Reprieved, she led the way into the living-room, glad she had kept the gas-fire on low, so that the room was comfortably warm, glad she had set the table with the Darvel lace cloth, the good china, the silver Apostle spoons, the two chrysanthemum heads she had salvaged from a sheltered corner of the cold garden.

'Well?'
'I've got a job.'
'*Reporter?*'

'No. Sub-editor. They have a senior man retiring. Bob Kent thought I could have a bit of a trial run.'

'Oh, great. Oh, marvellous,' she said. She watched him jealously as he spread his hands to the fire. He had not been keen initially to apply to the *Bellnoch Herald*, but Dr Ewart had backed her up about not going back to the heavy drinking scene in Glasgow.

At last, as though thawed by the heat, his face relaxed its tense expression. He held out his arms.

'How about a kiss for the great man, then?'

She put her arms a little shyly round him. Recently they had touched little. They had been careful and kindly, even loving, but touch had been something they shied away from. Now she leaned her head against his chest and gave a great sigh. 'Oh, Tom, maybe it's all going to come right for us.'

'I'll not be under much stress.' He hooked up her chin and reassured her. 'I'll get home early in the evenings. There's just one other thing I have to tell you, before I go into details of my interview. Eric Heggie's had a heart attack. I met his agent on my way home.'

Heggie was the ex-miner who now represented Dounhead in Parliament as Labour MP.

'How bad is he?'

'Not too bad. They've taken him to hospital. But whichever way it goes for him, it looks as though there'll be a by-election. Eric's getting past it. His agent said as much.'

She sat down on legs that had suddenly become cotton wool.

'Doesn't make any difference.'

'Yes, it does. If it comes to it, I want you to stand again. I don't want you to give up the nomination.'

'Tom!' Her voice was sharp and adamant. 'We've been over all this. My mind is made up.'

'I think you would get in.'

'You really think so?'

' "There is a tide in the affairs of men" – and women. You can't let it pass.'

'You forget. Poor Eric Heggie's not ready yet for the boneyard.' She gave a relieved laugh. 'Let's hope he won't be. You gave me a bit of a turn there.'

She pushed him towards the table. 'I've got chicken broth, steak pie, trifle. How does sir like the sound of that?'

He rubbed his hands obediently and sat down. 'Great.'

In the kitchen, dishing up, she found her fingers were

trembling. People made good recoveries from heart attacks these days, didn't they? She put out her mind the picture of the last time she had seen Eric Heggie, a worn-looking man in his sixties. He had sounded fed up with the electorate, with his party, with the government and what it had failed to do for Scotland. Maybe he would regard this as an honourable get-out. But she shouldn't even be thinking along these lines. What mattered was Tom getting the job. She had to support and encourage him in the days to come. In some ways now he was as timid as a child, uncertain, easily discouraged. It was as though they were rebuilding him, piece by jigsaw piece. The doctor said he would not be the same man again. More realistic about his capabilities. She hoped he was right. She prayed the Bellnoch job would give his spirits the boost they needed.

In the old days, they might have had some wine with the meal. She would certainly have put some sherry in the trifle. Now she wouldn't risk even that. While they ate, he outlined what his salary would be, discussed the sports copy he would chiefly be subbing and the people he would be working with. She saw that he was seeking reassurance that he was not suffering too much in status. 'The *Herald* is a good county paper,' he told her. She nodded. 'The week wouldn't be the same for a lot of folk without the *Herald*.'

Halfway through the meal he threw down his fork and knife. 'Hatches, matches and dispatches. Births, deaths and marriages. That's all it is. Really.'

'So is *The Times*,' she coaxed.

He started eating again. 'I'm nervous, I suppose.'

'Don't be. You'll be fine. Keep telling yourself how well you've done.'

'Only with your help.' He looked at her, with that half-embarrassed expression he wore when he wanted to express something emotional. 'My love,' he said. 'With *your* help.'

She went out and made the coffee, the tears trembling on her lashes till she dashed them brusquely away. She went back in, snapping off the main light, snapping on the small lamp above the television set and finally switching on the set itself. It flickered into scenes from the war in Vietnam and she switched channels to a comedy show.

They sat holding hands on the sofa. She tried to stifle her disquiet at his thinness: it reminded her of her father. It would take time, that was all. She must be patient. When the comedy show was over, they switched off and sat talking, more animatedly than they had done since he had come home from hospital.

'Where do you think Crispin is?' She said this often, sometimes wistfully, sometimes with a crackling anger. Tonight he detected no overtones either way, more a yearning optimism.

'The last card was from Istanbul.'

'He might be on his way back.'

He said nothing. They were both afraid of what might have happened to their son in the meantime. The drug culture had claimed so many victims. They comforted each other by remembering what he had been like as a little boy, when he had belonged to them, dwelling selectively on the good, the funny times. And as often happened, yearning and anger grew in her till she said, 'Where was he when we needed him?'

'He had to sort out his own problems.'

'What problems?'

'Kids nowadays care more about what sort of people they really are. Not with putting on a face or acting a role. How can that be a bad thing?'

'Does Crispin care what goes on inside *me*? Or doesn't it matter?'

He drew her to him. 'There's one thing, Ellie. We are closer now than we've ever been. That's for sure.'

'Yes,' she said tenderly. She curled her feet up under her and huddled against him, glad of his physical presence.

In bed he turned her towards him. She touched him, kissed him, wanting to fire him with her own urgent, nascent sexuality and quickly succeeding. 'Nobody could be closer,' she whispered. Her body opened to him, her mind swam, shimmered, exploded with the old, the remembered ecstasy. It had been a long time but afterwards, she thought shiveringly, it had been like touching bone. She knew now where Tom had been in those terrible weeks in hospital. And now she had to drag him up from that place. The connection had been made.

The bus stopped at the scratched and battered shelter in Dounhead Main Street. Someone had written on the side 'Send the Pope to the Moon'. The two young people descending the bus steps looked round, as if indeed it were a lunar landscape *they* saw. He wore a dirty goatskin coat, with colourful embroidery down the front, frayed jeans and white plimsolls. He was bearded and his hair fell halfway down his back. She wore a long, indeterminate frock and a shabby jacket, both of which had seen the light of day many years before, possibly before she was born. Her hair was long and curly and she wore round, silver-rimmed grannie glasses, giving her an earnest air.

They held hands as they walked with the curious, loping contemporary gait past the chip shop and the Co-op hall, the solid clump of council housing, till they came to the street with the greystone cottage.

'Maybe I should have written,' said Crispin as he went in the gate. 'I hope,' he said belatedly, looking nervously down at his companion, 'that they'll be pleased to see me.'

When she had brought them in, wept, fed them, scolded and questioned them, Eleanor Wishart sent her son and his girl-friend Lally to bed. It did not matter to her that they were 'living together', as they put it, and sharing a bed out of wedlock. It didn't matter that their dusty feet would soil the white candlewick bedspread or that very possibly fleas would seek fresh pastures in the eiderdown she threw over their weary bodies. He had come back all of a piece. He was hungry and filthy and tired, but it had been her son, her Crispin, who had looked back at her from those sunken sockets of eyes. Wherever he had been, whatever company he had kept, he had survived. The small American girl he had met in Afghanistan was of lesser importance. She would accept her, if need be, if it was the price of laying nightmares. Sitting in the kitchen with tea she had made without realizing it, Eleanor shook with rage, laughter and relief.

But before Tom came back that evening she had stormed into action, making both Crispin and Lally take baths, arbitrarily removing their clothes for washing and providing them with a makeshift wardrobe, even hastening to the Co-op before it closed to buy them plimsolls and throwing the smelly predecessors into the dustbin.

'How could you, Crispin?' she raged.

'We've been travelling.' He said it easily, refusing to be caught up in her anger. In a failed attempt to soothe, he said, 'Don't make it too heavy a scene, Mother. We don't want to be caught up in your bourgeois values again. Don't try to change us.'

'But you stink!' she howled.

'Not any more,' said Crispin reasonably.

'Now listen to me,' she heard herself shouting at him.

'Your father has been very ill. While you were seeking your mantra or whatever all over the place, the man who fathered you nearly died. When he comes in, you and Lally have to spare *him* any heavy scenes. I won't have him upset. He'll want you to cut your hair to a reasonable length, he'll want you, as I do, to get some kind of a job and – ' with a look at the silent Lally – 'he may very well feel that you and Lally should regularize your union. That's the way we do things in Dounhead. Do you hear me, Crispin?' She stopped, appalled at the shrill note of hysteria in her voice.

'Mother.' Crispin's note was steady, unwavering. 'Do not try to run my life. My life is my life.'

She wanted at that point to scream at him to get out, but she didn't want him gone before Tom came home. She sat down with them over endless cups of tea and coffee and tried to piece together their travels, their experiences, their philosophy. To her it all seemed open-ended, inconclusive, infuriatingly inarticulate and vague. Said Crispin, 'That is how it's meant to be.' To Eleanor, they were like two adult children, irresponsible, obtuse, immovable.

To her astonishment, Tom's reaction was much less violent than her own. Even on the first night, he opened up to Crispin and Lally about his alcoholism in a way he had not done to her. He did not seem to mind the sponging on their own fragile resources. He was gentle and supportive with Lally, who would not eat meat or let them kill the dozy, late wasps coming in the kitchen window. It was in Eleanor that the conflicts raged and it was because of Eleanor that after a week Crispin and Lally talked of moving out.

'Where will you go?' Eleanor heard the familiar wailing note in her own words.

'We thought of Aunt Camilla. Maybe we could squat in part of the old hotel – it's not used for anything, is it? We could perhaps in the end have a commune, grow our own food – '

Eleanor looked at them helplessly. She dug into her purse and gave them the few notes she could spare. She felt as though she had mothered a changeling. The boy who had left university had been tense, argumentative, still in touch with the world of jobs and ambition. This one gazed back at her with his equivocal, teasing smile, a maddening easy-going child with a mysterious girl playmate. Where were they going? Not down her road. When they had left she

305

washed the white bedspread and hung the eiderdown out in the frosty sun.

Camilla, it turned out, was not averse to the two scruffy young people who took up abode in a ramshackle downstairs room at Calneggie. The windows had already been stove in by summer vandals. Crispin replaced these and Lally hung up curtains of sorts that she bought at a jumble sale. They spent hours on the seashore, gathering driftwood for the big open fire. Crispin could be seen digging and hoeing a small plot in front of the mansion, much to the amusement of the locals who were gently tolerant of the hippies now dotting the West Coast landscape like shabby crows.

'Camilla must be doted,' fumed Eleanor. But she had a place to fit Crispin into now, a frame for his life, and it was better than the days when they had not known where in the world he laid his head, or even if he were still alive.

Tom had stuck to the job at the *Herald*. There were times when he came home silent and brooding, and she knew something at work had upset him – perhaps a thoughtless word or an imagined slight. But he was slowly putting on flesh and with encouragement from Mairi and Robin their social life picked up again. Eleanor found her own regime of easy domesticity hard to bear. It was difficult to go back to being the kind of rigid, houseproud creature she had been soon after her marriage and yet, perfectionist by nature, she scoured and polished rooms that did not need it.

It was Tom who came back to the attack about her political involvement. He had stayed her hand about giving up the candidature and when Eric Heggie announced his intention of retiring from public life, he urged her not to give up the considerable ground she had made in the constituency and to try once more. She dismissed his pleading out of hand.

'Are you trying to become some sort of martyr?' Tom argued furiously.

She was very calm. 'I'm settling down. It's time I did.'

'To keep an eye on me. Scarcely a life's work. And what's more, a sacrifice I repudiate.'

'What would you do if I were down at Westminster all week?'

'Only when Parliament is sitting. And you'd be home at week-ends.'

'Not always.'

He said diffidently, 'I know I haven't been properly involved before. But I could hold the fort for you here, take folks' complaints. My job doesn't stretch me. You know that.'

Still she would not have given in had people in Dounhead themselves not urged her to reconsider her decision. They refused to countenance any other Scottish Nationalist candidate: it had to be Eleanor Wishart or nobody.

One evening while she was washing up after the meal the doorbell rang and she answered it to a middle-aged man in a prosperous overcoat.

'You don't know me?' The man smiled. 'I'm Eddie McCafferty. I've just bought a wee shop. Newsagent and tobacconist.'

'Come in,' she invited, still mystified.

'You'll not remember the McCaffertys. Went away to the Fife coalfields. But your da kept me out of jail once. Never mind when. A long time ago. The time of the Spanish Civil War. He was a good man, Eleanor, one of the best. I've come to say to you: stand for us. He would have wanted it.' It all came blundering out at a great pace and she had a fleeting elusive memory of the huge sprawling family in the slum clearance scheme, whose father had died on the way back from harvesting in Canada.

She put the man off. She had the feeling he had wanted to come back and show himself as a success as much as he had wanted to encourage her candidacy. His politics were passionate, muddled and obscure.

Yet his visit had the effect of making her more restless than any other source. The strength of her response to his plea shook her. Could she really be *needed* then? She sought her mother's advice and found Mairi only too pleased that she was at last turning her mind outwards again.

In the end she agreed to stand. Support for the Nationalists had begun to waver again, and Labour had won back a measure of popularity. It was unlikely she would get in, but just to be back on the hustings was exhilarating. She owned wryly it must be something in the genes. Personal worries shrank back into proportion.

If Crispin had opted out in his search for head-space, as he called it, he was no different from many others of his generation. And she could see now how the world needed gentleness, reflection, that the life cherishers and small-is-beautiful people might do more to conserve the earth than the head-on-ers like herself.

It was one of those strange inconsistencies which riddle political life and confound the pollsters that returned her to Westminster in the end. The carefully chosen Labour man had been too didactic, his ties and his manner too flashy. The Tory man had been too honest about unemployment, saying it would take a long time to cure. Something had worked like yeast through the Dounhead voters, something compounded of sympathy, folk memory and a kind of magical rapprochement between the woman and the hour.

All went well for the first six months. Her fears about Tom appeared unfounded. Mairi made sure his meals were taken care of when she wasn't there and Tom's journalistic qualities helped him in dealing with the constituents who called in Eleanor's absence.

She had consigned the bad times to the past when he began drinking again. He made light of it, of course, saying it was social, obligatory, that he could control it now. She did what she could. She lived with it. He went back into hospital for another dry-out. He was well for quite a long time. But she knew drinking was a part of Tom now, that he would not, could not give it up. It was a fact of life, like her growing Parliamentary presence, like her new skills in committee. There was a composure and acceptance in her now that was not hardness or ambition. When they talked about Women's Lib she knew what they were getting at, but she liked Crispin's word better; head-space. In a strange way, this was what her son and his generation had given her.

CHAPTER NINETEEN

Before she left London, Philip had been mooning about her minuscule flat again, talking about setting up home together 'within or without marriage', as he put it.

She had sat next to a tweedy, over-friendly young Dutchman on the plane coming up, making no secret of her hostility. He and others like him had brought up huge tracts of the Highlands, a kind of Clearances in reverse.

He had cheerfully ordered her a gin and tonic and said in good English, 'And what alternative have you? You are beggarman's country. Your steel, your cars, your ships, they have all gone phtt! Phtt! Phtt! Your government have spent twenty per cent more on you than on England and to what purpose? More unemployed, more emigrants.'

She had turned to stare out of the plane window rather than risk further provocation. Ten years in Parliament and in truth, she thought, I might as well have saved my breath to cool my porridge. It had been the anniversary of Tom's death yesterday – four years to the day – and that had depressed her. She would have liked to turn to the placid, self-satisfied Dutchman and say, 'Wait till we have independence!' but it was no certainty that even devolution would come or that either would supply the answer. In the spring, 1979 – a referendum, but if less than forty per cent of the people wanted it, the Scotland Bill giving the country its own Assembly would go out of the window once again. The last time it had done so with 350 amendments, which was laughable if you had a mind to see the funny side.

Funny how at times like these Tom's memory was so important to her. He had tried so hard to hang on, to be of help to her. Weak silly tears still rose in her eyes. She missed him so. But at the same time it was as though he were there, putting a bit of backbone into her, urging her on with his sly, sconcing wit.

She was going to need the backbone this afternoon. She was good at fighting for other people, but now it had come down to her own, she was shaking like a tyro. If Crispin did not get the go-ahead for his Dounhead project, she didn't know what was going to become of him and Lally and the kids. Her grandchildren. Katie and Fay. They would leave the country, in all probability. And she was sick of people leaving. This time it felt like her own life-blood draining away.

We've convinced the world we still have a national identity. Funny how she could hear those words spoken in Tom's voice, and see his face as he spoke them. Was that all the Party had done before it had sunk in popular favour? She had almost begged him. *Isn't it enough? You've proved you can't sweep away that identity by saying that television and Marks and Sparks have made people the same the country over. We aren't, and it would be a sad day if it were true.*

She wished she had been able to keep her poise and tell the Dutchman that. We are fighting for our very existence, she could have told him. Twenty-one areas of multiple deprivation in Britain and *eighteen* of them in Scotland! It would have sounded like special pleading and he would not have been sympathetic. To the outsider, it must look as though Scotland had brought her troubles on herself. He might have said, 'Serve you right.' Serve who right? The politicians, the planners, the people? Who had to take the blame? Historians will tell you, she could have argued, that man for man Scotland has done more to create the modern world than any other nation. So what happened? Must we go gently into that good night? Must we cry *Suas Alba* just once more before we disappear into the mist?

As the hired car sped towards the Central Hotel in Glasgow where she had arranged to meet Crispin and Lally she made a final effort to shrug off her despondency. They were making the old Royal High School in Edinburgh ready for the Scottish Assembly. Was that likely if devolution were not almost a cast-iron certainty? And although jobs were hitting rock bottom, due to rationalization and new technology, investment was stirring again. Even if it meant being a little Switzerland – clocks and tourism – did that matter? She would like to take some of the doubters to East Kilbride, to the National Engineering Laboratory there. Maybe survival for some would depend on how they were learning to save energy, precious fuel, there. The Scots hadn't given up being an inventive people. It wouldn't be just clocks and holiday-makers.

Maybe Glasgow wasn't the place to come for reassurance. What a press it had had of recent years! Hard city. Rotting city. Vandal city. The worst slums in Europe and curved roofs on the factories to keep the destroyers off. She couldn't yield up her stubborn, irrational, defensive love for it. In the East End they were trying so hard to make a go of things. Painting railway arches, planting trees, building factories. If they could fight back, so could she.

The children saw her first in the hotel lobby, and jumped on her, kissing her, their small skinny arms hugging the breath from her, their silky hair tangling across her face. She turned laughing from them, her spirits immeasurably lightened already, towards Crispin and Lally. Like the children, they wore homespun, hand-knitted clothes. 'Ethnic chic,' she said to Lally, touching her short plaid cape. Lally smiled gravely. She took her self-sufficiency with a serious pride that brooked no jokes.

As the lunch, her promised treat, proceeded, she wondered if Crispin was right to think of uprooting his little family from Calneggie and moving back to the so-called industrial belt. He had said there was little option. With Camilla, who had, after all, been the presiding spirit, now being cared for in a nursing home, and the village school threatened with closure because of a paucity of pupils, the area offered little in the way of stimulus for the children. They loved it there, but they were, he averred, like little feral cats, in need of taming.

His imagination had been caught by the way the government-sponsored Scottish Development Agency had taken up the cause of the small business, encouraging service as well as manufacturing industry and even offering premises rent free for a year or two in the most run-down areas. It had been Mairi who, in reminiscent mood, had taken them all down to Patie's old Dounhead workshop during the last family get-together, talking about the cars that had been made there and the dreams Patie had dreamed. The notion of starting up a car rehabilitation workshop had been born there and then.

Eleanor watched her son with a good deal of jealous, covert pride. She felt he was growing into his skin, that the time had come for him to stretch himself. The men from the Development Agency and the Regional Council, whom he was hoping would agree to fund him, would surely see that. Encouraged at first by Camilla, he had been rebuilding vintage cars for several years now at Calneggie, lovingly restoring near-wrecks to a new and shining beauty. He had also been carrying out experiments with a prototype battery car, but had been desperately hamstrung for lack of funds. Funny how she and Tom had thought he would be a lawyer and how the family engineering skills, from the old railway engineer, Paterson, and the motor engineer, Finn, had skipped her generation but renewed themselves in Crispin. Funny and sobering, the trap of the gene machine.

Crispin, she realized, was one of a new breed none the less in that he took life at his own pace, refusing to be bull-dozed into false notions of 'getting on' or 'making his way in life'. He and Lally had calmly abstracted for themselves a mixture of Eastern philosophy and Western psychology which made life tolerable for them. They were thoughtful, kindly, unselfish, with many friends who came and went from the small West Coast community, practising meditation, dis-

311

cussing poetry and religion, making music. Eleanor found them all very direct and somewhat serious. But then humour was often an evasion, she had found. Especially Scots humour, which could be cruel, abrasive and wielded by the iconoclasts like a savage club. Crispin's politics were selective, mainly concerned with ecology. Both he and Lally had helped in the campaign to prevent nuclear waste being dumped in Loch Doon and both were now campaigning against the building of the biggest hydro-electric power station in Europe at, of all places, Loch Lomond, arguing that extra power could be generated by uprating the existing scheme at Sloy. They had come a long way from the two disorientated waifs who had returned from their world travels in the 'sixties and one of Eleanor's greatest joys was that they had a solid, loving, joyful marriage, against all the odds in these divorce-ridden unhappy days.

'Maw, you haven't heard a word I said!' She had been coaxing the mischievous, elfin Fay into eating up her pudding but turned now towards Crispin's anxious face. 'We'll have to get cracking. We must get to Dounhead in good time.'

Sitting in Crispin's elderly, well-cared-for Morris with a granddaughter on either side of her, Eleanor stole glances at the Glasgow they passed through on the start of their journey. Walls still bore rude exhortations directed towards Ally Macleod, the football manager who had dashed the chauvinist dream in the World Cup and performed a brutal, necessary lesson in national chicken-counting.

She felt her heart contract at the slummy tenements, the drab little shops, the shrunken little men of indeterminate age walking the streets, jobless. 'Talking bunnets', as one of those merciless comics dubbed them. An English friend recently up on a visit had confessed to being glad when the time came to leave Glasgow, a city full of hard-faced menace and aggression he had felt. Could that be so? Could strangers not see the deprivation that spawned the hardness, or the cheerful attenuated stamina that fought it?

The same sense of ghostly loss haunted Dounhead. No beauty. No trees. No *brio*. Why do we persist? she wondered, yet knew the answers were there, in the children, in Crispin and Lally.

It had been arranged they would meet the officials at her mother's home and then go down to the site. She knew the moment Mairi came to the door that something had happened. Her mother warmly but absently hugged the children, her eyes seeking Eleanor's with an expression that was almost pleading.

'What is it, Mother?' she demanded.

'Eleanor, it may be a shock to you. One of the men is Geoffrey Benson.'

She repeated the name stupidly, feeling a hot blush of embarrassment flood her neck and face as though she were some silly schoolgirl.

Her mother whispered urgently, 'He's come up to Scotland to live. At Bearsden. I think he's nervous too. I thought I'd better warn you.'

She shot her mother a hasty, grateful look, and, composed on the surface at least, walked ahead of the others into the big, cheerful sitting-room. Her step-father kissed her and she held out her hand to two grey-haired, bespectacled, earnest men in turn before she found her grasp returned by Geoffrey Benson.

Was this what time did to them all? There was nothing cruel about the changes in the man she had once loved. He was still slight, trim, his hair scarcely touched with grey. He had just grown a little more ordinary, unremarkable, punctilious, stereotyped.

'My dear Eleanor! What a pleasure to meet you again.' He looked in two minds to kiss her but she put on her Scots WASP expression, the one with which she intimidated senior civil servants, and said formally, with the right note of subdued friendliness, 'Geoffrey! I never thought to see you here!' We must have a talk later.' She moved towards the table and took papers from her briefcase, to indicate this was an occasion of business and that the protagonists had no time to waste.

She had the feeling that the mood was not altogether promising. But Crispin had marshalled his arguments carefully and put his case with care and passion. Mairi came with them to the old workshop (which had been used for many trades since, including a bakery), her face broody with memories as she recalled Patie's work and the encouragement he had had from her grandfather. Dounhead House had long since been demolished, but she tried to bring alive for them the day Patie had ridden a borrowed car round the drive and declared he would never work or live anywhere but Scotland. Maybe something touched the official heart then. was always difficult to know. But the conversation began to take an upbeat, more constructive turn and she could see from Crispin's face he felt he might be in with a chance.

Robin and Mairi had laid on afternoon tea and it was then Geoffrey seized the chance to talk to Eleanor. He joined her at a window-seat, jerking his thumb in Crispin's direction and saying, 'He puts a good case. And so do you.'

'I never miss a chance to bring work to my constituency. I don't need to tell you how badly it's needed.'

'No.' He gave her the brief, equivocal smile she remembered as being so much a part of his nature. 'I haven't missed your battles in the House. I tell all my friends I once knew you.'

'How boring for your friends!' she teased him.

'I have been here for three years – '

'I never thought of you as leaving London – '

Their words ran over each other. He took a careful bite of shortbread, brushing invisible crumbs from his knee and said, 'It must amuse you, just a little, this small exodus in reverse. I believe some six thousand a year. The south-east has become top-heavy, so impossible to lead the complete life in.'

'I'm delighted by it. I think we make a great, combustible team. Maybe a New Age of Enlightenment is coming – it did us no harm at all the last time it happened, after the Union of the Crowns.' She stopped in a little confusion, regretting the word combustible. 'What does your wife think of life up here?'

'She loves the space, the physical freedom, the pace of life.'

'That's good.'

'We have two girls, both married, and a son at university.' He looked at her with a kindly, intimate expression she found disconcerting, then put down his cup with a decisive movement. 'But see here, Eleanor, I am not altogether happy about your son's proposals. The logistics of the situation point towards heavier investment, heavier industries, in this area. Traditionally – '

'Time we broke with tradition. And besides, I'm fed up with pie in the sky. Those industries, that investment, may never happen. Crispin's ideas will. If not here, somewhere else.' She could feel that her face had gone frozen, her whole body taut.

'Could you come to my office tomorrow? It's important discuss some of the long-term implications for Dounhea with you. Or must you get back to Westminster?'

'No, I am paired at the House for the rest of the week.'
She looked over at Crispin, talking with such animation to
the other two men, and then at her mother and Robin. She
wanted to do this for them. And for Dounhead. It wasn't
much, but she had learned from Lally and Crispin the importance of the particular, the individual. 'I'll come and see you
tomorrow,' she said briskly. She looked at her diary. 'Shall
we say two o'clock?'

'You see,' said Geoffrey, 'bringing in these small-scale affairs
to a place like Dounhead is a bit like putting a poultice on a
pimple when great boils are needing treatment all over the
place.'

'What a charming metaphor!' Eleanor could not help laughing. 'I haven't convinced you more delicately then that
it's better to light one small candle – '

'Than to curse the darkness?' He threw down his pen.
'Well, of course you have. But it's a committee decision in
the end.' He held her look. 'I'll see what I can do. For old
times' sake.'

She felt the tension drain slowly out from her. She had
done all she could and now her trained politician's mind
knew the case was more likely won than lost. An office girl
brought in a tray with tea and biscuits and she heard Geoffrey
tell her he would be going out for half an hour with Mrs
Vishart and felt the girl's curious, half-impudent stare rest
on her before she left the room.

'Where are we going?' she demanded, sipping the hot tea
gratefully.

'Let's walk along by the river. It's such a lovely afternoon.'
He took her in his car to Glasgow Green. As they travelled
along the Trongate, he said in his precise, scholar's voice,
'Edmund Burke once called this the finest street in Europe.
Did you know that?'

She said gaily, 'No, but I did know that Daniel Defoe
once called Glasgow the beautifullest little city he had ever
seen, which doesn't say much for his sense of the grammatical.'

When they got out and walked he held her elbow at first,
his hand gradually slipping almost possessively into the
crook of her arm.

'Do you sometimes think of the old days at Calneggie?'

Somehow she had been dreading the question a little. It made her shed too many of memory's skins. It made her too vulnerable.

But she answered him truthfully, 'Oh yes, I do.'

'Shall we sit here?' He indicated a bench in a pool of sunshine. He studied her candidly, like an artist running a critical eye over a canvas. She saw the half-smile waver from his lips as he turned away. She put her gloved hand on his on the slatted seat. 'What about you?'

It was a little time before he turned and then he didn't answer her directly. 'Do you find,' he said conversationally, 'that there are people in your life who are like – like signposts, like landmarks? You might only meet them briefly, but you know from the moment you see them their influence is going to be altogether disproportionate to any others?'

'We didn't meet briefly,' she protested.

'Taken out of a lifetime, our time together was short. Yet there's scarcely been a day I haven't thought of you. Wondered about you.'

'Geoffrey.' She was near to tears.

'Heavens!' he said. 'I didn't mean to upset you. I've lived a good life. I've been very happy. Yet I couldn't resist bringing you out here today so that I could have you to myself for a little.'

'I'm flattered.'

'I remember you running along the sands at Calneggie, the wind fanning your hair out behind you and your face sharp and glowing from the cold.'

'Well, I think this is unnecessary torture,' she said bluntly. 'I don't want to remember that. I want to remember my husband.'

'Yes,' he said more soberly. 'Yes. Perhaps Rowena would take a dim view of this, too. I don't care. As time gets shorter I'm prepared to be a lot less scrupulous about friendships.'

'Really?'

'Yes, really.'

'You don't mean affairs?'

He was silent.

'Those too? Since you were married?'

'One. No, two. They were both with girls with a little bit of you in them.'

'I don't believe you. And to think you were once a rather churchy young man.'

He grinned at her slowly and she could feel something

inside her turn over, like a little acrobat in a glass ball turning somersaults while she looked on with delight and love. 'You've changed and yet you are still the same.'

'It's lovely here,' he said. 'Isn't it?'

She knew he wasn't talking about the immediate scene. 'Yes,' she agreed.

'I won't go back to the office this afternoon. I'll take you to the Art Gallery and show you the incredibly vulgar Dali and the beautiful Impressionists.'

'I haven't the time.'

'Oh yes, you have,' he said quietly. 'And besides, they do marvellous scones. I'll buy you your tea.'

She wasn't greatly at home in the Art Gallery. The Impressionists were all he had said they would be, but she did not understand why she liked them and when he tried to explain she felt the gaps in her consciousness like great desolate windy spaces. It was the same with music.

'I'm basically an artisan soul.' She tried to explain her attitude.

He shook his head, but she persisted. 'You've been to Dounhead. You know what it's like there. I suppose I grew up with most of my contemporaries, thinking the arts were fripperies. Except for the cinema.'

'Well, maybe they *were* fripperies, when it was a case of bare survival. Look, I'm impressed by your son. I'll see he gets all the help and encouragement possible. It might even be feasible to build a new place for him.'

'No. Don't do that!'

'Why not?'

'The old one has family associations that mean a lot to us.'

Shops and offices were closing when they said their goodbyes in the centre of Glasgow. She was going home to Dounhead for the night and returning to London the next day.

'I hope I'll see you again,' he said, kissing her cheek. 'It would be nice if you could come and meet Rowena and the family.'

'I'd like that,' she said, feeling the warm touch of his fingers fall away from hers.

She took the train back to London the following evening, glad to have secured a sleeper. Her mind busy with constituents' problems, she remembered something Geoffrey had quoted to her from some newspaper clipping: 'Devolution will not bring tranquillity.'

She was looking forward to telling Philip Mackenzie about her visit home. He was her friend. They went to the opera and the theatre together, quite often, and she fed him at her flat. It was better than being lonely.

She felt that both her life and her country were about to enter one of their more volatile phases. Anything could happen. Good. Good. She did not greatly care for tranquillity.

The place for that was the grave.

Howard Spring

In 1938 his most famous book, *My Son, My Son*, was published; it was a world-wide success. Since then all his books, without exception, have been bestsellers and have earned Howard Spring a high reputation as an author of universal appeal.

'He is not afraid of stark drama, and he writes with real feeling.' *Sunday Times*

MY SON, MY SON £1.25
ALL THE DAY LONG £1.25
FAME IS THE SPUR £1.25
I MET A LADY 80p
RACHEL ROSING 75p
SHABBY TIGER 75p
A SUNSET TOUCH 50p
THERE IS NO ARMOUR £1.00
THESE LOVERS FLED AWAY 95p
TIME AND THE HOUR £1.25
WINDS OF THE DAY 75p

FONTANA PAPERBACKS

Fontana Paperbacks

Fontana is a leading paperback publisher of fiction and non-fiction, with authors ranging from Alistair MacLean, Agatha Christie and Desmond Bagley to Solzhenitsyn and Pasternak, from Gerald Durrell and Joy Adamson to the famous Modern Masters series.

In addition to a wide-ranging collection of internationally popular writers of fiction, Fontana also has an outstanding reputation for history, natural history, military history, psychology, psychiatry, politics, economics, religion and the social sciences.

All Fontana books are available at your bookshop or newsagent; or can be ordered direct. Just fill in the form and list the titles you want.

FONTANA BOOKS, Cash Sales Department, G.P.O. Box 29, Douglas, Isle of Man, British Isles. Please send purchase price, plus 8p per book. Customers outside the U.K. send purchase price, plus 10p per book. Cheque, postal or money order. No currency.

NAME (Block letters)

ADDRESS
